COPYRIGHT ACKNOWLEDGMENTS

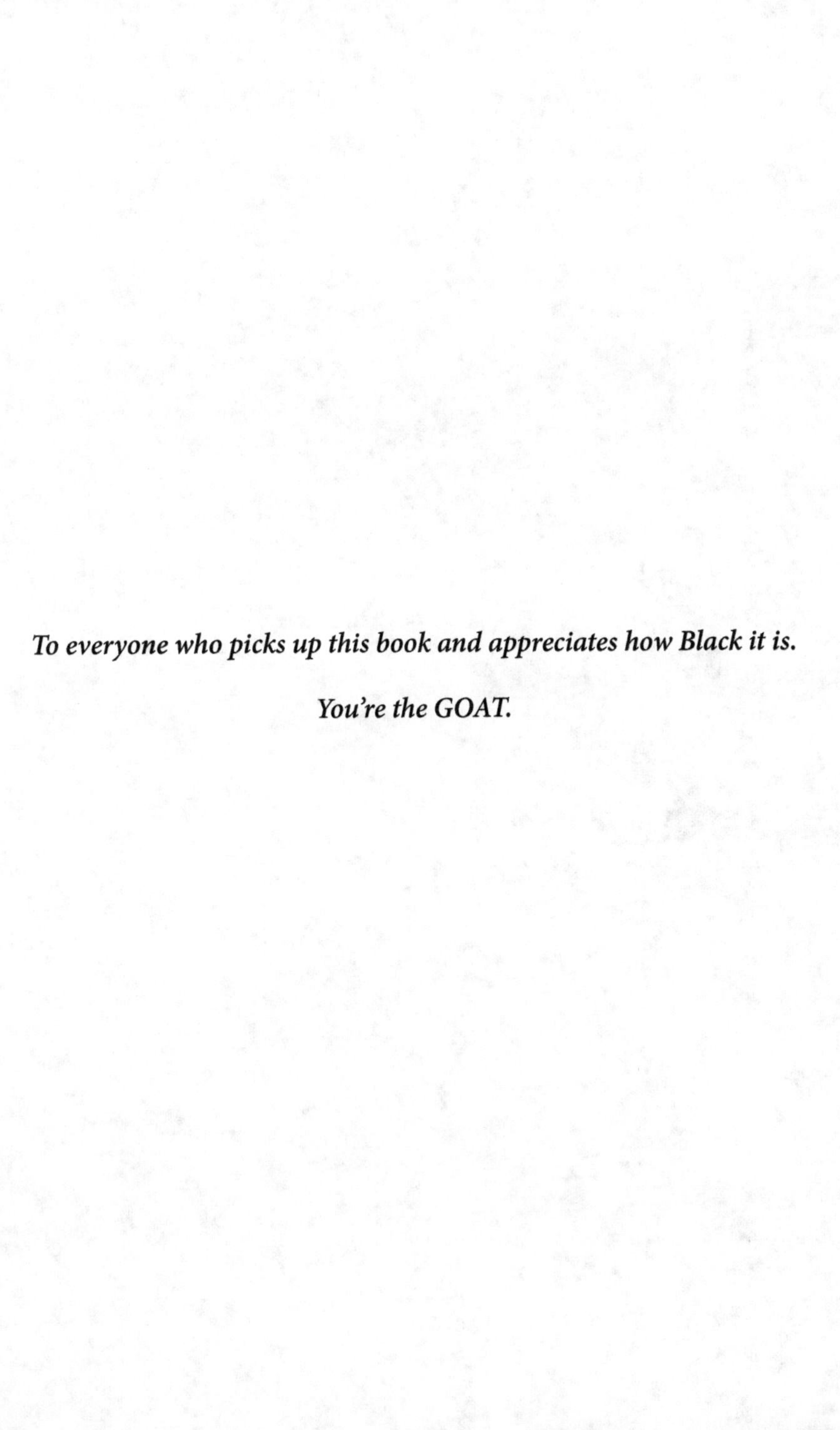

To everyone who picks up this book and appreciates how Black it is.

You're the GOAT.

TABLE OF CONTENTS

MAGIC IN THE MELANIN

A Black Fantasy Anthology

Presented by the Melanin Library

TODAY, WE ARE GENERALS

BY TATIANA OBEY

ART BY PLAIDPUMA

399

THANK YOU FOR READING

423

MAGIC IN THE MELANIN

INTRODUCTION

This will be the Blackest book you ever read.

At least, that is our goal.

Everyone who contributed to making this anthology a reality is a Black author, artist, or creative — and that was by design. Because I believe, with every fiber of my being, that Black creators should be celebrated, and I don't say that simply because I'm a Black author myself.

I say it because we live in a world where we are treated as undeserving. Even while our creative contributions are being pillaged by other cultures, we're expected to prove why we are worthy of being in a space. And even then, we still create. We craft worlds from scratch and pour our souls onto the page, challenging the world to see us as we dare to see ourselves.

And if that isn't the purest form of magic, I don't know what is.

So, this anthology is our magic — honed and refined and presented to you in the hopes that you will see how wondrous our creations are. This collection is what adult fantasy looks like when it is unapologetically Black. When the stories of Black creatives are not stripped down and compressed into a box of generic storytelling in order to appease an audience of readers who will, nevertheless, complain about being unable to connect with our characters, or refuse to understand how our characters could interact with their world the way that they do. These stories are for all those who dare to see color and appreciate it for all the beauty it brings into the world.

Because our worlds are beautiful.

Beautiful and unexpected and breathtaking — when we get the chance to write them. Too often, Black authors are relegated to writing stories of pain, suffering, oppression and self-hatred in order to get a foothold in the publishing industry, because that is what the world demands from us. More often than not, that is all they will accept from us. But we are more than just some diversity checkbox to be ticked off of someone's list.

We are the sparks that set fire to the world.

And that is why this book exists.

Magic in the Melanin: A Black Fantasy Anthology is what fun and freedom look like when Black authors are allowed to spill their talents across the page, uninhibited. When they can stretch their creativity beyond the boxes they've been placed in to write stories about warriors and mermaids and priestesses without having to appeal to a society that actively works to exclude their existence.

The goal of this anthology is to create a space for us to be whole in a world that only wants fractions of who we are, therefore, there will be no instances of racial oppression in this book. And, if that doesn't make you want to read this anthology, I don't know what will. So, I'll say it again: *in this book, you will not find any commentary on race, racism, or systemic oppression.*

Our reason for excluding racial oppression is simple: we want every reader who ventures into these pages to feel welcomed. For them to laugh, swoon, and feel for the characters they'll meet. For them to be thoroughly entertained. Because that is why we, as authors, pick up the pen — so that we can write stories that move people, resonate with them, and offer a little bit of hope, light, and joy to the people who read our stories.

So, with all that being said, we hope you enjoy this book. It is a collection of fantasy stories from authors who write in a variety of styles, with themes that range from mythical and romantic to dark and unsettling. We do not expect every reader to love every story — that would be unrealistic. But we hope you appreciate every Black author, artist, editor, and narrator who touched this project and worked to breathe life into it. That you walk away from this anthology with a new appreciation for the Black authors who dare to tell their stories and include themselves within them. And that, as always, all your books are full of melanin.

— C. M. Lockhart (Chelsea)

Founder of Written in Melanin

Owner of the Melanin Library

Author of books featuring Black girls who aren't all that nice.

ASH OF THE CINDERS

BY L. PENELOPE
ART BY IJEOMA OSSI

ROMANTIC FANTASY AND FAIRYTALE RETELLING

The invitation lay in a place of prominence in the foyer of the crumbling seaside manor sitting on a scarred wooden table between a fine, but slightly chipped crystal vase—damage Ash had been blamed for but was actually his stepbrother's fault—and a bust of the Grand Emperor Hodari, whom Lord Dawit somewhat dubiously claimed as an ancestor.

Ash longed to touch the fine parchment. He admired the craftsmanship and the flow of ink on the page, but didn't dare allow his fingers to graze it. He knew it would be velvety soft, the golden lettering—created by a palace mage—would feel almost liquidy to the touch. In another lifetime, he and Jamila used to watch the palace letterer at work producing correspondence for the queen, both children marveling at how it was done.

Now the invitation pulled at him, pulsing like a dull ache as he chopped and hauled the wood, loaded coal, mopped the floors, repaired the crumbling wall, and patched the glass where a pane inexplicably fell out of a window casing that had been there since before Erendil was born. The manor's decaying elegance always caused a pang of resentment deep within. Thoughts of restoring the place to its former glory and carefully renovating every wall and floorboard with love were his constant companions.

In the kitchen, as he sliced onions for the old cook whose arthritis left him barely able to complete the task, he shared what he'd barely allowed himself to consider.

"The invitation says *all* eligible bachelors." His deep voice was hushed so his stepfather and stepbrothers couldn't hear him, though they almost never lowered themselves to enter the kitchen of the manor.

Erendil, propped up on a chair with a pile of pillows at his back, blew out a breath. "So, it does. And you want to go, child?"

Ash hummed and started in on the potatoes. He had his father's formal suit that his mother had secretly kept. It had remained hidden from his stepfather, who hated any mention of Ash's late father. Since the invitation's arrival, Ash had stayed up late at night in his attic room, after he'd completed all his and Erendil's chores, altering the jacket.

The quality of the suit was good, but he was a few inches taller than his father had been and broader about the shoulders. While not a professional tailor, he had enough skills over the years from mending Dawit, Chidi, and Tambo's clothes that he did a passable job. The suit didn't need to stand out, just not get him kicked out of the ball.

"Well, by decree of the queen, you should definitely be there," Erendil said. But the tone in his voice was speculative. He was likely thinking the very same thing that Ash was. Would his stepfather let him go?

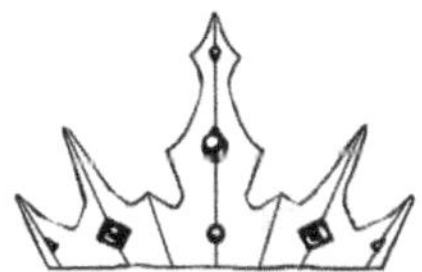

Ash had been given no notice of the dinner guests until they were on the doorstep. Each meal was already stretching the meager contents of the larder to the limits, so feeding two additional mouths was next to impossible. Thin soup it was.

Erendil would be blamed of course. There would be a tirade about making Lord Dawit look bad in front of guests, but Ash would take the punishment the way he always did. He could no more let the elderly man go hungry than he could stop breathing. Not after what the cook had done for his mother during her final days.

As he brought the heavy-laden tray into the dining room, the people at the table took no notice, their chatter continuing.

"It's a dangerous ploy," Lord Busan was saying. His wife, Lady Fuza, fluttered her lashes at Ash as he set her bowl before her, but he ignored it. He had to remain on his guard around her, as she always tried to back him into some dark, shadowy corner of the manor when she visited.

"I am paying you good money to get this done, Busan." Dawit's gravelly voice was harsh. "Will this Tanzanite Crest of yours ensure that Princess Jamila chooses one of my sons to be her king consort at the ball?"

Ash nearly dropped the empty tray. He struggled to keep his face neutral, knowing if he belied his horror at the suggestion that it would not go well.

Fortunately, he stood behind Fuza, so her eagle eyes were not on him. The others barely spared him a glance, as usual. In their minds, he was just a servant; one of the two left to tend the sprawling estate that had once been grand and beautiful.

"I will sell you the charm, Dawit, never fear. I just urge you to take care. It is very powerful juju and in the wrong hands it could backfire spectacularly."

Dawit snorted, his arrogance bleeding through his posture and expression. "Then it is good that it will not go into the wrong hands."

Instead of heading back into the kitchen to prepare and plate the final course—a paltry mini tart that had used the last of their flour—Ash detoured to the foyer, to the invitation, its gold lettering glinting up at him in the candlelight.

He snatched it off the table and stuffed it into his pocket. His so-called family was willing to use dark curses to trap the princess in a loveless marriage with a feckless man, and Ash was not going to stand for it. He had no illusions about capturing the princess for himself, but he could warn her and protect her from what was coming.

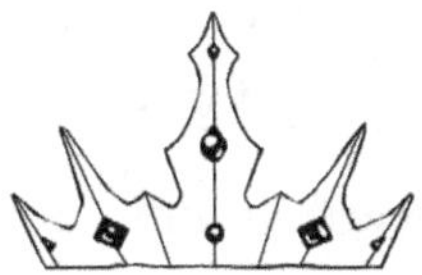

"What. Is. This?" Lord Dawit's frosty voice asked several days later from an unusual spot next to the fire.

Ash's heart iced from the chill. In his meaty paw, the man held the suit jacket that Ash had been painstakingly letting out to fit his frame.

"That is mine," Ash answered through gritted teeth.

"And where exactly do you think you'll be wearing a garment so fine? Perhaps to the ball?" Dawit held up his other hand, which bore the invitation. His scowl was dark as a thunderstorm. However, Ash stood his ground.

"The invitation is for every eligible bachelor in the land. So yes, I was planning to attend."

Ash tightened his jaw as Dawit smirked. "I'm sure you know that *eligible* means those of royal blood."

"That is not what it says." He tried to keep his voice reasonable.

Dawit considered the jacket in his hands. "The craftsmanship on this is quite good. Have you been stealing money from us?"

Ash's eyes narrowed. "No. That was my father's." Pride rang out in his voice, but instantly he knew it was the wrong thing to say. Dawit's fist tightened on the fabric, skin taut against his knuckles before he tossed the garment into the fire.

"No!" The bellow exploded from Ash's chest. He dove to the fire, but Dawit grabbed him around the waist. Ash easily tossed the smaller man aside, but when he pulled the fabric from the flames and beat it against the stone of the hearth to put out the fire, it was already half charred. Not salvageable.

"Why?" he raged at the man who loomed above him. "Why would you do such a thing?"

Dawit slowly gathered himself, straightening his clothing. "You are the son of a shoemaker. You are not good enough to attend a royal ball. It was only your mother's beauty which inspired me to overlook the stain of her first marriage and marry her anyway. But you need to learn to stay in your place."

With that he twirled on his heel and left the kitchen.

"It was my mother's wealth, which you have all but squandered, that inspired you to marry her," he said through the haze of anger covering his vision.

Ash stayed there on his knees, the remains of his father's jacket clutched in his grip for a long, long time.

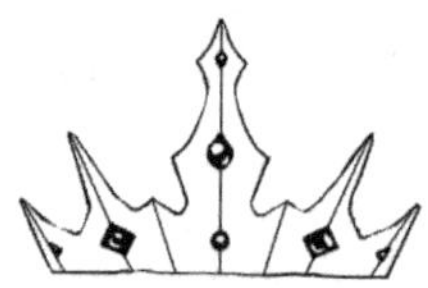

Erendil found him by the cold fire in the morning. "What's wrong, child?"

Ash showed him the remains of the garment but did not say a word.

The old man lowered himself onto the bench and sighed. "You should have left here long ago. Right after your mother passed on to the afterworld and that fiend cheated you out of your inheritance." He held up a hand when Ash would have responded. "I know you stayed to care for your mother's land. And for me. I understand and am grateful, but I wish you had been able to spread your wings some more."

Ash shook his head stubbornly. "I promised Ma I would look after you. You eased her transition so much, gave her so much peace, and I know it cost you."

Erendil hadn't been so sick before his mother's passing. The old man, a member of the ancient Aquatikin race, had used his magic to aid and calm his mother's final days. But it had taken something out of him.

He stroked his tightly coiled gray beard. "An Aquatikin's magic is finite. Most can only use it once in their lifetime and it must always be used in the service of others. It was my pleasure to help your mother find peace. We find purpose in service, and I would not have changed a thing."

Ash's eyes grew misty. "You deserve to spend your life here next to the sea and not in some distant inland water preserve. I won't abandon you."

Erendil looked up, tears in his eyes. "I see that. And you don't know what a gift it is."

The praise warmed him, but the pain of Dawit's actions would take a long time to fade.

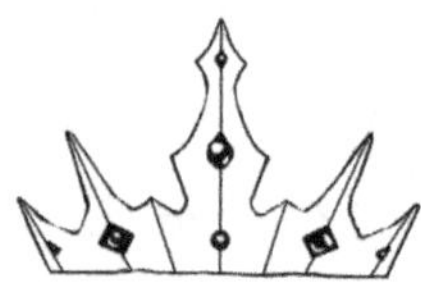

The day of the ball dawned bleak and dreary. A harsh wind blew in from the sea with the promise of rain on its heels. Ash resentfully did his chores, unable to stop thinking about Dawit's plans for the princess.

When evening fell, a carriage arrived to ferry Lord Dawit, Chidi, and Tambo to the ball. They must have used some of their last few coins to hire the vehicle, Ash thought, as the four mares pulled away.

Then he raced back to the kitchen to change his dirt-encrusted boots for his only other pair, which were worn but clean.

"Just what do you think you're doing, child?"

"I'm going to find a way to the palace and warn Mila."

"*Mila*?" the old man said, brows raised.

Ash's cheeks warmed. "Princess Jamila. I—I knew her as a child when my father was the royal shoemaker. I'm sure she doesn't remember me, but I feel duty bound to at least warn her. How could I sit by and let Dawit and those idiots use dark magic to trap her?"

"So you're planning on going to the royal ball dressed like that?"

The skepticism in the man's voice had Ash looking down at himself. The gray-brown pants covering his legs were worn and frayed, and his shirt was so thin from many washings as to be nearly see through. His stepfather did not actually pay him; Ash earned a little here and there doing odd jobs for neighbors, repairing equipment, hauling junk, or using his talent for building things out of scraps. He had no funds to buy appropriate clothing for a ball. "It *is* a masquerade. Besides, I was going to try to blend in with the servants."

Erendil snorted. "Masquerading as a pauper is certainly an innovative costume. But, I'm guessing even servants in the palace dress a far sight better than that."

Ash shrugged. "I'll find a way. If you're trying to stop me—"

The man held up a hand. "No, I'm not trying to stop you. I will help."

"How?"

"Sit."

Impatience tugged at him, but he trusted Erendil, so he sat.

"Where is your father's jacket?"

Ash swallowed the lump in his throat and pointed to the shelf next to the fireplace where the neatly folded charred fabric lay. Erendil retrieved it and held it up.

"All right. Let's see what we can do."

The Aquatikin elder scooped a cup of water from the bucket near the door and peered into it, gray brow furrowed. Then he began speaking in an ancient tongue. Soft, sibilant words ran across Ash's skin like silk.

The water in the cup bubbled and frothed, then shone with an ethereal golden light. That same light began to shine from Erendil himself. For a moment, the man's form shimmered, and Ash caught a glimpse of the fish that lived within—dark eyes, iridescent scales, powerful fins. The image faded, and Ash's vision whited out.

When he could see again, the clothes he was wearing had transformed. No longer was he clad in well-maintained rags, now he wore a suit of the same high quality as his father's. Gold epaulets and gleaming buttons framed the well-fitting garment. Black pants fit his tapered waist and perfectly encased his muscled thighs. And his shoes…

The shoes bore the same delicate hand stitching that had made his father one of the most sought-after shoemakers in the land. The craftsmanship had inspired the queen herself to hire him.

Ash's eyes were so wide, he couldn't even blink. He rose from his chair and whooped, then grabbed the old man in a hug and spun him around.

"Put me down, child," Erendil complained, beating at his back.

"How can I ever thank you?"

"You don't need to. You have been thanking me for years with your actions and your care." The old man's voice was thick, and Ash's eyes misted.

"The suit also has a few surprises." Erendil listed the magical properties of Ash's new outfit to his captive audience.

Overwhelmed, the younger man smoothed out the buttery soft fabric. "Now, I just need to get to the palace in time."

"Don't worry. I've called in some friends to help. Come and see."

Ash followed Erendil outside into the cool evening. The sea was almost black in the twilight, and from the shore a tiny tornado kicked up. Soon two horses pulling a carriage were visible. But the horses were unlike any Ash had ever seen before.

Their front halves were very much horse-like, with coats of spotted gray and blue. But the back halves were essentially fish tails, thick and powerful and apparently able to work on land, much like a snake.

"Are those... seahorses?"

"Of a kind. They are kelpie draught mares. Highly intelligent water horses. But they can only be on land for a short time. You must leave the ball by midnight for that is when the horses and the rest of the magic will fade... I'm sorry I cannot do more." His breathing was shallow and his brown complexion seemed almost gray.

"This is more than enough." Ash's voice held wonder. Carefully, he wrapped his arms around the man once more and smacked a kiss on his cheek. Erendil swatted him away, then shooed him into the peculiar carriage that appeared to be crafted out of orange coral.

In moments the seahorses were off, galloping at full speed toward the palace.

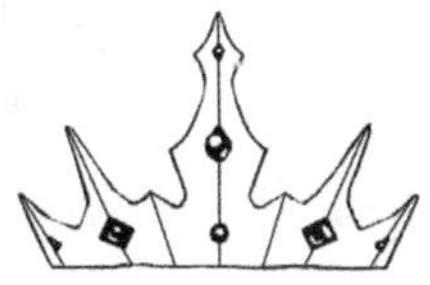

Jamila held her breath as the guards passed her hiding place behind the billowing curtains. Music from the ballroom was so loud that her brains rattled. But if she was expected to continue this charade for the next few hours, she needed a break. If one more smarmy, smiling lordling uttered the same series of compliments—in the same order, as if they had studied from a single manual—she was going to scream right in his aristocratic face.

This ball was her mother's idea. After the disastrous ending of her betrothal to the prince of Dawnhaven, Queen Aziza had been both furious and desperate. In seven generations, there had never been a non-married queen of Emberglade. And while her mother had many years more left to rule, tradition dictated that Jamila find a groom before her twenty-fifth birthday—one short month away. Hence the ball.

Of course, that meant dealing with dozens of simpering, obsequious, king consort wannabes practically falling at her feet to lick her gem-encrusted shoes. Each turn around the dance floor had been worse than the one before.

The pair of patrolling guards was currently at the furthest point in their rotation around the ballroom. It was go time. Jamila lifted up the skirt of the ridiculous pink confection of a dress her mother had insisted she wear and raced outside into the gardens beyond the ballroom. The voice of her lady's maid calling out, "Your Highness?" nearly made her stumble, but she didn't look back. Just held up her hand giving the signal that she needed a fifteen minute break. Enora would cover for her.

There was a hidden courtyard, Jamila's favorite place in the entire palace grounds, where she could take a brief reprieve. Collect her wits before she headed back onto the ballroom's dance floor to be assaulted by the courtly attentions of the lordlings.

The door to the secret space was hidden by a fall of vines, and the palace gardeners only occasionally remembered this place existed. Inside was a small rectangle of paved stone, bordered by wild flowers growing freely. An ancient fountain in the center was the focal point with its cracked statue of some mythical water creature leaping towards the air. The fountain had been dry for decades, and Jamila had filled it with dirt and planted a variety of flowers there with her own hands.

A place of such untamed beauty, so at odds with the rest of the perfectly manicured grounds, did something to restore her soul. It always had. There had only been a handful of people she'd shared the courtyard with, almost no one besides Enora and a few trusted friends knew of its existence, so when she opened the secret door to find a suit-clad man standing on the overgrown pathway, her heart jumped into her throat.

"Who are you?" Her tone was far more rude than she'd intended, it's just that so few things surprised her anymore.

The man spun around. He was tall—so tall, and so broad, with massive shoulders that were somehow in perfect proportion to the rest of him. His suit was impeccably tailored. She'd seen so few large men in clothing that truly fit them well and the task that jacket was performing in covering those shoulders and the breadth of his arms was impressive.

A plain black domino mask obscured his features, but highlighted the strong jaw. The interior of the courtyard was lit only by the ambient lighting from the gas lamps on the other side of the wall, so he stood somewhat in shadow. But despite the alarm she'd felt upon first encountering him, she took a step forward.

"Your Highness," the man rumbled and bowed low. "Forgive me for disturbing you."

"It seems that I have disturbed you. How did you get in here? Almost no one knows of this place."

"I came to urge you to be cautious tonight," the man said, ignoring her question. "There is a plot by one of your noblemen to use the magic of a Tanzanite Crest to enspell you into choosing a particular man to be your king consort."

The mystery of his presence took a backseat to this revelation. "Dark magic? Who would dare? And how did you come by this information?" She took another step toward him, drawn forward as if by a string around her middle. The weak lighting did nothing to assuage her curiosity about what exactly he looked like.

"Lord Dawit and his sons." The name was vaguely familiar. Some minor aristocrat that no doubt wanted a vast upgrade in his circumstances. But to sink to such forbidden magic… Chills pebbled her skin.

"Do you have a way to protect yourself against such threats?" the man asked.

He was certainly good at evading the questions he didn't want to answer. "I can tune the protective charm I wear to detect such a thing. But it helps to know the type of dark magic, so your warning is of great help."

He nodded as if this confirmed something he already knew. Her eyes narrowed. She was certain she'd never seen this man before, but he knew her secret courtyard. Had seemed to be expecting her here, not in the ballroom. Should she be afraid? Was some important sense of self-preservation within her broken because fear was the furthest thing from her mind?

Though news of the scheming aristocrats was deeply troubling, she had faith in her protective charm. Curiosity now grabbed her in an iron hold. Who was this man?

She took another step closer, and he took a matching step away.

Music from the ballroom filtered through the air as the musicians ended one song and moved on to the next. Jamila tilted her head. It figured they would play her favorite dance while she was out here on a break.

Another step forward brought her into the shadows with him. Closer now, but in the darkness, the hope of making out his features was gone.

"This is my favorite song," she said wistfully.

The man paused, looked back toward the ballroom and then to her. "Would… you like to dance?" The question was spoken almost too softly to hear. As if he wanted her to be able to pretend she hadn't heard. Oh, but she had.

Delight filled her, and she held out her arms. His full lips curved upward. Then he walked into her embrace and placed a warm hand at her waist. The heavy strength of it was like a band of comfort surrounding her. He moved her competently through the steps, though it was clear he did not dance often. Still, even his slight stiffness was better than the smooth, practiced charm of the men she'd been shuttled between all night long. There was something authentic and real about him. Something almost familiar, like she had done this before with him, maybe in a dream.

"Will you tell me how you found this place?"

"The ballroom was overwhelming." Her head came up only to his chest so he tilted his face down until his voice was a breath brushing her cheek. "It was far more crowded than I'd expected. I came for a walk in the garden and something about the spacing of the walls didn't seem right. There had to be something hidden here. It was just a matter of finding the door."

The words shook loose a flash of memory. She'd heard those words, or words like them before.

The first time she found this place, it had been with Ash, her long ago friend. The son of the palace shoemaker. In fact, wasn't it Ash who'd actually found the courtyard? He'd had an eye for space and design. The boy could build anything out of scraps, like the dollhouse he'd constructed for her from the discarded cartons of the weekly food shipments.

She peered up into the face of the man she danced with, searching for familiarity. She had not seen Ash in nearly fifteen years. Could the slender boy have sprouted into this muscular behemoth?

"What is your name, sir?"

But instead of answering, he pulled her into a spin that had her heart racing. "Would you settle for a secret instead?"

Her skin warmed at his playful tone. "What kind of secret?"

"Only the best kind for the princess."

She pressed her cheek against his chest and inhaled. "You do not wish to give me your name?"

"My name is not as valuable as a treasured secret."

"Very well then," she sighed. "Though you know I could issue a royal decree for the information. What is this treasure?"

"This suit is enspelled." He removed his hand from her waist for a moment, leaving the area almost bitterly cold. Then he flicked his wrist toward the fountain and its mysterious statue. The cracks in the old stone began to glow and water spouted from the creature's mouth in an arc. It fell in a stream which moistened the soil around the flowers in the base.

Jamila gasped in delight. "Are you a mage?"

"No." He shook his head. "But I have befriended an Aquatikin and recognized the fountain as the handiwork of their kind."

She looked at the sculpture again with this knowledge in mind. "I've always wondered what that was. Of course it must be an Aquatikin."

"When you are queen," the man said, spinning her around again, "perhaps you will revisit the way they are treated. Shuttled off to preserves far from the sea when their 'usefulness' has ended. It has always bothered you, has it not?"

Once again, the pulse of familiarity beat within her. "It definitely has. When I have more influence, I do want to change things. But I must ask, you came to the ball to vie for my hand in marriage. How am I to know whom to choose if you do not give me your name?"

Those upturned lips stuttered and fell. "I came only to warn you, princess. I have no designs on your hand. I would not be an appropriate choice for king consort."

A heavy weight of shame shadowed that statement. Jamila longed to unravel and unpack his words. No one she'd met so far had awakened the feelings of interest she now bore.

The song came to an end and they stopped moving, but Jamila still clung to his shoulder and waist. She yearned to close the polite space between them and fully enter his embrace, but he stepped away, removing their points of contact. She was about to actually issue a royal decree for his name, when the courtyard door swung open.

Enora stood silhouetted in the doorway. "The queen is looking for you," the young woman stage whispered. Jamila rolled her eyes.

All she'd wanted was a few moments of peace. Well, she'd gotten them, hadn't she? Peace and curiosity and a whole lot more.

She turned to bid the man goodbye, but he was gone. Retreated into the darker shadows? Or had he known about the other courtyard door?

The princess took a deep breath and steeled herself to face the crowd again. She *would* find him again, and when she did, she wouldn't let him leave without giving her his name.

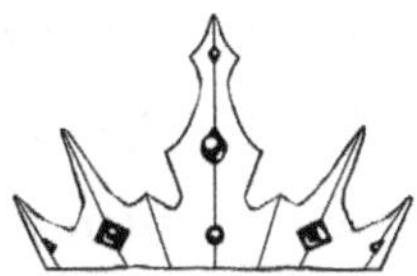

Ash leaned against the wall sucking deep breaths into his lungs. Mila was… incandescent. She had been delicately beautiful as a young girl, with rich mahogany skin, wide-set doe eyes, and a softly rounded nose. Adulthood had refined her features and made it so she was almost impossible to look away from.

She'd wanted his name and he had deflected. Did some part of her remember him? He'd been tempting fate by reciting almost exactly the same words he'd given when she'd first asked him how he'd found the courtyard all those years ago. He both did and did not want her to remember him.

What name could he have given anyway? Ash of the cinders? He was no one now, not even the shoemaker's son. Just a servant in a dilapidated manor. But he had done what he came here to and delivered the warning. Now, hopefully, the princess was alerting the guards and his stepfather's plans would come to naught.

Back in the ballroom, he spotted Jamila marching up to the queen, who stood just in front of the dais. Ash was ready to turn away, conscious of his time ticking down. It was nearly midnight, however, his progress was halted when he spotted Lord Dawit's purposeful march towards Jamila with Chidi in tow. The gods only knew where Tambo was.

Rage struck when his stepfather bowed to both a smiling queen and a scowling princess. Jamila was speaking, motioning aggressively with her hands. But where were the guards? Why was no one arresting the men?

Even from this distance, the Tanzanite Crest was visibly pinned to Lord Dawit's lapel. It glowed with a vibrant blue light. Ash realized the queen's vacant smile and loose-necked nod must be a result of the magic. The woman was not normally so agreeable. Realization swept over Jamila's face too and her jaw dropped.

From what Ash had overheard, the crest was only effective for short periods of time, providing a gentle, but insistent compulsion towards the user's purpose. It would not last long enough to, for example, take over an entire kingdom. But it looked like it was enough to sway the queen into pushing Jamila to dance with Chidi, apparently against her will.

Ash was moving toward them, cutting through the crowd as quickly as he could. He got glimpses of the queen's face, the vacant smile turned harsh as she bit out sharp words to her daughter. Jamila looked around for help. But the guards standing nearby weren't lifting a finger. Their first loyalty was to the queen, especially if Jamila's orders contradicted her mother's.

The princess herself didn't appear to be under the spell. Did she wear the same protective amulet she had all those years ago? The small crystal pendant was likely hidden below the neckline of her dress. Still, Ash could not truly breathe a sigh of relief until his stepbrother and stepfather were far away.

Chidi swung Jamila out onto the dance floor, impervious to her stiff limbed posture. She looked like she was still searching for escape strategies. Ash put on a burst of speed, racing the clock to get to the princess.

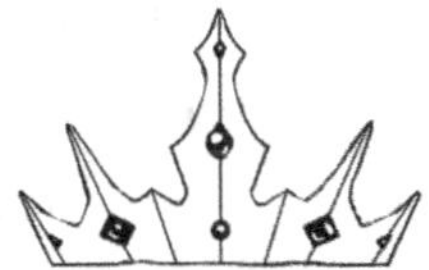

The lordling before Jamila smelled of cheese. There was nothing at all wrong with cheese, she enjoyed eating it quite a lot, but the scent of it on human skin was off-putting to say the least. Rage flowed through her veins at what she'd just endured. Lord Dawit had used dark magic on the queen of Emberglade, forcing her to ignore her daughter's objections and make her dance with this gouda-scented idiot.

The young man leered down at her, the dark blue mask he wore tilted crookedly, and his gaze dropping to her modestly covered chest like he was trying to see through the fabric.

At least she was wearing her amulet. She had already spoken the words to tune it to protect her from the dangers of the Tanzanite Crest. Why her mother was not wearing her own defensive charm was a mystery. It likely hadn't matched her outfit. The queen's vanity could potentially doom their entire queendom.

All Jamila had to do was make it through this dance without causing a scene and then alert a set of guards not within Mother's hearing or better yet, find one of the palace's martial mages. They would swiftly handle the dark magic users.

Just as she resigned herself to this indignity, the little cretin before her moved the hand that lay sweatily on her shoulder to the back of her neck.

"Exactly what do you—" Her words cut off with a gasp. Her amulet! He'd unclasped it and now it was sliding down to the ground.

Jamila jerked away from him, anger rising. "How dare you?"

The lordling, whose days on this land were numbered, grinned maniacally. "When we're married," he started, but whatever he was going to say was lost to the slap she launched at his cheek.

Anger darkened his eyes. Jamila readied herself to slap him again, when a voice called out, "Step back from her!"

It was Lord Dawit. The man's son had maneuvered them to the edge of the dance floor so that Dawit stood just a few paces away. He held the stone that had been pinned to his lapel and his forehead bunched in concentration.

A beam of blue light shot out of the infernal gem. Jamila instinctively ducked to avoid being hit by the magical blast, when a huge body flew in from the side, deflecting the stream. It bounced off his wide back and dissolved in a fizzle of gray smoke. When the man from the garden fell to the floor, vibrations rumbled beneath her feet from his weight.

Jamila knelt at his side as royal guards rushed toward them. "Are you all right?" she asked, breathless.

Lord Dawit let out a scream of frustration and the Tanzanite Crest glowed brighter, indicating another burst of dark magic was coming.

Her protector, still on the ground, whispered something that sounded like, "Bastard." Then took off his shoe and flung it at Lord Dawit, hitting the man squarely in the forehead and taking him down. The beam of dark magic shot harmlessly toward the ceiling.

As the guards surrounded her, the ornate clock at the edge of the ballroom began to toll the hour. Midnight, thank the gods. This dreadful ball would be over soon.

Assuring the guards that she was unharmed, she searched for the man who had saved her. But he was nowhere to be found.

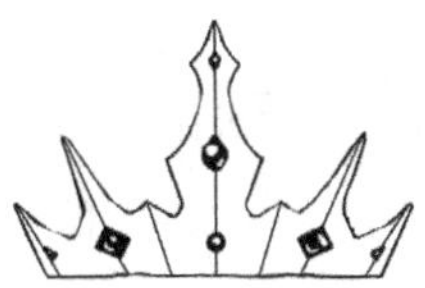

Ash walked back to the manor having lost a shoe, and his ride, but with a sense of satisfaction that couldn't be replaced. His mother's girlhood home was finally his, his stepfather and stepbrothers having been arrested after their stunt at the palace.

But his triumph was bittersweet. He returned to find Erendil bedridden after such a hefty use of his magic. "It was worth it," the old man said, and Ash hoped it was true.

The next week was spent nursing Erendil and cataloging what was needed to bring his mother's home back to its former glory. And perhaps, every now and then, wondering how a certain princess was doing. Who she had decided to make her king consort.

After seven days, it was clear the old man was not going to get any better. "Take me to the sea, child," he rasped. "It's where I am supposed to be."

And so Ash complied, carrying his frail form the hundred paces to the ocean.

"It was the honor of my life to know you and your mother. I am proud to have given both of you my magic," Erendil said as he lay in the waves. In no time at all the emaciated frame of the sickly old man transformed. Brilliant, shimmering blue scales encased his legs, which formed into a single, powerful tail. Those scales extended up his chest. His arms retracted into two smaller flappers. The giant fish—the likes of which had no mundane counterpart—eased itself into the water.

With a final splash, Erendil was gone.

Wiping what must be spray from the ocean out of his eyes, Ash trudged back to the manor to find a gilded carriage in the drive and a royal messenger knocking on his front door.

"Sir, is this your home?"

"Yes," he answered cautiously.

"I need you to try on this shoe," the young man said.

Ash stared at his own shoe in a velvet-lined box in the messenger's hand. "What?"

"You haven't heard about the princess's decree? She's been searching the queendom for the owner of this particular piece of footwear."

A spark of hope lit within Ash's chest. He swallowed, not wanting to allow it to catch fire just yet, as he slipped off his boot and placed his foot in the shoe.

A bright light enveloped him, and the scent of the sea invaded his nostrils. When the light faded, he was dressed once again in the immaculate formal suit he'd worn to the ball.

The carriage door opened and the young woman who alighted smiled brightly at him.

"Ash?" she said, voice filled with wonder.

"Yes, Your Highness?" She was so lovely, his eyes hurt.

She nearly tripped on the gravel drive racing into his arms.

Ijeoma Ossi is an illustrator inspired by folklore, mythic history and the supernatural. She is passionate about promoting African stories, and her client work includes book illustration, graphic novellas, picture books, visual development (character and background design).

Her art has been featured in literary magazines such as Moon Cola Zine, Isele, and Omenana. She has worked for brands such as UNICEF, FEMNET x Oxfam UK, Kugali, University of Bristol, and LoloTalks.

She is open to working on picture books, middle grade books, graphic novels, history and mythology non-fiction, and supernatural fiction (horror, YA fantasy).

Portfolios: https://achalugo.carrd.co/

Leslye Penelope is the award-winning author of the Earthsinger Chronicles. The first book in the series, *Song of Blood & Stone*, was chosen as one of TIME Magazine's 100 Best Fantasy Books of All Time. Equally left and right-brained, she studied filmmaking and computer science at Howard University and sometimes dreams in HTML. She hosts the *My Imaginary Friends* podcast, co-hosts the *Ink & Magic* podcast, and lives in Maryland with her feline dependents. Visit her online at: http://www.lpenelope.com.

Other books by L. Penelope

Earthsinger Chronicles

The Bliss Wars Series

Daughter of the Merciful Deep

KEEPER OF THE SPIRIT GATES

BY CELESTE HARTE

DARK FANTASY

CONTENT WARNING FOR WAR AND DESCRIPTIVE VIOLENCE

Exana stepped out from the great halls of the temple to look out into the sky. Birds took flight in the pattern of arrowheads as they left this season to take refuge in another climate. The sky went on and on, and Exana took pleasure from the fact that she couldn't see it all at one time. No matter how far one traveled, they would never see the sky in its entirety. Whenever Exana looked up, there was something bigger and greater than her. Sometimes, it was good to feel needed, but Exana craved a moment to believe that she was entirely unimportant.

Reality broke her moment of reprieve. Exana looked down again, and she knew avoiding her duties meant abandoning her peace of mind. Born a medium with the ability to see and hear the dead, she was rigorously trained by the elderly woman who once presided over the temple.

So when Exana beheld the rivers of blood that coated everything below the temple steps, and spread across the hills and tall grass, she was fully prepared. Soldiers limped, crawled, and wailed. Women cried for their children, and children wandered aimlessly, their eyes glazed over from the horrors they'd seen. Exana breathed again. She didn't know if her duty really mattered in the grand scheme of things. After all, these were the spirits of dead soldiers that had already served their duty. Citizens whose souls were lost in the wake of greater acts of violence. The real fight was out there on the battlefield. If Exana helped these spirits or simply moved on, few would notice.

Exana could hear all sorts of voices, not just from the dead. All ghosts were spirits, but all spirits weren't ghosts. Everything had a voice. For most, listening to the voices of the otherwise inanimate was a skill that one trained for years to obtain. But for Exana, everything wanted to start conversations. Exana's master saved her by teaching her to stop the flow of the constant rush. She could now deafen her second pair of ears, able to control when conversations started and ended.

There was pleasure now in tending to spirits that had waited long to talk. The Hills complained about fleeting flowers, the River sang of its joy when full, and even the Temple sometimes grumbled in disgruntled admiration of its inhabitants.

Ghosts, however, were not as easy as dealing with the spirits of land and air. Ghosts used to be people, and people held resentments that followed them after their passing, especially if they died in anguish. Mediums came to the temples to help such spirits resolve their grievances and pass to the other side. To leave them as they were was to open the world of the living to curses and strife caused by ghosts that refused to leave this realm until their revenge or griefs were satiated.

But most ghosts that came Exana's way were merely confused. Many didn't know they were dead and needed to be told so their spirits could move on. Sometimes they wanted to complete something before they passed to the other side, like seeing a loved one once more. Only sometimes did she come across a spirit that died angry; tortured, raped, or murdered. She lived in a community small enough for these deaths to be rare.

But that was before the war.

Time and space were only vague concepts to the dead. A person that died miles away could manifest here, drawn to the spiritual power of the temple. Exana was practically a beacon, due to her strong innate powers. Not even the other mediums at neighboring temples drew the attention of all the spirits she did.

Every day she saw a new spirit dragging its own arm, or an old man searching for his lost son. The Hills, Forests, and Rivers cried about the blood that stained them. She followed through with her duties each day just for the sake of ridding herself of these horrible sights. She could only look up into the sky for so long before she had to look down and remember that as long as this war waged on, she would always see death and anguish unless she did something about it.

Exana took her staff in her left hand, long false nails wrapped around the shaft. Her nails extended long enough to nearly be the length of her fingers, dipped in silver. An anklet of bells rang at her right foot as she walked down the steps of the temple, and her plaited hair ran down her chest, over the bright orange cloak she wore over her shoulders. Soldiers miles beyond were fighting a battle every day, leaving Exana to fight a different battle in their wake.

Exana turned from the scene before her and entered the temple. She walked down its long halls, her brown, bare feet padded against the marble tiles as she passed torches that bathed the space in a warm, orange glow. Not too much light, though. A medium worked best in some measure of obscurity.

The temple she looked after was small. Acolytes from larger temples sometimes came to help with maintenance, sweeping out leaves or dusting pillars, but today she was alone. She crossed the short hall to her meditation chamber in silence, save for the soft jingling of the bells around her ankle.

Her chamber was not lit by torches. Instead, a spiral of candles circled toward the room's center, their faint light barely illuminating the painted mural of the Gate on the back wall. For she was its Keeper.

Hundreds of lights flickered against the dark as she stepped around the flames with ease. Her robes fluttered past, but never caught fire. She sat in the center of the room and regarded the lights.

Instead of completely closing her eyes, her eyelids stayed slit open, enough to see the candlelight as a blur. Her attention focused on her breath as she watched her consciousness sink, ever so slowly. Mediums had to split their awareness between two realms, seeing where the spiritual realm met the living, like two pieces of paper held together in front of a burning light, the contents of both overlapping each other to come into full view.

She entered a trance through a gradual transition. Her breath hitched and changed in rhythm. Her heartbeat slowed, to the point the span of time between beats could have held a dozen. This used to scare her, but now Exana knew the experience well enough to not be afraid.

She kept her lids half-open, gently directing her attention to the Candles. When she spoke, her request was made to the Candles, themselves. "These Candles I have lit to represent the soldiers that fight and have fought on the battlefield as war rages across these lands. I work as but a servant to two planes of existence. May my deeds be a balm to the wounds of our hearts while this war continues on. Please, I ask you, let the fire of each candle represent a dozen souls. Show me those that have died this day."

A chill swept across Exana's skin, though the room had no windows. She could feel the change in temperature against her back as every flame in the room blew out. Exana heard the torches crackle and extinguish as the smell of smoke filled the air.

Exana's mouth went dry. "Wh-who? How? This can't be possible."

Only silence met her. Exana's mind reached out, her awareness expanding. Past the Candles, past the stone walls. Like an eagle, she cast her senses up high, to feel beyond the Temple, across the Fields, out to the Trees.

"What's happened?" She wanted to ask the Wind, the Trees, even the Sky, if it would answer. But once her mind went past the walls of the temple, her nose stung with the stench of death. She thought the sky was a refuge before, but with her senses heightened, she saw that it choked with agony. So many spirits drifted through the air. The sun shone on a bright day, but from here, it was like the rays of light couldn't penetrate the blanket of miserable spirits floating aimlessly.

Exana's bones shook, her lungs tightened. She had no time for questions. Sweaty hands gripped her staff as she raised it above her head. There were too many souls to do this neatly, so she would have to act quickly.

"Wearied souls, you've gathered here, drawn by the powerful symbols and rites that make this place a safe haven. I am the Keeper of the Spirit Gates, here to guide you to a better place than this."

She felt the attention of thousands turn to her, and a chill went down her spine. It was dangerous to call this many all at once, but she had little choice. With this many tortured souls, she wasn't sure there was enough spiritual protection in the world to shield herself from them all.

"Come," she said, steeling her voice. "As a conduit, I shall guide you through the Gates that will lead to your next resting place. Come to me."

A frigid air swept across her form. Her awareness sunk back down into her body, and through slit eyes, she watched the room fill with ghosts that did not walk; they ran. They phased through the walls, descended from the ceiling, and crawled out of the floor, all moaning, crying, and screaming. She felt a strong gust, but it was not the wind. The sound of creaking wood filled the air as Exana knew the painted mural behind her was shifting and the Gate was opening wide, sucking at the air as it did, drawing the spirits in. Exana knew this was happening, but she couldn't turn to see. Her vision flashed with grim crimson as images of violent last moments overcame her. She saw what these souls saw before they died. So much blood spilled from lives that ended too quickly. When tears flowed down her cheeks, for a moment, she thought the blood had poured out from the vision and fell from her eyes.

The air that the gates pulled in turned eerily cool, and Exana felt icy tendrils claw at her heart. Her heartbeat was slowing even further. She was reaching her limits. If she held the Gates open too much longer, she'd be in danger. But she was well-trained, and knew how to keep herself from being overused. "Enough."

With that single word, the phantom bodies halted, arrested by an invisible force. These walls were reinforced with ritual and prayer, preventing spirits from doing whatever they wished within. As Exana finished her ritual, they scattered like leaves in the wind.

Slowly, she allowed herself to come out of trance. The gust weakened as she heard the otherworldly creak of the Gates closing, abiding her will. Finally, her breath came more easily, and her heartbeat picked up a steady pace. But she was exhausted. Her skin felt cold and clammy, and her stomach ached like she hadn't eaten in days. What she'd done wasn't nearly enough to keep her safe tonight when the spirits would be at their most wily, especially now. She was in no state to fend off haunting spirits tonight, even with protection. As tiring as it was, her safest option was to replenish herself with food and meditation and come back so there would be less spirits to worry about come nightfall.

She wiped at the drool that had dribbled down her chin. She used her staff to help her to her feet, then trudged across the room like a feeble old woman. Just as she stepped out of her chambers, she jumped as a young man almost ran into her. Then she groaned, because he was a ghost.

"I'm sorry, I didn't mean to disturb you," he said. If Exanna was less experienced, she would have confused him for living, like she did as a child. He looked younger than her by a few years. Maybe 16 or 17 if she had to guess. He had curly hair and expressive doe eyes. His brown skin was a few shades darker than hers, and he was dressed in plain clothes. But Exana now knew the slight signs that differed the spirits from the living when they manifested themselves. The whites of his eyes gave off a soft glow, and his plain clothes fluttered with a non-existent breeze. His voice reverberated slightly, like he was speaking from within an echo chamber.

On any other day, Exana might have greeted a guest more warmly, but she was too vulnerable. Then again, these days she was often too vulnerable for warm greetings, to the spirits or otherwise. She offered a weak smile. "I'm afraid the temple is closed for the rest of today. I'm the only one here, and there is too much to do with the war going on."

"Oh," the spirit said, looking sheepish. "I'm sorry to trouble you, but if I could only have a moment. I wanted to light a candle for my younger sister, to light her way to the other plane." A quivering smile touched his face, and Exana saw the familiar sight of grief cross his features. She was watching as this man was trying to process a painful goodbye. "It's just— I know she's lost. She's always gotten lost chasing something, playing in the forest, getting distracted. I always told her to stop, but—" he choked up, then swallowed. "She doesn't have anyone to guide her right now. Our parents have already moved on. Just one candle, please. I need to know she's crossed safely. It's important to me."

He surprised Exana when he fished into his pockets, most likely for an offering, but she waved the gesture away. She knew what money was worth to a ghost when they passed. She put her hand on his, and he flinched as her false nails lightly brushed against his skin. "What's your name?"

"Kyo."

She nodded, then gave a deep sigh. Her work still wasn't done. "Well, Kyo, I've just finished a very lengthy ritual, so give me some time to recover. But I'll help you. We can send your sister off properly together."

He grasped her hand with both of his. "Thank you," he said sincerely.

Exana gave him a soft smile and pulled away, and felt an odd warmth in her chest as she did. Something about meeting Kyo made her feel a little stronger as she left him behind and strode outside of the temple. To her relief, she didn't see nearly as many soldiers out now. The limping figures slowly faded out of focus, the cries dying down. She'd have relative peace for now.

The idea of helping Kyo made her feel a little lighter, though, despite her fatigue. Nowadays her work had become so impersonal, sending off spirits with no names or relatives. The idea of helping Kyo send his sister off lifted her heaviness with a sense of purpose. People taking care of each other in the wake of destruction shone a small beacon of hope she could cling to. It would have to carry her through to endure tonight's perils and tomorrow's uncertainties.

The wind breathed over the grassy fields, and she heard the Wind's voice whisper, "Well done." Gratitude from the Wind washed over her. The Grass Fields that brushed against her calves seemed to fortify her legs in support, and she heard the Hill moan a soft, "Thank you," for alleviating their burden.

"So," said Kyo from behind her, startling her. When he noticed, he grimaced. "I'm sorry—"

"—It's alright. You may as well go… home," she said, unsure of where exactly he came from and landing on a word that didn't assume. Ghosts didn't always know they were dead, and finding out was a shock. She wouldn't tell him to return to his realm if he didn't know what it was, so she would play it safe for his sake. "I'll conduct a ritual for your sister later tonight. I have another ritual to do at that time anyway, and I'd rather begin my night helping you say goodbye to your sister."

"I was just wondering if you needed any help. I noticed you were all alone, and… I hope you don't mind my asking, but aren't you a little young to be a practicing medium?"

Exana sighed, putting her clawed hand on her hip. Well, at least he knew he was dead. "I've been able to see and hear for a long time. I had to learn quickly."

"Well, if you won't take money, at least let me offer you my strength." He offered a hand, then pursed his lips, and there was more misery in his eyes than some saw in a lifetime, much less in a little more than a dozen. "I'm here to help save my sister, but really I suppose I was the one that got lost this time. Truth be told, I didn't realize I'd died until I heard your call. But I didn't see my sister when you finished your ritual, and I got worried about her."

"If you know you're dead, why did you offer me your coin? Surely you got it from family members who believe in paying the dead's way in the afterlife. Here you're trying to pay just to have me point your sister in the right direction. I don't have any influence over what happens on the other side of the Gate."

"I died looking for my sister," he said, face stern. "Our village was attacked in the middle of the night. I didn't see— everything went up in flames so quickly. Laya must have ran for the forest when she saw the flames, but I don't think she got away. They burned the trees and—"

"—A fire?"

Kyo barely acknowledged Exana's interruption. "I looked for her. I couldn't find her, I couldn't— she died alone."

Exana felt the grief and guilt that poured off of him in waves, but she could read between the lines of his story. "You did too, didn't you?"

Kyo bit his lip. "But they found my body. That's why I have this." he pulled out the single copper coin he was laid to rest with. It might have been all his remaining loved ones had to give. "I don't deserve this. I can't move on and leave my sister deserted. I thought if I could pay my way to a better afterlife with this, I could at the very least show you thanks. If you won't accept my coin, let me lend you strength with part of my energy, then. Let me do something. Don't make me feel like a useless older brother."

His response surprised her. She'd never had a ghost offer her something for her services before. She wasn't sure she saw her services as really being *for* the ghosts, as selfish as it sounded. It was for her own peace. But could one really be selfish in doing such a thankless act? It left her exhausted. She had no one out here since her master died. Not even ghosts stayed to see her. The land spirits were too singular in nature to be true companions. The spirits were to be revered, and that was the only way to handle them. She'd never known a spirit to revere her in kind.

Emotion warmed her chest at the unnecessary gesture. She didn't need his help. She would eat, have some tea, ground herself by the stream perhaps, and come back later to light a candle for his sister, then let them both through the Gate. It was intense, and it was brutal to do this every night so long as men at the boarder couldn't decide what side of the line was theirs or not. Whether or not Kyo helped tonight out of many nights was of little consequence. But she realized that if she was selfishly helping ghosts pass to the next life for herself, perhaps he was selfishly trying to help her as well. He wanted to feel like he'd done something in thanks for her help. He wanted to help his sister himself and be a good older brother, even after he'd passed.

Exana found herself nodding and allowed him to come near her.

Just then she heard a strangled cry. "No!" Another ghostly soldier came running. Unlike Kyo, who had presented himself to Exana with his form unmarred, it was obvious that this man was dead. A thick cut blazed a red line across his neck. His uniform was soaked in his own blood from the collar down. Panic was etched into his dark features, and he ran, not like the spirits hastening to the other side, but with a pointed purpose of getting to Exana. "Stop! This spirit means to deceive you, my lady!"

Exana frowned, looking to Kyo, only for the spirit to raise his hands, confusion on his soft face. "I don't understand."

Without explaining, the soldier stepped between Kyo and Exana, bloodied blade raised. "Don't be fooled by his appearance," the soldier warned. "This is a malefic spirit, seeking revenge."

Exana's eyes flicked between the two. Her clawed fingers twitched, but she kept her calm. "I assure you, I am no amateur medium. As easily as I can pass a spirit through my Gates, I can dispose of them when they cross the line. Please, calm yourself. This place is a safe place for the spirits, but that permission is a privilege, not a right. Fighting of any sort will get every participant expelled."

"He is the enemy," the soldier insisted. "The filthy Nabodian who cut me down now seeks aid from my country's own medium to get into an undeserved afterlife." Rage twisted his dark features as he spat on the ground. He gripped his blade with clenched fists. "He would sap your strength and leave you unable to broker passage for your countrymen to the other side."

Kyo still seemed lost for a moment, but then recognition eclipsed his features. "I remember you now." He looked down at his hands. A machete appeared in them, scarlet blood dripping down its edge. Kyo's hands became stained in red, and his face turned sullen and dark. "I did," he murmured. "I did kill you."

The soldier turned his attention to Kyo. "You play the innocent, but you were a soldier, just as I was. How dare you bring yourself to one of our sacred mediums in your plainclothes, rather than in the garb of your military, the way you died?"

As the soldier spoke, Kyo's clothes changed. He was now wearing a uniform as well, a red the same color as the blood that trickled down his fingers. White war paint was brushed across his upper lip and dotted on his forehead.

Kyo curled his lip, heat in his tone. "Now I remember. You were part of the attack. You were in my way. I was trying to find my sister, and you were blocking me."

"Was it not enough that you took my life? Now you would cheat your way into safe passage through the Gate by one of my own?"

Kyo's voice cracked. "I never wanted to be in this damned war! They put a sword in my hand and told me to fight. I got to come home from the battlefield for the first time in years and then the fire started."

"You have no right to the mediums of a country that doesn't belong to you. Find your way by some other means. Or you will taste defeat a second time."

Kyo sneered, and the irises of his eyes changed from warm brown to piercing white, his form shifting with his emotions. This was getting out of hand. "I was the one that killed you, remember?"

"Enough," Exana said, pushing the soldier aside. The fire left Kyo's eyes once she was in his sight again. She placed a hand on his cheek. "You're not a killer," She insisted, forcing him to look into her eyes rather than his enemy's. "You approached me as you saw yourself: a caring older brother." She turned to the soldier. "Lower your weapon. Whatever strife you carried in life shouldn't burden you in your afterlife. Let him go."

When Exana turned back to Kyo, the blade had vanished from his hands, and he was back in his plainclothes. His eyes glimmered with wetness.

The soldier gave an incredulous scoff. "My lady, you would side with your enemy rather than a soldier who died for you?"

Exana put Kyo behind her to face the soldier. Suddenly the events from this morning started to make sense. "You died because you burned down his village, and littered your country with countless souls of the dead. Don't carry the sins of your country by defending pointless violence when it got you killed along with your supposed enemies."

The soldier sneered. "We were within our rights. Karthera will retake the land of the Nabodia and expel those wayward people that wandered in, as they do everywhere. A people not even civilized enough to make permanent residence anywhere. They scurry about the land like rodents with no purpose but to eat and breed on whatever land they happen upon. This is our land and they should be expelled, forced to continue their ways elsewhere."

"And you?" Exana cocked her head. "You wandered here just the same as he did. Are you not on my land? Do you not also seek passage through my Gate? And what of the afterlife? Whose land is that? You repeat the senseless babble of men who made you feel justified, even as you died. But this is *my* temple, and you will leave this place."

The soldier leveled his sword at Exana, and his irises turned white like Kyo's did before. A black halo wafted off of his form, and his presence turned menacing. His eyes fixed a punishing gaze on Exana as his body became swallowed in shadow. "You are a traitor to your people, and your practices are foul. You willfully let the undeserving pass through your Gates. A medium? Ha. You may as well be a whore for the dead."

Kyo tried to push past Exana, but she held him back, her clawed hand extended. "I'll handle this," she assured him, though the pleasantness in her tone had gone. Kyo made the wise decision of stepping back.

She turned to the soldier. "I don't even know your name." With a single swipe of her silver nails, the image of the man's sword split into ribbons like it was made of silk instead of steel. "But when I'm done with you, you won't either. Your last mistake will be underestimating me."

The soldier charged her, and with a swift movement, she clawed at him, nails slicing through the inky smoke that wafted off of his body. But his spirit regathered to her left and threw himself at her.

Exana passed her staff to the other hand and batted him away at the last moment, but he'd gotten too close. A chill swept through her right side, sinking to her bones. A shiver ran through her, and her breath hitched.

"Miss!" Kyo called.

Exana held out a hand. "Stay back."

Dead spirits shouldn't fight. Once the soul left the body, its form shifted freely outside of its earthly shell. It made spirits change with their moods and emotions, and turned them dangerous when they got out of hand. Kyo would only turn himself into an enemy if he tried to help her now.

But she would need to finish this quickly. Her ritual from earlier left her weak, and she couldn't risk letting this fight last long. Hefting her staff, Exana directed it at the soldier. *"Come,"* she said, her words penetrating the air like a knife. Her command drew the soldier like a puppet on a string, yanked from his stance and pulled him towards her waiting claws. She impaled his shadowy chest.

A white grin spread across a smoky face. "We will not be gotten rid of that easily."

Exana's eyes widened. The soldier's body bubbled, and faces

pushed out of his form, gurgling and overlapping each other, like a boiling pot of human features. His form grew around her claws, and soon he was towering over her, with a dozen white eyes blinking across his body, peering down at her. The air turned icy, and Exana's fingertips turned numb with cold. A shiver broke across her body and a cold sweat streaked down her face. Suddenly she couldn't move, as if frozen to the spot. It was hard to think. *He has the army behind him*, was the only thing her mind was able to grasp.

The soldier spoke a single word with a thousand voices as he raised a hand that constantly shifted form. "Whore."

A quick hand pushed Exana out of the way and sliced across the shadow with a glowing white blade. The dark spirit wailed and retracted as Kyo stood in between Exana and the monster, his machete in hand.

"That will be the last time you say that word again in her presence." Kyo turned to Exana, eyes glowing white. "I'm sure you aid countless spirits every day. Let someone help you for once."

Kyo touched her shoulder, and strength pumped through her body. Warmth spread, melting the icy cold that gripped her before. Her thoughts flowed, and she could breathe again. Her silver nails glimmered and lengthened. The end of her staff glowed.

Exana understood.

The darkened spirit wailed, and at the same time that Kyo stepped back, Exana propelled herself forward. Her movements were quick. Her lengthened claws ripped across the spirit's body, a blazing hot white that seared through the blackness and rippled the air like she was swiping across a pond. The spirits within the dark mass split, separating into screeching phantom shapes that wavered through the air.

Exana spoke, "I am the Keeper of the Spirit Gate, and by the power of the spirits that protect this land and empower my will, I banish you."

The spirit did not vanish with a screeching wail or a scream. But a whisper came through the breeze, and like a candle snuffed out, the spirits were silenced. They were there, and then they were vapor, an empty sigh that the wind carried away. The afterlife would not have them, nor would the living world. They no longer existed. Such was the right of a medium to deal with a baleful spirit that broke the sacred laws of her boundaries.

Exana's nails retracted to their original size, and the end of her staff dimmed. She turned to Kyo. "A spirit has never done that for me before."

Kyo's sword vanished, and his eyes shifted back to their soft brown. "My people's beliefs are built on gratitude. We thank the priests that honor our dead, and we thank the beings of the world beyond with coins for passage. I could not go without thanking you, as well."

Exana made a fist with her right hand, feeling the leftover strength pulsing through her blood. This day was exhausting, but somehow Kyo had made himself a beacon of light in an otherwise lonely and dreary routine. What filled her now was the resolve to let his story end the right way. The world lost a noble soul on the day he died, but she would see him cross to his next story safely, as well as help him honor his dues. "Let's go light a candle for your sister."

She led Kyo back into the temple, and she went through the rites that called a wayward spirit to guide them back. Kyo watched as she lit a candle and rung a bell, speaking soft words to draw his sister from wherever she'd gone missing to come back to her brother.

It didn't take long for a young girl with a halo of afro hair bouncing on her shoulders to come running. Exana could see why he'd missed her. She was dressed in rags, and her hair was matted in some places, but the look on her face was one of a child who was too loved to notice anything she lacked. She leaped into her brother's arms. Laya, Kyo had called her before. "Kyo!" Laya shrilled.

Kyo took a long moment to hug her back. "I told you not to go running off by yourself all the time," he said, voice cracking.

She gave him a coy smile of a child used to getting away with everything. "Well, you found me in the end, didn't you?"

Kyo chuckled, then pulled out the copper coin from his pocket and pressed it into his sister's hand. "Take this. You'll need it."

She nodded reverently, clutching the coin with tiny hands. "Aren't you coming with me?"

"Not yet. But I'll join you soon," he said, and Exana raised an eyebrow, wondering what he was implying.

The little girl nodded. "Alright! See you soon, Kyo!"

Laya darted for the Gate, and Exana had to say a quiet word to open it for her before she comically ran into the closed doors. Exana chuckled and shook her head as the girl disappeared behind the mural that shifted its paints to close its gates again, and a soft breeze washed over them as it did. Then she turned to Kyo. "Why don't you go through? You may not be able to pay your way, but I'm sure there are other ways for you to get across."

Kyo shook his head. "I'd rather stay and help you."

Exana huffed. "You? Help me?"

Kyo crossed his arms. "It doesn't look like you have any friends around here. And you need someone to remind the spirits that pass that they should give something in return for your help. Energy should be an exchange, not a loss." He touched her shoulder, and she felt a brief moment of that warmth and power from before. "They should at least replenish the strength you lose by passing so many on. Especially in the midst of a war where you show yourself impartial to either side."

Exana evaluated him for a moment. She wasn't used to anyone thanking her. She wasn't really used to being around anyone.

"How long do you plan to stay here?"

Kyo gave her a soft smile. "Perhaps long enough for us to see my sister again together. She'll wait. And I'm sure spending a human's lifetime aiding a medium will make up for the coin I cannot pay."

Exana was at a loss for words. "You can't possibly mean that. And what if I don't want you here the rest of my life?"

Kyo shrugged. "I'll go if you ask. But I don't think you will."

"And why's that?"

"Because you need a friend. And so do I."

Exana crossed her arms and bit her lip. At her silence, Kyo held out his hand. "May I?"

Perplexed, Exana nodded. Kyo closed his eyes. "I bind myself to you as an aid and companion to protect and stand by you as I am able."

The air shimmered, and Exana watched in awe as golden lines traced the air, hooking through Kyo like a string, then connected itself to Exana.

"I've never seen this ritual before," Exana admitted as the golden strings faded, wondering if they came from rituals unique to his people, or if the magic was universal to any that knew its secrets. She suspected the latter.

"No one has shown you gratitude before, either. My father was a priest, before he died. He had spirits that helped him, as well. It's not a foreign concept."

Exana tried to make herself believe that this was unnecessary. She'd gone this long without help. Why change anything now?

But the things he'd said resonated with her. She always thought she became a medium for herself, to stop the visions from driving her mad and the voices from keeping her awake for days on end. Her duty served to preserve her own well-being, but that didn't mean she should allow others to take her services for granted, either. Her job needed not be thankless.

"I accept," she said, and after a heartbeat, added, "Thank you."

Kyo grinned.

Celeste Harte

Celeste Harte is a sci-fi and fantasy author out here making worlds and taking names. She's the author of the **Dragon Bones** trilogy and an upcoming D&D inspired high fantasy novel. She's a freelance technical writer and copy editor, as well as an illustrator for book covers, character art, and children's books. Her favorite way to relax is with a good anime or manga, and she loves playing Elden Ring. Learn more about her at https://celesteharte.com/

Other books by Celeste Harte

Conquest

Rising

Uproar

THE PROMISED ROAD: A TALE OF NAHWALLA

BY OMARI RICHARDS
ART BY MELANIN ECLECTIC

SWORD AND SORCERY

CONTENT WARNINGS FOR DESCRIPTIVE VIOLENCE
AND PREGNANCY

Twenty men were not enough to protect the caravan. There would be too many gaps in their formation that any group of mounted attackers could exploit. Twenty was too precarious a number, it meant every man mattered. Should one or even two lose heart and flee, their strength would easily diminish.

Arazaki could only sigh and adjust his greaves. He had brought these concerns to Queen Sizakele Morowa three moons ago when she ordered this procession. He had used every rhetorical technique he had learned in his fifteen years of serving and protecting the high caste to change her mind and avoid possible disaster. He had used flattery, charm, fearmongering, speculation, conjecture, comparison, and religious tenets, none of it worked. If anything, the self-declared Queen of the Cwatha Peninsula only seemed to dig her heels further into the idea. Not even the thought of losing their precious cargo seemed to sway her.

"Our cause is true and just," Queen Sizakele had insisted. "The goddess Omutonzi would not turn Her back on us. She will guide us down this road and to Her temple. Our faith will shield us and the precious cargo."

"If faith was all that was required, then why do I wear armor into battle?" Arazaki scoffed under his breath. He scowled at himself. He knew better than to voice such thoughts aloud. With the high caste and their games at court, even when you thought you were alone, you never were. Fortunately, the men and their servants seemed too preoccupied with securing the carriage and triple checking its wheels and spare wheels like he had ordered to pay his grumblings any mind.

"Sir," a young strong voice said, snapping Arazaki from his thoughts. "We have completed inspecting the carriage and believe it is safe for the queen and the precious cargo." Arazaki raised an eyebrow.

"You believe…. Isisila?"

Isisila dipped his rather small and overly round head, likely repeating the words again in his mind to find the error. Sweat from the heat and the task had already begun to undo Isisila's face paint. His brown-red foundation remained solid but the white spots that covered his cheeks, the bridge of his nose, and forehead were beginning to appear uneven. Fortunately, the thick dark lines painted down his eyes and to the side of his face to keep the sun from his eyes remained solid.

Isisila cleared his throat after a moment's consideration.

"Pardon my mistake, sir," he said. "We *know* that the wagon is suitable and safe for the queen and the precious cargo."

"*Confident*, Isisila," Arazaki said, shaking his head. "We can only be confident in these things. Blind faith kills just as much as doubt does."

Isisila sighed and scraped at the dirt road with his foot. "These precautions would not be needed if the queen had taken the sea or river routes like you and the councilors suggested."

"Our duty is to protect the high castes," Arazaki said, gripping the younger warrior's shoulder. "Not to question them. We leave that to the councilors."

Isisila's lips remained tight. "Was King Kganelo this difficult during your years of being his personal guard?"

Arazaki squeezed the hilt of his straight sword, and hoped his face did not reflect the twist in his stomach. In the corner of his eye, he could almost see the blood storm Kganelo's throne room became at their final encounter.

"Worse," he said. "Kganelo was an Owuo and with their giants' blood it often took the entire castle just to move one toe. We should consider ourselves fortunate that we do not have to resort to such measures with Queen Sizakele."

Arazaki rolled his shoulder. Talk of his former captor and mentor aggravated the burns on his back.

"I doubt even the most stubborn of Owuo would dare to enter Sangeya Forest on foot at night without Mutulu to guide us," Isisila grumbled.

Arazaki glanced up at the orange and purple hued horizon. Nolitha, the sun, was near the end of her daily journey across the sky but tonight her husband Mutulu, the moon, would not appear. Once every month, Mutulu lost his battle against the darkness and needed to restore his strength, leaving them without his light. It was a time for reflection, rebirth, and prayer. But it was also a time where demons, evil spirits, and magic were at their strongest without Mutulu's light to keep them at bay.

Arazaki had yet to encounter a demon during these nights. But he had encountered several brigands who were emboldened by the darkness. Many of them, who were often deserters or former warriors of deposed rulers, took refuge in Sangeya Forest. The only time they weren't fighting, robbing, and killing each other was when they were fighting, robbing, and killing every traveler who entered what they considered their territory.

Outside of his occasional offerings to Varasha the Sentinel, for the sake of the men, Arazaki was never one for prayer. Tonight however, he prayed that the bandits and brigands found another group of foolish travelers to torment. Though he wondered which god remained to hear it.

"We stay close, we stay together, we survive," Arazaki said, patting the younger man's cheek. "Can I count on you?"

Isisila nodded. "Of course, sir."

"Do not be so quick to give your feathers to the tortoise, boy," a gruff voice spat ahead of them. "Especially this one. I can see the flies on his tongue even from here." Arazaki nearly chewed through his lips at the sight of Mwanza Mapula. The elder warrior's reddish-brown skin emphasized his growing wrinkles and age-lines. Grey had long overtaken his short beard and his bald spot showed no signs of stopping. The former captain of the guard walked with a black molamu stick engraved with the various names and brief messages of his ancestors. Perhaps the only thing older than the molamu stick was the brown pangolin scale armor Mwanza clung to despite the growing ease and access of quilt armor and mail.

"There are neither lies nor trickery on my tongue when I say sticking together is how we survive," Arazaki said, meeting the elder's hazel eyes which burned with a permanent fury since Queen Sizakele named him her new captain of the guard.

"Sticking together," Mwanza sneered as though it were a curse. "Is that what you told King Kganelo before you abandoned your post and left him to die?"

Arazaki's hand quivered on his sword. The ten men Mwanza had chosen for the task formed a small circle around them, all wearing pangolin scale armor. To strike at Mwanza would risk losing their aid.

"You would have done the same in my place," Arazaki said through grit teeth.

"Cowards, traitors, and fools abandon their posts," Mwanza spat, tapping Arazaki's breastplate with the knob of his molamu walking stick. "It is easy to guess which one you are. Yet, I am expected to entrust our queen with you?"

Arazaki's jaw trembled. It was suddenly difficult to keep a steady breath. "The queen is fortunate then that you are here to drive your dagger in my back if I betray her."

"**When** you betray her," Mwanza said. "I've seen your type before, bastard. Clan-less, landless, no family, all you have are your selfish desires. You jump from place-to-place betraying everyone around you just to climb a single branch. You have our queen fooled but not me. You are simply waiting for your moment, you and that treacherous wife of yours."

Arazaki's blade sang as it flew from its sheath, the iron arc primed for Mwanza's short neck. A flat dull note rang through the courtyard. Arazaki flinched at the sudden stop of his sword. Rather than flesh, it had bitten into Mwanza's walking stick. A thin, toothy smile rippled across the old man's face as his left hand began to draw his sword.

"Save this foolishness for our enemies," a loud, clear voice declared from a distance. All movement and aggression ceased at the sight of Queen Sizakele. She was a pillar of gold and crimson. Her simple red dress and golden necklace and earrings caught the sun's fading light and reflected it onto the courtyard. The dark gray travel robe Arazaki had instructed her to wear did little to damper her elegant movements. Neither did her new short hair make her appear more like a commoner. Her face still held the sharp shape and high cheekbones found in the Morowan clan. Authority still radiated from her eyes. Her mother's golden crown only seemed to orient itself more to match the crown of her head.

"Did you not see, my queen!" Mwanza exclaimed. "Did you not see him draw his weapon against me?"

"As would I if you continued to spew your obscenities, Mwanza," Queen Sizakele said with a deep sneer. "Arazaki and Noluthando are doing a great service for not only the crown but for our people. You would do well to remember that."

Arazaki coughed in his hand to cover his smile at the sight of Mwanza's mewling. A quick glare from the queen cut whatever amusement he felt to pieces.

"I do not trust them, my queen…." Mwanza grumbled.

"*I* trust them," Queen Sizakele declared. "That should be enough. And if it is not, seek another ruler to serve. There are plenty to choose from in this fractured land of ours."

"None that I have protected and fostered since they were children," Mwanza said.

"Then act in a manner that I would expect from my trusted old soldier," Queen Sizakele said, before her face softened. "To know that, even after all this time, you still question my judgment, hurts me, Mwanza."

Mwanza froze. "It is not that at all! It's...we've been betrayed before, my queen. The treachery of Noluthando's father nearly robbed us of everything, then Ayubu's attempt to sabotage your experiment..."

"And I have learned from those mistakes," Queen Sizakele said. "Have these past twelve years not proven that?"

Mwanza dropped to his knee so swiftly, Arazaki was sure he heard the bones pop. "Our land has known nothing but prosperity since you retook your mother's throne," Mwanza said. "I only wish to ensure that this prosperity continues."

"And it will, if we complete this journey. And to ensure that, we need Arazaki and Noluthando. Is that clear?"

"Yes, of course my queen!"

She nodded before facing Arazaki. "Please excuse my old soldier. At times I forget he will forever see me as the small girl of nine living years sitting on his knee and clapping her hands as he tells his war tales."

Arazaki immediately straightened his back as he spoke. "There is nothing to forgive, your highness. Lord Mwanza is well within his rights to be concerned."

"And you are well within your rights to be frustrated with him. There are certainly times where I am," she said before dropping her voice. "However, I will not tolerate any harm to befall my old soldier. If there is even a nick on his neck from your spear or any sworn to you, your service to me will be concluded... permanently. Do we understand each other?"

Arazaki sheathed his sword and gulped. "Yes, my queen, we understand each other."

"Good. Now, see to your wife, she had a difficult morning with the potions. I fear for her and our child."

Panic surged in Arazaki's stomach and heart. He crossed the courtyard and reached the stairs just as his wife emerged from the castle gates. He ignored that Queen Sizakele had draped Noluthando in a fine silk yellow gown despite his urging to keep to simpler traveler clothes to avoid attention. He looked past the large ruby ring on her middle finger, the final gift from her treacherous father. He held back his scoff at her large charm necklace of a red stallion, the symbol of the fabled Lady Nomathemba.

He cupped his wife's round face and looked her over, lingering on her large, swollen belly that carried the queen's precious cargo and the future of the Morowan clan. Other than swollen feet, a few loose strands of hair that escaped her headwrap, and her glowing skin which she said did not originate from divine acceptance of motherhood but from her constant sweating, Noluthando was as he had left her the previous day. Though it was not until he saw the full grin form on her lips, revealing the dimples in her cheeks, and heard her bright laugh, did he allow himself to relax.

"It is as I said, my queen," Noluthando said between chuckles. "My husband is both swift and attentive when given the proper motivation."

Queen Sizakele gestured to the gathered men. "It was not I who needed the reminder."

"But I imagine you needed the amusement," Noluthando said.

"Without question," Queen Sizakele said, removing her crown and placing it in a prepared silver lockbox held by Mfuneko, a tall warrior beside her.

"I'm a source of amusement now?" Arazaki asked.

"You've always been, my dear," Noluthando said with a smile. "Ever since the day you tripped and fell in the river."

"You mean when you pushed me?"

"Do you believe there is a difference? You were in dire need of a bath regardless." She wrinkled her nose at him. "And to be honest, you still are. Do you plan on using your stench to frighten our enemies away?"

Arazaki chuckled. Her sharp tongue was still intact. She was fine. "It would be a more effective weapon than bathing myself in lavender." He tapped her charm necklace. "Or relying on a fable for protection."

Noluthando placed a hand over the red horse charm. "Lady Nomathemba protects those who journey to fulfill their promises to others and travelers embarking on dangerous roads. What better protection is there?"

Arazaki sucked his teeth. "Inform me when the mystical lady provides you with a sword, armor, a spear, and a shield?"

She smirked at him. "She sent me you, did she not?"

"And your father?" he asked, nodding towards the ruby ring. "What is he protecting?" Noluthando spun the ring with her thumb, her eyes leaving his for a moment.

"My resolve," she said firmly.

Arazaki flinched and lowered his voice. "You endured the queen's…experiments for nine moons to ensure the heir suited her requirements. Her handmaidens could only reach four moons before they succumbed. And you still doubt your resolve?"

Nolu squeezed his hand. She bit her lower lip to keep it from quivering.

"We all need something to place our faith in."

"I'd rather reserve my faith for what I can see."

"It's not always a matter of sight."

He pressed his forehead against hers. "The gods have fled these lands, Nolu, it's only us now. You are all that I choose to believe in."

A soft kiss met his lips before Noluthando pulled away and pressed the charm necklace in his hand. "Wear it for this journey, you may become accustomed to it before long." Noluthando was entering the wagon with the queen before Arazaki could object. He sighed knowing that Nolu would not rest until he put it on. Once it was secured, he walked around the wagon twice and nodded towards Isisila. In four breaths, they were all mounted. Arazaki gave the signal.

The castle gates opened and Sangeya Forest awaited them.

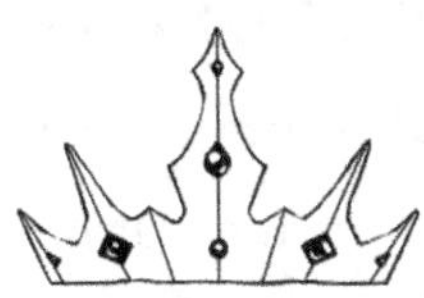

Every time the child kicked, Noluthando spun her father's ring. She still remembered when he awoke her in the early hours shoving the ring in her palm, and imparting frantic final words to her before the guards delivered him to his execution. She didn't see it. She had buried her face and ears in her pillows. It didn't help. Her father's screams had engulfed the castle as he was burned alive for his treason. A treason she had exposed to Queen Sizakele. A treason that would have eliminated the promised peace Queen Sizakele sought to deliver to the Cwatha Peninsula at the conclusion of her regional conquest.

What other choice did she have?

A bump in the road jolted the carriage and awoke the Morowan heir in her belly. The infant's blows had only grown stronger and more frantic in the last few weeks. The child must have sensed their gift day was near, or the heir was absorbing her own discomfort. It had become common for her sides to ache throughout the night as both she and the child fought to find a sleeping position where they were both comfortable. Arazaki had made it a habit to remain awake with her despite her urging that at least he rest. It was one of the many instances where he did not listen, and she was silently glad for it.

She would be gladder still for a full night's sleep, not dousing every surface with her sweat when she sat, and not running to relieve herself every three breaths. But this was how she fulfilled her duty and her debt to Queen Sizakele. This was how she ensured the queen's work would continue. If it went to ruin during the delivery, the Morowan clan and the Cwatha Peninsula would still have their queen. She carried this burden so that Sizakele was free to carry the land into peace and prosperity.

"You could deliver sixteen strong and powerful children for the queen," Arazaki had said during one of their many sleepless nights together. "And it still won't absolve you of your father's treason in their eyes…"

"It's not for my father or for the council that I do this," she replied in between winces.

Arazaki had furrowed his brow.

"I believe in her," she said. "As she believed in me when I informed her of my father's plot."

"The high caste feeds on belief like hyenas and vultures Nolu," he had said. "They turn us into rotting corpses in the sun as we wait for them to fulfill their promises."

"And how would you know this?"

"I've seen it," was his reply. "How do you know she will deliver this peace?"

"I've seen it," she answered. "On the horizon. In my prayers. In my dreams."

"And that's enough?"

"Sometimes, it's all we have."

"Such an unpleasant sight," Queen Sizakele said, shaking Nolu out of her memories. Noluthando wrapped her hands around her belly as the carriage jolted again and the heir unleashed another round of swift kicks.

"What sight, your highness?" Nolu asked when the heir settled.

She peered out the carriage's small window and moved the thick gray cloth that covered it, which Arazaki said could halt arrows, and peered out to Sangeya Forest.

Cones of fading sunlight shot through the thicket, illuminating the only completed road through the forest. The trees were entangled and clumped together as if Omutonzi was rushing their creation. Few creatures scurried in the bush, but several groups of vultures circled above, it did not take long for Nolu to understand why.

Corpses, fresh and old, along with bones and skulls had been hammered into the tree trunks. Symbols identifying the bandit groups responsible were either painted or carved onto the bones with further messages declaring territory and for invaders to stay out written in either red ink or blood. Nolu did not wish to know which was correct.

"Once the peninsula declares me their queen, cleansing this putrid place will be my next campaign," Queen Sizakele said as she closed her window.

The ease in her voice made Noluthando shift in her seat. She spun her father's ring. "A valid and needed conquest, your grace," Nolu said. "But after five years of war to unite the peninsula, the men, our coffers, and our resources will be exhausted. Would it not be better, to regain strength, reestablish trade routes, and solidify the territories that you have won before attempting another campaign?"

Queen Sizakele placed her sharp chin atop her interlaced fingers and gave Noluthando a hard stare. "What good are trade routes when our roads and waters are unsafe for caravans to pass?"

Noluthando held her gaze. "What good are these conquests if you cannot hold them? Your—*our* experiment to create your heir has angered many, both high and low caste alike, your grace. Many call it a perversion of Omutonzi's gift of life. To force an exhausted army to march, even if it is to clear the way for trade, would prove them right, that our queen cares little for life and only seeks her own ends."

Queen Sizakele tilted her head and regarded Noluthando for a long breath. Nolu squeezed the side of her dress to keep her hand from shaking. She fought the urge to look away. She fought to keep her face still as the Morowan heir began to torment her sides with kicks.

After what felt like days, Queen Sizakele eased in her seat and laughed. "Your tongue truly knows no fear or deceit, Noluthando, only the truth. And my ears welcome such a bounty." Noluthando could not hide her relieved sigh.

"You are right, of course," Queen Sizakele continued. "To push into Sangeya Forest now would only strengthen the position of Ayubu and his supporters. A paid soldier has some loyalty, a hungry soldier has none. The path forward will be one of grain, rice, yams, and meat. I thank you for this counsel."

"I merely guided you to the wisdom you would have found yourself, my queen," Noluthando said, inclining her head.

"Flattery is meaningless to me, Nolu," Sizakele said with a frown. "I am served enough of that by the councilors, even your husband. What I need from you is to tell me what they will not. That is why when this task is completed and I am holding the Morowan heir, I intend to have you on my council."

Noluthando gulped. For a moment, the floor of the carriage vanished. She spun her father's ring faster.

"I have barely established myself as the Njongo of Khayakazi. I am just beginning to help the city emerge from the debts my father left behind. And I am a traitor's daughter. What voice could I carry on your council?"

Queen Sizakele squeezed her knee. "You have carried our future in your belly. And it is that future which will guide your decisions, not the petty squabbling and schemes that fester on every council. You see what others cannot on the horizon, Noluthando. When I came to you and Arazaki with my plan for an heir, he could only see the immediate pain, the immediate danger.

But you, you saw what could be. What ought to be. Deliver this guiding light to the council, and you will be more valuable than a thousand advisors."

"I am…unsure what to say, your grace…."

Queen Sizakele chuckled. "Say yes, so we may discuss other topics."

Her reply was sitting on her tongue, prepared to reveal itself to the queen when the carriage jolted with such force it slammed their heads into its roof. The back right of the carriage sagged as though it was depleted of the will to continue.

"Javangha's Fangs! Mfuneko, Mwanza, what is the meaning of this?" Queen Sizakele exclaimed.

"Snapped wheel! Snapped wheel!" came the chorus from the

caravan.

"Replace it, quickly!" Arazaki exclaimed.

In four breaths the carriage rocked. Noluthando clung to her belly. The kicks were getting more frantic. Pain ran up her body. Her heart raced. She latched onto the carriage wall and began the breathing she had practiced for months. The pain only expanded. She clamped her teeth together. Queen Sizakele rushed to her side and shouted for the men to stop, but the men seemed to pay her no mind. Noluthando squeezed the queen's hand, the world shrank only to the pain. A single word, however, managed to pierce her agonizing veil.

"Arrows!"

That was when the screams started.

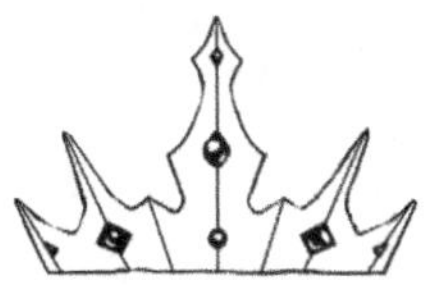

Noluthando's screams nearly knocked Arazaki from his horse. The screams of three men writhing on the ground with arrows protruding from their necks kept him in place. Arrows flew past his neck and knocked against his helmet like metal stones. The trap had been perfectly set. The brigands had dug smaller holes throughout the road, places they knew it would be difficult for a wagon or carriage to avoid. When the carriage jostled, it alerted them. But no damage had occurred, so they continued, becoming numb to the sight of the carriage bumping and rocking believing it to be a result of the road's poor condition.

All the while, the wheel's strength was weakening until the carriage struck the larger hidden hole that snapped the wheel, leaving them in range for the archers that awaited them. And the bandits Arazaki was sure would flank them.

He grit his teeth. He would be impressed with the trap if he wasn't so angry at himself. "Shields up!" Arazaki exclaimed, following his own command. "Encircle the carriage!" The men quickly galloped in place. The arrows thudded against their shields, but two more were unlucky with arrows striking their throats. Arazaki growled, in less than twenty breaths there were only fifteen of them left.

"Mfuneko! How many men do you need to replace the wheel?" Arazaki shouted to the tall warrior already hunched over by the broken wheel.

"At least four!"

"You'll have it!" Arazaki said and gestured to four men in red and white quilt armor to join Mfuneko.

"Stop rocking it!" Queen Sizakele exclaimed. "You're making her worse!"

Arazaki squeezed the reins. "Nolu! Can you hear me?"

"The baby is coming, Arazaki! It's coming!" she bellowed over her screams.

"Mwanza! How far are we from the temple?" Queen Sizakele asked.

An arrow flew past Arazaki's face and embedded itself in the cloth covering the carriage. Two more struck his raised shield.

"Another six miles, your highness!" Mwanza said, his shield blocking an arrow from taking another man.

"Isisila! You're our fastest rider. Ride to the temple and tell them we need their Rujindiri warriors and a healer priestess!" Arazaki said. "Wait for my signal!"

Another volley struck their iron circle. Another scream from Nolu pierced his heart. "Javelins!" Arazaki shouted over his heartache and pointed in the direction of the arrows. "Respond!"

Ten javelins sailed into the bush. A series of pained grunts and one man falling to the ground was their reward.

"Isisila! Go now!"

The younger warrior wasted no time. He kicked his horse into a gallop that trampled the injured archer on the ground. Isisila was halfway down the road when a group of fifty brigands on foot armed with spears burst from the bush forming a shallow line five rows deep. Enough to stop Isisila despite the old and damaged mail they wore.

"Mwanza! Take seven of your men and ride them down! Clear a path for Isisila! Wedge formation!"

The old soldier glowered at Arazaki for a moment before signaling for his men in pangolin armor to form the wedge. They thundered down the narrow road. The arrows from the remaining archers snapped against their pangolin armor. Their remaining javelins sank into the torsos or heads of the brigands and their horses smashed against the meager ground force. The brigands' numbers amounted to nothing when matched against the pangolin armor, spears, swords, and horses of the queen's warriors. Mwanza took the heads of three brigands and rode down two more, using Queen Sizakele as his war-cry. In ten breaths, the first line of brigands was either dead or dying. The rest would soon break.

But the brigands held. They began to swarm the warriors, attempting to pull them from their horses. Three men succumbed and their final cries were lost in the chaos. Arazaki craned his neck trying to find Isisila.

The younger warrior was caught between five brigands swiping at him and his horse with spears while he fended them off with his sword, trying to break through the melee. Mwanza's walking stick cracked two skulls as the old man galloped to Isisila's aid, his riders reduced to only four.

Behind Arazaki, Noluthando continued to scream. Three men propped up the carriage and Mfuneko scrambled to replace the wheel. Two more arrows whizzed past Arazaki. He growled and hurled two spare javelins. The archers dropped from the trees like stones.

A triumphant cry grabbed his ear. Isisila had broken through the melee. He galloped down the road, his exuberant smile visible even from a distance. Arazaki's muscles relaxed. He could see their way out on the horizon.

A single slash put an end to that.

Blood burst from the throat of Isisila's horse, sending both creature and rider to the ground. Isisila rolled out of the path of the thrashing horse and slashed the air with his sword but there was no foe in sight.

The young warrior yelled, circling in every direction but there was nothing, only the forest. He turned on his heel and began to run down the road towards the temple. Another slash ripped across the air. Isisila froze in his steps. His torso fell to the left. His head rolled to the right.

Arazaki's eyes widened. He couldn't even bring himself to cry out, the air had fled his lungs. He barely heard Mfuneko speak. He could only stare with a slacked jaw as Mwanza's remaining riders were cut down by the unseen enemy. A slash opened a gate of blood on the side of the old man's neck. Mwanza gasped, the fight and his life drained from his limbs.

The brigands reformed their line, confident smiles overtaking their bloodstained faces. Arazaki's stomach twisted. He drew his sword, but it was a twig compared to the wave of death before him.

"Arazaki!" Nolu exclaimed.

The pain in her voice sent a jolt through his body. He tightened his grip on his sword and straightened in his saddle. Lady Nomathemba's charm necklace surged with heat when he spoke. "Is the wheel fixed, Mfuneko?"

"It is," the tall warrior said, taking position on the carriage to drive the horses. Two more men laid dead beside the repaired carriage with arrows in their throats. The last two of their brethren had mounted their horses, glancing at him with uncertainty. Arazaki twirled his sword. A torrent of calm overtook him. For a breath, the fear that had gnawed at his stomach evaporated. The fog dissipated from his vision. Lady Nomathemba's charm necklace no longer burned. A certainty arose in his chest and flowed up his arm. He sheathed his sword; it wasn't what he needed.

"Mfuneko," Arazaki said, barely recognizing his own voice. "Spear."

He didn't look when the taller warrior pressed the weapon into his waiting palm. He heard Nolu's screams but it was a faint echo. He was suddenly aware of the wind against his neck. It carried the scent of palm wine, dirt, mud, blood, and sweat from the brigands and the men, but there was something else. A foreign, unnatural scent coming from the bandit's formed line. It was a thin layer of lavender that covered what smelled like a mixture of burnt wood and rusted metal.

Arazaki adjusted his grip on the spear and turned to the men.

"We break through, no matter what, understand?"

"We break through," the remaining men said in unison.

"For the queen," he said with a nod.

"For the queen," the men repeated with a growing vigor.

Arazaki thrust the spear into the air. "For the queen!"

His cry spurned them into a swift gallop. The carriage rattled along beside them. The brigands braced themselves and shouted war cries of their own. An arrow knocked against Arazaki's breastplate while another one found the man beside him. Arazaki barely felt the collision of their horses against the brigands. He saw Mfuneko swing his sword left and right, slashing through the throats and chests of the brigands while urging the horses to keep their gallop. Two enemies attempted to leap on the carriage but were promptly cut down by the rider at the rear. But his triumph was short-lived when he was pulled from his horse.

Arazaki gripped his spear, ignoring his slowly panicking horse, ignoring the chaos beneath him as the brigands swung and pulled at him. He shook his head and closed his eyes, searching for the scent.

A slight wind struck his face, and he felt it. A small distortion in the air to his left like embers in the distance. It was charging towards him.

Arazaki's eyes snapped open, and he thrust.

For a breath it appeared that his spear had struck only air.

Then, he heard a groan as his horse galloped past.

Arazaki looked over his shoulder and saw the form of a burly man with wild, unkempt hair flicker in and out of sight before his stunned men. In two breaths, whatever witchcraft kept him from sight, faded. He fell to his knees, his glaive rolled from his grip. The previously invisible brigand glanced down at the spear protruding through his heart. The brigand's final words were lost to Arazaki's ears, he only heard the brute's body drop to the ground and the triumphant cry of Mfuneko when they galloped through the gap in the brigand's formation. By the time the brigands gathered themselves to give chase, it was too late. They were too far ahead.

The forest rushed past, unaware or indifferent to the bloodbath that had occurred beneath its branches. But movement in the bush caught Arazaki's eye.

A horse was galloping beside them.

A red horse with an armored woman as its rider.

Arazaki's jaw slackened.

Their eyes met and she only gave him a smirk.

"I can see the temple in the distance!" Mfuneko exclaimed.

Arazaki tore his eyes from the rider. Relief washed over him at the sight of the Omutonzi Temple.

Mfuneko smacked the carriage. "We've made it my queen! We've made it!" Arazaki returned his gaze to the tree line. The rider and her red horse were gone. He squeezed the charm necklace and galloped towards the temple.

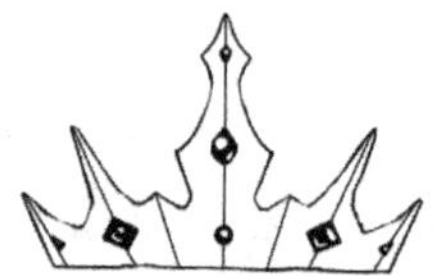

Noluthando only knew pain for what felt like days, perhaps weeks. She drifted between the waking world and unconsciousness. She breathed, pushed, rested, and pushed again. She cried out so many times that her voice fled her tormented throat. Banana wine was constantly forced down her mouth. It became the only taste she knew. Priestesses dressed in purple robes with silver headbands circled her like vultures feasting on a carcass. They submerged her in a warm pool of water, cut into her flesh, turned her to her side, smothered her with ointments and creams, and washed her with more water.

Her only tethers to the waking world were Arazaki's firm grip on her hand and his voice that cut through the fog of pain, drunkenness, and darkness. Once, during a rare moment of ease, he urged her to open her eyes, and she saw a priestess holding a small crying bundle wrapped in a Morowan red cloth. Noluthando felt herself smile before the darkness overtook her. But had it been a dream? Did she dare to hope?

Finally, Nolitha blessed her with a sunrise absent of great pain. Her hoarse groan echoed through the rotund stone chamber. A sharp pain ran up her side when she attempted to sit up. Noluthando winced and laid back down, perhaps it was for the best. Fatigue filled her bones and muscles after that small burst of motion. She went to stretch her arms but felt a weight on her hand.

Arazaki's hands were intertwined with hers. His forehead rested on his wrist with Lady Nomathemba's charm necklace wrapped around it. A faint trail of dried drool decorated the corner of his mouth. But even in sleep, he did not cease his rhythmic chanting.

"Which god is fortunate enough to have earned my husband's prayers?" she asked. Arazaki stirred and his face immediately brightened.

"Whichever one brought you back," he said and gave her hand a slight squeeze.

She managed a small grin. "Brought me back…? Did I go somewhere?"

He stroked her cheek. "You did," he said softly. "But thankfully, it was not for long."

Noluthando leaned into his touch. "From what I can remember, you had a difficult time as well. What happened out there…?"

Arazaki grimaced and shook his head. "I'm still attempting to understand it myself. The temple's Rujindiri warriors captured a handful of the brigands and questioned them. So far, we have learned they were not brigands at all, but trained mercenaries hired to halt the caravan."

"Hired by who?"

Arazaki shrugged. "That is the next question. Mfuneko and I each have our guesses. I say it was Lord Ayubu. It would make sense he would attempt to sabotage the experiment by any means in the name of the goddess. And who else has the copper and gold to hire archers from the Dikejiaku Guild? Their arrows devastated many of the men. They nearly found me several times."

"Dikejiaku archers usually don't miss," she muttered.

Arazaki glanced at Lady Nomathemba's charm necklace. "You're right, usually they don't."

"What does Mfuneko think?"

"With the presence of the mercenaries' invisible fighter, he believes King Jaruntaka of Ogesha had a hand in this. You know how he and his vultures like to tamper with magics and spirits that should not be tampered with."

Her thumb stroked his palm. "It doesn't matter, Arazaki."

"You're right, I suppose it doesn't for now. You're safe, the queen is safe, and..." She passed a hand over her stomach that no longer swelled. Panic shot up her back. "T-the child! What happened to—!"

"The priestesses needed to cut the child from your belly. It looked uncertain for a few days."

"However, Princess Othamela Morowa defied Javangha's coil and only grows stronger with each passing breath," Queen Sizakele said from the door, clinging the baby to her bosom. Two priestesses in purple robes flanked the queen as she entered. A smile greater than any Nolu had seen was plastered on the queen's face.

Riches already covered the Morowan heir. She was swaddled in a bright yellow silk blanket that resembled gold. A golden bracelet, larger than Othamela's wrist was held in place by Queen Sizakele's hand while a golden lion pendant was draped over the baby's neck. Nolu lacked the will to inform the queen of the risk of choking for Othamela.

"Your majesty is pleased, then?" Nolu asked while the priestesses examined her from head to toe.

"Beyond pleased, Noluthando," Queen Sizakele said, cooing to her daughter. "You, the both of you, have done me a great service. I shall not forget."

"We seek to serve you, your grace," she and Arazaki said in unison.

"I welcome your service," Queen Sizakele replied. "I can only hope future births will be an easier process."

Nolu and Arazaki glanced at each other.

"Future births, your grace?" Arazaki asked.

"Of course!" Queen Sizakele said at once. "This cannot be a singular occurrence. My entire line cannot rely on a single heir. We shall seek out others like Noluthando, whose bodies can endure the potions and treatments required to carry a proper Morowan heir. And we shall seek men like you, Arazaki. Strong and reliable men to provide their *ase* to my chosen vessels. You all will live on in the bodies of over a thousand heirs born outside the wombs of Morowan queens, who shall never know the fear or pain of childbirth."

Arazaki bit the corner of his lips and glanced at Noluthando.

"A…bold plan, your grace…" Nolu muttered. "I…I was not aware of the grand scale of your vision…."

Queen Sizakele adjusted Othamela in her arms. "That is hardly half of it, Noluthando. I envision a time where Morowan princesses will never have to watch their mothers perish in childbirth. A time where marriages are not compromised by barren wombs. I hope I can rely on you, Noluthando, in guiding these chosen women."

Noluthando licked her dried lips. Her head spun with all that the queen had revealed. She stared out her window at the distant horizon. Nolitha rose over the dense forest filled with mercenaries, brigands, and death. Her rays spread across the peninsula, towards the mountains to the west, the savanna and desert to the north, and across the vast oceans to the east. Everyone knew her light regardless of how it came to them, regardless of what had occurred just days before. Nolitha's light could not, would not be stopped. She found there was only one proper answer.

"Yes, your grace," Noluthando said firmly. "I shall aid you in this vision." Arazaki raised his eyebrows but said nothing.

Queen Sizakele turned to Arazaki. "I hope I can rely on you as well?"

Nolu squeezed her husband's hand.

"Of course, your grace," he said. "You will have my service in this matter."

"Excellent. I promise you both, neither of you shall want for anything from this day forward," Queen Sizakele said with a wide smile. "Ask anything of me and it will be yours."

"For now, your grace..." Nolu said. "I would like a moment with my husband."

"Of course, get your rest. There is much work ahead of us," Queen Sizakele said and with a wave of her hand dismissed the priestesses from the chamber before shutting the door behind her.

Noluthando eased back into the bed, unsure when she had found the strength to sit up. On the small table beside the bed was her father's ring.

"Javangha's Fangs..." Arazaki muttered, squeezing Lady Nomathemba's charm necklace. "What did we just agree to, Nolu?"

Noluthando took a deep breath, enclosed her father's ring in her hand, and dropped it. "The future, Arazaki," Noluthando said. "We've agreed to believe in the future."

Omari Richards

Britney is a visionary artist specializing in creating captivating, fantasy-inspired artwork that celebrates Blackness and sparks wonder. With a passion for blending blerd culture and intricate details, her pieces amplify the voices of the underrepresented while embracing vibrant, colorful narratives.

This passion led to the creation of Melanin Eclectic LLC, a brand dedicated to "putting the Black in Fantasy" and encouraging unique self-expression. Britney draws inspiration from anime, books, comics, and all things nerd, crafting illustrations that resonate with dreamers and adventurers alike.

To connect, collaborate, or inquire about custom artwork, reach out via melanineclectic@gmail.com. Explore her portfolio on Instagram @shopmelanineclectic.

Omari Richards is a debut novelist who specializes in Sword and Soul style epic fantasy. *The Kimoni Legacy: Initiation* is his first novel. He is currently writing *The Tales of Nahwalla* short story series, Book 2 of the Kimoni Legacy and a Black Mermaid Urban Romantasy Novel.

Other books by Omari Richards

The Kimoni Legacy: Initiation

TO KILL A LIVING NIGHTMARE

BY D.L. HOWARD
ART BY ANNAIT LJ

DARK FANTASY

CONTENT WARNINGS FOR DESCRIPTIVE VIOLENCE
AND DEATH OF A LOVED ONE

Jolted awake, Bikani struggled to move. She found herself pinned to the bed, her chest being crushed by the weight of a crimson-eyed creature. Its gaze pierced hers. Its mouth stretched open, unveiling a terrifying sight of rows upon rows of razor sharp teeth. Her lips parted to scream, but nothing came out. A silent sound—only heard inside of her head.

Heart racing, she tried to shove the monster off her chest, but no matter how hard she tried, the creature wouldn't budge. It snapped at her, breath pungent and vile, its lips hovered mere inches away from her face.

She closed her eyes as the unsettling feeling of dread sunk its claws deep into her, refusing to let go. *"It isn't real. It isn't real,"* she chanted silently. With all her strength, she willed her right arm to grab the moonstone amulet around her neck. The warmth of the stone filled her, chasing away the cold. The creature revolted as Bikani gathered the dream magic, took aim, and flung it at the creature with her mind. It screeched and hissed as her magic engulfed it. Leaping off her chest, writhing in pain, it hit the floor, flailing and flopping. The monster let out a piercing scream, filling the room before it disappeared into the darkness.

Bikani gathered her wits, shot up out of the bed, and assessed the situation.

She was in the waking, not a dreamscape.

Noctis shades shouldn't have been in the waking.

The lingering remnants of darkness slowly dissipated, but it left behind the disconcerting feeling of being watched. Her eyes darted to the corners of her dim room. The soft glow of early dawn filtering through the small window chased away the shadows and gave her a sliver of relief for now. She said a silent prayer asking for protection and guidance because a gnawing discomfort was settling in her gut.

Wiping her face with the back of her hands, she glanced at her pillow, then tossed it to the side. Bikani searched for her dreaming stone until she found it and froze. Absolute terror washed over her as she stared at it. The oval stone was as black as the darkest night, with swirling shadows instead of the usual soft, but vibrant, moon pearl color. No wonder the shade slipped through the dreamscape.

Her stone had failed.

"It can't be…" she whispered nervously. Bikani grabbed the smooth stone and winced. The blistering heat bit into her palm, then sent waves of agony up her arm. She dropped the stone onto the bed, no longer wanting to touch it. She searched around her room, found a piece of cloth, and used that to pick up the stone and studied it.

There wasn't a drop of color in it. The stones always had color. It was the first thing they were taught as children. Reiterated when she started her training as a dreamwalker many moons ago.

Unbidden to Bikani's mind, fragments of an old prophecy's opening lines surfaced to the front. Words that were passed down for centuries. Many had forgotten them throughout the kingdom, but not there in Umoya. Even the children learned the words and their meaning.

When unending night begins to rise,

Dreams will fade under obscured skies.

Darkness born from nightmares deep,

Will plunge the world into restless sleep.

There was no other choice. Bikani had to speak to her. The old woman would know what to do.

"Mama Eshe is looking for you," Bikani's mother said as she handed her a plate of fried bread, fish, and fire roasted vegetables. She had just walked into the kitchen, following the delicious smell of her mama's cooking. Her stomach grumbled with hunger, but she didn't have time to sit and eat. "She came to me in my dreams. Said you must see her at first light." Bikani ignored the suspicious glance from Bayam. "Find it mighty strange she couldn't get to you in yours."

Bikani silently reached for a piece of warm bread, filling it with fish, roasted peppers, and onions. She bit into it, breaking her fast. Hoping the full mouth would keep her from speaking, knowing her mother would've erupted if she'd known a noctis shade was in their home.

"I don't know, Mama." Bikani took another bite, then spoke with her mouth full. Bayam's face contorted with disgust. "I'm still training. There's no telling why she couldn't reach me."

"Hmm…." Bayam said before placing fruit into a basket. "That's always your excuse. You've been training going on twelve years now. If you can't tell me, say you can't. There are things walkers like you and mama must keep to yourselves. I get that, but still. Something ain't right. She wasn't herself and neither are you. Hurry na. Go see Mama Eshe. Take this with you." Bayam lifted the woven basket she had just filled with food and handed it to Bikani.

She wasted no time and snatched the basket from her mother, ignoring the hiss Bayam made. Something else was bothering her mother, and she had a feeling she knew what it was. Probably the same thing bothering her. "I'll let her know. I'll see you later," Bikani said, then rushed out of the house.

Umoya was a large village in the southwestern corner of Obari Kingdom. What made Umoya special was its location—nestled between the Spiritwoods and the Raha River, it was a lush landscape with fertile lands, but it was the dreaming stones and the Spiritwoods that made Umoya different from any other place in Obari.

As Bikani made her way through Umoya, people waved at her. She acknowledged them, but she was too absorbed in her thoughts to see the tired and weary looks on the faces she passed.

Bikani veered from the main road onto the path leading to her grandmother's cottage, which sat between the border of the forest and the river. The house was Bikani's favorite place, and the sound of the rushing waters brought a smile to her face as Mama Eshe's cottage came into view.

The cottage always seemed like it was hiding secrets within its walls, shrouded in mystery. Made from timber taken from the Spiritwoods, the dwelling blended seamlessly with the natural landscape. Bright flowering dreamcatcher vines snaked up the exterior walls while thorned mistbushes framed the large windows. The place was like a second home to Bikani.

"'Bout time you showed up here," Mama Eshe fussed, when Bikani reached the edge of her garden. "We've got things to do."

"I got here as fast as I could," Bikani said, while she watched the woman tend to her starlight blossoms and aurora lilies.

"Hmph," Mama Eshe grunted without bothering to look up. "Your stone go dark?"

It was more of a statement instead of a question. "Yes."

"Can't remember your dreams, can you?"

Bikani shivered, remembering the shade, but not her dreams. "No"

"Cause it was no dream. True dreams don't cause the stones to go dark. 'Dem be nightmares. Corrupt and malevolent. We must be careful, or we'll fall into the endless sleep when we lay down at night. Never wake up again." Mama Eshe placed the small shovel into the ground, then dusted her hands on her skirt. She finally glanced at Bikani. There was something in her gaze and Bikani couldn't discern if it was fear or regret.

"It's happening. I hoped not in our lifetime, but all the signs are there. 'Tis why I couldn't reach you. But I felt its touch on your spirit."

Maybe it was both, Bikani thought.

"It's the prophecy, isn't it?" she asked.

"Yes, child. It's the prophecy. And if we're not careful, Mavi, Weaver of Nightmares, might escape her prison."

Bikani shivered at the thought of Mavi getting free from the dream realm. She was a dark entity who preyed on mortals and twisted their dreams into terrifying nightmares, while feeding on their fear.

Her grandmother shunned the help Bikani offered to get off the ground.

"We need to call a meeting. Gather everyone. Weave a spell of protection around Umoya. If it's happening here, then it's happening elsewhere. Come on. Time's running out."

Upon entering the home, they touched the protection sigils that were intricately carved into the door frame. Once inside, all around were shelves built into the walls filled with old tomes. Scattered across the tables were ancient, yellowed scrolls. It looked as if Mama Eshe was searching for something amongst their pages before being called off to do something else.

The spacious home had vaulted ceilings with thick, exposed beams, woven rugs covering the floor, and a large stone hearth to Bikani's right. Tapestries adorned the walls, and the scent of dried herbs filled the air. Bikani could still feel the old magic that was imbued into the house seams by her ancestors.

Mama Eshe grabbed an empty leather satchel and handed it to Bikani. "Fill this with dreaming stones and dreamweed. Something tells me the king will come calling soon."

"The King? Why?" Bikani asked.

Mama Eshe scowled. There was a hint of bitterness in her tone. "Mmhm. Something ain't right with the dreamwalker by his side. He's no good. I warned the king about him, but no, King Rashaken is stubborn. He don't listen to old women like me."

"Most men are, grandmother."

"That they are," Mama Eshe smirked. "Glad you're paying attention. Now fill the bag. We need to be on our way."

Bikani rushed through the house, grabbing essentials, and shoving them into the satchel. They left for Umoya immediately, passing villagers who looked like they hadn't slept in days. She mentioned it to her grandmother, but all Mama Eshe did was touch the amulet she wore around her neck and shook her head.

In town, they followed the stone path to a large circular building with a high roof made from spiritwood and brick. Carvings above the Great Hall's entrance depicted the village's history, with wooden sculptures on each side of the door, representing the sky god, Kyatu and the earth mother, Nyara.

Inside, Elder Sanaa was removing the window coverings to let in light, her eyes widened at the women's arrival. With one glance, Bikani noticed Sanaa looked like the others.

"What did you dream?" Mama Eshe asked, not bothering with normal greetings.

"Dreams didn't come last night, Dreamweaver. Sleep was a distant memory. Shadows with red eyes watched me," Sanaa said. "There's trouble brewing in Umoya."

"Yes, there is," Mama Eshe agreed. "Where are the other elders?"

"You haven't heard?" Tears welled in the corners of Sanaa's eyes.

Mama Eshe's gaze narrowed. "Heard what?"

"Found out moments ago. Jomo and Suri can't be awakened."

Bikani gasped. "The endless sleep!"

Mama Eshe's face crumbled at the news. Her shoulders slightly slumped before they recovered. Suri and Jomo were her closest friends. The news was devastating, even if she refused to show it. Her voice carried a sorrow Bikani was unfamiliar with.

"Then they're already lost. We need a meeting. We can't let their sacrifices be in vain. Hurry and call the villagers here. We need everyone to set a new protection spell among us. We gon' need every soul."

Sanaa went to the center of the hall and touched the runestone, activating the beacon. Light burst through the opening in the roof, alerting everyone to the hall. Slowly, villagers trickled their way in. The four remaining council members arrived and seemed as bad as Sanaa. Exhaustion etched on their faces, each one looking worn down.

"Grandmother," Bikani whispered. "Was the council attacked in the dreamscape last night?"

"Mmhmm, except we were better prepared for it than they were."

Bikani shook her head, remembering the noctis shade, and the two elders lost to the endless sleep. They weren't dead, but it was a death sentence. Their bodies would waste away and eventually succumb to the final sleep. "We're lucky no one died—yet."

"It's inevitable," Mama Eshe said, walking away wrestling with her solemn thoughts.

The dreamweaver caught the gaze of everyone. "Sisters and Brothers of Umoya. From the moment we exit the womb, we're taught about the age of waking nightmares. We learn if we aren't careful, we'll descend back into that chaos and pain. All our lives, we prayed these troubles wouldn't come during our lifetime. 'Tis why we're gathered here now. We must cast a protection on our village. Protect our people, so we won't lose any more to the endless sleep."

Sharp gasps rose, creating a wave of surprise that rippled through the crowd.

"We'll go to the sacred tree," Mama Eshe declared before she pushed through the crowd. "We'll call upon our ancestors there."

Guided by the Dreamweaver's words, the gathered villagers sensed the urgency of the situation and followed her along the winding path that led them to the sacred tree at the heart of Umoya. Located on a patch of land that never changed, no matter the season. A serene place filled with life, powerful magic, and a deep connection to the spirits and earth.

The dreaming tree soared high—its canopy stretched as wide as ten people. Its thick, midnight-colored trunk was rough to the touch. Ancient stories said it was the first tree, started as a tiny seed, placed in the dirt by the earth mother, Nyara, herself. Here, the spirits of their ancestors dwelled, and villagers tied their wishes and dreams with dreamcloth to the blue, luminescent leaves with hopes of them coming true. The only place where they could seek protection from the encroaching evil.

Engraved stones encircled the tree's base, bearing symbols known only to the Dreamweaver. Elders guided the villagers to form circles around the tree, handing them sacred instruments for the ceremony. Four villagers with the strongest spirit magic positioned themselves at the cardinal points of power to amplify the spell.

With a flick of her wrist, Mama Eshe's clothes transformed into her ceremonial white. She lifted her carved wooden staff high. Around her, villagers clutched their shakers, and held their drums. Their eyes fixed on the Dreamweaver as the ritual began. Bikani stood beside her grandmother, anticipation swelling within her.

The call of the drums started with a steady rhythm. Its deep, resonant beat mirrored the heartbeat of the earth, inviting their ancestors to lend their strength. Tiny wisps of light flickered around them before joining the circle as the ancestors heeded the call—without their strength, the protection spell wouldn't be enough.

Bikani and Mama Eshe touched the tree. Power flowed through them and through it, promises of aid made from their loved ones now long gone. They turned from the tree and swayed to the beat of the drums, surrendering to the sound.

Mama Eshe's rich voice cut through the daylight as she traced a shimmering pattern in the air. "Ancestors, hear us, spirits get wise."

"Guard us from the shadow's rise," the villagers responded, their voices blended into the morning air. As they chanted, their bodies moved in synchronized rhythm. The drumbeats quickened; the air crackled with energy.

"From the depths of time, your strength we claim!" Bikani cried out. As she twisted her hands, a brilliant blue fire danced in the sky, creating complex geometric patterns before vanishing into thin air.

"Protect us from night's dark flame," the villagers echoed, hands raised high.

As the spell progressed, the villagers spiraled around Bikani and Mama Eshe, dancing an invocation to the old gods and revered ancestors. The magic was strong, and as the spell climaxed, Mama Eshe thrust her staff into the earth. The ground shook and rumbled from the force.

"Shield us with your light. Through dreams and waking, day and night."

Shadows around the dreaming tree emerged. Malice gleamed in their eyes. A collective gasp rippled through the villagers. Mama Eshe remained unwavering. Indigo colored fire licked up and down the staff, blazing bright. The energy within the circle pulsated. A warm blue glow emanated from the tree and grew, encompassing the villagers, and eventually overtaking the entire village of Umoya. The air hummed with power and through the spirit users, the collective magic of the people and their ancestors strengthened the protective spell in place. As the brightness filled the village, the shadows with red and golden eyes shrieked in defiance and recoiled, their forms dissipating like mist.

The echoes of their chanted spell slowly faded away. The drums slowed to a stop. All was silent. Mama Eshe's salt and pepper locs fell in her face as she bent her head—the dreamstones and shells woven between her strands made soft clinking sounds. She pulled in a deep breath, then slowly exhaled.

"Thank you, ancestors, for your guidance and protection," she said. "This circle is complete."

A solemn faced man dressed in the King's colors stepped out of the shadows. His presence caught Bikani's attention before Mama Eshe turned to meet his gaze, the tension in the air evident. Her grandmother beckoned him towards her. "Let Maril, the King's messenger, through."

The villagers parted ways, allowing him to close the distance in mere steps. He reached Mama Eshe and offered a respectful bow, handing her a scroll sealed with the royal insignia.

"Dreamweaver," he began. His voice was calm, yet carried a note of urgency. "King Rashaken requests your presence at the palace. He insists it's of the utmost importance."

Mama Eshe cut a glance at Bikani before turning the scroll over in her hand. She said nothing as she broke the seal and quickly read what was inside. After she finished reading the letter, she handed it to Bikani.

"We will come," Mama Eshe finally replied.

Daylight faded to twilight and the uneasy sense of mortal danger grew. Each mile to Sokari was steeped in tense silence that pressed on Bikani's nerves. It was hard to ignore the fear etched on the soldiers' faces. It mirrored what was in her heart.

"Sokari is another hour away," Maril said, bringing his horse in step with Bikani and Mama Eshe. "We will go straight to Ki—"

A blood-curdling scream pierced the air, cutting his words off.

Bikani and the others spun in their seats, eyes widening as they watched two of their soldiers being dragged across the ground, into the trees by slithering, sinuous shadows.

"After them!" Maril pointed towards the retreating monsters. "We must save them!"

"No!" Mama Eshe reached behind her, grasped the familiar grip of her carved staff, and swung it in a wide arc. The staff's tip halted inches from the messenger's chest. Her eyes pierced his, silently commanding him to stay put. Her horse sidestepped slightly, sensing the sudden tension in the air. "If we give chase, we will never make it to the palace. We'll die. Noctis shades travel in packs. They're more dangerous when they have the scent of blood."

"We can't leave them!" another soldier shouted. His horse nickered nervously. "They're our friends."

"This is only the beginning. Sometimes sacrifices are to be made." Mama Eshe lowered her staff and secured it on her back. Bikani knew once her grandmother's mind was made, there was no changing it. The dreamweaver turned her horse around, holding the chestnut gelding steady. "You can go for them if you want, but me and Bikani are going to the palace. With or without you."

Soon as her grandmother spurred her horse into action, Bikani followed suit. Thundering hooves and clouds of swirling dust marked their departure. When she glanced back over her shoulder, a few soldiers went towards the forest, but the rest, including Maril, followed them.

It didn't take long to hear blood-curdling screams as they dashed away from danger.

By the time they had reached Sokari, the sun had set. Its towering walls loomed over them as they entered the city. Maril shouted as he took the lead, galloping at a relentless pace without slowing down.

"Make way by order of King Rashaken!"

The guards leaped aside as Maril led them through the gates. Sokari was a dizzying blur as they raced to the palace, dismounting swiftly before being escorted to the king.

Bikani was struck by the throne room's opulence, but it was King Rashaken's commanding presence that held her attention. Queen Amira, in royal blue and silver, sat expressionless beside him. Stone-faced nobles watched as Bikani, and her grandmother approached the dais.

King Rashaken's piercing brown-eyed gaze tracked their every move, while Bikani discreetly extended her magic, probing the source of her sudden unease.

"Dreamweaver Eshe," the king's voice boomed. "So glad of you to come on short notice. You know why you've been summoned?"

Mama Eshe bowed respectfully   her expression unreadable. "Yes, Your Highness."

"The stones are failing," the king said. "We've lost members of my council to the endless sleep."

Mama Eshe nodded. "I'm sure the unfortunate situation is happening kingdom wide. Even Umoya has not come out unscathed from this so far… Your Highness."

Behind the king, Bikani spotted his dreamwalker, Azeem, whose sneering gaze was fixed on her grandmother.

"If you had been more vigilant in safeguarding the veil," he scoffed, voice dripping with contempt, "perhaps we wouldn't be facing this mess."

Mama Eshe shot him a sharp glance, her eyes flashed with restrained anger. "And perhaps if your dreamwalker were more adept, Obari wouldn't be on the brink of destruction."

King Rashaken held up a hand. Golden rings on dark fingers glistened under the light, silencing all. "Now is not the time for this, Azeem. Don't speak unless spoken to. We must work together to protect Obari."

Azeem scoffed. He crossed his arms across his chest but said nothing else.

The king glanced at Mama Eshe. "I know you understand the urgency. It's the prophecy, isn't it?"

"'Tis the prophecy I warned you about many moons ago. Because I'm an old woman, you didn't listen to me. Azeem doesn't know how to maintain the seals to keep us protected. He always had a strange way about him. When I voiced my thoughts, you sent me away." Mama Eshe cut a hateful glance at Azeem. "You listened to him and now look where it has gotten us. Many people will die. I pray the gods, and our ancestors welcome them with open arms."

The king silently agreed. "I was wrong. Believe me, Azeem will answer for his mistakes. What type of ruler would I be if I can't admit my failures? I'm listening now, Dreamweaver. What will you do?"

"We'll go through the veil. Enter the realm of dreams. Stop Mavi before she escapes her prison in the dreamscape." Mama Eshe frowned. "Unfortunately, I will need use of your dreamwalker."

Bikani opened her mouth to speak, but a sharp glance from Mama Eshe silenced her instantly. Azeem protested loudly, but it did no good. The king's decree was clear: Azeem would accompany them. The dreamwalker's face bore no sign of defeat, but there was a dangerous glint in his eyes.

"As you wish. Take a few of my soldiers with you. They'll protect you on your journey back to Umoya tonight." King Rashaken beckoned his general to him. "Maril, go with them and return with good news."

Fist over chest, Maril promised he would.

"Then it's settled," King Rashaken said. "You have my blessings, and may the ancestors guide you."

Bikani glimpsed golden and crimson eyes in the trees, though nothing attacked. An uneasy silence hung in the air, and it didn't sit right with her spirit. But it was Azeem's constant complaints about helping a "backwater village" that grated on her nerves the most.

It was just after midnight when they arrived in Umoya. Instead of stopping at the hall, they continued towards the Spiritwoods. The roads were empty except for the peacekeepers who kept watch at night.

"Grandmother," Bikani said when they reached the border of the forest. "Are you sure we need him?" The women glanced at Azeem. "When I see him, all I see is darkness."

Mama Eshe reached for Bikani's hand and squeezed. "Not now." She looked at her affectionately before speaking again. "This night will be trying for us all. Remember everything you've been taught. Pull from it and have your magic ready at a moment's notice. You're a dreamweaver, like me and your ancestors before you. Stronger than me. Stronger than Azeem. Focus on your awareness of your surroundings and pray for guidance. We'll need it."

The way her grandmother spoke troubled Bikani. She wasn't as strong as her. The woman was invincible and always has been. She stared hard before nodding. "I'll remember and do as you say."

"Good. Now let's get this done before that idiot has an apoplectic fit."

Bikani laughed before following the old woman inside the Spiritwoods. "I would love to see that."

Wispy tendrils of light flitted in between the group as they trekked through the Spiritwoods. Some soldiers attempted to grab the wisps, but Mama Eshe scolded them.

"Those are spirits of our ancestors who refuse to move on and prefer to stay here for now. They lend us wisdom, strength, and protection; therefore, we protect them. Don't touch unless they give you permission," she said.

The Spiritwoods were called such because spirits dwelled there. Few recognized its true nature as the gateway to the dream realm—a sacred place guarded by Umoya's dreamweavers and guardians.

Silver tendrils of moonlight pierced the canopy, lighting the path to the sacred altar. Bikani knew the trail by heart, yet this time it felt different. As they ventured deeper, the silence intensified. An eerie stillness enveloped them. No wildlife. No wind. Nothing.

"We're almost there," her grandmother said before going silent.

After a few minutes, Mama Eshe stopped in a clearing where the full moon illuminated the giant black stone altar. Its star-speckled surface, usually beautiful, now filled Bikani with trepidation.

She edged closer to Mama Eshe and whispered, "The stone shouldn't feel as such."

"Never thought I would see the actual gateway," Azeem murmured, before he shoved the soldiers away from him who were blocking his path to the altar. "It calls to me."

"Get away from the stone," Bikani shouted.

He whipped around, snarling at her. For a second, she could have sworn his eyes flashed red. She recoiled at his vehemence. "Stay in your place, child."

"Who in the *ether* are you calling a child?" Her anger swiftly rose like the tide in the ocean. A violet glow engulfed her entire body. Bikani lifted a hand, prepared to strike with an orb of dreamfire, but her grandmother's gentle touch doused her anger.

"No," Mama Eshe whispered. "Let him go."

Bikani started to argue, but the look on her grandmother's face stopped her. They turned in time to see Azeem reach the stone. A sinister laugh escaped him as his hand extended towards it. Then he vanished as if he had never been there.

"Ancestors protect us," Maril prayed behind Bikani.

"Fan out. Don't get close to the stone or stray too far lest you get lost in the darkness of the Spiritwoods," Mama Eshe warned.

Maril and his soldiers fanned out, some faced the altar, while others faced the encroaching darkness of the forest, while Bikani and her grandmother approached the stone.

"What happened?" Bikani asked. "How'd he do that?"

The dreamweaver shrugged. "Guess we're about to find out. Now, hand me the bag with the stones and dreamweed. We'll enter the dreamscape properly."

On the groove of the altar, Mama Eshe placed the dreamweed into the ceramic bowl. She ignited the herb and wafted the smoke towards herself and Bikani. Inhaling deeply, they chanted the incantation to open the dreamscape.

Soon, the air shimmered before them, and an opening appeared. "I'll take a few of these stones and you'll take the rest. Place them in your pockets. They will protect you. Help you get back to the waking."

"You mean, it'll help *us* get back to the waking."

Mama Eshe's smile didn't quite reach her eyes. "Yes, I meant us."

"What aren't you telling me?" Bikani implored.

"I've told you everything. We go to fight Mavi." She lifted her staff. "I have this. You don't. Not yet. In due time." Mama Eshe looked to the shimmering portal. "Let's go."

She said no more and stepped through the opening, leaving Bikani behind. In her soul, Bikani knew her grandmother was keeping something from her and she suspected it was serious. Glancing back at the soldiers, Maril saluted her with a fist over his chest.

"Travel well, Dreamweavers," he said. "May the ancestors guide and protect you."

Dread seeped into Bikani's bones as they crossed into the dreamscape. What was once a reflection of the waking was now a distorted version of it. Muted. Gray. Darkness had warped the peaceful dreamscape into a place of nightmares. Above, the inky night sky was a swirling mass of shadow and storm, blotting out any light. Lightning flashed silently in the distance. Blackened gnarled trees with twisted roots ominously towered over them. Its branches reached out like skeletal fingers and the leaves rustled with a malevolent whisper.

Shadows in the thick fog contorted into misshapen shapes that danced at the edge of their vision. The ground was a cracked barren wasteland with jagged fields of rocks stretching out as far as Bikani could see. The rocks had an unsettling, sickly glow that pulsated with a strange, unusual darkness. She grabbed the amulet around her neck and held it, seeking its warmth.

Mama Eshe shook her head in disbelief. "As I suspected. Still, we must forge on to the heart of this monstrosity."

Bikani's heart pounded as she and her grandmother traversed the nightmarish landscape. Each step echoed in the oppressive silence. They pressed forward, as darkness swallowed what they left behind. Lurking horrors and ember-eyed creatures stalked them from the shadows. Bikani was acutely aware of the dangers that waited for a moment of weakness.

As they progressed deeper into the twisted landscape, everything assaulted Bikani's senses. The weight of the shadows beneath their feet, had each step sinking them further into the depths of darkness. The overpowering stench of death and decay was heavy which made her want to retch. A faint, eerie scream lingered on the wind, heightening the fear bubbling inside as she remained on edge. They still didn't know where Azeem went when he crossed over.

"What happened here?" Bikani asked.

"Mavi has awakened and escaped her prison," Mama Eshe stopped walking. "We can't let her escape the dreamscape. She can never step foot into the waking realm."

"It's exactly like the prophecy said…" Bikani's words trailed off as her gaze followed Mama Eshe's line of sight. In the near distance was the largest tree she'd ever seen. It was a grotesque mirror of itself.

"We've made it to the heart finally." There was a sad note in her grandmother's words.

"It's just like the dreaming tree in Umoya."

"Its reflection. Underneath it is where Mavi was imprisoned."

Bikani noticed an outline of a figure forming in front of the tree and suspected she knew who it was. "It would seem that we've found Azeem."

Darkness slowly bled into the dreamscape as they approached the heart where Azeem stood. His robe billowed in a gust of freezing wind. Shadows clung to him, his eyes gleamed with hatred and malice. In the dim light, his lips curved into a deceptive grin as he withdrew a pulsing red talisman from inside his tunic.

"You shouldn't have followed," he hissed.

As the darkness deepened, Azeem began a low, guttural chant. The shadows around him grew even thicker. He closed his eyes as if in prayer, focusing his entire will on the shard in his hand. The sky rumbled as he spoke his invocation while the air trembled with anticipation.

"Stay close," her grandmother whispered, pulling Bikani closer to her. "Look. The dreamscape is changing."

Bikani glanced around as everything changed before their eyes. Despite her grandmother's presence, she felt uncomfortable.

"Grandmother," Bikani murmured. Her eyes widened when the silhouette behind Azeem fully formed. "Are you seeing this?"

Mavi materialized behind him. She spread her hands high to the darkened sky—waves of darkness slithered out of her palms as she released it into the dreamscape. Skillfully twisting and shaping it into one of her perverse landscapes.

"I see it," Mama Eshe said. "Nothin' we can do about it now, but make sure she doesn't leave this place." Her grandmother's hands glided gracefully through the air, weaving her threads of power into the very fabric of the twisted dreamscape. The familiar feel of Mama Eshe's magic rippled all around, then exploded outwards. It hit a wall of roiling black mist and the mist consumed the dreamweaver's light, blotting it out of existence.

Her magic had failed.

Azeem's dark laughter echoed between them. Flashes of lightning danced across the sky. "You have no power here, Dreamweaver. Not anymore."

Mama Eshe lifted her glowing staff. Light pooled around it as she summoned her power once more. The expression on her grandmother's face was set with grim determination. Brilliant streaks of her dreamfire magic slowly clashed with Mavi's ever-growing shadows.

Mavi emerged from the shadows that protected her. Her deep ebony skin shimmered like polished onyx. Eyes fathomless like the void. Her thick, long hair cascaded down her back like a waterfall. An ethereal beauty that was the embodiment of evil. Her presence was like a physical weight that pressed down on the two, suffocating them with fear. The Weaver of Nightmares advanced on them.

"I will not be imprisoned again," Mavi promised.

The ground beneath them shifted as Mavi unleashed her wrath, turning the dreamscape into a black abyss. Bikani felt like she was falling, tumbling through endless shadows. A scream tore from her throat. The oppressive weight crushed down on her. Her fingers trembled as she reached for her magic, desperately searching for the familiar spark—but nothing answered her call.

"Bikani, it's not real!" Mama Eshe cried out. She swiftly positioned herself in a fighting stance in front of Bikani. "I don't have time to hear speeches. If we gon' fight, then let's fight. I got more important things to worry 'bout!"

Bikani grabbed the moonstone around her neck. Everything became clearer. Bikani took a deep breath, then exhaled. Grounded, she whispered to Mama Eshe, "I'm alright."

Azeem sneered as he summoned the darkness to him. "And you will die, old woman. You and your apprentice. Your line will fa—"

Tired of hearing Azeem talk, Bikani slipped away unnoticed in the chaos of another blast of darkness. She broke into a sprint towards him. In one fluid motion, she dropped to the ground, her braids splayed out beneath her, hands clasped tight before her. Bikani flung her clasped hands apart, palms up, as a torrent of dreamfire erupted from her hands. Blazing forward in a searing arc, it struck Azeem, knocking him upward and back. He shrieked as flames engulfed his robe, and he was knocked back into the shadows

Bikani hurried to her feet and shrugged. "What? You said we were gon' fight."

Mama Eshe barked out a joyful laugh. "That I did, granddaughter. Now, come help an old woman."

"You're not old," Bikani said, rushing back towards her grandmother.

Mama Eshe hesitated but kept silent.

Together, they poured their strength into fighting the dark, pushing back against Mavi's relentless encroachment. The shadows only grew, devouring the light as it slowly turned the dreamscape into a nightmarish abyss.

"Keep fighting. Don't let go," Mama Eshe murmured.

Bikani's heart stammered as she watched Mavi stand at the nexus of the growing shadows. Her figure wreathed in darkness, her smile— wicked and unyielding. She reached deeper within and matched her grandmother's light with every ounce of dreamfire magic she had.

It wasn't enough.

What felt like hours were only minutes. Mama Eshe turned to Bikani, her voice filled with pain and love. "Granddaughter."

Bikani looked at her. "Yes?"

Mama Eshe shoved the dreamweaver's staff into Bikani's hands. Bikani's eyes widened. "No, don't do this!"

"It's the only way." In a mix of ancient tongues, Mama Eshe spoke the words of transference. "Ancestors, grant me a place among you. Bestow upon Bikani our collective strength and wisdom, that she may claim this power as her own and rise as *the* guardian dreamweaver destined to restore balance."

A shadow flickered at the edge of Bikani's vision. She turned around just as Azeem's blade flashed in the darkness, and with ruthless precision, he buried it deep into Mama Eshe's ribs, then disappeared into the shadows.

Mama Eshe stood there for a heartbeat, her breath hitched, as she reached to feel where the dagger was still buried. She touched the wound, feeling the wet bloom of blood beneath her fingertips. Slowly, she turned, gaze falling on Bikani, a bittersweet smile on her face. She staggered forward, then sank to her knees.

"No," Bikani whispered, the word catching in her throat. "No, no…"

Mama Eshe's breath came slowly, but she still called on their ancestors. She whispered ancient words. The dreamscape shifted as she wove her dream magic one final time. The darkness was forced back, allowing light into the world enough to send Mavi recoiling backwards with ear piercing screams.

"Stay strong, Bikani." Mama Eshe's eyes softened, lingering on Bikani with fierce pride. "I-I love you."

As the transference of power completed, Mama Eshe took her last breath and toppled to the ground. The magic she once held wrapped around Bikani like a cocoon, infusing itself with her essence. It surged through her, wild and ancient. All the knowledge and wisdom of her ancestors filled her. The last gift from her grandmother was the most precious and priceless of all.

For a moment, Bikani couldn't breathe, couldn't move. Pain exploded in her chest. A sob clawed its way up her throat, but she swallowed it. Forcing herself to stand as Mavi's mocking laughter filled the air. The sight of her grandmother's still form carved into her heart. Her mind spun, refusing to believe, but when Mama Eshe didn't stir, the weight of reality crashed over her, leaving a hollow hole in her heart.

The retreating shadows returned, swallowing the light Mama Eshe had conjured into the dreamscape. Filled with hurt and anger, Bikani's white hot resolve fueled her.

With newfound power coursing through Bikani's veins, a swirling storm of azure colored energy crackled around her. She tightly gripped the staff, then with a renewed determination, charged towards Mavi.

"You don't have what it takes to defeat me!" Mavi surged forward to meet Bikani, unleashing a blast of dark energy at her.

Bikani lifted the staff just in time, a shimmering barrier sprung to life as Mavi's blast of dark magic hit it. "Then I will do my damndest to destroy you!"

They collided in a tangle of arms and legs, falling to the ground and rolling over each other. Both got back to their feet, but with the power of her ancestors and fueled with anger, Bikani fought with everything she was.

With a swift kick to Mavi's legs, Bikani followed it with a quick throw of dreamfire. Mavi shrieked in defiance as she was hammered with dream magic. The two attacked each other without abandon. She had forgotten about Azeem, who hid within the shadows.

Tiny wisps of light whispered in Bikani's ears, "Behind you, Dreamweaver!"

Bikani spun around in time to catch Azeem right as he lifted his hands. With revenge on her mind, she unleashed a barrage of dreamfire, incinerating Azeem in a blinding flash. Leaving nothing but ash in his wake.

An intense force exploded within Bikani, the surge nearly consumed her. Her body trembled; the weight of the raw magic flooded her senses. The dreamfire within her blazed hotter than ever and her heart stuttered at the power she was channeling. Then a soothing, comforting presence in the fiery storm settled within her.

The spirit of Mama Eshe stood at her side. "You are not alone, granddaughter. We do this together. We will always be with you."

Tears strolled down Bikani's face. The phantom touch of her grandmother's hand over hers gave her strength. Together, she harnessed the power and shaped it with purpose. The dreamfire surged through her, guided by her ancestors. She lifted the staff right as Mavi lunged at her. With a cry that echoed through the twisted dreamscape, and with every ounce of strength she had left, she let loose the power. The raging tide of dreamfire erupted from her staff, then spread, quickly consuming the dreamscape. At the center of it all, Mavi tried to retreat but was held by the spirits of Bikani's ancestors, her voice a wail of fury and pain. In a searing blaze, the dreamfire tore her apart.

Her essence scattered to the winds.

Bikani stood in the wreckage of the dreamscape, her breath coming in ragged breaths. What was once a nightmare, now filled with light. Bikani knelt beside Mama Eshe's body and placed a hand on the old woman's chest. "Thank you, grandmother. For everything."

With her other hand, she pulled out a dreaming stone. It was back to its normal color, allowing Bikani to breathe a sigh of relief. She whispered the incantation to depart the dreamscape, landing back in the glade with her grandmother's body.

Maril ran to her, "It's done then," he said before stopping in his tracks when he noticed Mama Eshe. With a sad glint in his eyes, he bowed in reverence. "She died a warrior, Dreamweaver. She will be honored!"

Bikani nodded, then looked at him. "The nightmare is over—for now," she whispered. "However, Mavi's darkness wasn't destroyed entirely, because the shadows are never truly gone."

Annait LJ is a 25-year-old digital artist. She's been practicing her craft for three years using Procreate. Before that, she spent ten years learning to draw with a pen and paper. She prefers drawing humans and plants, but will dabble with animals.

D.L. Howard is a fantasy author who weaves beautifully chaotic worlds where magic is untamed, myths come to life and the heroes can't always be trusted. When she's not conjuring the latest dark world, you can find her wielding her camera like a magic wand, capturing untold stories through her lens or chasing inspiration in far-flung corners of the globe. Fueled by an insatiable desire to craft magical worlds, she pours her deep love for all things mythological and fantastical into her creations. Follow D.L. Howard's immersive universes filled with magic, danger, and unforgettable characters @ dlhowardwrites.

Other books by D.L. Howard

The Unholy Witch Wars Series

TRUE NATURE

BY SHAKIR RASHAAN

SUPERHERO FANTASY

CONTENT WARNING FOR MILD INTIMACY

We're glad you're gone, just make sure you stay gone.

Gideon Montgomery couldn't remember a time since he moved in with Uncle Jessie and Aunt Selena, in his hometown of New Orleans, that he didn't hear some damning proclamation levied against his parents. His uncle made it seem like he was the catalyst for their deaths and his current living situation at every possible occasion.

I'm almost sorry your parents left you with us. You've been nothing but trouble since the day we took you in.

He wasn't a bad kid, despite their claims to the contrary. He'd earned a full academic ride to attend Hampton University, which was no easy feat, and was working through an advanced pathology degree at UCLA after graduating from the "Home by the Sea," which was even more daunting. But, for some inexplicable reason, they'd harbored this unhealthy hostility toward him. Now that he was separated from them, the future and its brilliance were within his grasp.

Gideon's parents died in a plane crash when he was fourteen. According to the reports, engine failure and extreme fog conditions brought their aircraft down into Lake Michigan—not far from their home in Highland Park. It left him broken, rudderless for a couple of years as he questioned the Almighty, wondering if he'd done something to cause his parents to be taken from him.

If it wasn't for his best friend, Tera Matthews, and her parents becoming extended family, Gideon wasn't sure he would have survived his teenage years. He was thinking of them as he left the parking lot of the Powell library, where he had done his best to research information for yet another final paper due on Friday. He was hoping to ask his best friend out after finals.

Fate had other plans.

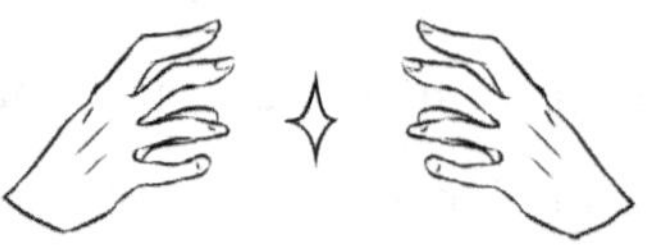

A bright, blinding light greeted Gideon as he awakened from what he thought was a blackout. The last thing he remembered was driving home to his off-campus apartment, letting Tera, his best friend and roommate, know he wouldn't be long, when sirens blared in the distance. He scanned the area but had a hard time determining the direction they came from. He didn't think anything more of it and hit the accelerator, entering the intersection. The sudden, fast-approaching roar that accompanied the sirens came first, followed by the ear-splitting sound of impacting metal and broken glass.

A public address system blasted in the distance before he focused on the distinct sound of a patient monitor. The incessant beeping was enough to shake him from the thick haze, and he reached for the monitor to turn it off—until a delicate hand intercepted his reach.

A nurse sat at his bedside, checking the rest of his vitals and writing the results onto a clipboard. She smiled as he blinked a few times to get a better gauge of his surroundings.

"Mr. Montgomery, I'm glad you're awake. I'm your nurse for this shift, Mena," she says as she introduces herself. "I don't know how it happened, but you survived. Your girlfriend said you would."

Gideon raised an eyebrow. He had trouble figuring out her explanation. "Survived? Where am I? What do you mean, 'girlfriend'?"

"You were involved in an accident a week ago. You're at Cedars Sinai Hospital in the ICU," Mena replied. "A chemical tanker was stolen from a facility just outside of the UCLA campus. The police were in pursuit and, unfortunately, the chase ended when the tanker jackknifed. Your car was caught in the crash."

So, that's the roaring I heard with the sirens. "And you mentioned my girlfriend… I don't have a girlfriend."

Mena shot a puzzling glance at him for a moment but waved him off as she continued writing. "It might be the Dilaudid talking, but she's been at your bedside every day since you arrived. Tera, I believe is her name."

Gideon breathed a sigh of relief. Tera always seemed to be right there when he needed her most. "Tera isn't exactly… well, that is to say, we've been best friends forever, but she isn't my *girlfriend*."

Mena grinned, taking some mild delight in his discomfort. "If she isn't your girlfriend, then it must be one hell of an act. She's advocated for you, and she was your primary ICE contact, according to the EMTs who transported you here."

He nodded, remembering the precautions they took as the "significant other" if either of them was hospitalized. Normally, her parents were medical powers of attorney, but they were vacationing on the other side of the world.

The on-call doctor entered his room, examining his notes as he glanced at Gideon.

"Mr. Montgomery, my name is Dr. Wells, and I'm a part of the team that has been monitoring your progress over the past week. I have to say, sir, you put up one hell of a fight to stabilize. I'm still trying to understand how anyone could've made it through what happened to you."

"What exactly happened to me, doc?" Gideon asked. He sat up in bed as best he could, but still needed answers. "I mean, no one has really been all that forthcoming with the details. And for that matter, where is Tera? Shouldn't she be in on this conversation?"

"Now, you know there's no way I wouldn't be here, baby." Tera entered the room, picking up on the conversation in mid-stride. "I left explicit instructions for the staff to let me know when you regained consciousness."

She slipped by Dr. Wells and grabbed a chair to sit next to the bed. She moved Gideon's locs from his face, caressing his cheek as she stared into his hazel-green eyes. "Sorry, doctor, please continue."

Dr. Wells cleared his throat as he continued to check his notes. "The good news is that you'll be out of here soon, but we need to run some more tests. Your bloodwork is coming back inconclusive. We need to know what's happened to you."

Gideon sat up in bed, grabbing Tera's hand in a subconscious move. "Inconclusive? What's going on? Is there something I need to worry about?"

"No, not according to the specialists we spoke with." Dr. Wells pushed his glasses up on his nose. "The truck that was involved in your accident spilled its payload, an experimental formula that was derived from a newly discovered isotope, which, according to the CytoDyne spokesperson—the company that owned the truck—was created by accident."

"Wait a minute, speak English. I'm a reasonably intelligent human, but what you're saying is going over my head."

Dr. Wells paused for a moment to sit down on the other side of the bed. "It supposedly was tested on certain animals and humans who were in vegetative states. The formula is rumored to have induced telekinetic abilities inside the hosts once they regained cognitive ability."

Gideon's eyes widened as he squeezed Tera's hand. He switched his attention between them, the fear evident as he tried to understand what happened to him.

"So, I didn't die, but now, I might be a metahuman? I think I need a minute to process."

Tera patted her hand on top of his, turning his face to hers with an index finger. "It will be fine, Gideon. We'll speak to the representatives at CytoDyne so that we can get to the bottom of things."

"I know this is a lot to take in, Mr. Montgomery, but I assure you that we will use every available resource to help you figure out what has happened," Dr. Wells tapped his knuckles against the railing as he rose from his seat. "The specialists came in from their headquarters in Chicago to analyze the results."

Gideon shrugged. This was more than he could wrap his head around. "What do they need from me?"

Dr. Wells acknowledged his cooperation. "They're not entirely sure that the formula works, or what the outcomes may be if it does. Outside of the formula that absorbed into your skin, the rest of it was deemed irretrievable. You're technically the only sample they have to draw any conclusions. I'll see you once the results are made available to me."

Mena stayed behind to finish documenting his vitals. He took note of how form-fitting her scrubs were, doing his best to keep his more lustful thoughts to himself. He did his best to not be too obvious, but

Tera caught him, playfully tapping his forearm.

"You know better than to flirt in front of your 'girlfriend,' babe," she whispered to keep Mena from hearing. "I know she's cute, but you're already 'taken,' you know?"

Gideon grinned as he caressed her arm. "Are you jealous? You know anyone who I have any interest in will have to go through you anyway. You're my best friend. Any woman who wants to be with me will have to deal with that."

Mena made her way out of the room, smiling at their banter. Gideon stopped in the middle of their conversation and turned his attention to her. "Thank you for everything, Mena, I guess I'll see you in a few hours for the medicine rotation?"

"Indeed, you will, Mr. Montgomery," Mena responded before turning on her heel to leave. The next moment, she flinched and rubbed her butt, startled as though someone pinched her. "What in the world?!"

Tera and Gideon turned toward the door, wondering what happened. "Are you okay?" Gideon inquired, watching as Mena looked around like she might have caught her scrub bottoms against the doorknob.

"I'm not sure, it felt like something touched me. That's weird, but it has been a long day," Mena replied, dismissing the incident. "I'll see you later, Mr. Montgomery, and you too, Ms. Matthews."

Once Mena left the room, Tera shifted her attention to Gideon. "Okay, what happened, and did you have something to do with it?"

Gideon raised his left eyebrow. "I have no idea what you're talking about, I didn't do anything."

"Stop playing. Something happened, and considering the inconclusive test results, we have to look at every possibility," Tera stated. "She wasn't near anything when she reacted like someone had touched her. What were you thinking about when that happened?"

"I swear, I wasn't thinking about anything," Gideon protested before he shook his head, blushing as he stared at her. "Okay, so, maybe I was thinking about finding out how soft her butt might feel, but I knew it would be inappropriate, so I put it out of my mind."

Tera thought about what he'd described, and after a few moments, she leaned in close to him. "Okay, let's test that theory. Think about how I would feel in your arms."

Gideon shook his head. "What's that gonna prove? I'm not doing that, Tera. It would be too weird."

Tera gazed into his eyes, the purpose of her words landing with the force of a wrecking ball. "Come on. How would I feel if you really thought about touching me. It's not like you're actually doing it, you're just thinking about it."

"Tera—"

"Touch me… please."

Gideon closed his eyes, succumbing to her request. He focused on her face, reaching out to caress her cheek. The look on her face surprised him; she leaned into his touch, much like a woman would when she wanted to feel her man's touch.

He continued down to her neck, watching her smile as she took his hand and gave it a gentle squeeze. The look she gave him both warmed him and scared him at the same time. *It shouldn't feel this good, but it feels so right.*

Tera shook him with enough force to wake him out of his trance. "Stop… okay, you can stop now… Gideon, snap out of it."

He stared at her like it was the first time he'd seen her all day. "Tera, what just happened?"

The shocked expression on her face was enough to freak him out. He watched as she touched her face in the exact places that he thought about doing in what he thought was a dream sequence. "You touched my face and my neck… but, I mean, I don't know how to describe it. Your hands were by your side the entire time. How is that possible?"

He took her hands in his, pulling her to him, close enough for her to lean the rest of the way and kiss him. "I'm not sure how else to explain it, T. I think that chemical compound Dr. Wells was talking about might have given me telekinetic abilities."

Tera's eyes widened, realizing the consequences of his words. "We need to keep this under wraps until we can get to the heart of the matter, okay?"

Gideon nodded. "We need to talk about the other thing that happened when I touched you, Tera. I'm not an empath, but I know what I felt."

Tera blushed, nodding at his observation. "We'll have time to talk about that later. Right now, we need to focus on how this happened to you, and what this has to do with CytoDyne."

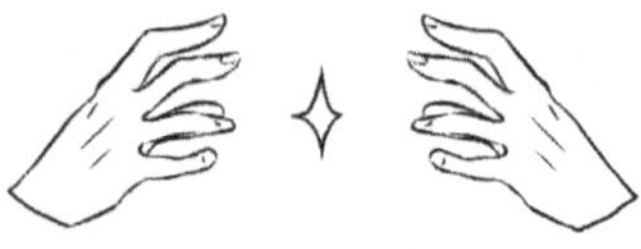

The intense buzz around Cedar Sinai was intense as CytoDyne researchers tried to find any metaphysical changes within Gideon's bloodwork. Despite the crash, Gideon emerged with only a concussion and minor scrapes—no broken bones, no lasting damage, which baffled the doctors, and the inconclusive tests only deepened the mystery. A week later, Gideon was discharged.

Back at their apartment, Tera dug into CytoDyne's background, uncovering connections with various government agencies, including the Centers for Disease Control and Prevention and the Food and Drug Administration. When she mentioned a subsidiary—Psyke Genesis—Gideon froze.

"I know that name," he said, voice tight. "My parents worked there. The logo... I remember it from their badges."

Tera touched his cheek, wiping away a tear. "There's no mention of your parents, though. Are you sure?"

"Almost certain." Gideon stood, heading to the closet where his parents' things were stored. As he sifted through the boxes, two of them lifted, hovering in mid-air.

"Gideon!" Tera shouted, breaking his concentration. The boxes crashed to the floor. "Did you know you were doing that?"

"No. I… I'm sorry, T," he muttered. "It happens sometimes when I'm not thinking. All of this scares me. I don't know what's happening to me."

Tera knelt beside him, holding him close. "We'll figure this out. Together."

Gideon looked into her eyes, noticing more than just concern—something deeper, stronger. "Tera… what's going through your mind right now?"

Tera never spoke a word, she simply straddled his lap and kissed him, her hands framing his face. He lost himself in the intensity of their embrace, feeling her tongue searching for his, curling around each other, exploring as their lips continued their own dance. The taste of strawberry lip gloss mixed with unexpected tears brought him back to his senses, causing him to pull back.

"Hey, why are you crying?"

"I… I didn't mean to rush things like this," she stammered, burying her face into his shoulder. "But when I thought I'd lost you in that hospital… I couldn't wait anymore."

Gideon grabbed her hair and pressed his lips against hers, pulling her deeper into his body, feeling their shared heat the entire time. She broke for a moment, giggling while caressing his face, placing kisses all over his face before they slipped back into their own private party.

As their embrace deepened, everything around them faded—until Tera broke away, giggling. "Um, baby… we're floating."

They were four feet off the ground. Gideon's heart raced. "I didn't mean to—"

"I trust you," she whispered, stroking his back. "Just lower us… gently."

Once they were safely on the floor, Gideon studied her face, wondering if he was still dreaming. "Is this real? Did we really do what I think we did?"

"Well, to be honest, I was ready to do more, but making love on the ceiling would have set the bar pretty high for anything we did moving forward, " Tera replied, continuing to plant soft kisses across his lips. "So, are we gonna talk about what this actually means between us or nah?"

He chuckled, looking toward the ceiling before his gaze met hers again. "So, how long have you… I mean… wanted to do this?"

Tera pressed her forehead against his, letting out a sigh as the question landed between them. "If I'm going to be honest, I would say since I first laid eyes on you."

His eyes widened, trying to understand the weight of those words. "I thought I was the only one in this, T. I never made a move because I thought you only saw me as your best friend."

"I did. But seeing you in that hospital… I realized how much I love you. I'm desperately in love with you, Gideon Montgomery."

Gideon blinked, her words sinking in. He smiled wide, his dimple pronouncing itself on the left side of his face, but then he dropped his head against her chest. "I love you too, T. I've wanted to say it for so long. But how can we be together when I don't even know what I'm dealing with, or what's happening to me?"

"You're not dealing with this—*we* are dealing with this." Tera took his chin and lifted it so he could meet her gaze. "Now, let's go through your parents' things so we can figure out where this trail leads, okay?"

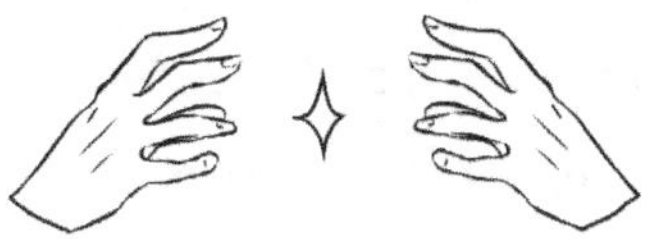

Gideon never thought in a million years he'd return to New Orleans, but the files he and Tera uncovered changed everything. His parents had been key players in Psyke Genesis Labs, planning to buy control before their sudden deaths. What's worse, he learned he was the sole heir to a trust that was worth millions and was being managed by his aunt and uncle until he turned twenty-five—the same aunt who resented him, and the uncle who abused him.

As they pulled up to his aunt's house, memories hit him with the force of a tsunami. He gripped the steering wheel, unsure if he was ready to face them after all these years. Having Tera's hand on his calmed him, if only for a moment.

"They don't know who you've become, Gideon, and they will see it whether they like it or not."

Gideon nodded, leaning over to kiss her lips. "I'm ready to deal with them. It's time we worked it all out. They have some explaining to do."

They walked up to the door, hand in hand, having a hard time taking their eyes off each other. Gideon knocked on the door a couple of times, squeezing her hand to steel himself against whatever would happen next. Tera lifted his hand to her lips, placing a quick kiss against the back of his hand, preparing herself for the conversation.

When Aunt Selena answered, she adjusted her glasses to get a better look, and when she realized Gideon stood in front of her, she clasped her hand over her mouth in surprise. "Oh, my God, Gideon? I'm so happy to see you. I never thought I'd see you again."

He was taken aback, looking around to ensure he wasn't being pranked. "Happy? The last time we spoke, you said you never wanted to see me again."

"I was wrong, for all of it. I allowed so much to happen to both of us," she explained. "I divorced him a few years ago, after he tried to steal from your trust for some other woman he was cheating on me with."

Gideon's eyes widened as his anger flared. "You knew about the trust and never told me?"

Aunt Selena sighed. "I wanted to, but Jessie… he constantly bullied me into submission. So, to make up for things as best I could without angering him, I had money sent to you at Hampton to make up for the difference in tuition that the scholarship didn't cover."

Gideon gazed into his aunt's eyes, torn between anger and a longing for answers. Tera squeezed his hand, nodding her encouragement for him to find his voice. "I want to believe you, Auntie, but where were you when I needed you?"

"I'm here now, my love," she whispered, pulling him into a hug. "Things should've been different. It's taken years of therapy to unpack it all, to realize where I went wrong. You're my sister's only child. I should never have allowed anyone to treat you so badly. Can you ever forgive me?"

Gideon flinched as they embraced, taking him back to all the times that Jessie mentally abused her, finding ways to talk his way back into their lives. He couldn't believe how one-sided things were, and it helped him release all the anger he'd built inside.

"I forgive you," he said with tears streaking down his cheeks. "But I need answers. A lot has happened since the last time we saw each other."

"I'll do whatever I can, " Aunt Selena stated before she turned her attention to Tera. "I'm glad he has you. He couldn't have picked anyone better."

Tera blushed as she kept her grip of Gideon's hand. "How in the world could you have known? We just declared our love a week ago."

She touched Tera's arm and smiled. Tera closed her eyes and saw flashes of her future. Witnessing her wedding day, with Gideon by her side. Their kids as toddlers, two boys and a girl. "Wait a minute, how did you… I mean, was that what I thought I—?"

"Yes, child, we have the gift of sight," Aunt Selena explained. "Your mama did too, Gideon. That's why she worked at Psyke. She was trying to understand us—to understand you. It's a slight possibility that her research developed something."

"Auntie, I was in an accident, and… I have a feeling it unlocked something else in me," Gideon said. "If what you're saying is true, I don't just have the gift. There's something I think I need to tell you."

"Yes, baby, you do, but in due time. There might have been something else already inside you, but your parents never got a chance to figure out what it could've been." She took a deep breath to gather herself. "I'm convinced your parents were murdered because of whatever they discovered, but I don't have any proof."

Before he could ask another question, a deep rumble broke the quiet of the neighborhood. The sound of approaching vehicles grew louder, making Gideon pause and glance at Tera. His muscles tensed, and an uneasy feeling settled in the pit of his stomach. He knew something wasn't right.

They turned toward the street, noticing several black SUVs screeching to a halt in front of the house, and armed soldiers dressed in tactical gear poured out, weapons drawn. The insignia on their uniforms was unmistakable—CytoDyne. Gideon's pulse quickened. He hadn't expected them to find him so soon.

"Stay behind me," Gideon murmured to Tera as he stepped forward, instinctively positioning himself between her and the soldiers. Aunt Selena stepped out onto the porch, her eyes widening with recognition and fear.

"Gideon, what's going on?" Aunt Selena asked, her voice low but tense.

"They're here for me," he replied, his voice hard. "CytoDyne wants to take me in."

The lead soldier raised a megaphone. "Gideon Montgomery, by order of CytoDyne, you are to be taken into custody. Do not resist."

Gideon's jaw clenched. "You picked the wrong day to try this," he muttered under his breath.

The soldiers advanced, weapons trained on him. Gideon's mind raced. He hadn't fully grasped the extent of his abilities, but he knew he was capable of much more than they anticipated. His aunt had hinted at it. He could feel it, the strange power thrumming beneath his skin, begging to be unleashed.

The lead soldier took another step forward, and Gideon made his move.

In an instant, his hand shot out, and with a mere thought, the earth trembled. A shockwave rippled from him, sending two soldiers flying backward. The others hesitated, startled by the sudden display of power, but quickly recovered, raising their weapons to fire.

Bullets zipped toward him, but Gideon raised his hand again, creating an invisible barrier that deflected the projectiles like they were nothing more than raindrops. The soldiers tried to regroup, but Gideon was already a step ahead. With a twist of his wrist, he focused on the nearest SUV. It levitated off the ground before rocketing toward the squad, scattering them like bowling pins.

Tera watched in stunned silence as Gideon moved effortlessly, commanding the very air around them. She had seen glimpses of his power before, but nothing like this. He wasn't just defending himself—

he was in complete control.

One of the soldiers tried to flank Gideon, but he reacted without even looking, throwing his left hand to the side. The soldier was lifted off his feet and slammed into the side of the house, knocked out cold.

Tera reached out to him, concern etched on her face. "Gideon, you have to stop. We don't know the limits of your abilities. If you use too much energy, you might—"

"I'm fine," Gideon replied, his voice calm despite the chaos around him. "I'm just getting started."

The last few soldiers scrambled for cover behind their vehicles, but Gideon had no intention of letting them regroup. He focused his mind on the lead SUV, and with a sharp gesture, it crumpled like a tin can. The remaining soldiers, realizing they were outmatched, shouted for a retreat. They scrambled back into their vehicles, speeding away with tires peeling out.

The air grew still again, and Gideon lowered his hands, his breath steady despite the adrenaline pumping through his veins. Aunt Selena stepped closer to him, her eyes wide with admiration and worry. "Gideon, that was... are you okay?"

Gideon looked at her, his gaze intense but softening. "I told you I've been... changing. CytoDyne must have realized what I am, and now they want to use me—control me. But I won't let them."

Aunt Selena, still standing in the doorway, nodded as her expression turned serious. "This must have been what your mother was explaining to me. If CytoDyne's after you, it's because they know what's inside of you. They won't stop coming for you until they have it."

Gideon took Tera's hand, his resolve hardening. "Let them try." He looked back at his aunt. "We need answers. If CytoDyne is behind this, we're going to take the fight to them. I'm done running."

Tera squeezed his hand, nodding in agreement. "Then let's get started. Whatever's coming, we'll face it head-on."

With the threat temporarily gone, Gideon turned back to Aunt Selena. "You said there were people who might have wanted my parents out of the way. CytoDyne—were they involved?"

Aunt Selena's expression darkened. "I wouldn't be surprised. They've always had their fingers in dark places and bought the company after your parents died. But there's more to this than we may yet realize, Gideon. And we will need every bit of your abilities to uncover the truth."

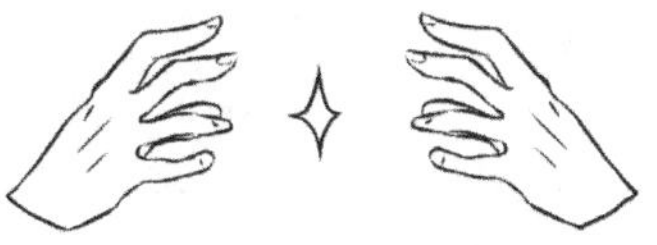

The low hum of the ceiling fan barely masked the weight of the conversation about to unfold. Gideon sat across from Aunt Selena at the dining table, its polished surface reflecting the tension between them. The room was bathed in the warm, golden light of the late afternoon sun, casting shadows on the walls. Tera leaned against the counter, watching the exchange closely, her presence a steadying force in the room. The air smelled faintly of the jasmine tea Aunt Selena always brewed but had forgotten to pour. No one was in the mood for comfort drinks today.

Aunt Selena folded her hands on the table, her eyes scanning Gideon's face as if she were looking for something—a sign, perhaps, of what he intended to do. The weight of their shared history hung between them, unspoken but heavy. She had been distant since Gideon's parents died, guarding her emotions like a fortress, and Gideon had grown used to her cold, protective demeanor. But now, something in her eyes had softened, cracked by the reality of what they were facing.

"I need to ask," Aunt Selena began, her voice low but firm, a quiet storm gathering behind her words. "Are you absolutely sure you want to go after CytoDyne?"

The question lingered in the air, heavy and sharp. Gideon met her gaze, his jaw tightening as he considered his response. He already knew the answer, but hearing it asked out loud brought a fresh wave of anger to the surface.

"They killed my parents," Gideon said, his voice rough with restrained emotion. "I'm not letting that go. They used my family and tried to use me. They're not going to stop unless we make them pay for it."

Aunt Selena's expression tightened. "And what about you, Gideon? If you go after them, there's no turning back. You've seen what they're capable of. You've barely scratched the surface of your power. You go after them now, and you'll need more than just anger to win this fight."

Gideon clenched his fists under the table, his body rigid with frustration. He knew she was right, but the thought of doing nothing—

of letting CytoDyne continue unchecked—made his blood boil. He wasn't a child anymore. He wasn't going to sit on the sidelines while his family's legacy was torn apart.

"I can handle it," he said, his voice hard. "I don't care what it takes. I'm not stopping until they're destroyed."

Aunt Selena studied him for a long moment, her face unreadable. Then, with a slow, deliberate movement, she reached into the drawer beside her and pulled out a thick, worn folder, bound with an ornate ribbon, along with a laptop that rested beside the folder. She set it on the table between them, her eyes never leaving Gideon's face.

"If you're serious," she said quietly as she powered up the machine, "then you're going to need resources. More than just what you and Tera can scrape together." She paused, her fingers brushing over the folder as if she were weighing a decision that had been years in the making. "This is the trust your parents set up for you. The one they left in my care."

Gideon's breath caught as he keyed in the credentials to log in, his eyes flicking to the site on the laptop screen. This was the only tangible connection to them he had left. He hadn't expected it to come into play so soon, and he'd put the idea of it out of his mind.

Aunt Selena continued, her voice steady but tinged with something that sounded almost like regret. "The terms were clear. The trust wouldn't be released until you turned twenty-five, or until certain conditions were met. But given everything that's happened... I'm willing to change that."

Gideon's eyes snapped back to her, surprise flickering in his expression. "You'd sign it over now?"

Aunt Selena nodded. "If it means stopping CytoDyne—if it means making them pay for what they did to your parents, to my sister—I'll sign it over early. All of it."

Tera straightened from where she'd been leaning, her eyes narrowing as she watched the exchange. She could sense the gravity of what Aunt Selena was offering. This wasn't just about money. This was about trust, about rebuilding the bridge that had been broken between them for so many years.

Gideon hesitated, staring at the screen with a bit of apprehension. "How much are we talking about?"

Aunt Selena opened the account and stepped away from the screen. Gideon scanned the information and felt the air leave his lungs. The numbers were staggering—more than he'd ever imagined. Tens of millions, all carefully invested and protected over the years, enough to bankroll a war against CytoDyne and then some.

"This is what they left for you," Aunt Selena said, her voice soft now, almost reverent. "They didn't just leave you with a legacy of power, Gideon. They left you with the means to protect yourself—and to fight back."

Gideon stared at the screen, the weight of it settling on his shoulders. He could feel Tera's eyes on him, her quiet support radiating across the room. This wasn't just a financial decision—it was a declaration. If he took this, if he accepted the trust and everything that came with it, he'd be fully committing to the fight ahead. There would be no going back.

For a long moment, the room was silent.

Gideon's throat tightened, and for the first time in a long time, the anger he had carried began to loosen its grip. He didn't want to stay angry, and she was the only family he had left. He needed that anchor to ground him. It could make all the difference.

He nodded slowly, swallowing the lump in his throat. "We'll do this together," he said, his voice steady. "But after this… we're rebuilding us, too. I don't want to lose you again."

Aunt Selena reached across the table, her hand finding his. "We will. I promise."

Tera, who had been silent throughout, finally spoke, her voice gentle but firm. "Then let's bring them down. Together."

In that moment, a new resolve settled over them. The battle with CytoDyne was coming, and it would be brutal. But they had something stronger than power or money—they had each other.

And that was how they would win.

Shakir Rashaan has been conjuring stories for the past fifteen years and is best known for creating lavish worlds and introducing readers to topics they've never encountered before. When he isn't conferring with characters, new and old, inside of his "NEBU Universe," he can be found binge-watching series on various streaming platforms. Shakir currently resides in suburban Atlanta with his wife, a daughter currently in grad school, a Jack-Chi named Teddy, and a Jack-Pit named Akila. Find out more at www.ShakirRashaan.com.

Other books by Shakir Raashaan

The Sageborn Prophecy Cycle

The Nubian Underworld Series

The Kink, P.I. Series

WE'RE GOING ON A GOD HUNT

BY C. M. LOCKHART

ART BY KARISSA

DARK FANTASY

CONTENT WARNING FOR DESCRIPTIVE VIOLENCE

"Does it bother you?"

The question was quiet and smoky, as his voice always was, but still just loud enough to be heard. He sat with an ankle across his knee on the smooth edge of a boulder that hadn't existed a half hour ago and let his jade eyes follow the two women walking across the silent battlefield. He hadn't expected them to pick a fight with sentry angels the moment they arrived in heaven, but he was too fascinated by them to be surprised.

"The hell are you talking about, Jennings?"

Jennings' smirk stretched into a smile at her response. Shirley never gave a straight answer to his questions — it's part of the reason he felt compelled to ask so many of them. She was sharp-tongued and skeptical that way. Even after six months together, traversing first the realm of demons and now the heavens, her fingers never strayed too far from the leather-bound grip of her staff, and he found it a constant source of amusement that her trust never extended any further than necessary. Her brown eyes narrowed at him, deepening the tiny crow's feet around her eyes. Her gaze was unforgiving as she watched him with the same level of caution she afforded her enemies.

"If you got time to ask questions," Barbara said, dropping her axe, cleaving the head of a fallen angel from its shoulders, "then you got time to help us." Its feathers fluttered around her from the force, and Jennings couldn't pull his gaze away. Their once golden hue was gone — soaked through with crimson and tinged with the black stain of corruption. The feathers were a dark reminder of the blood-stained path that remained before them. "Or you plan on watching us do all the clean-up on our own?"

"That is exactly the plan," Jennings said, his smile pulling even wider into a toothy grin. "I am merely a humble scribe," he said, lifting his shoulder. "A walking vault of recollection, if you will. I would be of no use to you on the battlefield."

"That's the truth," Shirley said, rolling her eyes before whispering a quiet prayer that turned her staff to a spear. The red light of her magic coated her body and followed her blade as she pulled it through the tender flesh of her fallen enemies. It gave her the strength to behead creatures that, were they still alive, would have been able to crush her with a single blow. Both Barbara and Shirley were covered in bruises. Their armor was discolored from the gore and their flesh swollen from the hits they'd taken. But still, they remained. The death of every enemy would be confirmed.

They would not let humanity perish.

It was an odd thing for Jennings to bear witness to. Over the millennia he'd been alive, he'd never encountered humans who remained true to the oaths they swore to the gods. Sure, in the throes of youth, they all carried dreams of heroism and grandeur — swearing loyalty and fealty to the mystical creatures in exchange for power and glory. They were little bundles of potential, just waiting for a chance to prove their worth to the gods. But youth was a fleeting thing. And the promises of a child often fell apart under the crushing weight of adulthood. The desire for greatness waned into the desperate need for survival, and the blinding light of hope dimmed until nothing but a cynical reality remained.

It was a story he'd seen play out a million times and seldom was it ever any different. Every few hundred years, an outlier would be born — a human who remained true to their oaths — but they often lacked ambition and failed to reach the heights of glory they strived for. And then, in fifty years or so, they were gone.

If he blinked too fast, he'd miss their entire life.

But the women in front of him were different. Every time he thought they'd succumb to the weight of their circumstances, they proved him wrong — defying every silent expectation he had. They were beautiful, blinding lights of inspiration woven into the dull tapestry of humanity, and it pained him to know that in a century from now, there wouldn't be a soul alive who would remember their names.

It might take longer than that — maybe two centuries, or three — but their kind was short-lived and forgetful. In a dozen generations, there would be no one left to tell the story of Barbara and Shirley, the two women fighting tooth and nail against the corruption of the gods. And he needed to know if that bothered them. History would either hate them for killing the gods, or forget them altogether. And though Jennings didn't make a habit of growing attached to humans, the idea of time erasing Barbara and Shirley from the world as if they never existed birthed a flurry of emotions in his chest he couldn't say he was fond of.

Before he could open his mouth to press the question further, though, they finished beheading the angels and turned to take their next steps forward, and he knew it was of no matter to them.

They did not do this for glory.

That much he understood.

What dodged his understanding, though, was why would they hunt gods for any other reason? It was baffling to him, but as they walked away from the battlefield, he pushed off the boulder the angels had hurled at them and left the question behind.

"Well," Jennings chuckled, examining the pearly white gates that creaked open for them, "we've broken into heaven. What will you two do now?" Jennings' long purple tail swished behind him in anticipation and his pale green eyes darted around the bustling town that came into view once they passed through the narrow opening. "It won't be long before the absence of those sentry angels is noticed."

"We're headed to an inn," Barbara said, rolling her shoulders back. "Our apprentice should be there with some useful information. And some of us," she said, throwing a glare at him, "actually did something today. We're tired."

"What are you glaring at him for?" Shirley asked. "It's not like you contributed much more than he did."

"The hell I didn't!" Barbara snapped, spinning to face Shirley. "By my count, I took down four more angels than you did."

"I took down their leader," Shirley shot back, keeping her voice even as she led them down a street crowded with souls.

"With my help," Barbara added, leaning forward to hiss the words at Shirley. "Your little saint's magic ain't all that useful up here, now is it?"

"It will always be more useful than whatever power of the demons you wield," Shirley said, frowning and turning her nose up at the idea of ever so much as touching the weapon Barbara carried.

"It's an axe!" Barbara shouted, drawing more than a few gazes. "And I use it in accordance with Rovannah's will," Barbara stated, for what Jennings felt like was the millionth time since he'd set out with them. "But that don't matter to you, do it?"

"Of course it does," Shirley said, scoffing. "I respect the will of the gods. I just don't know why Rovannah would gift you with such a," she glanced at the axe and almost gagged from the miasma coating the blade, "heinous thing."

"Don't speak about Remalda like that!"

Their bickering continued and Jennings tuned them out. He'd learned that being at odds with each other was their natural way of being, and his attention was drawn to the souls around them. Like the demon realm, humans who had completed their mortal lives resided in the heavens. Tiny silver wings sprouted from their backs rather than the horns they would have acquired in the demon realm, but in any place, humans were humans. They milled about, concerning themselves over meaningless things. It's why most of them would never ascend to become true angels or demons — they never left behind the worries that made them human.

Barbara and Shirley were no different.

They were still alive, so they had neither wings nor horns, but they concerned themselves with things much bigger than their own lives — they carried burdens they should have never laid claim to. Even covered in blood and armor as they were, they had no issues blending in with the crowd. All types of people arrived to heaven in unusual attire, and to everyone else, they were just two middle-aged women who went about minding their own business.

Shirley was slender. Tall, with light brown skin, high cheekbones, arched brows, a sharp gaze, and a blunt cut bob that never had a single hair out of place, even in battle, she was a saint who favored the red and white robes of her goddess over any other dress. And no matter whether she was having dinner with nobles or cutting out the tongue of an errant demon, she remained elegant.

Barbara was her natural opposite. She matched her in height, but she had every curve that Shirley lacked. Her brown skin was dark, her eyes were round and bright, and her full lips usually curved upward into a grin that was bigger than her afro whenever Shirley wasn't around. She was a demon hunter by trade and the master of the dark war axe, Remalda. Forged in the depths of the demon realm by the immortal blacksmith Juri, it had two blades and spewed the miasma of a thousand demons with every swing. It was a powerful work of pure wretched perfection and Jennings stood in awe of Barbara's power whenever she swung it.

Shirley's staff had a name too, but Jennings had been far less interested in a holy weapon forged by angels, so he hadn't bothered to commit the name to memory. Both weapons were gifted to them by the gods and had the curious ability to disperse in a burst of magic, returning to them the same way. Jennings could only ascribe the strange magic to being a blessing from the gods, but it puzzled him.

"Excuse me!"

Jennings' musings were interrupted by the small woman, who stared up at him with wide eyes. Her shoulder had collided with his in the crowded streets, and now she stood frozen — in awe or fear, he couldn't tell. But he smiled at her nonetheless and nodded as he stepped around her.

"Pardon me," he whispered, flicking his tail at her. "I didn't mean to be in your way."

Had she been a demon, she would have blushed a dozen shades of violet at his smile. But she was an angel. So, she gaped at him, and Jennings was reminded that he was the one who drew unwanted attention in the heavens. With his long, narrow tail, polished black horns, pointed teeth, sharpened nails, and jade eyes, he stood out like a sore thumb — never mind that his skin was the palest shade of lavender and his short, curly afro was the same shade of green as his eyes.

In the demon realm, he was considered a heartthrob in his prime — educated, articulate, and well-dressed, with a gift of knowledge and charm. But in the heavens, he was little more than a sideshow freak, and it almost made him laugh at how eager the crowd was to scurry away from him.

"What are you doing, Jennings?"

Barbara's words were heavy with irritation, but even as annoyed as she was, Jennings still found her to be the most incredible beauty he had ever seen. Her hand was on her hip, and her bright eyes were narrowed at him — not a single trace of affection to be found in her gaze. But any form of her attention was enough to get both his hearts pounding, and he grinned as he hustled over to where she stood.

"Apologies," he said, clasping his hands behind his back. "We've arrived?"

"This should be it," Shirley said, her gaze tracing over the soft curve of white letters on glass as she handed a small slip of paper to Barbara, who glanced at it before nodding.

"Let's make this quick," Barbara said, rolling her shoulders once more. "Theo probably didn't get us much information, clumsy as he is. And I want a nap."

"Doubting him already?" Shirley asked.

"Not like he was deserving of much faith to begin with," Barbara snorted, rolling her eyes.

"Well, anything is better than nothing," Shirley said, pushing open the door to the inn.

"And this is where your apprentice is meant to be?" Jennings asked, his gaze trailing over the three-story building made of white brick, gold trimmings, and large windows. It was welcoming in a way that made him want to turn around and return to the hazy twilight of the demon realm, but he knew better than to voice his complaints. Neither of the women in his company would care to listen.

"Why else would we be here?" Shirley asked. "Assuming he hasn't managed to behead himself in some way, he should be inside."

Her words were sharp, but her tone was soft — kinder than anything she'd said to him in the six months he'd known her, and Jennings' curiosity was piqued yet again. He wanted to meet the person who could round out all of Shirley's sharp edges, and he glanced over to Barbara with his eyebrows raised. She smirked and clapped him on the back as she followed Shirley inside.

"Sorry Jenns," she said, using the nickname he'd come to grow fond of. "You won't be the favorite anymore."

"Was I ever?"

"Over me?" Barbara asked before letting out a low laugh. "Absolutely."

Jennings didn't know how to respond to that. Despite his close proximity to them, he'd never been able to understand the complexities of their relationship. They bickered incessantly, but trusted each other implicitly. He'd witnessed it in every battle they fought. When it came down to matters of life and death, they were in perfect sync. But the moment they stepped off the battlefield, every word had a retort and every button they had was pushed.

Through many clipped stories and brief explanations, he'd pieced together that their history went back much further than the moment they decided to save humanity. From what he understood, they'd known each other since they were children. They'd never been fond of each other, but they'd always been thrown together. In school, they were roommates, sparring partners, and committee chairs locked in a rivalry that only grew more intense with each passing day.

The only thing they never seemed to compete in were matters of the heart.

Shirley, to Jennings' surprise, was a heartbreaker. With a taste for damsels in distress, she left behind a doe-eyed, doll-faced girl in every realm and sector they visited.

Barbara, naturally, was her opposite. She enjoyed tall men of few words with unwavering convictions. And Jennings liked to think he was the kind of man she could love, but her heart was still bleeding for

Hubert. She'd been united with him for fifteen years before Roxandra — a goddess of fertility, corrupted by envy and greed — had taken his life. She'd devoured his soul, ripping it into indecipherable pieces before consuming him. By the time Barbara returned from her demon hunt, nothing of Hubert remained. So, she swore to cut down every god who dared to stumble off the pedestals the people put them on — starting with Roxandra.

And Shirley, ever a devout follower of the righteous Chrysandra, couldn't stand for corruption among the gods, so she'd joined Barbara on her crusade.

Their logic was baffling to Jennings.

Barbara and Shirley hadn't spoken a word to each other since they'd graduated school until their apprentice arrived, but now they were killing gods together and bubbles of expectation rose in Jennings' chest at the idea of meeting the man who had brought them back together. He'd tried to coax information from them, but all he knew was that the apprentice was named Theodore. He was a young man of about twenty who served the god of love, Justinizen, and had a rare affinity for both holy and demon magic. Other than that, he was a mystery. And as Shirley checked in with a hostess who pointed them toward a narrow hallway leading to a room in the back, Jennings was near bouncing on his toes. He kept in close step behind them, and his grin grew wide as the door swung open.

"You're here!"

Theodore's voice was soft, pitched higher than Jennings had

anticipated, and as he crowded into the room behind Barbara and Shirley, the bubbles in his chest popped — leaving him disappointed. He'd hoped to find another impressive human, but Theodore was anything but that.

He was underwhelming.

Slim, with pale brown skin, coarse black hair slicked back to the nape of his neck and muddy brown eyes, he was the furthest thing from what Jennings had imagined. His smile was wide, and his cheeks flushed pink with his joy as he wrapped his arms around Shirley, who, to Jennings' surprise, returned his hug. He was a tiny thing — even at his full height, the top of his head didn't reach Shirley's chin and Jennings could almost mistake him for a girl.

"Hello, Theodore," Shirley greeted him, returning his smile.

"Theo," Barbara said, also grinning at him, "I'm glad to see your head still attached to your shoulders."

Theodore turned beet red as he scratched at the back of his head and forced out a stiff laugh.

"That was one time," he whispered. "I wish you two would forget that."

"Not a chance," Barbara said, laughing as she extended her fist to him and he bumped his against hers. "You get the information we asked for?"

"About that," Theodore whispered, his eyes darting away from Barbara's heavy gaze. "Actually, I —"

"Of course you would begin interrogating the boy as soon as we lay eyes on him," Shirley huffed, cutting a glare over to Barbara. "At least address the demon in the room first."

Every eye turned to Jennings, and he pulled his shoulders back as he awaited his introduction. Jennings had lost all interest in Theodore, but he couldn't help but beam under Barbara's attention — his long tail swishing back and forth behind him as he waited for someone to address him.

"You two are traveling with a demon?" Theodore asked, his eyes wide.

"A pleasant turn of circumstance," Jennings said, dismissing the unspoken question of how he'd come to join their company. "The name's Jennings," he said, bowing with a flourish. "A pleasure."

"Great," Barbara cut in. "Pleasantries are behind us. The information, Theodore?"

"Oh," Theodore said, flushing again. "The thing is… Roxandra…" he said, scratching at the back of his neck, "she's actually…" he blushed a deeper shade of red and Barbara narrowed her eyes at him.

"She's what?"

"If you would let the boy talk, he'd probably tell you," Shirley quipped.

"Maybe if you pressed him more, he wouldn't be so nervous about answering simple questions," Barbara shot back. "You're always too soft on him." Shirley opened her mouth to say something else, and Barbara held up her hand, cutting her off and returning her attention to the flustered boy standing between them. "Answer the question, Theo. The goddess is actually what?"

"She's his wife," Jennings said, answering the question their apprentice tried to avoid. All eyes returned to him, but this time, his face was stony. His jade eyes overflowed with light as he read the story of Theodore's life as if he were an open book. It was a convenient gift to have, but one he rarely chose to use. He preferred to earn a person's secrets with his charm rather than steal them away with his abilities. But he held no respect for Theodore and disliked the way his hesitation angered Barbara. So, Jennings didn't spare a second thought about stealing from Theodore. "It seems the boy here meant to be faithful to your instructions and acquire intel on the gods, but his heart was weak against her…" Jennings smirked and let a low chuckle slip under his breath, "overwhelming charms."

"Explain yourself," Shirley demanded, her gaze hardening as she looked down at Theodore, who trembled where he stood.

"I'm sorry," he whispered, shaking his head. "But Roxie, she —"

Before he could finish his sentence, a blue orb surrounded him, trapping him and his words inside. His eyes grew wide, and he looked to be begging for forgiveness as his teachers reached out for him, but the bubble popped before they ever got close, and he was gone. They stared at the spot he'd been standing in, frozen in shock. Teleportation was something only the gods could do at will, and Theodore's remorse only confirmed what Jennings said.

Theodore was a traitor.

Barbara was the first to break the trance when she kicked the table they'd never had the chance to sit at. It was bolted to the floor, but the metal leg still bent under the force of her kick and Jennings had a fleeting moment of compassion for the table as it continued to take the brunt of Barbara's fury.

"Calm yourself," Shirley said, her serene voice cutting through the room. "Destroying the furniture won't bring him back or alter anything about the situation. And we already have to pay for the table," she added, a sigh slipping out of her as she glanced at the warped remains.

"Calm myself?" Barbara asked, her words incredulous. "Calm myself? How in Rovannah's name am I supposed to keep calm?" Each word rose in volume until she was screaming, and Jennings had no doubt that every ear out front had heard her.

"It's unwise to take the gods' names in vain while in heaven," Jennings warned, his pale green eyes darting around the room as if one might appear before them. "I can see you're unhappy, but I would still encourage you to remember where we are."

"And now look what you've done," Shirley said, pinching the bridge of her nose. "You've gone and made me agree with a demon."

"Cause that's the worst thing that could ever happen," Barbara said, scoffing.

"No," Shirley corrected, sighing, "the worst thing that could happen is our apprentice and information broker gets corrupted and now we have to storm the pearly gates of the gods without knowing a thing about them," Shirley said, turning to leave. "But that's what we're doing, so clean yourself up and get some sleep," she ordered, pulling open the door they'd walked through less than five minutes ago. "Tomorrow, we're going on a god hunt."

The next morning, Jennings stood with Shirley and Barbara outside the gleaming white gates of the gods. They extended into the sky beyond what even he could see. Shirley stood on his left, clad in her saint's robes that had been altered to stop just above her ankles with high slits up the sides, and Barbara stood on his right in her dark blue armor with black trimming that looked like it was designed more for an assassin than a tank like her. The women summoned their weapons and he chuckled.

"And this apprentice is truly worth all this effort?"

"Of course he ain't," Barbara said, frowning at him. "This was always the plan, Jenns. Ascend to heaven. Kill Roxandra," she stated, her eyes focused on the giant gate in front of them. "And take down anyone who stands in our way."

"We'd have enjoyed a bit more preparation before this moment," Shirley added, cracking her neck, "but it can't be helped. What's done is done, and we must press forward. Corrupted gods cannot be allowed to reside in the heavens," she said, her words growing dark. "We will not allow it."

With those words, Shirley closed her eyes and began whispering a prayer under her breath. As a denizen of the demon realm, Jennings could never understand the words an exceptional saint like her uttered to the gods, but he knew enough to take several steps back. A crimson light bloomed beneath her feet, spreading out like the spilled blood of her enemies. When it was three feet wide in every direction, she opened her eyes and the color drained away, leaving the glowing white runes of a language Jennings would never be able to comprehend. When it was done, she pointed her staff to Barbara, whispered a single word, and jerked her staff through the air toward the ground as if she meant to split Barbara in half. The magic pooled at her feet shot over to Barbara, climbing up her legs and over her shoulders, staining her dark blue armor purple as she gripped her axe tighter and grinned.

"Knock, knock!"

Imbued with the strength of ten thousand warriors of old, Barbara swung her axe at the towering white gates. They resisted her slash at first. A barrier of the gods protected them from intruders like her, and the blinding white light pushed back against the dark blue stain of miasma, but it was no match for Remalda. The demon poison ate away at the barrier until nothing was left. And when Barbara swung her blade again, Remalda cut through the gates with a grating screech before sending the whole thing crumbling to the ground. Shirley erected a barrier around them as the pieces of the gate fell and Jennings couldn't help the laugh that escaped him as he stood in awe of their raw power. And this was only the beginning.

"Let's go," Shirley said, as the last of the debris settled and allowed her to release the barrier. She followed behind Barbara, and Jennings pulled up the rear. The destruction of the gate was more than enough to draw the attention of every guard on duty, but they were stunned into silence when they realized it was only two human women who stood before them.

"It's just them?"

The question was asked in disbelief by one of the towering guards. They were no less than ten feet tall and stood like giants before Shirley and Barbara, but that meant nothing to them.

They seized the moment.

Barbara broke out into a sprint before launching herself through the air toward the first guard. She swung Remalda, using gravity and her boosted strength to cut the lesser god in half from shoulder to hip in one swing. Crimson blood shot into the sky, raining down on them as the severed guard hit the ground in two pieces. The other guards watched on, dumbfounded, but Barbara and Shirley never stopped moving.

In the few seconds it took the guards to collect themselves, Shirley had already summoned the blinding white fires of Chrysandra and lit the guard on her right aflame. The fire would never burn the righteous, but it devoured the flesh of the iniquitous and he screamed as he burned. The cries of a lesser god like him sounded more like crashing gongs of thunder than a wounded being, but Shirley's focus never wavered. She didn't budge from her spot, even as the remaining three guards charged toward them.

Barbara faced them, a wide and wicked grin on her face as the miasma of Remalda clawed its way up her arm, darkening the purple edges of her sleeve to black and turning her brown eyes blue as the poison seeped into her veins, adding to her strength and speed. Most humans would succumb to its effects in mere moments, but Barbara was an extraordinary woman with an extraordinary blessing and Jennings watched with muted glee as she shot forward like a bullet, swinging Remalda to slice into the ankles of the lesser gods charging toward them.

Like their comrade, they let out thunderous roars of pain, but Barbara never hesitated. She used the momentum of her last swing to spin her body around and release Remalda, sending the axe flying through the air and letting it bury itself between the eyes of the guard closest to her. His head rocked back and another geyser of crimson blood shot into the air as she summoned her axe back to her hand in a burst of light. His body fell back into the two remaining guards, but they sidestepped him to keep limping forward.

"On your left," Shirley said, her voice calm even as she lifted it over the noise of battle. Barbara said nothing in return, but targeted the guard on her right. She let Remalda disperse in another burst of light and used the strength Shirley gifted her earlier to launch herself at the guard. He was unprepared for the woman to wrap her legs around his neck and shove her whole fist into his eyeball. The black sludge of corruption darkened his blood, sending inky trails of his blood oozing from the socket as he wailed in pain and stumbled back, dropping the shield and sword he carried in an attempt to pry her off.

But Barbara was ruthless.

She summoned Remalda in the hand shoved inside his skull and yanked it out, cutting through his head and leaving him dead long before his giant body hit the ground. The guard in Shirley's sights flailed and burned inside her ring of fire and Barbara rolled her shoulders back as she approached.

"Finish him," Shirley said, dropping the ring of fire as the guard fell to his knees.

Barbara needed no further instruction and was more than happy to swing Remalda towards the guard's neck. And like the gates of heaven, she cut through his flimsy barrier of protection. With her boosted strength and Remalda's miasma, she sliced through his tendons and bones as if she wielded a hot knife against butter. His head rolled from his shoulders and, like all his comrades before him, his body collapsed to the floor.

With the final guard lying motionless on the ground, his charred eyes watching from where his head rested by the crumbled gates, Barbara led their small trio deeper into the home of the gods. As they navigated the sprawling hallways, Jennings couldn't contain his amusement. They were covered in the blood of the gods and walked with the confidence of the devil herself as they strode down the long halls.

As they traversed the home of the gods, they learned there were, in fact, two gates. They'd already taken down the one separating the lesser gods from the humans and angels. The second gate separated the true gods — those who came into existence, created the world, and would exist after it — from the lesser gods, the ones who relied on the prayers and worship of humans to survive. And it wasn't hard to tell which ones were touched by corruption — the lesser gods either whispered a blessing over them or summoned weapons against them.

Rivers of crimson and ink ran through the home of the gods, bursting through doorways and flooding the streets of heaven. Jennings wished he could see the terrified reactions of the humans and angels at such harrowing signs, but he would never dare pull his eyes away from the women in front of him. It wasn't until they reached the final door in a corridor devoid of light that they stopped. Shirley illuminated their path with a gentle light at the end of her staff, but as they gazed upon the warped and cracked door before them, she put it out.

"Are we in agreeance?" Shirley asked, glancing over to Barbara, who snorted in response.

"Aren't we always?"

Shirley chuckled before tapping the end of her staff to the door. Jennings couldn't tell if it was already feeble and would have fallen apart at the slightest touch or if Shirley had used a prayer to rupture it, but the door turned to ash at her feet and she stepped over it behind Barbara who, as usual, led their way into battle.

The room they entered was both expansive and suffocating. It was large, but all the light and color had been sucked out of it. With plush couches, thick rugs, a large fireplace, and crystal chandeliers, lavish would have been an understatement. And it wasn't difficult to imagine what charms Theodore had succumbed to when the apprentice in question was an eager participant of the debauchery taking place beneath the sheer curtains of the canopied bed.

"Course this is what would do him in," Barbara muttered, stalking forward.

"He was blessed by that no good Justinizen with a yearning heart," Shirley added, stepping up beside her. "We should have known better than to believe he could resist temptation."

Barbara sucked her teeth before reaching out and yanking the canopy down. The room filled with shrill screams and the blue light of orbs popping as the three naked women surrounding Theodore disappeared. He was left alone with the voluptuous woman on his left, who had been more of an observer than a participant. His face turned a dozen different shades of red before draining of all color as his expression morphed into one of horror. He scrambled to cover himself, but there was no point. The woman beside him had no modesty as she crawled over him, her gray skin shifting with an undercurrent of blue light. Jennings assumed the teleportation magic had been hers and he bit back an amused smirk as she glared at them.

"What are you doing in here?"

"Roxie, no," Theodore hissed as he threw his arm out to hold her back. "Those are my teachers."

"So, this is the infamous Roxandra," Barbara said, giving the naked goddess a once over. "I'm disappointed, Theodore, but not surprised."

"If a harlot was all you were looking for, you should have remained in the human realm," Shirley added, curling her lip in distaste. "There are plenty of women who would have adored a face like yours."

"Really?" Theodore's eyes lit up and Jennings almost felt bad for the boy when the goddess next to him screeched in rage.

"Harlot?" she repeated. "Who are you calling a harlot? I am the daughter of Alexander Devine!" Roxandra shouted, crawling across the bed despite Theodore's attempts to stop her.

"And who is he?" Barbara asked, lifting a brow. "Never heard of him."

"Never heard…" Roxandra blinked as she sat back on her knees to place her hands on her wide hips. "He is the true god of dereliction!"

"Dereliction, you say?" Shirley asked, lifting her own brows. "Does he perhaps lead others to abandon the light?"

"Of course he does," the goddess said with pride as she pushed out her chest and Theodore groaned behind her. "He's the true god of corruption and I —"

She didn't get to finish her sentence before Remalda cut through the air, cleaving her head from her shoulders, just as it had done to every other enemy it encountered. Her head bounced on the mattress before landing next to Theodore, who was now as pale as the sheets he laid on. He ignored the blood of his dead wife soaking into the mattress as he lifted his gaze from her severed head to Barbara and

Shirley. Tears slid from the corners of his eyes as they circled the bed to approach him.

"I'm sorry," he whispered. "I'm sorry."

"Your remorse is worthless, Theodore," Shirley said. "Apologies count for nothing when you were intentional about inviting corruption into your soul."

"Repent and maybe Justinizen will forgive you," Barbara said, hefting her axe overhead. "We won't."

With that, she swung her axe, and Jennings watched as she beheaded her own apprentice without batting an eye.

"Was that necessary?" he asked. "Could he not have been reformed?"

"A soul as weak as his was not worth saving," Shirley stated, breezing past him and out of the room. "He would have simply fallen again."

"And," Barbara added, smirking at him, "we know who the real problem is now."

"Yes," Shirley agreed. "So, let's finish this up and leave this wretched place," she said, flicking her blood-soaked sleeve away from her as if that would cleanse it, "the stench is beginning to turn my stomach."

Barbara laughed, but followed her through the dark hallway, anyway. It was quiet now, so Shirley took the lead. The only gods that remained were those lesser ones, untouched by corruption. Barbara was a few steps behind Shirley, and Jennings moved to catch up to her, matching her stride as they moved toward the second set of gates, deeper into the home of the gods.

"May I ask you something, Barbara?"

"What is it?"

"Does it bother you?" Jennings asked, his mind once again caught on the one question he could never seem to find an answer to. "That no one will remember you, I mean."

"I thought you swore to remember us?"

"Yes," he nodded. "I will, but… you are fighting gods for the sake of humanity, and I am a demon. Why do this if not for the honor and glory that come with that feat?"

"Who needs glory?" Barbara asked. "I'm killing gods because I hate them."

"But your mate has been avenged, hasn't he?" Jennings asked. "And you still feel the same?"

"Hubert's soul may be able to find peace now, but that don't change nothing about the gods," Barbara said, scoffing. "They sit up on high and play with humanity like we're nothing but toys. And when we refuse to worship them, they take and take and take from us until we have nothing left," Barbara said, glaring at the world. "They were meant to protect us. Love us. And I will cut down every god who has forsaken that." She shook her head and scoffed. "Besides, I know what I've done. That's enough for me."

"So…" Jennings whispered, his eyes growing wide as a grin pulled at his lips, "you do this for your own satisfaction?"

"What other reason would there be?"

"None, I suppose," he said, chuckling. "Let me ask you another question."

"You're working my nerves, Jenns."

"This one will be quick," he promised. "Would you ever consider being courted by a demon?"

The question took Barbara by surprise, and she barked out a laugh before looking him over from the corner of her eye. He'd wanted to ask her the question a hundred times, but had never had the courage to put his hearts on the line as he did now. But after watching them take down gods like they were mere children and behead an apprentice they both cared for, he didn't feel as if he could afford to be a coward any longer. Barbara would stride into the future whether he kept pace with her or not, and he straightened under her scrutiny. His face flushed and his tail twitched with nerves, but hope swelled in his chest when the corner of her lips curved upward.

"Where did that come from?" she asked, shaking her head.

"I want to know you better."

"So you can scribble personal things about me in your history books?" Barbara asked. "No, thanks."

"I only wish to remember you for myself," he whispered.

"You're serious," Barbara said, her words lifting in surprise. "I guess Rovannah's got a few surprises in store for me yet."

"You'll allow me to court you, then?"

"Ask me when I die and make it to the realm of demons," she said, waving him off to continue walking. "Cause ain't no way I'm making it back up here."

"I'll hold you to that," Jennings whispered with a smile.

"If you two are done?" Shirley asked, waving her hand at the looming gates in front of them. "There are more pressing matters at hand than Barbara's pending fall into disgrace."

"Come on, Jennings," Barbara said, swinging Remalda up to her shoulder with another wicked grin painted across her face. "We're going on a god hunt!"

Karissa is a freelance illustrator and character designer from Philadelphia who loves to make character art based on fantasy, mythology, and magical things. She also loves books, games, anime, and any story or show with vampires!

If you'd like to get in touch or would like to discuss collaborations and other illustration inquiries, please send an email to cryling.arts@gmail.com.

C. M. Lockhart writes stories about Black girls who aren't all that nice. Her debut novel, *We Are the Origin*, was released June 2022, and her latest series, *The Lady Widow*, is her first venture into the sci-fi genre. She is the owner of Written in Melanin, which encompasses a podcast and YouTube channel of the same name, founder of the Melanin Library, host of the Melanin Chat, contributing editor of *Magic in the Melanin: A Black Fantasy Anthology*, and co-founder of the DNF'd Book Club. More information can be found on her website, https://WrittenInMelanin.com

Other books by C. M. Lockhart

We Are the Origin

We Are Dying Gods

The Lady Widow Series

MAMA CACTUS SKY

BY MOSES OSE UTOMI

FABLE FANTASY

CONTENT WARNING FOR MISOGYNY

When I look up, I see the same sky as everyone else. Mama Cactus spreads her arms out then up, branches out wide like a candle holder, leaves straight up like candles. That's where she keeps all her water, in those leaves. Sometimes, when we're all struggling out in this desert of ours, she cries, and her leaves weep down onto us and make the ground grow green a little bit. Those are the best days, cause we celebrate with good food and good music and lots of dancing. I love those days, but it's been a real long time since we had one.

I think Mama Cactus is sick.

"Mama Cactus don't need water," the Gardeners tell me. It's they who live around Mama Cactus' trunk and make sure kids like me don't carve all manner of dumb things into her—hearts and oaths and that sort. "She a cactus. Know what that means?"

I don't, if I'm being true. But I don't tell them that. I just go and come back another time with a little bucket of water and try to pour it out at the bottom of her trunk so her roots can suck it up. But they stop me and send me on my way.

"Mama Cactus don't need water," Daddy tells me when I ask him about it. "She old as time itself—she find a way."

I believe him, but I also think maybe Daddy's wrong this time. So I watch Mama Cactus real close, day and night, to see if maybe I'm seeing something that nobody else is seeing.

And I do.

I think.

You should know Mama Cactus is five hundred feet high and almost as wide. She makes shade for our whole village. If She didn't, this desert of ours would scorch us up quicker than quick. Sometimes, the adults go out past Her shade, but never for long. Because even at night, when the sun isn't so mean, there's Ngota-Balivhi. She's a big old owl, near as big as Mama Cactus. Ngota-B only moves around at night, and she'd swoop us up if it weren't for Mama Cactus' spines ready to stick into her.

"Mama Cactus don't need water," my friends tell me at school the next day.

I'm not the best student, but I pay just as much attention as they do—they got no right to tell me what's up and down.

"You don't know that," I say back.

Then they really go after me, the way friends do.

"She a cactus, you unbrained goo-goo."

"This boy get half marks in agriculture but go and tell us how to keep Mama Cactus."

"What Mama Cactus need most of all is for you to shut up."

I argue back and we spend a while doing that until teacher promises us all a backsiding.

That night, I climb up top my Daddy's house and look out across this desert of ours, and I think maybe I'm wrong and everyone else is right and I should think about other things.

Then, out in the distance, there's a shadow sliding over a mountain top. It's a big thing, even from so far. Big enough to block out the moonlight the way it does, but moving too fast to be a cloud.

The shadow stops half way from the horizon, hanging over the desert. I can't make sense of the shadow's shape, so I look up to see what it's coming from, and there is Ngota-Balivhi. All six of her wings buzzing to keep her in place. Her ears rotating this way then that. Two sinkholes dug in her face, and her eyes glowing from deep inside. Wild eyes. Murderous eyes.

Unlike her ears, those eyes aren't moving. They're locked in a bloodstopping stare, watching us.

Waiting.

"Ngota-Balivhi don't wait," my friends tell me the next day at school.

But those meat pies don't know what's in or what's out.

"I saw her with these very eyes," I shoot back. "She was waiting for something."

Then they really go after me, the way friends do.

"What a big ol' owl like her gotta wait for?"

"This boy get quarter marks in animals but go and tell us how Ngota-B live her life."

"Must be she waiting for you to die, peepee head boy."

I argue back and we spend a while doing that until teacher starts waving that stick of his.

"Ngota-Balivhi don't wait," Daddy tells me. "You telling me you the first to put eye to her?"

It's true what he says—we all know the big owl is out there, but no one of these days has ever seen her. She moves too fast and too quiet, the way owls do, so even if you spend all night gazing at the sky, the best you'll see is a quick flash like a shooting star.

Daddy says it must be a regular bird made big by lighting or distance or something, but I think maybe he's wrong this time.

That week, we all go down to Mama Cactus' trunk to say goodbye to one of our sisters, Emi. Emi is actually one of my classmates' sisters by blood, but she's me and Daddy's sister by clan. When I see her standing under Mama Cactus, she's all swelled up with that baby of hers, looking ready to pop. Never have I seen a baby before so I'm real excited, as you can imagine. Emi, if I'm being honest, looks a little bit scared. That makes sense—making a baby is a serious thing, and Daddy always told me that it's the toughest thing in the world. Too tough for boys and men.

Emi also looks proud, though. Daddy says I used to have a sister by blood—a twin sister, even—but she died before I got to make memories of her. So when I look at Emi, I pretend she's that long gone sister of mine, and I'm happy and worried for her. I don't know her so well that I can speak to her, but if she were my sister by blood, I would like to think I'd go up and squeeze her hand and say something that only she and I could hear like, "I'm so proud of you, sister, and I love you, and I can't wait to meet this baby you been working on for so long."

Luckily, my classmate—who Emi actually *is* his sister by blood—goes up to her and does that very thing, though I can't hear him. But after he finishes whispering to her, she cries and they hug and she looks even more nervous, but somehow even more proud, even more determined.

This is the last time any of us will see Emi. If the baby were a boy, she would come back to us, but the nurses say the baby is a girl, so we won't see her again. The Gardeners will bring the baby back to Emi's Daddy to raise it, and Emi will become part of the land, part of Mama Cactus.

The Gardeners lead us in prayer, then we all salute with our hands on our hearts. When Emi returns the salute, all the seriousness of the moment goes away and we cheer real crazy as she goes off around the other side of Mama Cactus.

Then we all leave. But before Daddy and I go back home, I want to talk to the Gardeners.

"Ngota-Balivhi did what?" they ask.

I tell them again. "Did you not see?" I ask, because I know some of them stay up all night. But then I look up and I realize that they're so far under Mama Cactus that they can't see much of the sky at all, not like me on top of Daddy's roof out on the edge of the village.

The Gardeners all look at each other, real worried judging by their faces. They take Daddy aside and talk to him in quiet voices, and he nods. Then they all shake hands the way men do, and Daddy puts an arm over my shoulder and walks me back home, promising to cook me some puff puff because he knows it's my favorite and because I 'deserve it'.

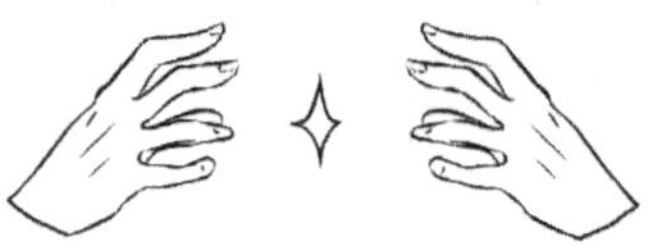

Daddy tells me I can't go up on his roof any more, so I try to be a good boy and listen to him. But each night I still go to the edge of the village and I look out across this desert of ours and I watch the shadow shade over the mountains, closer and closer to the village before fading away. I know it's Ngota-Balivhi, and I feel like she knows it's me who's watching her, like we got an agreement to meet there every night and not say a thing.

But during the day, when Ngota-Balivhi isn't around, my eyes keep going back to Mama Cactus. She's looking more and more sick to me. Some of her green is making for yellow, and her trunk is starting to look like its got cracks in it, like some of it is about to break off.

This time, I know better than to tell anyone. I try again to sneak her a drink of water, but the Gardeners stop me. Instead of taking my bucket and sending me on my way, though, they take my bucket and grab me a chair. Then, believe it or not, they start talking to me like I'm one of them, asking me about school and my friends and all that. I ask them the same, and they tell me they don't go to school, but they do got friends. Some of them even got sisters by blood who they miss, and they talk about that. One of them, a big, serious guy with a mustache I don't think much suits his face, even had *three* sisters, which I think has gotta be a record, and he says he's better off without them, but the other Gardeners all make jokes about how much he misses them, so I think he's lying.

"I wish I still had my sister," I say. The Gardeners made having a sister sound so fun. "Can I get her back?"

"If you have a shovel," one of the Gardeners says with a smirk. But that makes all the other Gardeners go quiet and look at him in a funny way, then they smile at me and send me home.

At night, back in my bed after telling Daddy I was playing late with friends—which is true because I think the Gardeners are my friends now—I wonder if Mama Cactus can die. If people can die, why not cacti? It would be a sad thing to no longer have her big branches and leaves overhead, protecting us. Though I realize it probably wouldn't be a sad thing for very long, because Ngota-Balivhi would swoop down and gobble us all up quick as quick.

What a mean bird she is.

My eyes are all heavy and my brain is starting to go real quiet when there's a big sound. A voice. Someone is speaking, but it's all loud and rumbly like thunder and it shakes our whole house and Daddy bursts into my room to check on me and he's got so much fear in his face that I almost think I need to check on myself to see if I'm okay. The sound only happens once, but it's so damn scary that I can hear its echo in my heart, over and over and over, this awful strange thunder that speaks but not in a human voice. And when I try to go back to sleep, this little body of mine is still shaking from being afraid, and that echo keeps on in my heart until it seems like I'm starting to make sense of it—like me and the voice are speaking the same language—and I think I know what it's saying.

"WHO."

But it's not like how me and Daddy and us villagers say 'who'. It's much different.

It's a threat.

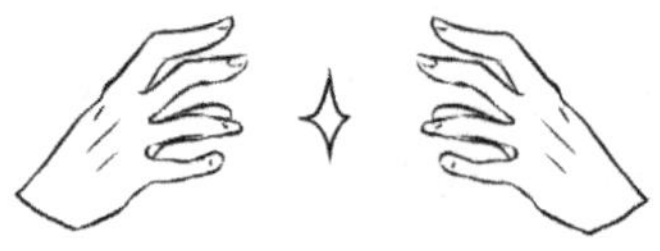

We all wake up to one chaotic scene, let me tell you.

Some of Mama Cactus' trunk fell off.

The Gardeners won't tell us a thing, but I know it must've been Ngota-Balivhi's great big owl "WHO" that shook it loose. As loud as she was, I'm glad she didn't shake all our heads loose from our shoulders.

The whole village gets together to help chop the piece so it's smaller and then we distribute it to families to use however they want. But no one really knows what to do with it. Mama Cactus' trunk isn't supposed to break like that. It feels too sacred to use for anything, so me and Daddy just put our chunk in a corner and try not to look at it.

If we're looking at the sunny side, everyone now believes me about Mama Cactus being sick. They still don't think she needs water, but big wins are made of little wins, Daddy always says, so I'll take this little win and hope it grows.

The Gardeners are worried about more of her trunk falling off—they told us this first big piece almost crushed one of them—so they move back from her trunk and set up a fence to keep all of us away from it too. I go back with a bucket of water hoping they'll let me, their new friend, through the fence. They don't. They just take my bucket and tell me to sit and start asking me questions about how I knew Mama Cactus was sick and all that. But when I tell them again that she just needs water, they still don't believe me.

"Mama Cactus don't need water."

That night, Ngota-B hits us with another "WHO" and that about ends life as we know it. The whole village is out in the street in the pitch black dead of night, too afraid to risk sleep. A bunch of Gardeners come out to tell us it's all okay, but a whole other gang of Gardeners is running around like warring cats, putting on armor and hoisting spears and things like that. That only makes everyone more afraid, including me, because it looks like they're getting ready to fight Ngota-B, which makes about as much sense as my big toe fighting the edge of a door. The whole village is distraught and asking questions, but the Gardeners are saying "stay calm! stay calm!" and we're saying "no!"

I see my classmate—the one whose sister by blood is Emi—and he's crying and saying that he misses his sister. It's a real sad thing to see because his Daddy is consoling him, but it's obvious to any two eyes that his Daddy's love is not the right salve for this particular wound, and that if Emi were there, she would know how to heal him.

I feel all kinds of bad for him until the whole world suddenly thrums like we're all sitting on a great big guitar. We all vibrate, and I throw up more than once because my guts are vibrating too and it's about as uncomfortable as I've ever been. Somehow, we all know to look up, and we do it just fast enough to see Mama Cactus shivering from the impact of Ngota-Balivhi, who is filled with spines all over her torso and the inside of her six wings and even along her talons. The big owl is so close and hovering so low that I can see the discharge leaking out of her wild eyes.

People really panic then. Everyone just starts running. Not toward home. Not away from the village. Just running like the sun won't rise if they stay still, and we all spend the whole night running and hiding and praying and realizing—I mean everyone else, not me—that Mama Cactus is indeed real sick.

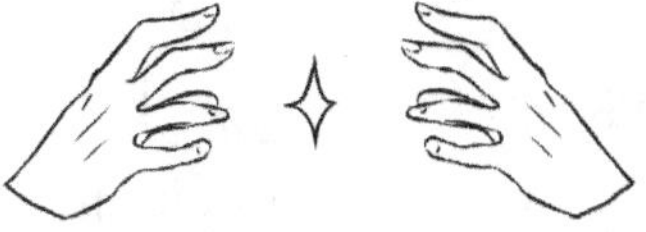

There's a whole new type of person that comes about in the next days. I call them Sad Boys, but they call themselves the Toothsavers or Sootplayers or something like that. But these Sad Boys just walk around the village in all white trying to convince everyone that Mama Cactus is what they call a false prophet and that Ngota-Balivhi is the True God, so I guess we should all stop eating chicken? I don't really pay much mind to their spewing because I realize that I've been right about this whole thing from before there even was a thing, so at this point it's up to me to solve all this before Ngota-B comes back down and gobbles the village.

I gotta get Mama Cactus water.

The Gardeners are real busy these days. For the first time I've ever seen, they get together and practice fighting. They got nice armor and spears and such, but when they practice, it don't look so different from when me and my friends play-fight at school, so I don't think Ngota-B will be much worried about them. One time, I see a Guardian throw their spear at a bunch of straw stacked and sculpted to look like Ngota-B and the spear bounces off the straw like if it were solid brick. I can't tell if it's the spear or the Gardeners that's weak, but I know Ngota-B is a whole lot thicker than a pile of straw.

The Gardeners are too busy to stop me from getting to Mama

Cactus, but Daddy won't let me out of his sight, and for good reason. The whole village has gone mad as a spoiled fruit merchant, and he don't want me out and about where people are getting hurt. I tell him that I want to play with friends or deliver sugar to the neighbors, but each time he tells me no.

So my only choice is to sneak out.

Two days have come and gone. The village is saying that Ngota-Balivhi must be plucking out all those spines that stuck her, but once she's done she'll come screaming back. The Sad Boys tell us that Ngota-B will snack us all if we don't repent and stop eating chicken. The Gardeners tell us they're ready while they practice with spears that aren't half as long or strong as one of Mama Cactus' spines.

I know that only Mama Cactus can keep us safe.

Daddy isn't sleeping anymore so far as I can see, so I decide that if I want to sneak out, I need to do something to make him feel calm. He's always drinking tea, but he has this one box of tea leaves in the top cabinet that in all my years I've never seen him peek at, so I assume they must be his most special tea. I climb up to the top cabinet and take out some of those special leaves and, while he's out in the front house, real worried like everyone else in the village, brew him a nice cup of calm down.

I can see suspiciousness in Daddy's face when he takes the cup, but he thanks me all the same and gives me that head rub and kiss he likes to give when he thinks I'm sad. He blows on the tea for a bit—at this point, I'm inside the house watching him through a window—

then takes a sip. It's all kinds of weird what happens after that because Daddy starts brushing his wrist against his face like a grooming cat, except his wrist got some wetness on it. I've never before seen Daddy cry, but I think that's what I'm watching. Daddy is crying. And he says something in the saddest little voice: "Trigona." I don't know what that word means, but it sounds like a name, so I gotta assume it's some woman Daddy knows, maybe a tea lady I've never met.

After a few sips and tears, Daddy comes back inside and sits in his favorite chair and keeps drinking the tea with a slumpy look on his face. Then, just as I'd thought up in this brain of mine, he closes his eyes and falls asleep.

So I'm on my way to Mama Cactus.

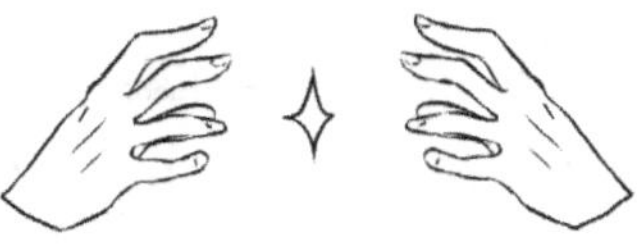

I take two things with me: a bucket of water and a saw. The bucket of water because Mama Cactus needs water, and the saw because I'm thinking it'll be easier to cut through the fence than climb over it.

It's not so far a walk to Mama Cactus, but there's a bucket weighing me down and my heart is going **brrr brrr** and I keep stopping cause I think I hear the Gardeners coming for me, but it's always a bird or a door closing or some other thing. I always thought I was good at being sneaky, but let me tell you, I don't like all this stress. No, no, not for me.

By the time I get to the fence, I'm all sweat and nervous shakes. I push and pull on the saw, chewing through the wood rods of the fence bite by bite until there's a hole big enough for me and my bucket to crawl through. Then, quick as quick, I'm on the other side, walking down to pay Mama Cactus a visit. No Daddy chasing after me, no Gardeners in sight, just me and She getting close to each other.

I've never touched Mama Cactus before. I guess none but the Gardeners have. Now that I'm all up next to her, I see how maybe I seemed a bit silly before with all my "Mama Cactus need water" preaching.

Mama Cactus is a real stout lady.

When I touch Her, it's like I'm touching the ground—just as hard, just as unmovable. By my eye, a hundred men could link hands and still not be enough to wrap around Her. I feel safe next to Her, like I feel next to Daddy, but also real small—like when I'm next to Daddy. I wonder if maybe that's just the way of things, like maybe being small is being safe or maybe you only get to be safe when you're small. That's why no one believed me before. If Mama Cactus were small and weak, maybe everyone would have noticed early that She needed help, like I did. But since She's big and strong, no one thinks to take care of Her.

"Hello Mama Cactus," I say as I rub her trunk. "I know You sick, so I bring You some water."

I'm just about to pour out the water at her roots when I hear some sound. It's all muffled like talking through the thickest pillow there is, so I can't make sense of it, but I can tell it's soft and steady, rhythmic.

It's coming from inside Mama Cactus.

I think a little bit that I should just water Her and be on my way. It's already night, and if Daddy wakes up, he's gonna flip the whole village over looking for me.

But I think mostly that I should check out what that sound is.

As hard as Mama Cactus is, I worry I'm not strong enough to saw a hole through Her, but after just a little bit, I see the saw teeth taking good bites. So I keep it up. Push then pull. Push then pull. The saw digging into Her a tiny dip more each time. Feels like hours pass, but I know I can be impatient, so it's probably more like minutes before I push my saw and it breaks through Mama Cactus' skin, leaving a thin line of black air.

Now I can hear it proper. Humming.

Not just one voice. Dozens all rolling together real smooth and gentle and pained and hopeful, high hums sitting on low ones, and together they all sound like maybe someone dropped a stone off from real high and it's falling in this patient way. Like it's resigned to falling and it knows how falls end, but it don't mind too much.

All that sound washes over me like a sunset, exchanging a bright day for dusk.

So I keep sawing.

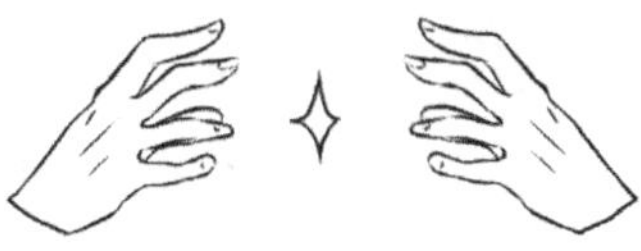

My palms are raw and cracked by the time the hole is big enough for me to climb through. I know I don't got a thing to worry about, but I take the saw and bucket with me like a spear and shield, just in case.

At first, I can't see a thing. It's all dark, just humming sounds and the smell of life. But I let my eyes learn this new place, and soon the darkness isn't so dark, and I'm looking around at a world like nothing I've seen before. It goes up up up forever, so far as I can see. A bundle of white ropes dangle down from the forever ceiling and stabs down into the soft soil.

And all around—radiating out from the center in staggered rings, their faces raised and eyes closed—were women.

I walk around them, and I don't think my jaw closes not once. More women than I knew were real, all just standing around. I stop by each one, and I can hear that they're all humming different kinds of hums, but when I step away and listen to them all together, it becomes that single falling sound again.

I recognize two of the women.

The first was my classmate's sister, Emi. I'd seen her just a few days ago, so she was fresh familiar. She stands in the same way as the others, with her face up and eyes closed and mouth humming. Her face is shining. Not shiny, like there's light on her face, but *shining* like there's light coming out of her.

The second looks like me.

At least a little. We got a mirror at home that I sometimes stop by to give myself a look-look, and this lady's face is a little bit like I'm standing in front of that mirror. Not everything—her cheeks more puffy, her chin more sharp. But the rest is so similar that I spend minutes in front of her, with no mind of what to say or do.

She never looks back at me. None of them do. I know it don't sound very sensible, but it feels like maybe we aren't in the same room. I'm inside Mama Cactus, but they're *inside* Mama Cactus in a different way, and I think they can't see me where they are. They all stay stuck with their faces up and eyes shuttered and, looking at them longer and longer, I see that they all look dry. Different levels of dryness, from a little bit parched to real dangerous. Like they're soon to die if they don't get some water in them. The Mama Cactus I'm in feels a little bit moist inside, but they must be in a different place with how dry they look.

But Emi looks properly watered. Her cheeks aren't all dipped in like some of the dry ones, and her closed eyelids don't got those plump veins throbbing in them. So I waddle my bucket over to the woman who reminds me of me, as she's one of the most dry ones, and try to open her mouth up.

But when I reach up to touch her jaw, my hand pokes right up through her face. Like she's just air. I tell you, this is a real confusing thing for me, but when I think about it, my brain begins to make sense of things. When I pull my hand back, her mouth opens anyhow. And when I scoop a hand of water from the bucket and pour it down into her mouth, the water just splashes on the ground, but I can see the swallow in her neck.

Then it's like her whole everything is born again. Skin fuller, eyes unsunk, hair moistened, a bud blooming before my eyes. By the end, her mouth is closed again, but instead of a flat line, she's got the ends turned up the littlest bit so it looks like she's dreaming about something real good. Then she starts humming again, but it's different now. Sounds more floaty, like a bubble drifting up and up to the sun.

I go to each of them, especially the ones who look most dry, and I give them each a scoop, and it's the same thing as the first woman, where it's like a whole new person is born. With each one, the music changes a little bit, and by the time I'm done, the whole sound is different. Inside Mama Cactus, a joyous hymn hums.

And just like that, I'm crying. I'm not one to cry too much—last year, I cried less than any of the other boys in school—but hearing the women fills me up with a really proud feeling. Sad, but proud. They must have been so thirsty. But they stayed stood up anyway, giving their power to Mama Cactus. I'm crying because I wish I could help them more, but it's like Daddy says: some things are too tough for boys and men.

Somewhere outside Mama Cactus, people are screaming so loud that even from a distance I can hear it over the humming. It reminds me of when Ngota-Balivhi attacked, so my heart is thinking that she's back to finish us all off. I should be afraid, but now that I've seen up close the women who protect us, even Ngota-B don't scare me.

I go look out through the hole and all I see is a group of Gardeners in a reckless sprint down the hill, running straight at me. They stop real quick to unlock the gate, then they're back to running again, shouting out as loud as they can.

But it's not just them.

Out past the fence, it's like the whole village has come out. A half ring of people all looking up at Mama Cactus, and they're all shouting too. I wish I could hear better, because not a word they're saying is clear to me, it's all a jumble. They don't seem upset, which is what I would expect on account of I cut a hole in Mama Cactus—in hindsight, a real risky move. They actually look quite excited to my eye, like they got some good news to share. So instead of hiding, I stick my face and arm out the hole and give a little wave.

And there's a swell in the sound, everybody's energy all snatched together and rising.

They're cheering.

And pointing up.

Curiosity takes control of me, so I squeeze out through the hole to see what they're all seeing. When I finally land outside and look up, I expect to see something unexpected, but it's just Mama Cactus. The same Mama Cactus as always, except now she's not looking so sick. In fact, I'd say she's looking real alive. Her trunk is already growing anew in the spots that had fallen away before, her branches are unfurling wider every second, and her leaves—they've been shrunk the last few days, some of them snapping in dryness and plummeting down to the sand—are proud soldiers, standing at attention, alive and green and plump like a baby's cheeks.

Mama Cactus is back.

Everyone gives me a hefty rain of cheers, tussling my head and lifting me onto their shoulders, and it's like no one even remembers I cut through the fence and Mama Cactus because they're so happy. Even when Ngota-Balivhi comes back to hover over us, everyone gives a defiant cheer because they know that now—again—Mama Cactus can tell that old bird to tread lightly or eat spines, so we all feel all kinds of joy and safety and warmth for each other. Even Daddy don't punish me.

When they ask what I did, I let them know it wasn't me at all. I tell them that it was the women. All their sisters and mamas and friends. They're all flavors of surprised to hear the women are alive, and I tell them all about the inside of Mama Cactus, and how the women hum such a beautiful sound, and how it's like they're there but they're not there, and how they were so dry, like they hadn't had any water in just about forever.

At that last thing, the Gardeners look at each other the funniest way, like when there's no palm wine at the party and your uncle arrives and everyone asks him where the palm wine is. Then there's a kind of all-together thing where the whole village realizes that people called Gardeners are probably meant to do more watering than fighting. The Gardeners can't explain how they forgot what they were supposed to be doing, but they got the good sense to look real ashamed about it.

I can't be too mad at the Gardeners, though. Or anyone else. Everyone was warning me and they were right: Mama Cactus don't need water.

But the women of our village do. Now that we know that, The

Gardeners made a little door in Mama Cactus' trunk, and each of us goes in to visit our sisters and mamas and wives and friends as often as we like to give them the water they need. And they don't need too much. Just a little bit. Just enough so they can keep doing what they have always done for us—holding up that big cactus sky of ours.

Moses Ose Utomi is a Nigerian-American fantasy writer and nomad currently based out of San Diego, California. He has an MFA in fiction from Sarah Lawrence College, and is a winner of the Ignyte Award and the Hurston/Wright Foundation Legacy Award. His works include the young adult Fantasy novel *DAUGHTERS OF ODUMA,* the fantasy novellas *THE LIES OF THE AJUNGO* and *THE TRUTH OF THE ALEKE,* and various short stories. When he's not writing, he's traveling, training martial arts, or doing karaoke—with or without a backing track. You can follow him on Twitter (@MosesUtomi) or Instagram (@profseaquill).

Other books by Moses Ose Utomi

The Forever Desert Series

I THINK I WANNA KISS HIS SISTER

BY LA PURVIS

ART BY DESTINY

ROMANTIC FANTASY

CONTENT WARNING FOR ROMANTIC INFIDELITY

If there was one thing Maia hated with all of her soul, it was morning. The glow from the sun clams were so bright that she thought her head would split in two. Which didn't even sound possible and yet somehow here Maia was, contemplating a life on one of the surface levels. Then the ear grating sounds of her shell phone ringer echoed with the sea currents.

The feeling that her skull was going to crack got so bad that she felt nauseous. She snatched the atrocious device from the side of her kelp bed and turned it off, not even looking to see who was calling. They should know better than to be calling so early on a rest day.

Although, Maia couldn't remember exactly why she had gotten so drunk in the first place; her last memory was talking to the bartender at Wayward Sip.

Maia sat up quickly, but regretted the motion almost immediately. As she struggled to keep the sickness from expelling out of her body, memories of the night prior filled her mind, and she remembered crying over her fiancé and being comforted by the bartender, Hezi. She had offered Maia something impossible. But as Maia dragged over her net purse and looked inside, sure enough there was a glowing golden apple sitting prettily next to her halimeda algae skincare cream.

Hezi told her she would know what to do with the apple, but as she stared down at the glimmering fruit now, all she wondered was: what in the Nine Seas was she supposed to do with this? It didn't even look edible.

Maia would have to go back to Hezi and complain about her lackluster gifts that couldn't even be considered decent hangover food. Honestly, who did she take Maia for? After the fifth glass Maia didn't even remember standing up from the stool she'd been at. And now she couldn't understand why these damn sun clams wouldn't get out of her room.

Groaning, she finally turned her attention and acknowledged them.

"Why are you here? Don't you have someone else to disturb? Shoo already!"

Maia waved her hand at them and threw some kelp in their direction, but they continued floating along as if they didn't realize she was speaking to them.

"Hey! I know you hear me." She stood up and waved her hand at them some more, making them scatter, although most of them stayed out of her reach. Maia was ready to chase after them if she had to, but the sound of pounding fists hitting the entrance of her cave made her stop. Her brows drew together in confusion as she swam through the cave channels to the front. Her cave was one of the few she could find within the coral reefs. With the entrance hidden, it made it harder for other unwanted visitors to find her. However, that didn't stop everyone.

What she wasn't expecting was to see Caol hovering just outside. His large arms crossed over his puffed out chest, looking intimidating. They almost made his equally large head seem smaller than it really was. Before she knew anything about his baby mama, the sight would've had Maia melting at his fins, but right now all she wanted was to get more sleep and then go yell at Hezi.

"I didn't think you'd be by today," Maia greeted.

Caol's brows drew together and his nose twitched.

"What's that supposed to mean?"

Maia yawned and stretched her entire body before leaning against the wall.

"It means I didn't expect you. Why?"

He scoffed. "Are you kidding? Where have you been? I've been calling you."

"Have you?" She looked back into the cave, in the direction that she left her shell phone, before turning back to Caol with a shrug. "Sorry. It's early. Did you need something?"

"Need something?" He let out one sharp chuckle. "Are you playing with me right now?"

Maia blinked and sighed a little as she rubbed her head. "Listen, Caol, I drank last night… a lot… and I'm having a little trouble remembering everything right now," she peeked one eye through the small space she made between her fingers. "So could you, pretty please, go a little easy on me, and just tell me what's up?"

When Maia fluttered her eyelids, Caol scoffed and looked away, his lips pursing up into a pout.

"You really forgot our rehearsal meal?" He had the nerve to sound affronted.

"Rehearsal meal?" In Maia's foggy memory, there was one that suddenly came into her mind.

That's right. The wedding was tomorrow. The event she'd been hoping, for months, would just stay an awful figment of her imagination, was finally looming right around the corner. And Maia still wasn't ready for it. She had come to terms with the fact that her happiness was not a factor that needed to be considered when it came to her duties and the survival of the Empire. But marrying Caol, knowing he spent most of his nights with his baby mama, while Maia's heart ached for another, was eating her alive. That was how she ended up at Wayward Sip. In front of Hezi. And in possession of that apple that still sat ominously upon Maia's bed.

Caol snapped his fingers in front of Maia's eyes, making her jump.

"Did you hear me? Are you that hungover? This is why I keep telling you not to drink."

Maia scoffed and shook her head. "You can't tell me what to do."

"Clearly, you don't ever fucking listen."

"Don't talk to me that way."

"Look," he held up his hands defensively. "I'm just worried about you. That's all. There's no reason for you to flip out on me because I'm concerned. Isn't that what a merman is supposed to do for his property?"

"Your… property?" Maia blinked and crossed her arms, looking around for where in the Nine Seas all his audacity came from. "You're saying… that I, Maia, Imperial Princess of the Nine Seas, Daughter of Emperor Yuval and Revered Empress River, am your property?"

"I'm a Prince too, Maia. We were born to uplift one another and be a united force against the turmoils of the Nine Seas. We're together, are we not?"

"I'm sorry… did you not leave me in the middle of the night to go and 'help' your baby mama?"

"I told you what that was about!"

"She couldn't find her shell phone?" She threw up her arms. "Are you serious? How dumb do you think I am? How else did she call you? Did she go out in the middle of the night and bum one off some random merfolk to call you? Get out of here!"

"You're being ridiculous," he sighed, rubbing his forehead. "I went there to make sure my children were alright. That's all. She calls me in the middle of the night and you don't expect me to go and make sure they're good? That's crazy and you know it."

"You know what?" Maia chuckled humorlessly and rubbed her nose. "Forget it. I got you something. Let me just go get dressed and bring it to you."

Caol looked surprised at her sudden shift, his brow bones raised high on his head. "You got me something? What for?"

"Oh, just cause," she waved him off with a flirty smile before she turned and swam back into her cave. Once back into her room, she noticed her bed maidens—four octopi that were all adorned with beautiful shells that signified their ranks within the royal palace—were now cleaning up her room, but had stopped once they noticed the glowing golden apple amongst Maia's old clothes.

Maia smiled at them all as eight large eyes looked in her direction and she motioned for them to relax. She went and sat down in front of her mirror. All of the maidens came to sit around her and assist in getting her ready. None of them asked questions, but Maia could sense their curiosity. As she stared at her reflection, they painted on the luminescent makeup, which aligned her eyes and circled around her head like a crown, before sliding down the center of her face to her chin. The makeup glowed against her black skin and onyx scales as she moved her head from side to side, feeling satisfied with the outcome.

She smiled and framed her face without touching it.

"Thank you, Titi. You always know just how to make me look beautiful."

Titi responded without hesitation. "You are naturally beautiful, My Lady. I merely accentuate that beauty."

Maia waved her off and after they finished painting more delicate lines down the extended spine of her dorsal fin and along the base of her tail, she slid a pair of fishnets onto her legs and the maidens assisted her with the rest of her outfit—a long dress with an a-lined skirt the shape of a jellyfish bell. After she was deemed presentable, the maidens swam over to the hidden tunnel that connected Maia's home to the main palace, and held open the large rock for Maia. However, Maia shook her head.

"I won't be going with you all that way. I'll be heading over with Caol," she told them. "Go ahead without me and let my father know we're coming."

The maidens bowed to Maia and went through the tunnel without her, being sure to reseal it behind themselves. Once they were gone, Maia drifted down and scooped up her net purse with the golden apple stowed inside, and swam back up to the front entrance.

Caol was pacing back and forth as he waited, his eyes trained down on his shell phone, and Maia wondered what had his interest. But she dared not ask. She wasn't sure she wanted to hear the answer. He clearly didn't care about lying to her.

Maia swam right up to him, startling him into nearly dropping his phone, and she smiled. She could see him winding up to yell at her, but before he could get out a word, she held up the apple, and to her complete shock he immediately appeared stuck. As if this was his first time ever seeing anything in all of his life. It wasn't at all what Maia expected. But, if she were being honest with herself, she didn't know what she had expected at all.

This apple felt like nothing she had ever held before. It was indescribable. It touched down into parts of her she wasn't sure she wanted it near for fear of exploring them herself. So when Caol reached for it, Maia didn't hesitate to give it to him, relieved to let go of the fruit as soon as possible.

Caol examined the apple closely. His eyes wide and his mouth hanging open, Maia began to wonder if his face was stuck like that.

"Where did you," he started to say as he went to hold the apple in both hands, but the fruit scattered into thousands of tiny golden flakes that infused into his skin.

Both of them jumped in shock at the sight, neither one expecting that reaction. Caol looked at Maia accusingly.

"What kind of trick is this?" he demanded.

Maia held up her hands and backed away, shaking her head. "Whoa, hold on. I don't know what just happened there."

"What—?"

"I don't know," she shook her head. "I really don't. How do you feel?"

Caol blinked and took stock of himself. His hands patted along his arms and down his torso, he felt along as much of his meaty tail as he could reach, and shook his legs. When it was clear there was no obvious distortion, he breathed a sigh of relief.

"The same."

"The same?" Maia's brow bones raised high on her face. "No difference?"

"No," he said matter-of-factly. "Actually, I'm pretty excited to get going, so… shall we?"

He held out his arm to her and his tail was already wiggling to move. There was no question about where the apple had come from or why she had given it to him, just a barely contained excitement over their plans. And as Maia slid her arm into his, she could feel his entire body vibrating.

Maia would have to remember to ask Hezi about those apples of hers later. Caol was like a completely different person. He couldn't swim straight, ran face-first into three bed maidens, bit his tongue almost any time he tried to speak, and he almost had his tail cut off by one of the closing tunnels of the main coral hall.

She wanted to laugh, but as they hovered before the Emperor and Empress, with Caol's tail fin stuck inside one of her mother's most prized vases, Maia couldn't pull her eyes up from the floor. The entire rehearsal had been a disaster. Caol couldn't remember what he needed to say when prompted, dropped the ceremonial jelly drinks, insulted the royal minister, and somehow managed to knock everything down within his range. If there was any mercy in the world, the floor would swallow her whole so that she could escape.

Caol's sister, Marlow, was there, wearing a sea glass dress that jingled every time she moved and her red hair was braided down past her waist. As beautiful as always, looking at her made the ache in Maia's chest grow. Marlow was surrounded by her fellow companions—who were all whispering in hushed, amused tones—her eyes were also aimed at the floor, but there was a stiffness in her tail that was not usually there. Maia knew that look and she hoped she could be around for when the explosion happened.

Marlow was always the one trying to keep Caol in check so he didn't dishonor their family. When she found out he had a baby mama, Maia watched her tear into Caol for a week trying to figure out who exactly it was, but he never confessed. She had begged him for answers, begged him to get rid of the problem before they became an issue. She even begged him on behalf of Maia. It was not a good look to have the Prince of the Jolnear Expanse with secret children no one knew about.

At one point, she had thought it was Maia that had gotten pregnant. Marlow had approached Maia and demanded to know what was happening, but Maia hadn't even known that Caol was seeing someone else. It had taken Maia off guard and she broke down in front of Marlow, and Marlow spent the rest of that evening apologizing and comforting Maia. It was bittersweet. Marlow had always been the better one of the two. For years, Maia admired the way Marlow handled herself and dealt with strife with the epitome of grace; and for years, she had secretly dreamed that Marlow had been the one their parents had arranged for her to marry.

As Maia's eyes lingered a bit too long on Marlow, she heard her mother clear her throat.

"You did wonderful, baby," Empress River said, reaching her hands out to Maia.

Maia swam up and grabbed her mother's hands, kissing her knuckles, and rested on the arm of her mother's throne.

"Thank you, mommy."

Empress River leaned her head closer to Maia's ear and whispered. "What's going on with that one?" she nodded towards Caol.

Maia sighed and shrugged her shoulders.

"Your Majesty!" Caol screamed, making everyone jump.

"Caol!" Marlow hissed. She swam over to him and placed her hand on his arm, every movement holding all the poise of her princess status. But Maia noticed the tight grip she had on his arm and the way his tail shook. "Watch your tone. Remember who you're speaking to."

Caol dropped his head and in that same instance one of the large clam lights fell from the ceiling and smashed into the back of his head, his tail drooped, and her mother's vase decided then to slip off and crash into one of the platforms below.

Maia's hand slapped across her mouth, Caol stayed completely still, Marlow's jaw hung in disbelief at the sight, and everyone else was so quiet you would think it was only the five of them in the room.

"M-m-my apologies, Your Majesty. Please forgive me. I don't know what's happening."

Her mother hummed, unamused, and cut her eyes away from his direction.

Emperor Yuval brought the end of his trident down against the throne platform and all the excess whispers ceased.

"Let us move to the morning room and begin the meal. The rest of our party has already gone ahead and are waiting for us. We should not linger here and waste the day."

They all followed the Emperor through a shell encrusted cavern that led to a room just a little smaller than the throne room. There were more clam lights floating around the room and dotting along the window openings, and sea shells and sea glass twinkled in the morning glow of the Ekriviel Palace.

As Emperor Yuval stated, there was a group of individuals already waiting respectfully around the table, one of them being Caol's and Marlow's father, and once they saw each other King Davey smiled brightly, his red hair danced around his head like a cloud as he waved at his children.

"Father?" Marlow said. "I thought you were leaving to deal with other business?"

"The business can wait. Emperor Yuval asked for me to join you all for the meal as well. Why? Don't you want me around?" He laughed jovially and Marlow bowed her head.

"I apologize if that's how I made it seem." She lifted her head and gave him a dazzling smile that made Maia stare once again. "Of course I don't mind you being here."

Empress River also smiled at King Davey as she greeted him. "I am very glad you were able to stay with us for longer, old friend."

"For you, my dear Empress, I would move oceans." King Davey then bowed to Emperor Yuval. "How about you, ya old merfish?"

Emperor Yuval chuckled and approached King Davey. "It's impossible to see you anymore. You hardly ever come out from the Jolnear Expanse these days. I have to use all the time I can get."

"Yes well, you know how things can be sometimes." King Davey stated to which Emperor Yuval nodded.

They all took their seats and the food was served shortly after. Maia somehow found herself in the middle of Caol and Marlow and the energy was tense. Maia tried to keep her attention on her plate but Caol had somehow managed to spill three more jelly drinks, break a cup, and drop an entire plate of mollusca.

After a while, Emperor Yuval wiped his mouth and stood up. Everyone stopped what they were doing and turned to him. He held a glass in his hand, but he wasn't making a toast. He stared down at his jelly drink for a moment before looking at King Davey.

"We've been friends for quite some time. Have we not, Davey?"

King Davey chuckled and nodded his head. "We have indeed, my friend."

"We've fought many battles together and worked together to

settle the turbulences within the Nine Seas. You assisted me with my struggle to temper the Empire and you've been a great source of advice whenever I need you. I have immense respect for you as an individual."

King Davey laughed and waved off Emperor Yuval. "Please, Yuval. No need to get all sentimental on me."

Emperor Yuval smiled, but continued. "It is because of our friendship that I'm saying this now. As you know, for years we talked about our children marrying, even going so far as to announce it at Maia's coming-of-age ceremony, and I've always felt confident in that decision… until recently."

"Wait. What are you saying?" King Davey asked.

"I'm saying that your son is not suitable enough to marry my daughter."

King Davey stood up affronted, Marlow dropped her fork, Caol choked on the dorado he was eating, and Maia stared at her father wide-eyed. She had never expected to hear such words come from his mouth. It was one of the main reasons she'd kept Caol's philandering and illegitimate children a secret.

She dared not say a word, too afraid that might wake her from this dream she must've been having.

"Why is my son not suitable? Because he's dropped a couple of things at the table? Maybe made a fool of himself at the rehearsal? Be reasonable, Yuval. He will do better tomorrow. This is ridiculous."

"From the sounds of it, you must be completely unaware of your son's dealings," said Emperor Yuval. King Davey made no retort to that.

His brows pulled together as he looked from Emperor Yuval, to Caol, Maia, and Marlow, trying to gather some kind of insight. "I, however, have learned a lot over these past couple of weeks. I have a duty to protect not only this Empire, but also the future of my daughter. And while I was willing to let it go for a moment, something inside me just won't let me allow this marriage."

"You were… investigating my son?" King Davey asked.

"I did," nodded Emperor Yuval. "He's meant to be the next one sitting upon the holy diasis and will become my son. Friend or not, I couldn't allow that without knowing who he truly is. And I'm glad I did," he said, narrowing his eyes. "It appears your son has already made a grandfather of you, old friend."

There were gasps of shock from almost everyone in the room apart from Maia, Caol, and Marlow, all of whom were now staring at the table without moving a muscle. Emperor Yuval turned his attention fully onto Caol.

"Do you deny it?"

Caol stood from his seat and stuttered over words that refused to leave his mouth.

"Speak boy," King Davey demanded.

"I—" Caol choked.

Marlow and Maia looked at each other from the corner of their eyes. They had promised one another not to speak a word about Caol's transgressions and Maia had kept her side of the promise for Marlow's sake. As they looked at one another, Maia gave her head the barest of shakes to say it wasn't her, and Marlow repeated the action. Neither one of them had told any maidens. How did they find out?

Caol finally stopped choking and bowed his head to the Emperor. "Y-your Majesty. There must be some mistake. I would never—"

"So, you deny it. I thought you might," Emperor Yuval interrupted. "That is why I waited until today. I want you all to bear witness to the way this boy lies to even the Empire."

"I-I'm not! Your Majesty, please, hear me out!"

Emperor Yuval turned to one of his octopi maidens. "Fetch my trident. I left it in the throne room."

"Your Majesty!" Caol dropped his head all the way to the sea floor, past the three shell platforms that resided under the dining table platform they were eating at. "Please! I would never disrespect the Empire, or your family for that matter, in such a disgraceful way. They were lying to you, I swear!"

"The maidens were lying. That is your excuse?"

Caol shook his head, his voice growing weaker the more he tried to deny anything.

"It's not excuse. N-no excuse," he corrected.

"No?" The maiden had returned with his trident and when Emperor Yuval had it in his hand, the pressure from his power thickened the room.

Marlow's hand suddenly grabbed Maia's, and though it surprised her, Maia squeezed her hand back and didn't let go.

Emperor Yuval turned his attention to the table, looking past

Maia, to the girl sitting beside Marlow. Maia tightened her grip around Marlow's hand as everyone's heads swiveled to the trembling figure of Lady Afshaneh. She sat straight-backed and wide-eyed as she stared at her plate and kept her trembling fingers twisted in her lap. The moss veil atop her head was like a shroud around her body that she tried to keep herself hidden behind. But as the silence stretched on, she turned to Marlow.

"Your Royal Highness, please, i-it's not what you think!"

Marlow, upon hearing Afshaneh's voice, closed her eyes. Maia wanted to move closer and offer more comfort, but she didn't dare draw attention to herself.

"What I think is not what matters anymore," Marlow said coldly. "The Emperor is speaking to you. I warn you not to disrespect him."

Afshaneh stood up and bowed her head to the Emperor. "My deepest apologies, Your Majesty, please forgive me."

"Forgive you for what, exactly?" asked Emperor Yuval. "For attempting to ignore me? Or for disrespecting my daughter?"

"I—" Afshaneh bowed lower. "It was never my intention to disrespect any of you."

Empress River sighed. "The same excuse. If I hear either one of you make one more excuse, I will have our guards go out and seize the child and bring it back here to be killed right before your eyes."

"NO!" screamed both Caol and Afshaneh.

"Please, Your Majesty," Afshaneh begged. "Forgive me. Please forgive me. Don't go after my children. Please."

"Ah," Empress River chuckled. "There's more than one, is there?"

Afshaneh froze, and Maia could hear tiny pearls dropping to the sea floor. She looked over and noticed Afshaneh's trembling was so bad she couldn't stay still. This was not what Maia wanted at all. She sighed and released Marlow's hand. Marlow looked at her, but Maia stood and drew everyone's attention.

"Papa…"

"Did you know about this?"

Maia nodded. "I did. Well… some of it."

"What did you know?"

"I knew he had children with someone else and I knew they were still seeing one another."

Empress River asked her softly. "Why didn't you tell any of us?"

"Because I did not want to draw attention to it. The unification between the Empire and the Jolnear Expanse has long been awaited by many. I did not wish to disappoint anyone."

"Oh, my dear girl," Empress River sighed. "You are not the disappointment. Willing to sacrifice yourself for the good of the people. The sign of a true leader. For that, I am very proud of you."

Maia bowed her head. "Thank you, Mommy. Either way, you don't have to do this."

"Why do you say that, baby?" Emperor Yuval asked.

"It's because of me," Marlow interrupted, standing up beside Maia. "She's trying to protect me. I found out about the affair. I told Maia about it. And I was the one who asked her not to say anything for fear of what it would do to our reputation. I never should've asked her when I could see how much bearing with it was hurting her. It's my fault your daughter kept this from you. I deserve to face punishment for—"

"No!" Maia snapped, grabbing Marlow's wrist without thought. "No, you don't. It was my choice. No one can tell me what to do. You know that, Papa."

"Well…" Emperor Yuval nodded in agreement.

"So, how about we all just take a breath, and calm down, okay?"

"You can't really expect us to just let this go, do you?" asked Empress River.

"No." Maia shook her head. "Of course not. But we don't have to bring the children into this. It's not their fault they were born."

Her parents both nodded and Maia released a small breath. Beside them, King Davey took large chugs of his jelly drink and slammed his cup down. He took a deep breath.

"This is beyond embarrassing. I don't even know what to say."

"It is not your fault, my friend," Emperor Yuval said, patting King Davey on the back. "Sometimes our children just know how to get the better of us."

"I know we can't let his transgression go, but if we could at least spare his life, for old times sake?"

Emperor Yuval nodded. "It seems that is what our Maia wants as well. So, perhaps we can come to an agreement."

King Davey released a breath. "I thank you." Then he turned to

Maia and bowed his head to her. "Your Imperial Highness, my thanks go out to you as well."

"I'm just glad we can avoid unnecessary bloodshed," Maia admitted.

"Agreed," he nodded slowly. His eyes drifted down towards her hand that was still gripped tightly around Marlow's. "Perhaps… another arrangement would not be disagreeable for everyone?"

Maia snatched her hand away from Marlow, making them both jump. King Davey blinked. And to Maia's horror, her parents seemed to have noticed as well. Had she made herself too obvious? Had she made a mistake trying to defend Marlow? But then again, she wondered, would her true feelings really bother anyone? Either way, that wasn't something she wanted to admit to others before she could admit it to Marlow herself.

No. She needed to get Marlow alone.

Right now, however, Maia focused on the still bowing Caol, bringing everyone's attention back to him.

At some point, Afshaneh drifted down to kneel on the floor beside him. They stayed quiet but the comforting way Caol's tail wrapped around her from behind was obvious for all to see. Emperor Yuval swam down to the seafloor to be at closer eye level with them and the party followed him down. Maia and Marlow stayed close together, but neither one of them looked at the other.

Emperor Yuval banged the end of his trident against the ground and told them to stand, and after a minute Caol moved, bringing Afshaneh up to stand with him.

"Are you going to keep denying your relationship?"

"No, Your Majesty," they said.

"Good. Then my judgment is this… Not only are you no longer fit for my daughter, but from now on, you are no longer Prince of the Jolnear Expanse, and from this point on you and your descendants will be banished from the Nine Seas."

Caol and Afshaneh gasped.

"But… Your Majesty. You can't be serious! I-I know I messed up, but this is too far, don't you think? I… it's not like I ever harmed Princess Maia."

"And is that supposed to make what you did better? What if I had never learned of this? What were you planning on doing? Were you going to ascend to my throne and try to imprison my daughter to the palace with more lies while you gallivanted off to place your bits into whatever foolish merwoman opened her legs for you?"

Empress River laughed humorlessly. "Who's to say he hasn't already? We don't know for certain if this is the only one of his paramores."

"True."

King Davey sighed, his head shaking in disappointment. "Please, Your Majesties."

"Yes, my apologies, Davey," Emperor Yuval patted him on the shoulder. "I don't mean to drag this out. Would you like to say anything? He is your son. I will not change my decision, but I won't take this opportunity from you either."

King Davey's large brown eyes turned to look at his son. He sighed again, as if the whole world was pressing down on his shoulders. But then his shoulders tensed as he began to pinch the bridge of his nose.

"Father," Caol whined.

"There is nothing I can do and we both know that," said King Davey. "You should have come to me about this. But instead, you thought you were grown and decided to play games you had no business being in. Did I teach you nothing growing up? I know I told you to be smarter than this. Were you ever going to tell us about her? Were you ever going to take responsibility?"

"I was taking responsibility! I take care of my children."

King Davey's eyes looked like they were going to pop out of his head. "What about your duties to the realm?! Were you just going to go on living two lives? You've destroyed our name with your actions! Don't you care?"

"I didn't destroy—"

The slap King Davey delivered to the side of Caol's head knocked out his equilibrium and for a moment, he was floating with the stars. Afshaneh kept her head down as pearls silently slipped down her face. She didn't even move to help Caol when his body started to float. After Caol came too, he looked dazed and confused by what just happened. As if he couldn't believe he'd just been struck.

King Davey turned to Emperor Yuval. He was at such a loss for words he waved his hands around his head in disbelief and shook his head. "I really don't know what to say."

Marlow grabbed Maia's hand and Maia looked over to see Marlow staring at her with large eyes. Maia stared back for a moment, before locking their arms together and they leaned on one another as two pearls trickled down Caol's cheeks. If anything, they would be a source of solace for one another now, just as they had been before.

"Ease your heart," said Emperor Yuval who had been watching the girls as King Davey was shouting. "I think there may be a way for us to keep our unification and salvage your family name."

King Davey opened his mouth to retort, but then he followed Yuval's line of sight, and everyone else's attention followed. Eventually, everyone in the room was staring at Maia and Marlow.

The two women straightened and tried to understand the implications being made. Maia's heart beat rapidly within her chest as she dared to hope.

"Yes," King Davey nodded. "I see. It could work."

Empress River sighed and crossed her arms. "How about one of you tell us your thoughts so the rest of us can know as well?"

"Yes, my dear," laughed Emperor Yuval. "I was merely pointing out the fact that Davey has two children. Why would we have to absolve the entire arrangement? Everything is already in place. The entire empire has been invited to witness. Canceling so last minute would not be proper. Do you not agree?"

"No, it makes sense," Empress River said, contemplatively.

"Wait," Maia interrupted. "Are you all suggesting what I think you're suggesting?"

"You can't be serious!" Caol shrieked. "Y-you're going to give my place to *her*? What right does she have—"

"Silence!" shouted Emperor Yuval and King Davey. Marlow jumped and tightened her grip around Maia's arm. Maia patted her hand and neither of them let the other go.

"You no longer have a say in any proceedings having to do with the Empire," Empress River coldly said.

"Remove these two from my sight," demanded Emperor Yuval. Caol and Afshaneh pleaded as they were dragged out by the palace guards—a trail of pearls followed their path. Their outraged screams echoed through the caves and Marlow trembled. King Davey wore a face of disgust at the shouting and shook his head.

"I failed him somewhere. If only I knew how."

"Don't be so hard on yourself," said Emperor Yuval. "You can't always win with them."

"No, I suppose not," sighed King Davey.

"Let us move on to more productive thoughts. Like tomorrow's wedding," suggested Empress River.

"Wait… mother…"

"What's wrong dear?"

Maia glanced at Marlow. "Can't we just… have a moment? This is a lot to take in."

"Of course, my love, have your moment. I'm going to go and handle the wedding changes."

King Davey rubbed his face. "Yeah, I'll have to make some alterations as well. I'll be back tonight, however. Marlow, come and find me then."

Marlow nodded and Maia didn't wait for any other command. She grabbed Marlow's hand and swam out of the morning hall. She led them all the way through the winding caves, into three other deep caves that eventually brought them to a private lounge room that Maia had stayed in every so often. The room sat within a large, hollowed out clam shell that looked out over the empire, but Maia didn't pay attention to the outside as she plopped down onto one of the sponge beds. Her head was hanging as she tried to gather her thoughts.

They were both quietly trying to wrap their heads around what just happened, but Marlow managed to whisper.

"I never expected he would be banished."

"No," agreed Maia. "Neither did I."

"He was so different today. I feel like nothing went the way it was supposed to."

Marlow was right. Nothing had gone the way it was supposed to, and that made her remember Hezi's words once more. She said that the apple would change things for Maia. Things Maia never would've guessed. It made her heart start its rapid pace all over again as she considered the future that was presented for her now. Had she actually somehow changed her fate?

A life with Marlow.

Wasn't that what she'd always wanted?

Maia lifted her head and saw Marlow perched at the edge of the clam shell. She was staring out at the empire with her hands held tightly in her lap. Maia swam over and sat down beside her, covering Marlow's hands with her own.

"Are you okay? I know this isn't what you had expected."

Marlow chuckled weakly. "No, I never expected to be the one sitting upon the holy diasis. I had come to terms with that. But now…"

"Now you're faced with not only that… but also being forced into a marriage with me." Maia squeezed her hands, desperate to comfort Marlow, even if her words cut. "I'm sorry—"

"What about you?" Marlow cut her off.

"Huh? What about me?"

"Don't you feel some type of way about all this? You're being forced into the situation as well."

"I never had a choice to begin with," Maia said honestly, looking at Marlow with an easy grin. "A lot of the major decisions in my life have been decided for me early on. That's why papa and mama let me get away with as much as they do. I don't put up much of a fight once I'm commanded. But… If I'm being honest, I don't feel as distressed about tomorrow anymore."

Marlow looked back at Maia, staring into her eyes. "You don't?"

Maia shook her head.

"No. Originally, I was against the marriage, but now… I feel like it's something I can look forward to. You and I…" Maia dropped her gaze for a moment, digging inwards for more of her confidence. "I've always thought that there was something different between you and I."

"You have?" Marlow's voice almost sounded hopeful and it drew

Maia's attention. She stared at Marlow. Eventually, her eyes dropped down to glance at Marlow's lips, before turning her attention back to her eyes. It didn't escape her notice the way Marlow's eyes mimicked the same path.

"Yes," Maia admitted. "I was attracted to Caol, but you were always the one I felt more of a connection to. I…" Her tail twitched in her nervousness and Maia had to shake herself calm before she could continue. She laughed, embarrassed.

"I could make you so much happier than he ever could," Marlow announced, moving closer to Maia. "You wouldn't ever question my loyalty. I could help you carry the burden of ruling over the empire and be there for you whenever the world gets too much… If you wanted, of course."

Maia reached her hands up and cupped Marlow's cheeks, her thumbs stroking soothing half-circles into her skin. There were so many times she had hoped to touch Marlow in such a simple way. There were many things she wanted to do with Marlow. So many wishful desires she had kept buried within her heart. Numerous hours of getting lost in her eyes and wondering what it was like to be on the receiving end of Marlow's affections. It was all Maia had wanted ever since her engagement to Caol. But never something she was allowed to explore. Now, unable to deny herself any longer, Maia moved in and pressed their lips together.

Marlow's kiss was soft and slow, drawing on Maia's desire and stoking the fires within. It brought a life to her that she hadn't felt for longer than she could remember. For the first time, Maia wanted to drown in these feelings that Marlow inspired within her. Maia wanted to look forward to the future and to plan for new beginnings. Anything that involved Marlow was now a welcomed opportunity of adventure waiting for them to experience together. And as Maia deepened their kiss, wrapping Marlow in her arms as they lost themselves in one another, she sent a mental thank you to Hezi for gifting her the golden apple.

It truly did end up changing everything.

Destiny is a medical doctor and art enthusiast. She enjoys making bright, colorful, and stylized character portraits showcasing beautiful Black people and is inspired by manga and anime. For inquiries about collaborations, art project or personal illustration please check out my page https://regulardestiny.carrd.co/.

La Purvis is a writer of Queer fiction and a lover of fantasy. She spends most of her time obsessing over dragons, getting lost in anime, kdramas, and true crime stories, and fighting a constant battle with insomnia. She is a contributing editor for *Magic in the Melanin: A Black Fantasy Anthology*, and the author of the upcoming debut novel, *May Chaos Reign Over You* releasing in 2025.

Other books by La Purvis

May Chaos Reign Over You

SICKLE CELL

BY JOEL ANTHONY HAMILTON

HORROR FANTASY

CONTENT WARNING FOR DESCRIPTIVE VIOLENCE

The howling wind yanks at the rusted doorknob of our wooden door, which violently rattles the frame that barely keeps it in place. The walls are made of ill-fitting planks running horizontally. The door is similarly constructed, but vertically. The floor and roof are patched where they gave way in the past. Their imperfections did a poor job at keeping the warmth in but excelled at letting in piercing gusts of cold.

Through the gaps and holes in the wood, I can see the snow swirl in one direction, stop, and then rapidly spin off another way. Along with the endlessly trembling door, the entire house creaks and groans, trying its best to remain upright. A sharp wind that snuck through the door makes me tense. My name is Hauron, and oh, how I hate the cold.

I shiver and turn toward a feeble fire that clings to life in a dark metal furnace. It lights the few feet in front of it in an orange hue. Anything beyond that point fades to brown and then black.

We have to keep the fire low, as our moderate stack of firewood has to last us until the storm passes. It is barely enough to stave off frostbite, especially with the cold air seeping incessantly through the walls, but we have no choice. I sit and look over at my grandfather, Cecil, wrapped in a tattered green blanket as he rests close to the furnace. He is frail and tall but seems shorter due to his curled position. Cecil wears a black beanie, and the tattered blanket hides his gray ensemble of thick socks, pants, and long-sleeved shirt.

He and I are the last of our once populated village. Others had moved on from this barren place but I had to remain with Cecil. The arthritis riddling his body is exacerbated by the cold. Going out into the bitter wind would surely shock his system too much. So, we stayed as the population of our village decreased. Some did stay, but eventually cold, hunger, or disease took them from us. The harsh environment and lack of trees forced me to deconstruct their homes for firewood. I had to burn the memories in their wooden frames just to stay warm. Once the houses were either used up or buried by snow, I had to venture far out to reach trees. But thankfully, at this moment, I am not outside.

I bring my legs up to my chest and hang my chin over my knees. All five-foot-eleven of my black, thin, twenty-nine-year-old frame is contained under a ragged green blanket. It is itchy but keeps the warmth in. Under that I wear a red, long-sleeved cotton shirt, faded blue-jeans, and layers of gray socks.

As I shiver under my blanket, I rub my forearms with my ashy hands, feeling the notches of scars. Along with battling the environment, I have to fight the wolverines that patrol this territory. They are bigger than average wolverines, just our luck. They range between one-hundred-and-fifty to two-hundred pounds, are three to four feet at the shoulder, and are four to six feet long. Their thick fur is mostly dark brown, they have occasional tan streaks, and their paws are padded to help them run on the snow.

They ravage our food stores and attack anything or anyone they view as food. Fighting them is a battle of endurance. Their hides are tougher than one would suspect, they are surprisingly quick-witted and agile, and are adept at maneuvering through the snow. If you hit them with a club, they get back on their feet and continue to charge. If you stab them, your knife might get through their hide, but will more than likely only come up with fur. They are insistent, and I have seen them eat people alive, undeterred by punches or assistance from any passersby. Their bone-crunching jaws just keep gnawing through flesh and bone until their prey simply pass out from the pain. The only way to survive an attack from a wolverine, at least that I know of, is to outrun it or lock yourself away and out of reach. Even though I hate the cold, freezing to death is second only to being eaten by a wolverine as ways I would hate to die. If you have nowhere to hide, not enough distance between you, or lack the endurance to run, a wolverine will eventually get you and you will be helpless to stop it from eating you.

I pass the time waiting out the storm by letting my mind wander and my gaze drift in the pulsing orange hue of the burning coals. That is, until I hear three strong knocks that stand out against the monotonous rattling of the door and creaking of the house. The incongruous sounds shake Cecil from his sleep. He slowly sits up, joining me as I also look toward the door. He then glances at me in confusion.

"Who might that be?" he asks.

I shrug, because our village is deserted and far from any other civilization. I stand, losing some of the heat I trapped beneath my blanket, and walk forward—my footsteps making the floorboards complain. Another three strong knocks stop me for a moment, then I continue toward the door. Through the cracks, I see swirling snow and a fluttering black cloak, but nothing else. I unlock the door and open it, squinting my eyes at the cutting wind. Oh, how I hate the cold.

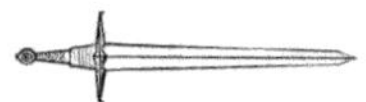

I hear Cecil shudder at the blast of cold that swept in.

"Come in," I say quickly. The man does so and I force the door shut against the push of the wind and relock it. Once I let go of the knob, the door begins to tremble again. Having lost the warmth of my blanket, I shiver. I examine the man before me. He is about six-foot-three, wears a threadbare cloak, long black pants, and—to my surprise—no shoes. His black cloak has a hood that drapes over his face. I am mystified. His cloak is too thin to shield against the frigid temperatures. He is black, like Cecil and I, but not ashy. The dry, cold air normally sapped all the moisture from our skin, but his ankles and feet look youthful. Even more surprising is that they are not frostbitten. Frostbite would set in minutes after walking through this environment without appropriate cover, yet he remains unaffected.

"Who and what are you?" Cecil asks as he also rises to face the visitor.

The man brushes back his hood to reveal an average, roundish face, a five o'clock shadow, and a bald head. A few thin scars mark his face, and his eyes are dark gray. He appears to be in his early forties.

"My name is Avinadale," he offers.

"I said who *and* what are you?" Cecil repeats.

I turn, unsure why Cecil is being so frank. Yes, it is odd he is barefoot and wears thin clothing, but it is our custom to let anyone in out of the cold. Let them in, keep the cold out, and ask questions later is how we normally went about things.

"My name is Avinadale and I—" He reaches behind his cloak and pulls out a dark, textured, red-and-amber-colored sickle with handles wrapped in thin black leather. I marvel at its varying tones as the light from the furnace seems attracted to it. The fireside stories I was told throughout the years let me know what he is before the words leave his mouth.

"—am a Sickle Cell," he confirms, as the wind howls more fiercely. I take a quick step back, causing the floor to creak, followed by slow, calculated steps until I was in front of Cecil. I could not believe a childhood fable stood in front of me.

"Please… it is just he and I. The food we have is in a bunker to the north and the only things we have here are firewood and blankets. We have no money, we have no jewelry. Please, do not kill us," I beg in a soft voice.

Avinadale stares at me for a few seconds before setting down his sickle and sitting with his legs crossed.

"The stories of us Sickle Cells are true," he says, "well, partly. I just wanted to find somewhere away from the howling wind to rest. I do not plan to kill you."

I untense and glance back at Cecil, who wears a stern look on his face.

"Partly true? What part of killing people is partly true? I have seen it with my own eyes. You go into villages and carve that half-moon-shaped weapon through the hearts of anyone you please. A group of murderers. What part of that is not true?" Cecil protests as he struggles to contain his anger with deep breaths.

"I told Hauron stories so that if he ever encountered one of you he would run. I also prayed he would never encounter or witness what I did all those years ago. I had hopes that you Sickle Cells had been wiped out or died of old age. However, here you are." He raises his nose in disgust.

Avinadale remains quiet for a few moments, listening, it seems, to the wind whistle and the door continued to jostle.

"Have a seat and I will explain," he says, looking at the floorboards. I motion Cecil to sit, despite his refusal.

"Listen," I whisper. "The last thing we need to do is get this guy riled up. Calm down." Cecil reluctantly begins to sit, as did I. We look at the man across the room, waiting to hear him out.

"It is true, we kill people," he says.

"See!" Cecil cries, but I quickly hush him, offering Avinadale a weak smile and nodding for him to continue, trying to keep the peace.

"But we do not kill without reason. You see, these sickles," he says, picking the weapon back up with his right hand and running his left fingers across it as he marvels at its colors. "These sickles are cursed. The blood of whoever wields the sickle changes, hence the name, Sickle Cell."

"But I thought Sickle Cell was a disease where red blood cells change into a sickle shape," I say, "that alters their function with life-threatening side effects."

Avinadale shakes his head. "The curse of being a Sickle Cell is slightly different. The cells in your body remain structurally the same, but your body becomes unable to provide or receive heat. As mammals, we are warm-blooded, can shiver to make heat, and can also warm up by being next to sources of heat, like your furnace. The curse of this sickle is that we lose these abilities and will freeze to death, unless we kill people with the sickle."

I am simultaneously curious and terrified. "Can you please explain more?" I ask.

Avinadale nods. "As you can see, I am barefoot and wearing thin clothing. An average person would freeze to death, but I am immune to the cold of the environment. Conversely," he sets down his sickle, stands, and walks to the furnace, opening it and grabbing a handful of coals, "I am also immune to the heat of anything I touch or the heat my body would naturally create." He dusts the hot coals off his hands and back into the furnace. Cecil and I watch with shocked expressions as Avinadale returns to his seat.

"When I kill people with this sickle, I gain warmth," he says. "However, it does not last forever."

I gulp. "How… how often do you have to kill people to stay warm?" I ask.

Avinadale shrugs. "Depends. Sometimes, every day. Sometimes, every few hours or minutes. Sometimes, years go by. It all depends on the sickle. However, when I begin to grow cold, I know it is time to kill again. If I do not kill, I will continue to lose warmth and frostbite will set in. Even if I set myself ablaze, I will freeze to death. It is a blessing, since I do not have to worry about the harsh environment or keeping a fire going. But the curse is having to kill people, or the impacts of not killing, when the sickle urges me to do so. I hate the cold, as I am sure you do."

Avinadale falls silent and we all sit listening to the door flutter in its frame and the wind try to knock down the house. Everyone just stares at the uneven, scuffed floorboards, unsure of what to say next. However, I catch note of a shivering sound and look up to see Avinadale has pulled his legs up to his chest and is rubbing his forearms, just as I did earlier when I was trying to get warm.

"No… no," he mumbles. My heart leapt into my throat. By Cecil's facial expression, he is experiencing the same. Avinadale is growing cold and he will need to use his sickle to stay warm.

"You have to understand," Avinadale says, "I do not like killing people. I do not like having to live this way but I… I…" Avinadale casts honest eyes at us, tears streaming down his face, "I just hate the cold," he says in a wavering voice.

I can understand. Well, partly. Growing up in this horrid environment made me despise being cold. It is cold when I go outside to use the restroom, cold when I wake up, cold when I go to sleep, cold when I eat. Everything is cold. I dream of being somewhere warm, where I do not have to battle the cold every second. For that, I would probably do anything to stay warm. But I cast that thought aside and focused on the sickle that lay before Avinadale. That sickle will be the death of us. Our lives depend on what happens next.

I could race forward and try to grab the sickle. I am not sure how strong Avinadale is but he has to be tough to beat. I imagine he fought many foes before me and probably surpasses me in strength. But then I begin to wonder what I would actually do if I got the sickle. *Could I… kill someone?* I wonder. *Even someone who would kill me?* I need more time to think. I need to stall.

"Av—Avinadale… How many people have you killed? How many other Sickle Cells are out there?" I ask, trying to buy myself more time to formulate a plan.

Avinadale buries his face in his shivering hands. As he does, I slowly rise and begin walking toward him and the sickle. I know this floor well and where it will and will not creak. I keep my eyes locked on him as I creep forward. The moment he moves his hands from his face or peeks from behind his fingers, I will race and grab the sickle. In the meantime, he begins to ramble as I slowly near.

"Hundreds. Hundreds of innocent people. Sometimes, one after the other. At other times, only single murders. I have to do whatever the sickle says or the cold will set in."

By this time, I am only a few steps from the sickle in front of him. I move even slower than before. One misstep and the floor will give away my approach.

"You heard him. How many other Sickle Cells are there?" Cecil asks.

I thank him telepathically, as me uttering anything will alert Avinadale to how close I am.

"I do not know. But please do not judge me for killing people. I try to pick someone elderly and sick. Someone who has already lived a good life or was suffering. You have to believe me. I am not a—" he stops, opening his eyes and freezing. I also freeze, as I have picked up the sickle and am halfway to a standing position. The sickle is a lot heavier than I imagined. I have to use two hands to hold it. The leather straps around the handle are easy to grip and are not as slippery as they look. I slowly stand and shift my weight to better hold the weapon and point it at Avinadale below me. Neither of us is breathing, and neither of us seems to know what to do from this point.

"Kill him before he kills us!" Cecil shouts but Avinadale and I remain still. His eyes are wide, seeking mercy. I can try and kill him right here, right now. But I am not sure if I can. I grip the sickle tighter, battling my will to live and my will to keep my humanity.

I yell, causing Avinadale to close his eyes, turn away, and continue shivering. He seems to be growing colder by the second but also does not want to watch his own death.

However, he opens his eyes when he hears footsteps racing across the squeaky floor. I cannot bring myself to kill him. Since I cannot kill the threat, I am going to get rid of the weapon that seems to be a bigger threat.

"Hey!" Avinadale screams as he scrambles to his feet and begins racing after me. Due to my head start and the small size of the house I reach the door, unlock it, and run out before Avinadale can get to me. Having left without putting on my snow boots, heavy coat, hat, or gloves, the blizzard outside blinds me with both snow and razor-sharp wind. Oh, how I hate the cold.

I quickly adjust and shuffle down the snowy steps and jump into the knee-deep snow in my socks and light clothing with a muted *crunch*.

"Hey!"

I hear Avinadale's muffled voice shout through the harsh, shifting wind.

I keep running despite my lungs burning, trying to grab breaths in the unforgiving air. I cannot gauge how far I run, but it feels like an eternity. My socks are soaked through and my feet are beginning to grow numb. Then, I feel a strong hand grip my shoulder and know I have been caught. I cannot think of how Avinadale has caught up to me or how I can fight him. My reaction is instinctual. I swing the cursed sickle back and low and then, with all the torque I can muster, fling it into the snowy beyond. All this happens in mere seconds, and by the time Avinadale pulls me back the sickle is gone.

He spins me around, picks me up by my shirt, hoists me into the air, and flings me to the side. I crash into the snow, my face feeling like it is being sliced by the frigid ice. I turn over to see Avinadale disappear into the cloak of winter, and I scramble to my frozen feet.

I have to get back to the house as soon as possible. My eyes dart around the snow as I stand, trying to regain my bearings. However, I cannot see anything. I cannot even locate the footsteps we made through the snow, even though they must be close. Along with my numbing feet, my hands are also beginning to malfunction, and frost is building on my eyelids, making it even harder to see.

Another hand on my shoulder sends me into a panic, making me think Avinadale found the sickle and returned to kill me. I shudder and crouch, bracing myself for death. But it seems death is to be delayed. A hand grabs my elbow and pulls me up. I squint to see a teetering light source, like it hangs from a swaying rope. But that is all I can see. I cannot even make out what or who exactly is gripping my elbow, but

I follow anyway. After a while, the snow is replaced by something hard as I walk up steps. Soon, the howling wind is muzzled as I hear a door close behind me. I still cannot see, as my eyelids are caked with ice and my walking is impaired by how frozen my feet are. But one thing I distinctly feel is warmth coming from in front of me. As I continue to be pulled toward the warmth, whatever or whoever guides me pulls me gently down so I can sit, my legs splaying out in front of me. I feel my thawing socks fight against being pulled off, but soon my frozen feet are exposed to the warmth. The ice covering my eyelids melts and I am able to open them. My vision is blurred for a few seconds afterward.

Once my eyesight returns to normal, I see Cecil going back and forth between the pile of firewood and the furnace, stocking it up.

"Cecil! That firewood has to last us—"

"Silence!" Cecil snaps.

I calm myself and see that he put on his snow boots, heavy coat, and gloves. He must have braved the snow, despite his arthritis and weakened state, to come get me. There is a lamp on the floor nearby. I assume that is the swaying light source that helped guide me through the snow. Once the furnace could be stoked no more, Cecil closes the door. He waddles to where I dropped my blanket, picks it up, and drapes it over me. He then pulls it tighter to make sure no warmth can escape, just like what he used to do when I was a child. Once I am swaddled, he returns to his blanket and plunks himself down, wrapping himself up. We sit in silence for a bit, listening to the fire crackle, the wind howl, and the door tremble incessantly. Cecil is the first to break the quiet.

"That was very brave of you," he says. "You saved us both."

"Brave? You were the brave one, coming after me despite your condition," I reply.

"We both did what was needed to keep each other alive," he states.

I smile but then turn back toward the rattling door.

"What happens if he comes back?" I ask, causing Cecil to shift beneath his blanket uncomfortably.

"Even if he is unaffected by the environment, he was shivering quite noticeably by the time he left. The curse of being a Sickle Cell. In his panicked, malfunctioning state he will find locating the sickle in the snow difficult, especially with the limited vision caused by the snow. It's easy to get turned around out there. I wasn't even sure I could lead us back," Cecil says.

"So, all we can do is wait?" I ask and Cecil nods his head once. I eye the fire raging within the furnace and am startled every time the rattling door makes a louder noise than usual, as the fear of Avinadale returning haunts me through the night. Neither Cecil nor I sleep as we wait for the storm to pass, or Avinadale to return, whichever comes first.

A few hours later, Cecil and I notice the door slowly stop its trembling and the howling wind subside.

"Looks like the storm has passed," Cecil says, giving a light stretch.

"And it looks like our adversary did not survive, or at least did not come back to finish us off," I reply, standing to stretch my stiff legs. By this time, the furnace is only emitting a low level of heat and the pile of wood has been reduced to a few pieces of kindling.

At times like these, most people would relax a bit. But us mountain people have to take advantage of every break in the storm. I put on three layers of new socks and lace up my boots, as does Cecil. Although he cannot take the bitter cold well, he fares well enough after a storm passes. We grab some heavy coats and gloves off the rack, their hoods lined with wolverine fur. Once geared up, we unlock the door and step out.

We are blinded for a few moments as the white snow amplifies the sunlight. Our eyes never truly adjust and remain squinted against the glare as we survey the treeless environment. After taking in our first gulps of sharp, cold air we split up to tend to our tasks. The air is frigid but manageable, however, even light gusts of wind make me pause and tremble. Oh, how I hate the cold.

Cecil goes to our storage unit to grab some rations for the day and checks the traps for any rabbits or other small game.

I go to the side of the house and pick up the icy ropes attached to a wooden sled. In the sled are a medium-sized hatchet and more rope. It is my duty to travel out and find firewood. So, I strap the ropes on my waist and set off.

The sled is light and glides smoothly over the fresh snow. The hard part is trudging through the snow, which is knee high. However, my clothing and years of doing this make this an easier task. After about ten minutes I strike something solid with my shin and yelp in shock. After a few rubs, the pain fades and I look down to see a dark, red-and-amber blade, partly exposed under the snow. I kneel and pick up the sickle. Thankfully, it seems I hit the dull end of the blade. I look around for Avinadale but see only white snow. Not knowing what to do, I toss it in the sled and continue.

After walking about fifteen more minutes, I encounter a small patch of pine trees.

I unstrap myself from the sled and use the hatchet to break off low-hanging dead branches. Once that is done I begin making notches in the trees, each strike causing a bit of snow to fall. The cold air and lack of trees make the sound of my monotonous work echo across the land.

The monotony is broken by a metallic *clunk* as the head of my ax strikes the tree trunk and falls into the soft snow. I sigh, knowing the only supplies I have to fix it are at the house. I take a second to catch my breath and I scan the area with my back to the tree. To the west, nothing but snow. To the north, a blurry, low-to-the-ground shifting figure. To the west… I pause and look back toward the north at the blurry shape. Against the white background it stands out like a sore thumb. I squint to fight the bright snow dazzle and as my vision focuses, I see it is an approaching wolverine. It is about a quarter mile away. It runs with a strange gallop; its right leg and shoulder bearing the bulk of each prance. It does not sink deeply into the snow, unlike myself. I can just make out that it is panting and it is headed in my direction.

I begin to panic. The house is too far away to try and make a run for it. It will surely run me down. I glance back at the trees but they are too narrow to hold my weight. All that I can do is stand and fight.

Looking at the sled, I see the sickle. With my ax broken, it is my only option. I move as quickly as I can through the snow toward it and strain to pick up the sickle with both hands. I steady myself and turn toward the approaching wolverine, which is now a mere hundred yards away. The closer it gets the more I am reminded how gigantic it is. It closes the distance and stops around ten yards away. Panting, it sniffs the air and moves its head up and down. It seems to be gauging how strong its opponent is, similar to what I am doing. Then, keeping its head low, it begins trotting in a tight circle around me. I turn, shifting my stance to watch its movement, gripping the sickle tighter with every second. This will be a battle determined by seconds. One bite will break my arm or femur. It will eat me alive. I can strike, but if I miss, it is all over.

Without warning it lunges, teeth bared and claws out. I swing, wide-eyed, and by sheer luck, the hook of the sickle digs into its torso, getting stuck halfway. Blood gushes out in a steaming freshet. The beast falls, landing on me. I am crushed for a brief moment before it rolls off, yelping in pain. It hisses and breathes heavily as it sprawls in the deep red slush it is creating until it ceases to move. I sit up, trying to catch my breath. As my breathing slows, I notice I feel oddly warm. I take off my gloves and still feel warm. Then I realize that killing something with the sickle is probably the action needed to enact the curse. And now I am a Sickle Cell.

"Hauron."

Cecil is calling to me in the distance. I set the sickle in the sled and cover it with my heavy coat, since I do not sense that I need it. I climb back into the sled's harness and begin trekking home. The wind picks up and as I near the house, another blizzard sets in. Even so, I am still warm. The blizzard's only impact is that it slows my progress back to the house. I put the sled, with the sickle, next to the house and scurry inside, shutting the door.

"Oh, thank goodness you are alright. What happened? What was that screaming about? And where is the firewood?" Cecil asks.

I sigh, not sure where to begin. And before I can speak, I feel my warmth fade and I begin to shiver. Knowing what is happening, my eyes track up to Cecil's curious face.

"What's the matter?" Cecile asks.

"Oh, how I hate the cold," I reply.

Dr. Hamilton is a researcher turned self-published author. Growing up he mainly did things to make his father proud. Following his passing, starting his self–publishing journey was the first thing Dr. Hamilton did for himself. He's published several books, including the *Mud Crab Kingdom* series, *Worth his Salt*, *Black Brilliance*, and *Oh, Sweet Plague of Mine*. He's received multiple honors and awards for *Mud Crab Kingdom*, such as the 2023 Readers Favorite 5 Star recipient, the 2023 PenCraft Book Award of the Cultural Fiction category, and several Indie Ink awards. Dr. Hamilton hopes to create books that inspire, uplift, and stretch the imagination.

Other books by Joel Anthony Hamilton

Mud Crab Kingdom Series

OF CELESTIAL FLAME

BY DOYIN ADERELE
ART BY MELANIN ECLECTIC

DYSTOPIAN FANTASY

CONTENT WARNING FOR DESCRIPTIVE VIOLENCE

Eba-Odan

Lower Quarter

5:30 owurọ

Early mornings have always been a staple in my life. Training at dawn with my father before he reported to his duties with the *Iwarefa*, going out to the *ọja* to buy ingredients for my mother to cook breakfast, then taking sunrise trips to her burial place after she passed. I thrive in the mornings, under the first light of the sun. Though today, before the sun has even shown its face, the humidity of the land already seems to have a suffocating tug.

The farmers in the grassy fields stop their work and stare as I drive by, the rumble of my bike disturbing their early morning toil. Despite it being the latest model, powered by pure electric energy, it's out of place in the rural area. I lean forward and accelerate, my tires kicking up dust in my wake.

"Almost out of the Lower Quarter. Will I need a charge?"

"ETA?" The technician in my ear responds. I look at the clock on my dashboard. I'll get there by sunrise.

"*Wakati kan.*"

"*Rárá*, you're set for the job."

I raise a brow, glancing at the battery life beside the clock. There are two bars left, which is usually good enough for two or three hours, but that's in the city where the machinery operates under perfectly regulated conditions. Out here, it's unpredictable, especially with the heat. Underneath my gear, my skin already feels damp with sweat.

I look over my shoulder, the sky-high adobe structures of the city shrink in the distance, its lights still a bright beacon in the morning twilight.

"Lieutenant Zira?"

I swallow my doubt. "Received."

"Good. Resume coms upon arrival."

Eba-Odan

Òkú Ilẹ
6:30 owurọ

Oku Ile, or the Dead Lands, demarcates Eba-Odan's borders. It's miles and miles of dirt where nothing lives or grows. LILO has run its energy domes out here for as long as it's been providing energy to the city, which is way before I was even alive. They pride themselves on their five decade-long operation. *"Agbara daradara fun lilo rẹ."* Efficient energy for your consumption.

The only structures visible in Òkú Ilẹ for miles are the four large sparkling blue-gray domes made of kẹrinla, the elusive material LILO uses to collect its energy from the sun. I've always wondered how they discovered it and its ability to create energy, but that's a secret they keep within company walls.

"I've arrived," I announce into my headset, slowing down at the borders of the domes. They're arranged in a circle, with a tall, narrow tower that stretches toward the sky in the center. Its highest point seems far above the *Iwarefa* House, which is the tallest in the city.

The tower's kẹrinla walls shimmer in the rising sun. Even surrounded by dark gray clouds of smoke caused by the flames that dance around its base, it looks beautiful. Static rings in my ear. "Approach the central tower and wait for instruction."

"Got it."

Before I kick off, I sit up and unzip my cloak, freeing myself from the thick, green material and allowing what little breeze there is to cool my chest. The speed of driving provides some relief as I start moving again. "The heat from the fire is intense."

"Respectfully, I'm glad it's not me out there, lieutenant." I roll my eyes.

Maintenance for LILO's energy systems is usually done remotely, however, yesterday the company alerted the leaders of Eba-Odan, the *Iwarefa,* of a fire at the central tower that needed immediate attention. No one is allowed in the Dead Lands except high-ranking servants of the *Iwarefa,* so they sent me. Being twenty-three would normally only qualify me for lower ranking positions in the guard, but as daughter of a warrior chieftain, blessed by Yemoja at birth, I was guaranteed swift advancement up the ranks at a young age. When I became a lieutenant, I made sure to live up to the expectations. I can't have the other members of the guard doubting me, which is why it feels good to be trusted with important jobs.

To get to the central tower, I weave around the long power tube that connects each dome. There's an opening near the northernmost dome where the pole begins to run uninterrupted for miles, straight into the city's power lines. As I ride closer to the tower, it grows hotter, sweat pouring down my face in streams and bringing a briny taste to my lips.

"*Olorun,* it's like a furnace out here—Oh my gods!" I swear as a small explosion rocks the area, the flames of the fire expanding and sending large sparks in my direction.

One hits my bike directly, knocking me right off. My head bangs against a rock when I crash into the dirt. I say a prayer of gratitude for the helmet on my head as my brain rings in my skull.

"Lieutenant Zira, are you okay?"

"Y-Yes, I'm fine," I groan, sitting up. The face shield of my helmet is cracked right across my eyeline. I pull it off, wincing at the sharp pain that shoots through my elbow. "Fire's a little rowdy."

I stand up. A few feet away, my bike lays on the ground, a black scorch mark in the paneling on the left side. Right where the battery is.

"My bike was hit."

"Does it still work?"

I lift it up with one hand so my right arm stays stationary at my side, and hit the start button. It rumbles to life, dashboard lighting up with a loud beep. The battery is down to one bar. "Yeah, but don't think there's enough power to get me back to the city."

"Battery must be drained. I can walk you through a power up in one of the domes after the fire's out."

I nod and turn the bike back off. When I lift my right arm, the pain is gone, elbow bending perfectly. I touch the cowrie shells around my neck as a thank you to my protector and then slip off my army cloak completely. The *aso-oke* vest top I wear underneath provides enough breathing room for my skin. I readjust my weapon on my back, the heavy weight of the ring blades a comfort even with the unlikelihood of needing them today. I trained with my dad for eight years to learn how to use them before I was finally able to get my own crafted for me at sixteen. I never part with them.

"Approaching the tower," I inform my nameless companion, reaching into the large pocket on my pant leg and taking out my sun goggles. The gold-tinted shade makes the fire look like the sun that it truly feels like it is.

"There should be a valve to the right when you walk through the entrance on the southern end of the tower. If you turn it, it'll release the water system. It's jammed and needs to be switched on manually."

I keep a safe distance away as I circle the tower, walking halfway around to get to the south side. When I reach it, weirdly enough the fire hasn't encroached on the door despite burning powerfully everywhere else.

"How is it not—" Boots crunch in the rock behind me. I whip around, my arms flying to my back.

A figure lurks near the dome to my left, wearing a dirty white jacket and a red scarf around their head. Their eyes are concealed by skinny white sun goggles with a red shade, but their exposed brown skin is dark and rich in the harsh sunlight.

"Who are you?!" I call, wielding my blades. Anyone who's out here alone can't be harmless. The person doesn't respond, but instead begins marching forward. "On behalf of the *Iwarefa* of Eba-Odan, I'm commanding you to halt right now!"

They don't stop, so I swing my right arm back and then sling it forward, releasing a blade. As it's whirring through the air, I send the left one flying after it. The person, who in closer proximity is clearly a man, stops moving as he unsheathes a spear from his back. My first ring cuts into his jacket sleeve. He winces but manages to block the second one.

I sprint toward him. The ring that struck him curves in the air and flies back toward me. As I run, I reach out and snatch it out of the air. I drop into a slide, dirt kicking up around me as I move into his space, grabbing the second ring off of the ground and jumping back up as I make another strike. Our weapons clang loudly against each other.

I jump back, holding my arms up defensively as I examine him. His fighting form is perfect, almost professional, and the spear in his hands looks military grade, at least the spear tip does. The handle is bound with sticks and wire, but the way he grips it, it looks sturdy. And familiar…

I lunge forward, but he immediately ducks low and aims his spear at my thigh. I spin out of his way as he slashes his weapon down. When I turn back around, a safe distance away, I see a braided piece of my hair on the ground between us, the cowrie shell once weaved into it now cracked in half. I grit my teeth.

"Lieutenant Zira, what's going on over there?" The LILO technician questions in my ear. I almost forgot about him.

"There's a—"

He attacks again. Despite being caught off guard, I block with both of my rings, wincing as my elbows take the shock. He pushes against me with his spear and I push back just as hard, both our feet digging holes in the dirt. He doesn't make a counterattack and I realize why when he lets go of his spear with one hand and reaches up to my face, ripping my headset off before I can even blink. He slams it onto the ground and it shatters into pieces.

"*Kilo ndamu e?* Are you crazy?" I yell, finally jumping back. "You're attacking a lieutenant of Eba-Odan's army!"

The man finally speaks. "God, I can't believe they sent *you* out here."

I blanch at the sound of his voice, my arms lowering.

"You—"

"I don't want to fight you, Zira Sàṣẹ́rẹ́." He drops his guard and takes the goggles off his face. I gasp.

"Mikah?"

Eba-Odan

LILO Energy Tower, Òkú Ilẹ
7:15 owurọ

Six months ago, Mikah Asaju was regarded as one of Eba-Odan's best warriors. He and I worked as lieutenants for the army, before that training side-by-side, as the youngest members of our battalion.

Six months ago, Mikah was assigned as interim security detail for

Ariyo Ojo, the head of LILO, whose usual guard had fallen ill. He was only supposed to work for the man for a week, but halfway through his service, Mikah deserted.

I only heard of the situation through second-hand accounts because I was on a mission in the northern mountains, thirteen hours out from the city, but the report once I returned was that Mikah had killed the head of LILO and ran. He was chased throughout the city by the army who swarmed Eba-Odan on motorbikes and army trucks. But Mikah evaded them, running on foot through back roads and escaping to the Lower Quarter on a stolen bike. The army followed him all the way through, intending to go until the end, but when Mikah fled into the Dead Lands, the hunt was called off. They kept security along the border for a month, but Mikah never turned up and was eventually presumed dead. No one can last more than a few days alone out there.

A lot of people were shocked that one man managed to escape an army of men, but they didn't know Mikah. I did. And I wasn't shocked. What shocked me was that he would commit murder. That wasn't the Mikah I knew.

"I-I thought you were *dead! Everyone* thinks that you're dead!" I exclaim in horror. The rational part of my mind is telling me that I'm hallucinating, that the heat has gone to my head. But another part, the part of me that never truly felt that he was gone—never truly believed that he did what everyone said he did—knows better.

"*Arewa,* you know I can't die that easily," he drawls, a cocky smirk crawling onto his lips.

"Don't—don't do that! This isn't funny, Mikah! Why did you pretend to be dead? What are you doing out here? Why—" I swear as tears well up in my eyes.

Mikah sobers. "I'm sorry, okay? You know I can't just go back there, they'll have my head before I can even explain."

"Explain what? Why you killed an innocent man?"

He flinches like I've punched him. He looks hurt. I immediately regret my words.

"You don't actually believe that, do you? You can't believe that, Zira, I would never—" I stab my finger into his chest.

"Then what really happened? Why did you run? You, out of all people, should know running makes you look guilty!"

Mikah touches my arm gently. I stiffen but don't pull away. It's strange to have someone's touch feel so familiar but foreign, like a ghost's.

"I'll tell you, okay?" He says, pointing with his spear at the LILO tower. "But I need to show you something first."

I search his eyes, his sincerity bleeds through as he begs me to trust him. I glance at the broken headset on the ground and sigh. I'm stuck here now anyway.

"Okay."

Mikah drops his hand, sheathing his spear. He starts walking toward the tower so I sheath my blades on my back and follow.

"Tell me though, how have you survived this long? You haven't been out here the whole time, have you?"

He shakes his head. "Definitely not. There's a slum, Bodija, that's just close enough to the Lower Quarter to be habitable. It's full of people who've fallen off the grid because of crime or poverty. I stayed there for a while. Then when the security at the border lightened up, I went to see Bayi."

"Your brother—I mean, half-brother?"

Mikah nods, sighing. "Yeah. To be honest, no matter how much I denied it in my past, he is my brother. Especially since he's been letting me hide out with his family in the Lower Quarter these past five months. Since no one knows about him, the royal guard never thought to look for me there. I guess I have you to thank for that."

I avoid his gaze, a frown taking over my features.

I don't regret not giving out that information when everything went down, even after being interrogated as one of Mikah's closest friends. But I still hate that I lied and went against all I stand for. I made a promise to serve the city in every capacity, yet in a crucial moment, I did the opposite.

Mikah thankfully doesn't push the subject. "Ever since everything went down, I've been coming out here every few days to check on any changes in the tower," he says as he leads me to the entrance I'd been directed to go through earlier.

"Why?"

"Because of this."

Mikah points above the door. There's a double circle with a cross in the center etched into the surface of the tower. I frown, immediately glancing down at the dirt. In the space on the ground where the fire's path is halted, there are an assortment of items neatly placed in a line. From my position, I identify smooth rocks, cowrie shells, chunks of fruits and vegetables, and sprinkles of grains. I can bet that if the fire wasn't burning, there'd be even more items laid out in a circle around the tower. Items for an offering.

"It's an altar," I say. An altar meant as a tribute for **all** the gods. Something like this isn't set up just for the sake of worship. Whoever made it has to be asking for something big. I look up, my head falling back as I follow the length of the tower into the sky. The heat of the fire stings my neck. The sun blinds my eyes. A sick feeling settles in my gut. "Don't tell me…"

"The day Ariyo Ojo died," Mikah begins. My head drops to look at him. His face is grim. "I was posted outside his chambers when his brother, Kola, came to see him. It was really early in the morning, so I thought it was a bit strange, but I let him in because he said he had something urgent to discuss with his brother. The conversation was loud and heated, it was hard not to listen in. Kola grilled Ariyo about how a deadline was coming up and Ariyo kept begging for more time because he was 'working on another way.'

"They spoke in vague terms most of the time, but I distinctly remember Kola shouting, *'The gods won't give us time, we need a sacrifice or they will take away everything!'*" The tightness in my stomach intensifies. I want to vomit.

"I came out here when I first went into hiding and it wasn't hard to figure out what they meant."

"LILO uses sacrifices to power the city."

"There's no way the gods would let the sun's power be used to this extent for free. It comes with a big price."

"Who else have they done this to?"

"Hopefully, not that many. When the brothers were arguing, Kola told Ariyo that the sacrifice wasn't needed often enough to waste time looking for an alternative. Apparently taking a life is not a very big deal to him," Mikah scoffs. "While I was hiding out in the Lower Quarter, I did a little digging into the Ojo family. The brothers were not the only children their parents had. They had an older sister who passed away when she was around our age, right around the time LILO formed as a company. When Ariyo was begging for more time, he told Kola that he couldn't give up another life like their father did when he founded the company."

"My gods, his own daughter?"

Mikah nods, jaw clenched as he glares into the flames. "Kola didn't share the same remorse. He told Ariyo he wouldn't let him ruin the company. Then I heard a crash and finally intervened. When I went inside, though, Kola had already killed him."

"But why'd you run?"

"I told Kola to surrender and took the knife from him. He seemed cooperative, but when I went down to check Ariyo for a sign of life, Kola started shouting for help and alerted the other security in the building."

My heart sinks. "He framed you."

"I had the knife and blood all over me, so it was easy. There was no way to prove I hadn't done it and who would believe that Kola killed his own brother? They basically run the whole city. Even I wouldn't believe it. I knew they'd have me killed immediately, so I ran."

It's a struggle to keep my relief internal. I don't want Mikah to see that I doubted him at some point. I think he'd rather me stab him in the chest than admit I thought he was capable of taking an innocent life.

"I can't believe this." I turn to the tower. "How did their father come across such a terrible ritual?"

And why human sacrifice? The usual requirements for a ritual are items that have strong connections to the deity the ritual is being conducted for. Not just any human will work— *"No one in your age class has a blessing from their patron deity as strong as yours, Zira,"* my mother said on my ninth birthday when my blessing was revealed. And I've heard it from everyone almost everyday since.

A chill runs down my spine. I think about how carefully crafted this mission probably was. LILO *requested* I take it on alone.

"Do you think the *Iwarefa* knows about this?" I ask aloud. I really want to ask if my father, Warrior Chief of the *Iwarefa*, knows. Whether he would allow such a fate to befall his daughter.

"I don't know, but even so, they can't just sacrifice an innocent life to keep the city running, especially if it's against the person's will."

I nod, swallowing the sting of fear that shoots through me. Not just fear of the fate that almost awaited me, but of my loyalty to Eba-Odan and how it might've made me agree to it if asked. That I can still see myself agreeing to it now.

I stare at the tower and watch the flames I was sent here to extinguish. Not with water, for a celestial flame will accept only what the gods demand, but with my body. Those flames should be burning underneath my skin.

"But…But what will happen without the sacrifice? The gods won't be happy if they don't get what they want. Darkness could fall upon our whole land, or worse." Mikah grabs my arm, jolting my gaze away from the tower and to him. His brown eyes darken like wet earth.

"Let them be angry! Let the world be *pitch black*. I'm not letting you die! Not for this." He doesn't let go until I nod, then turns away from me, running a hand over his face in frustration. "There has to be a way to do this without sacrificing someone."

I shake my head to clear the haze in my mind. *Loyalty from the blind is not noble.* Being a sacrifice for something without question would be stupid. There's always another way. Think.

The gods are not evil, they may not be easily pleased, but they wouldn't make it so the only way we could harvest the sun's power is through the death of the innocent. The gods love gifts that benefit them. A human death doesn't bring them many benefits.

"We need to find something better to give the gods in return for the sun's power. And it needs to be a one and done trade."

Mikah nods. "What's a big enough trade for the sun?"

"The gods love to be reminded of what's theirs," my father would

say when, as a child, I questioned him on the reason we have festivals dedicated to the gods. *"The land we inhabit is their creation and we must thank them for their generosity to us."*

I look beyond the fire, out at the expanse of Òkú Ilẹ, then at the glittering kẹrinla structures that surround us. I've always been impressed at the way LILO managed to make such barren lands benefit Eba-Odan. Maybe we can still do that on a wider scale. I turn to Mikah. "Your brother still sells ritual supplies, right?"

"Yes, why?"

"I think I have an idea," I tell him, already walking away from the tower. "I'll explain on the way, we need to get back to the Lower Quarter. My bike is fried, how'd you get here?" Mikah points towards the domes to the left. "We can take my bike. I borrowed it from Bodija to get out here."

"LILO won't just let this go, you know," I say as we start walking. "They'll come after me." If Kola killed his brother for this, he'll have no problem hunting me down.

"I've avoided them for this long. I think we can manage for just a little longer." Mikah shrugs.

"*Asan.* Your cockiness will get you in trouble."

Even when we reach his bike about half a mile out from the tower, I can still feel the heat of the fire as it intensifies, waiting for a sacrifice to consume. I force myself not to look back.

I grimace at the pile of metal parked in the dirt. Mikah's bike is a rusted yellow color, its engine clunky and covered with dirt from its exposed position under the seat.

"What is that?"

"An *okada*." Mikah laughs. "It's one of the oldest models of motor bikes. Definitely not as smooth as a LILO bike, but it gets you where you need to go."

"Can I drive?" I approach the bike, touching a worn handle. There isn't much displayed on the handle bars, just two gauges, one a speedometer and the other for gas. I climb onto the machine, testing my grip on the handles until it feels comfortable. There's no start button, only a single key in a slot.

"I'll direct you," Mikah says as he gets on the bike behind me, the long seat providing plenty of space for the two of us.

I turn the key and the bike roars to life, the ugly sound making me flinch. LILO bikes are relatively quiet, most noise coming from system alerts and the low hum of the battery. "Gods, you've really been using this thing?"

"It's nice when you get used to it." Mikah rests his hands on my shoulders. "*Oya, Jẹ́ ka lọ*. Use your foot to get it moving."

I kick the brake stand up and then push my boot into the dirt, rolling the bike slowly. The engine takes over then, jerking forward and sending us off, the tires sending dust up into the air around us. It's jarring how my body vibrates with the bike's rumble, and it takes me about twenty minutes to feel confident with steering the heavy machinery.

Mikah points out directions to help me navigate out of the

wasteland, easily finding his way around without a map. Six months is a long time. Plenty of time to develop a new skillset. Plenty of time to become a new person.

"Are you planning on ever returning to the city?!" I hope my voice isn't lost in the wind whooshing through our ears.

"Of course I am!" Mikah answers, leaning close so I can hear. He squeezes my shoulders gently. "I just need a way to prove my innocence first."

I bite my lip, nodding.

"You missed me, didn't you?" There's no need to look to see his grin.

"Of course not! I got to be the best while you were gone instead of tied for first."

"I always knew you were threatened by me."

We laugh, the wind carrying the sound up to the gods. The wind blows a warm breeze that crawls along the exposed lines of my scalp. The rumble of the bike below me becomes a steady rhythm underneath my thighs, which grip the seat as Mikah and I lean to the left and right to weave around craters in the ground. Somehow, this is more fun than riding LILO bikes in the city.

I ignore the thought that the feeling won't last long, clinging to the hope that I can fix the fire that burns miles behind us before it burns me.

Eba-Odan
Lower Quarter
9:00 owurọ

Bayi's house is a modest single level, similarly built to the rest in the Lower Quarter. It's strange to see. In the Main city, most of us live in stacked apartments, single homes were reserved for the upper class.

"Didn't know you were bringing a guest back," Bayi says when he opens the front door. With his light skin and brown loc'd hair, he bears little resemblance to Mikah.

"Hi," I greet as we walk inside. "I'm Zira."

His eyebrows fly to his hairline. He looks at his brother. "Zira? Like the Lieutenant of the army you're on the run from?"

Mikah sighs, nodding. "We can explain."

And we do. Since he already knows what led to Mikah's escape from the city, I tell him the reason I'm here and give a rundown of my plan. When I ask to borrow some of his store's supplies, he agrees without hesitation.

"I'll pay it all back," I say as he leads me into the shop.

"No rush, just do what you need to do."

The shop, while small, has an extensive stock. I grab a woven basket and start tossing everything I need inside. I feel bad at the amount it turns out to be, but if all goes well, it'll be worth it.

Mikah is sharpening his spear on the floor when I return to the house, something he does when he's stressed. Bayi walks in from the kitchen with a plate of grilled fish and plantain. My stomach grumbles, alerting me of how hungry I am. Before he can set the plate down on the table, a breeze wafts through the room as the front door swings open. A woman with a short curly afro, Bayi's wife, I assume, rushes in, guiding a small boy inside before her.

"The area is crawling with soldiers," she announces, shutting the door quickly. "They're screening everyone at the city border…" She looks at me in surprise as she steps into the living room, eyes darting between Mikah and I and then landing on Bayi. She sighs. "I'm sure you two have something to do with it?"

I watch as the little boy, Bayi's son, runs into his father's arms, feeling guilty for bringing trouble to their home.

"Yes," Mikah says, standing up to look out the window, I can't see anything from where I stand, so I'm hoping the soldiers haven't gotten deep into the neighborhood yet. "But we're heading back to Òkú Ilẹ, so gods willing, you won't be in the crosshairs."

"Actually," I start, making everyone look at me. I keep careful eyes on Mikah. "*I'm* going back to the Dead Lands. Alone."

He frowns. "What do you mean?"

"I'm going to do the ritual by myself and you're going back to the city."

"Zira—"

"Listen, you need to prove your innocence, right? And we need to make sure that LILO isn't poisoning the army and the *Iwarefa* against me. The more time they have, the more lies they can spread. Splitting up is how we make sure that can't happen." I pull a small iron ibis from my pocket, a charm that I've carried around with me since I was a child. I hold it out to Mikah. He takes it from my hand, a hard expression on his face.

"You go back to the main city and you find my father. In front of the *Iwarefa*, you must perform a small sacrifice to Orunmila, one of my dad's patron deities, with *eku ijebu*," I instruct, taking a handful of the hard grain out of the basket on my arm. I then hand him a scrap of paper with the sacrifice scribbled onto it.

The brutal Aje cannot eat ekujebu
You can't hunt me down
Disheveled chicken with clipped wings
Can't fly up to the roof
You are unable to bring me death

Ase

Growing up, my father always instilled in me the importance of this ritual, how it should only be used when absolutely necessary. I've never had to, even when it felt like I needed to. I didn't want to take advantage of it. But now is definitely the right time.

"Orunmila will expose LILO's secrets. This is how you exonerate yourself." Mikah clenches his fist, creasing the paper between his fingers.

"You've really thought this through, huh? You aren't gonna ask me if I agree?"

"I know you'll say no and I'm not taking no for an answer."

"You're so reckless, Zira! What will you do if Kola sics soldiers on you in the Dead Lands?"

I cross my arms. "I'll deal with them. I can handle myself."

"I know you can, but do you always have to put yourself directly in the line of fire? You're not invincible!"

"I'm just trying to help you!"

"I didn't **ask** for your help!"

I can't help but flinch at his outburst. The room feels deadly silent. Bayi and his wife don't say a word. Even their son seems to hold his breath.

Mikah lets out a frustrated sigh. "I'm sorry, I just—"

"I know you didn't ask," I say quietly. "I know you will **never** ask, but just **let me**, okay?"

"Fine, but I'm coming after you when I'm done."

I nod, expecting as much.

"You'll need to hide to get through security, Mikah," Bayi says, jumping into action. "I'll drive you in my truck. Let's go before they search here."

"Stay safe," Bayi's wife says as we head outside. "All of you." I smile at her gratefully. Bayi kisses her, planting another on his son's head before climbing into his truck. Mikah moves to follow, but I grab his arm. He turns around and I give him a stern glare.

"Be careful."

"This is your plan, remember?"

"I know, just…" I sigh, heart pumping worry through my veins.

Mikah's face softens. He interlaces our fingers. "I'll come back to you. I promise." I gaze at him silently. He raises a brow. Before I can overthink it, I grab his jacket and tug him close, slotting our lips together and kissing him with all I have. Mikah cups my face with his free hand, pressing his body closer to mine. His lips, softened with shea-butter, move earnestly, turning the tightness in my chest into something warm.

"*Arewa,*" Mikah breathes when I pull away. The nickname stirs up a whole new reaction in me. Combined with the intensity of his gaze, I have to suppress a shiver. "Do you know how long I've been waiting for that?"

"Seven months?" I ask with a smile, remembering the almost-kiss between us before I left for my mission in the north.

Late at night, the two of us were alone in the dark army mess hall, talking about nothing and maybe sitting a little too close. For a moment we silently swayed further into each other's space, mentally debating our course of action. Before we could settle on a decision, the sound of our fellow soldiers clamoring in the hallway startled us apart.

"Longer," he responds. I blink, stunned.

"Wha—"

Mikah shakes his head, nudging me towards the bike. "Later. You should go, the gods await your presence."

I take half a second to process before dragging myself over to the motorbike. I hook my basket on the bike handle and climb on. Over at the truck, Mikah jumps into the back, covering himself with blankets and baskets of supplies that Bayi's wife brought back. Bayi starts the truck and pulls away, rumbling toward the city.

I turn the key of my ride, letting the loud rumble calm me as I speed off in the opposite direction.

Eba-Odan

Òkú Ilẹ
10:45 owurọ

The heat of the fire is ungodly when I arrive. As I hop off the bike, I wonder how bad of a burn you can get from heat waves alone. Above me, the sky is abnormally dim, the sun somehow not shining as bright. There are no clouds, just a looming darkness.

There's nothing strategic about how I rush to toss the sacrificial objects through the tower's entrance. I use all my strength to hurl each item from my position ten feet away. The fire roars wildly each time something enters. It's my only sign that I'm doing something right.

*"**Divine spirits, I request your presence,**"* I say in Yoruba each time I throw something in. *"Accept my offering!"*

The fire grows more and more violent.

"Search the area!" A booming voice calls. LILO has arrived. Despite the voice's volume, I can tell they're still a distance away.

I keep going, moving faster, chanting quicker. Nothing has happened yet. I can hear the hum of multiple bikes and trucks closing in.

When my basket is empty, I drop it and rip the cowrie shell off my neck and chuck it into the flame. "*Mother, I come to you for protection.*"

Suddenly, the earth trembles and I trip. The tower creaks loudly, but doesn't fall. I turn, the trucks behind me steer in the wrong directions.

The quake stops.

I look down, my feet are not touching the ground. I'm floating up, above the fire, above the top of the energy tower. I can see all of Eba-Odan below me.

Around me, the skies are dark like midnight. Stars twinkle to life, illuminating the expanse. Then they begin to spin. Or I spin. I'm too dizzy to tell. I shut my eyes. When I feel steady, I open them.

Looming over me are hundreds of inhumanely tall figures, all with different faces and adornments. They stand like statues, the only indication they are sentient being their blazing eyes, eyes that are filled with roaring waves, thick green forests, or whatever parts of life they represent.

"Why do you call upon us, warrior?" A spine-chilling voice echoes in my brain. The Yoruba words are in an odd dialect that I somehow understand.

"I-I wish to make an offering, in return for the power of the sun."

"Your land already utilizes this power."

"I wish to offer something in place of an innocent life. I wish to give you our land. I ask that you rest your feet in Eba-Odan and use it as a gateway between your world and ours. My people will keep this place sacred for you. In return, we will continue to thrive under the rays of your burning sun."

I don't receive a response, but I'm not surprised. Instead, the stars around us begin to shine brightly, so brightly that I have to shut my eyes again. Then I'm falling, the wind whistling in my ears. I brace myself for the impact.

When it comes, it's not as hard as expected. In fact, I land in someone's arms, and they envelope me as we both hit the ground.

I open my eyes and the sky is back to normal, the afternoon sun high and bright. It's framed by the long branches of tall trees that now fill the Dead Lands. At their roots, thick grass grows from rich dirt.

"Arewa."

I shoot up, rolling off of the body underneath me.

Mikah winces as he sits up too. "Have you been doing extra training?"

I shake my head, smiling as I stand and pull him up with me. "You haven't been doing enough."

I turn away from him to face the group of soldiers that surround us. At the front of the crowd are my father in his *Iwarefa* robes and Kola Ariyo, restrained by the Captain of the guard. The fact that they're all here means I must've been in the celestial realm for hours. It felt like five minutes.

The crowd stares in my direction, eyes wide. I turn around, stumbling back in the face of the tall statues that surround the LILO tower. The fire is gone and in its place are physical images of the gods, similar to what I saw during the ritual, only these are clearly made of stone. I feel a wave of relief wash over me.

It worked.

"Zira," Mikah says softly. When I look at him, he wordlessly points down at my body. The outfit I once wore is gone. Instead, I don a short sleeveless dress with a black top and multilayer skirt made of handwoven wine and sand-colored material with intricately beaded trim around the edges. Cowrie shell bracelets are tied around my wrists and ankles and layers of beaded necklaces lay on my chest. What catches most of my attention are the faint white markings etched on my skin, wrapping around like bands down my arms and legs. My father approaches, taking both my hands in his. "Zira Sàṣẹ́rẹ́, the gods have chosen you to be high priestess of Eba-Odan."

What?

"Our land has become a holy land and it needs someone to be guardian of its sacred practices. Do you agree to serve the gods and the people of our city?"

My eyes dart to Mikah who smiles encouragingly. Then I look to the soldiers surrounding us, people I've worked beside for years. All of a sudden, they begin to kneel, bowing their heads in respect, and the full weight of this role falls over me.

But the weight isn't a burden, it's strong and reassuring, just as much as, if not more, than my position as lieutenant.

I look at my father and nod.

"Yes, I do."

He nods back, pride in his eyes.

"The city celebrates your arrival."

Eba-Odan

Main City

6:20 ọsán

It's the biggest celebration I've probably ever seen. The streets are lined with dancers and musicians, the air is thick with the scent of sweet and spicy festival foods. People watch the procession from the balconies of their homes, yet the roads are still filled. Even with the large crowd, the normal dry season heat isn't unbearable thanks to **Igbódù**, the Sacred Grove that now surrounds our city.

I smile as I step onto the glittering stone steps of the *Iwarefa*

House, the procession behind me continuing on through the city. Mikah saunters down from the top of the steps, meeting me halfway. He smiles, hands in the pockets underneath his agbada. The material is a luxurious black with gold trim. He has matching rings on his fingers and earrings in his ears. He looks good.

"Does the priestess have time to talk to a simple soldier?" He questions, not being able to hide his grin.

"That depends," I keep my tone playful. "If you meant what you said back at your brother's house."

Mikah frowns. "Hmm, not sure I recall."

"*Ode*," I smack his arm.

My insult doesn't deter him. He smirks and steps closer. "Maybe another kiss will jog my memory."

"You better hope it does." I hook a finger in his collar and drag him forward. The passion in our lips burns like godly fire between us.

Britney is a visionary artist specializing in creating captivating, fantasy-inspired artwork that celebrates Blackness and sparks wonder. With a passion for blending blerd culture and intricate details, her pieces amplify the voices of the underrepresented while embracing vibrant, colorful narratives.

This passion led to the creation of Melanin Eclectic LLC, a brand dedicated to "putting the Black in Fantasy" and encouraging unique self-expression. Britney draws inspiration from anime, books, comics, and all things nerd, crafting illustrations that resonate with dreamers and adventurers alike.

To connect, collaborate, or inquire about custom artwork, reach out via melanineclectic@gmail.com. Explore her portfolio on Instagram @shopmelanineclectic.

Doyin Aderele is a Nigerian-American writer who creates stories about the figurative and literal magic of her Yoruba culture. She earned a Bachelor of Arts degree in English Creative Writing from Rice University and when she's not writing, you can find her at home reading or at a concert featuring any of her favorite artists.

THE BANE OF THE DAMNED

BY SHELBY N. ROSE

SWORD AND SORCERY

CONTENT WARNING FOR DESCRIPTIVE VIOLENCE

Every story out of Isomare comes rife with fable, but of all accounts recorded about the famous Eidolon Assassin, one truth shines through:

He always gave his best works to the darkest hours before dawn.

Fireworks of dancing dragons and flittering bumblebees crackled brilliantly across the night sky. Country folk and city people alike flooded the square outside the palace gates in honor of the Verntide Festival, commemorating another survived winter and the first waves of spring. Set to last from dusk until dawn, it was said that the music and singing were loud enough to reach the hill country beyond the great kingdom's borders. The crowds danced through the night. Even the elders laughed like children as they drank in the infectious air of celebration.

Not one of them aware of the soul departing just a few streets away.

It was a narrow alley behind the cathedral where the Eidolon made his move.

He followed the trail of blood from the rooftops to finish off his prey. His target dragged himself down the cobblestoned passage with an outstretched arm, grunting with every agonizing inch.

Begging to be put out of his misery.

The Eidolon dropped into the alleyway, boots splashing in the sewage that let out ahead. He didn't need to shroud his steps as the festival's band spun a new jaunty tune. He unsheathed a sword from his back and let it scrape along the cathedral wall. The man's crawling turned desperate. But with an arrow planted through his thigh, another firm in his chest, and the last square in his opposite kneecap, there was no hope that this man would make it anywhere fast enough.

Or live long enough to hear the end of this song.

The assassin drew his blade's twin.

The man flipped over at the sound of swords, but the Eidolon was already there. He pressed a foot into the man's punctured chest, purging a groan from him. With the tip of one sword, the assassin drew back the man's shirt sleeve, revealing the black phoenix against skin the color of scorched sand. It was the same mark worn by every member of the Hasaran family.

"If you tell me where the rest of your family festers," the Eidolon said, "I'll let you live."

"I'm not afraid of you, Death-Bringer," the man wheezed.

The assassin almost huffed a laugh. Most thought themselves clever when facing the gleam of his reaper, but of his last thirteen victims, all of them Hasarans, eleven said something similar.

And of those eleven who claimed to be fearless, the Eidolon turned nine into liars before they died.

The assassin tipped his head. "Then you're allowed to make one final request."

At first, the Hasaran looked like he might deny the gift out of defiance, but after drawing a ragged breath, he nodded. "Only a coward allows a man to die while behind the shadow of a mask."

To see his face. Not an uncommon request.

The Eidolon knelt, pulling back the deep maroon hood to reveal a freshly shaved head and chestnut skin. Finally, he lowered the black mask from under his eyes.

Another round of fireworks boomed behind them, washing the Hasaran in blue light as he took in the assassin's face—the markings that lay there.

The Hasaran smiled.

Though he lay at death's door, nothing could deter the man's crooked, bloody grin. "Who do you serve, boy?" A laugh bubbled up in him, so rich, that he could barely get out the words.

The crowd's cheers swelled again, and the Eidolon brought down his blade with a vicious will, turning laughter into screams that went shattering and unheard through the night.

Ten. He'd exposed ten liars now.

That Hasaran clung to life another quarter-hour before he drew his last. And the Eidolon had made him regret every moment of it.

He'd left the body where it lay after he was done. Word amongst the street said some young couple searching for privacy found it shortly after, but by then, the assassin had been long gone.

Another Hasaran dead in only two weeks, the people were already whispering. *The Eidolon of Isomare rears his head again.*

In his bathroom back at the Assassin's Keep, the Eidolon dumped the last pitcher of warm water over his head, but even the roar in his ears couldn't drown out the words lingering in his mind.

Who do you serve?

The assassin gripped either side of the basin too tightly as water dripped off his face, neck, and chest back into the bowl. Opening his eyes, he blinked until his reflection focused in the mirror. But he wasn't looking at the scar cutting through his eyebrow or the familiar shadows laying under tired eyes, just the bold silver tattoo along his right jawbone.

Most of his victims who'd seen his face sneered or spat at him when they saw, ashamed that a man of his caliber had bested them. But over the years, he learned to take each jab in stride. He had come to enjoy the hatred in their eyes, but it had never been this. Never had he expected to be wholly diminished as he was last night.

The way that Hasaran laughed still raked down the assassin's spine. The sound was brash and full, as if the man was certain his fate in death was far better than any the assassin would experience among the living.

The great Eidolon of Isomare. Not a man in his own right but a drudge to be commanded. Because in this kingdom, the silver tattoos of a bastard meant he was destined to serve another until the day he died.

He had no idea what the ink said. He'd been told it was a transcription of his story in the Language of the First Dawns. But more believably, the priest that'd done this to him at thirteen likely put lines and dots that resembled the text for show. After all, it could not be his story. That would require every inch of his skin to tell.

The Eidolon backed away from the basin, stretching his neck. He headed into his bedroom and finished dressing for the day. Finally, he went to the trunk in the corner of his room to retrieve the sack he'd put there hours before. He slung it over his shoulder and went out into the hallways of the Keep.

The Harbinger would be expecting him.

Though he meant to leave everything behind, the Eidolon despised the way that encounter in the alley clung to him. He'd let that man cloud his judgment, and it caused him to brandish his blade in a way that was unbecoming of everything he was taught here.

To lose control was to lose yourself. For those who let the blade wield them would be better off lying in the grave next to their victims.

And it didn't help that last night was the first time in a while an assignment had brought him so close to the palace, forcing him to think of days he hadn't touched in eight years.

The twin suns were high in the sky across the lively courtyard of the Keep, and it seemed the other assassins could sense the Eidolon's terrible mood.

As he traversed the grounds toward the east wing, the Eidolon was usually stopped by a comrade or two, but today, the only ones brave enough to wave were the unaware apprentices.

The rest let him pass without a word.

He approached the door engraved with the Harbinger's customary signet—the mythical silver-winged doe—but stopped when he heard a woman's giggling beyond it.

He hesitated before knocking, thinking of backing away altogether in an attempt not to interrupt. Though she had to have known he was coming. They'd discussed the meeting only yesterday …

The Eidolon banged on the door.

The giggling hushed. After some moments of rustling, the Harbinger poked her head out the door. An older woman. She would never tell him her exact age, but he suspected she was brushing against half a century. Amelia Starborn, Harbinger of Death, was a foreigner in these lands, from a place past the hill country and beyond the western Peaks of Enberg. She had skin the shade of mahogany and was dressed in a silk maroon nightgown today. Her usually rolling dark hair was tied up and away from her face.

The Eidolon cleared his throat. "Bad time?"

"Never for you," she said before swinging the door open.

He followed her in, already steeling his face for what—*who* might be waiting inside. In the seven years he'd lived in this Keep, he was accustomed to her keeping the company of many—

"Lizards?"

Hundreds of them crawled along the floor, up the walls, and hung from the ceiling. Her bed was covered in the scaly creatures so thoroughly he wondered where she'd slept.

The Eidolon looked at Amelia. "Should I ask?"

The Harbinger sauntered to her desk at the far end of the room, sending reptiles skittering out of the way in every direction. "Some client thought it'd be funny to make his payment based on the rutting barter system. I was going to, you know, send one of you to obliterate his entire lineage."

"Naturally." The Eidolon cracked a smile, this being the fourth time she'd threatened someone's lineage this week.

"But I don't know," she said as she sat. "They're growing on me. Cute and very entertaining." She let out a satisfied hum before turning her full attention to him. "I trust last night went well?"

The assassin nodded, tiptoeing to the seat across from her. He waited for her to gather the record books from her drawer and put on glasses to scan her ledger.

"You're doing that thing again," Amelia mumbled after a while.

The assassin froze. He hadn't even noticed, but he looked down and found a thin line on his pants from where he kept unsheathing his hidden wrist blade against them.

Shit.

The keen ears of a falconed fox, that one.

The Harbinger peered over her glasses. "Something on your mind?"

"No." The Eidolon opened his sack and dumped the severed hand and head of his latest victim on her desk.

Amelia shot him a wary look. "Straight to business then." She took a pointer from her desk and turned the hand to see the tattoo. After examining it for a moment, she leaned in. "These cuts could have been cleaner," she murmured.

"I damaged my blade," the Eidolon replied immediately.

The Harbinger's eyebrow lifted. "Oh?"

"Mistimed a swing. Ended up having to yank it from a stone wall."

Of course, that was only *after* he'd discovered the same mangled work from letting his blade go wild, but clumsiness was a far safer embarrassment than admitting what overtook him last night.

Amelia's eyes didn't linger. "Then I trust you'll see it repaired before you go out again?"

He dipped his head. "I've already dropped it to the smith."

"Good," the woman said and went on. "Did he talk?"

"Quiet as a tri-horned mouse." Though he hadn't been particularly patient with gaining information.

Amelia clicked her tongue.

They'd been hunting the ranking members of the Hasaran family for weeks now—an assignment given to them by an anonymous client with deep pockets. The job was simple: dismantle the house and kill its leaders. Of any mission he'd been on, this was one he didn't have to lose sleep over. The Hasarans had been knee-deep in Isomare's crime ring since he was a boy. Countless murders, thefts, and their specialty: capturing young women and selling them to the eastern kingdoms for coin. With such vast profit on the line, Amelia had demanded her best, so she called for him. But no matter how many he tracked down and interrogated, not one could be persuaded to give up the rest. It forced him to pick off Hasarans one by one.

"We *will* get the rest … in time," Amelia said.

The Eidolon nodded. "I know."

"Is that what this frown is about then?" She gestured to his face. "You know, young men like yourself shouldn't waste so much time being grumpy. It ages the features."

"It's nothing to worry yourself with," the assassin told her.

"I doubt that." Promptly, a transparent-looking lizard crawled from the crevices of the Harbinger's updo.

The assassin raised an eyebrow but couldn't fight the amusement that tugged at his mouth. "The money, Amelia."

She waved a flimsy hand at him. "Yes. Yes. That's all you seem to care about these days." The Harbinger reached into another drawer and pulled out a large bag of gold. It was so big that the Eidolon waited for Amelia to take her share, but his heart seized when she slid the entire sum across her desk.

Given his reputation, his portions were usually sizable amounts, larger than anyone else in the Assassin's Guild would ever lay eyes on, but the bag she put before him was something else—entirely too much.

"This isn't my wage," stumbled from the Eidolon's mouth.

But the Harbinger shrugged. "If there's one thing I never mistake, it's my money."

"My cuts—they weren't clean. I don't deserve—"

"It's not like poor cuts make the man any less dead. You've done excellent work for me these past weeks. What kind of patron would I be if I didn't reward my best from time to time?"

But he knew that wasn't what this was about. "No, I won't take this."

"*You will.*" And before he could get out another protest, Amelia nodded to the door. "I'll send your next assignment, but for now, you may go." Dismissed. A leash yanked into perfect subjugation.

Who do you serve, boy?

When she saw the way his jaw clenched at her words, Amelia's demanding features turned curious. Concerned. "Dami—"

But the young assassin took his coin and headed for the door.

The Eidolon had promised to take the apprentice girls into the city to buy their first silks of the season.

With the way he'd seen them train, the young ladies certainly didn't **need** a chaperone to face the market, but they never minded seeing if his purse was willing to tag along.

And the Eidolon didn't mind them asking, either.

The youngest of the bunch—little Millie—hung on his arm as the near-horde paraded him from shop to shop. These hours away from the Keep was just what the Eidolon needed to gain some perspective.

He shouldn't have stormed out on Amelia like that—had regretted it as soon as the door closed behind him. But he figured letting the dust settle before returning would be best.

He watched the girls through another shop window for a while before his stomach reminded him that it was mid-afternoon, and he hadn't eaten since the night before. He signaled to an older apprentice that he would return, and headed toward the food mart.

When he wasn't being **The Eidolon,** he didn't mind letting his tattoos show. He could be another forgettable face shifting through the crowds. But he didn't even make it out of the materials district before he sensed something different today.

Someone was following him.

He turned down the nearest street, away from the mart.

A woman. Hooded. But he couldn't tell if she was armed.

The Eidolon slowed, zig-zagging through the crowds, and she followed him mindlessly. **Untrained,** he thought. And he was sure of it when he led her into a darkened alley with no foot traffic. She even did him a favor by closing the distance.

Quick as a bulladder, he turned and grabbed her, pinning his assailant with a forearm to her collarbone and a hidden knife against her throat.

"Damien, wait," she breathed.

He nearly dropped the knife when he registered her face. Though much older now, he'd recognize her button nose and dark, gold-flecked eyes anywhere.

"Leanna." There was no hiding the surprise in his voice as he let his arm fall.

Leanna rubbed her neck, voice unsteady when she said, "It's true what father says about you then? How you make your living?"

Eight years. They hadn't seen each other in eight years, and that was the first thing she had to say.

The assassin tucked his blade away. "I thought you were a rogue. Last I checked, it wasn't a crime for a man to defend himself."

Leanna made sure they were alone before she took off her hood. "From the likes of me?"

"From anyone," he answered.

She didn't seem to have a reply to that, but she finally met his eyes. Damien leaned against the crates stacked along the alley wall. "A princess shouldn't venture so far from the palace, Leanna. You might not be able to get the muck off." He leveled her with a glare. "What do you want?"

She hesitated, and Damien watched her eyes drift to his jaw, but then she said, "Prince Gavin was taken last night during the Verntide Festival. This morning, the king received a ransom note from the Hasaran House saying Gavin would only breathe for two more days.

Damien almost started at both of those names. If he remembered correctly, the little prince—crowned prince could only be ten years old.

"I would suggest paying the ransom."

"To do that would invite discourse of weakness. Instead, the king hoped he could retrieve him by other means. To employ someone. Like the Eidolon of Isomare."

Damien couldn't help the joyless laugh that escaped him. He didn't know why he hadn't guessed. There was no telling how the king knew his identity, but after all this time, why would they ever come looking for him if not to use him?

"Tell him I respectfully decline."

Leanna's eyes hardened. "Your king is asking for your service as a citizen of this kingdom—"

"You can tell *your* king that I'm not his thug."

Leanna looked away, mouth pulling tight. "You would be well compensated."

So much judgment in such few words that the assassin could hardly stomach them. "You think this is about money?"

But that was just it, he realized. She didn't know what to think of any of it, especially not of him after so long.

This thought made a bright anger rip through him. Damien stepped closer to the princess, closing any distance between them.

"Tell me, Leanna: did you ask your sovereign why it's you he sent to fetch me?"

To her credit, this time, she held his burning gaze. "I'm staying in the inn up the road for two more suns-rises should you change your mind. After that … Well, it won't matter then, will it?"

"I hope your king has a backup plan." The assassin turned to go, ready to leave her behind.

But before his foot touched daylight, Leanna spoke again:

"She was my mother too, Damien."

He hated the way his body stiffened at that. Hated that it wasn't anger, not really, that had caused it. Just the unfamiliar consequence of brushing up against his former self—the brother this princess once knew so well.

Damien straightened and replied, "Well then, it's good you have plenty of silk to dry your tears with."

The Eidolon sat on one of the inner roofs of the Assassin's Keep. The first sun had dipped below the horizon line, and he watched the second chase its twin into nightly oblivion. Familiar sounds of meeting swords rung out from the apprentices training in the courtyard below.

He leaned back on his hands, sighing.

For the first thirteen years of his life, Damien Valreece was the Crowned Prince of Isomare.

It had been Leanna and him for the longest time, as she was a year younger than Damien. But a decade after the princess was born, the king and queen announced they'd birthed another boy. Damien still remembered his pride in standing with his family before the kingdom. He was an older brother twice over, blissfully unaware of how that day would reshape the rest of his life.

On Gavin's second birthday, a drunk showed up on the palace steps demanding to have his only son now that the king had a true heir. He demanded to have Damien.

To this day, Damien didn't know what legitimacy the king found in the man's claim, but soon after, the royal guard took the queen, that man, and Damien to the dungeons.

And the queen knew. She'd always known that Damien was not the king's, but the son of a lover from her days before the palace. One she had not given up even after putting on the crown. Damien had to watch his mother confess that truth through the bars of a prison cell to the king, her only bargaining chip as she begged for Damien's life. She told the king that Leanna and Gavin were legitimate, but Damien was not.

Not long after, the guards took the queen and that man from the dungeon, and never brought them back.

Damien must have wasted away in that cell for weeks before they came for him, too. The king had indeed promised not to kill him, but Damien learned too young that there were other deaths in this life. Ones far less merciful than the kind he trifled with now.

Ones that had left him living but never quite whole.

The king and man whom he'd loved as his father, marked him and threw him from the castle as a common bastard with nothing but the clothes on his back.

To the people, the beloved Queen and Crowned Prince had suddenly passed from the rare scarlet plague. The entire kingdom mourned his death while they really spat on him in the streets.

Damien was too old not to have any trade, so no smith or apothecary would take him in. He was too young to use the only advanced skills he did have—swordplay and archery—to die for king and country on the battlefields of the eastern kingdoms. No draft officer could understand why he would even want to. But it was simple:

At least then, when he died, it would be with a full belly.

From future king to not having a bed to sleep in for just under a year. He barely got by on begging, and thieving when that didn't work.

Another small death. This time to his honor. But it was the only thing that kept the rest of him alive. That was until he tried pickpocketing the wrong foreign-looking woman.

Or the right one.

Amelia.

Had it not been for meeting her, her training him despite the markings on his face, Damien was sure he wouldn't be here.

She'd saved him from all those small deaths and a final one.

The Eidolon looked to the courtyard, where two apprentices were still training despite the quickening darkness. A slick move from one sent the other tumbling in the gravel, but the standing apprentice helped the fallen to his feet before continuing the spar.

Damien couldn't help but smile.

A moment later, footsteps echoed from the ladder under the roof hatch, and Damien heard her voice when that door opened. "You realize this is about the broodiest spot you could have picked to brood."

When he didn't reply, Amelia came to sit next to him. "How'd it go?"

"How'd you find out?"

"Please, don't insult me. You know my eyes are everywhere."

Damien shook his head. "The Hasarans have taken the prince. The royals wish for me to save him."

Amelia's eyebrows lifted. "Ooo, that is a juicy one."

But Damien's head hung lower.

Amelia traced a light finger down his jaw. "You don't owe them anything."

Damien grunted, and Amelia snorted right back.

"He's their only heir," Damien said. "If anything happens to him, the line is lost, so why come to me? Why not pay the ransom?"

"Aside from being incredibly stubborn, I would think the king assumes they'll kill the boy regardless."

"The Hasarans are bold but not stupid," Damien said. "They'd never make an enemy of the monarch."

Amelia tilted her head. "Maybe not normally, but they might if they discovered the client who employed us to dismantle them was the king."

The words hit Damien like a knife, stopping him cold. "**What?**" he hissed, his hand making a fist against his thigh. He'd been working for him—*serving* him this entire time. He looked over at Amelia. "Why didn't you tell me?"

"Money is money, Damien. Where it comes from isn't important."

That's how they'd known. Working so closely with Amelia, it

couldn't have been hard to find out what became of their bastard.

Damien shook his head, standing. "Still…" He ran a hand over his hair. "You should have seen the way she looked at me."

Amelia scoffed. "Don't be such a child. You have your reasons for doing this. Nothing she thinks should be able to sway that."

Damien thought back to the bag of coin. "Yes, though I wish you wouldn't help so much. I can earn my way out."

Amelia stood to slap him on the shoulder. "I know you can, but traversing this alone would be idiotic."

They stood silently for a while, admiring the ending suns-set. Then Amelia said, "You're going, aren't you? Somewhere in that head of yours, you think they can be redeemed?"

He didn't dare deny it. "Does that make me a fool?"

"Oh god no, not a fool. Something far worse." She smiled softly. "It makes you human." Amelia retreated to the roof door. "You should start your preparations."

"I can't very well let the boy die," Damien called after her.

"You could." The Harbinger threw a sly smile over her shoulder. "But the price wasn't right." She hesitated before descending the ladder. "You should remember humans are far more mortal than wraiths, though, so be sure *the Eidolon* goes to save him."

Damien dipped his head, returning that smile. "Yes, Harbinger."

He gave Leanna quite a fright when she found him crouched outside of her door, armed to the teeth the following dawn.

"How long have you been here?" She stared at him like he really was a ghost as he came inside.

Damien looked around the shabby room. Small. Not well-lit. The bed looked as if it had the potential for nightcrawlers.

Fit for a princess, indeed.

"You shouldn't be staying here without protection. If people find out, you'll be a targ—"

But the rest of those intended words died when Leanna pulled a small crossbow from under the pillow.

Damien cleared his throat, looking off. "Right."

Outside the room's window, the songbirds began their symphony as the second sun bled over the horizon line. Damien caught himself fiddling with his knives and forced his hands to still.

"You'll help then?" Leanna asked.

Damien took a deep breath. Yes, he really was doing this. "I assume you have a location?"

She nodded, reaching for the sack at her bedside. She took out a map and spread it across the bedsheets. "Our scouts followed the messenger back to this manor." She pointed to a spot on the edge of Carrigon Forest, the only strip of land separating the hill country from Isomare's eastern border.

"Why didn't you ask your scouts to retrieve Gavin then?" he grumbled.

But she ignored him. "They got some of the guards' rotations before I left, but not all."

Damien examined the entry points, or lack thereof, and the terrain surrounding the land …

"You're asking a single man to break into a fortress," he said.

"A trivial task for the **Eidolon of Isomare**, no?"

The way she sang the name was the definition of a challenge.

"I'll get it done. Just have my payment ready." He wasn't sure why he said it, but he couldn't deny the satisfaction he felt in the disgust that crossed her face.

"Don't worry. I wouldn't dare spoil your drunken brothel visits or whatever you assassins do."

He'd gotten under her skin, and she made sure to return the favor.

"I don't spend it," Damien said. "I save it."

She was still staring at the map. "What?"

"The money I earn—I save it."

"I'm sure."

He chewed the inside of his cheek. *What does it matter what she thinks?* But the thought didn't stop him from saying, "I save it so I can leave."

Leanna scoffed, looking up from the map with what he was sure would be more words to burn him. But she stopped, as if finally hearing. "Leave? What do you mean 'leave'?"

He wasn't hiding it, not when it was made so irrevocably clear that this world did not want him. Leaving had always been the plan.

"When I have enough, I'm going to travel over the peaks and keep going until I find a land that knows nothing of bastard tattoos or the Language of the First Dawns. I'll keep going until I find somewhere to start over." His hands balled into fists. "What I am might be difficult for you to understand, but it's all I have. My only way out."

The shock on Leanna's face was unmistakable as those words settled between them. This was all he had because they'd taken the rest, and now she came to spit on that, too.

Damien rolled his shoulders. "Don't worry about it. Forget I said anything. I never wanted your money." He pointed to the map. "Pick a rendezvous point, and I'll take care of the rest."

Amelia was right. He never needed anything from them then, and he didn't need her pity now—

"Damien." Leanna laid a gentle hand over his fisted one. But he didn't look at her until she repeated his name. "I … I'm sorry," the princess said. "It wasn't mine to judge."

And it never will be again.

Because he wasn't here to serve the king or the past that left him needing to prove that he was more than the discarded fake this world made him. Maybe Leanna could understand that. Perhaps she couldn't.

But reminding himself settled something in him, like an anchor to tether his spirit.

"Even if only by half, I'm still your brother. You—Gavin—you're still family." Damien opened his hand to squeeze Leanna's. "Mother wouldn't forgive me if I let anything happen to either of you."

She nodded, her eyes deep and suddenly indecipherable. "Thank you, Damien."

The Eidolon replied with a small smile. "Don't thank me yet." He gestured to the map again. "We've got a long day ahead of us."

Damien attacked the manor at midnight.

The layout was simple enough. There was no information on the lower level, but the scouts sufficiently detailed the main house and watchtowers for Damien to make his move.

Leanna was waiting to meet him in a forest clearing a mile from the manor, so he had to be swift. He did not enjoy the idea of her being alone in these woods.

Damien climbed the outer wall. Two guards stood watch, but before he pulled himself over, the assassin ended them with throwing knives. He pulled their bodies out of sight and continued on. He'd kill as little as possible tonight. Harder to remain undetected with a trail of bodies behind him.

He searched the place for nearly an hour. Damien went to the lower levels, but the storage chambers there were empty. He worked his way back up, sneaking through the halls, avoiding guards. He started to think Leanna's scouts had been misinformed, but then Damien came across a bedroom with four Hasarans guarding outside.

The prince bolted up in bed when Damien picked the lock and opened the door. The assassin gestured for the boy to come with a finger to his lips to keep the prince quiet. Gavin nodded and followed Damien barefoot into the hall. His eyes widened at the bodies surrounding the door, but Damien grabbed his hand.

"Sleeping," He reassured the boy. Then whispered, "Stay close to me."

Together, they traversed the manor back to Damien's entry point. There wasn't as much traffic coming out as going in. They'd been lucky. Soon, Damien was easing them down the manor wall.

When they dropped to the grass, Damien took Gavin's hand again, but the prince yanked it back. "Who are you?"

"A friend," Damien replied. "Your sister sent me to find you."

Gavin perked up at that. "Really?"

The young prince's naivety made Damien smile under his mask. Gavin's face had grown into an undeniable image of the king, and he had gold-flecked eyes like his mother.

After Damien nodded, Gavin allowed him to lead them into the forest. After a half-mile trek, the prince tired, complaining about his feet. Damien put his brother on his back and carried him the rest of the way. Not ten minutes later, Damien pointed to the tree line. "See that? We're almost there."

They broke into the clearing.

But it wasn't Leanna he saw first. Instead, there was a woman with sand-shade skin and flowing black hair. She stood out in the open, shaking hands with—

Leanna?

The first arrow hit Damien in the chest.

Gavin screamed as they both crashed to the forest floor. But the Eidolon was up in an instant. He kept the prince protected behind him with a drawn sword. He searched the trees from whence the arrow came, and though he could sense them, he couldn't make out any figures in this darkness.

"Eidolon," the woman standing with Leanna called out. "It's about time you showed up."

"Gavin, come." Leanna's voice was calm, though they were surrounded. Damien was so unsure of what was happening that he didn't stop the boy when he crossed the clearing to his sister.

The click of a crossbow came from behind him. Damien whirled and sliced down an arrow streaking toward his back. Too quickly, a second arrow sunk into his sword hand—

And the third in his calf dragged the disarmed assassin to his knees.

"I heard you've been looking for me, Eidolon." The other woman was crossing the clearing toward him.

At first, Damien didn't understand, but then the woman pulled up her sleeve to reveal a phoenix tattoo.

Hasaran.

But not just any branch, he realized. He'd heard the whispers in the street that the heart of Hasaran House did not belong to a patriarch but to a mother.

The woman smiled as she crouched next to him. "I'm right here."

The Eidolon struck. A hidden blade drawn, he swiped at the woman, but she parried him with surprising accuracy. Damien couldn't guard himself before a fist sent him sprawling in the dirt. Tasting iron in his mouth. The matriarch took his second sword and threw it across the clearing.

She yanked off Damien's hood but spoke to Leanna. "Consider the ransom paid in full, princess. You and the prince may go."

But Leanna didn't move.

Damien's eyes slid to hers. Even in the night, he could see her trembling, and more clarity struck like a hammer.

Why didn't he pay it? He'd asked over and over. But it was because the king couldn't. Because the ransom had never been money.

It'd been him.

"I'm sorry," Leanna said, holding his gaze. "I will tell the king." She spoke like it was meant to comfort him. "I'll tell him how well you served."

It was almost funny. He could not feel the arrows in him, but the agony that came with her words was sure and cavernous.

The Hasaran woman grabbed Damien's chin. "Did you think I wouldn't come for you after what you've done to my family?" She ripped his mask down, and after a moment, the matriarch smiled again. "And to think, the Eidolon of Isomare is just a man with no one to miss him."

Damien spat blood on the ground next to her, and the matriarch shoved him back. Groans from loading crossbows emanated from the trees, but the matriarch raised a hand.

"No," she said, standing tall. "This one belongs to me." She pulled a crossbow from the folds of her flowing jacket.

Damien tried to think—*breathe*, but every breath was harder to catch than the last and…

The matriarch aimed at his heart, finger tightening around the trigger—

A shriek tore out from the surrounding trees, and the matriarch's attention snapped to it. There was the sound of a loosed arrow, the thud of impact—

Damien saw the glint of a hurled dagger before it connected with the crossbow in the matriarch's hand.

Two weapons in the grass. One window to stay alive. Instinct lurched Damien across the clearing.

The matriarch was a split second behind. More landed arrows and cries echoed through the trees.

Someone was attacking the Hasaran archers. But he couldn't think of that or the fire lacing up his leg.

The matriarch reached the crossbow, but Damien slid for the dagger. He whirled on his good knee and swung—

His blade sunk into the Hasaran's neck.

The matriarch's body went rigid. Her half-aimed crossbow fell from her hands. Wide eyes jumped to Damien's as blood slid from her lips.

"You should have stayed in your hole," Damien said. Then he ripped that dagger across her throat.

The woman's body dropped like a stone.

Damien fell back. His head was too light, and even in gasping, there wasn't enough air. The night shifted around him without a tether; the only still, sure thing was the blade in his hands …

And the silver-winged doe he found carved into its hilt.

Footsteps approached Damien from behind.

"How'd you find out?" he asked, still dragging in stinging half-breaths.

Amelia answered. "You will learn one of these days, boy."

Relief came like a tidal wave. "Thank you."

Amelia crouched next to him, nodding while she examined the arrow in his chest.

"How bad?" Damien asked.

"You won't die." She grasped the arrow in his hand. "But you make a good show of it, don't you?" Damien grimaced when she broke off the shaft.

She was breaking off the other two when a shout came from across the field.

"Harbinger, I have them!"

The voice belonged to an assassin named Jotham, a skilled boy just out of apprenticeship.

Leanna knelt before him, hugging the prince to her side and shielding his face with a hand.

The ire that spread through Damien was unlike any he'd ever felt—numbing cold instead of a flame. And he was sure the princess saw the same when she met his eyes.

Amelia helped Damien to his feet, and when he approached, Jotham gave Damien his sword.

"You can still leave," tumbled from Leanna's mouth in a rush. "That's what you want, right? To leave this? Never see us again—"

The Eidolon silenced her with a blade to her throat.

Gavin couldn't see them, but the boy stiffened in Leanna's arm.

"Damien …" Leanna started again, voice uneven. "I did this. Kill me. Just let Gavin go."

"You're in no position to bargain." The Eidolon pressed that sword until blood started down her neck.

"Please, Damien! He *needs* his heir!"

Damien stopped—stuck beneath the weight of those words.

The night was quiet save for the wind and the hitching breaths of the prince.

He needed his heir … but not her.

Damien lifted Leanna's chin with his sword. "If I cut off your head and sent it back with the boy, would he raise banners in your name to get to me? Or would it be a hunting accident?" There was no delight in Damien's smile. "Perhaps the plague would return to claim a third."

But the princess said nothing, and that silence was too familiar—a story he'd watched play out before. His mother begging then. Her daughter begging now.

Damien let his blade down.

He turned away but did not catch Amelia's eye as he limped back to where the matriarch's body lay.

His hand was steady when he severed the head.

Damien threw the head at the princess's feet. "Go. Take that to your king. And never come looking for me again."

Leanna searched his face, perhaps for a trick, as if she were the one skewered and betrayed. Fresh rage set to claim him again, but Amelia was quicker:

"I would go, girl. Before he changes his mind."

Leanna glanced at the sword in Damien's hand, then shrugged off her cloak and covered the head. She released Gavin and quickly gathered him and the head up before hurrying across the clearing.

The prince tried to look back, but Leanna pulled him into the trees under the cover of darkness.

Damien kept watching the place where they disappeared.

"You … let them leave."

It was Jotham who broke the quiet.

Not a question, but he knew they were both waiting for an answer. Amelia trusted him, but that didn't mean she understood.

Damien's eyes caught on a pin shining in the grass. It was the royal crest that held Leanna's cloak. Damien lowered himself to pick it up.

"I swore long ago that I wouldn't use this new life to destroy my old family."

Jotham stepped forward. "Still, the royals go too far. To threaten the Guild. Nearly *kill* you. Damien, we *cannot leave* this unanswered—"

"I don't intend to," the Eidolon cut in, his eyes fixed on that crest.

He would take time to heal, but when he did … Damien, the former Crowned Prince, the bastard, the Eidolon of Isomare, had one last demon to lay to rest.

"I'm no kinslayer." Damien closed his hand around that pin. "But that vow is only bound by shared blood." He looked to Amelia. "I have my next target, Harbinger."

Amelia's lips hooked in a smile. "Then where do we start?"

Shelby N. Rose's origin story began in Dallas, TX, where she tore through every superhero story she could lay her hands on. In true Tony Stark fashion, Shelby graduated with a mechanical engineering degree from The University of Texas at Austin and a certificate in Creative Writing. Now, by day, she works in the tech industry. By night, she's either manufacturing new twists for her sci-fi/fantasy worlds or practicing her form in Muay Thai. Shelby currently resides in Austin, TX.

@the__ninety8

LOST IN THOUGHT

BY JAMES GETTYS
ART BY THE NINETY8

PORTAL FANTASY

CONTENT WARNINGS FOR TOXIC MASCULINITY, MISOGYNY, AND MENTIONS OF SUICIDE

The exact moment the magic died escapes me, but the pain of its absence stings like the first time every day. Especially when my wife rejects a ride on the Daddy Express, which is all the time lately, and whenever she does allow the rare opportunity of my train into her station it's like banging a mannequin from one of them expensive ass stores she loves to spend my money at. A complete one-eighty from the freak I could barely keep up with. Even the spark of our kisses done fizzled from a bolt of lightning to one of them tiny flashes when a plug enters a socket. Worst of all, she doesn't even call me "Daddy" anymore.

I suck my teeth as I flop onto my side of this overpriced king-sized bed and glare at Bae's back. Snatching that bonnet off and ruining the hair she cares so much about tempts me since she knows I'm laying here on brick and can't even be bothered to help, but that'd just make things worse and accelerate her leaving me. I know she's going to no matter how much she denies it, because somebody clearly pleasing her since she doesn't need me to. Once our daughter moves out, she'll follow her out the door and into that bastard's arms. She's probably thinking of him now. If only I could bust in and catch them.

Fuck. Good mood ruined. I stare at the ceiling and wish it'd come crashing down to take me out as quick as the dopamine flees. All the shit stressing me returns and weighs me down, reverting my brief joy back to endless pain that makes me want to cry. Anger fills me and strengthens me, keeping all that weak shit back. I can't be doing all that. If I did I'd be as bad as my daughter, Juryni. She used to laugh all the time and stick to me like a magnet, but now she stays away as if I'm one of them perpetually musty people, and always complains that "I'm so strict". Not my fault I know how these young boys think and I'm not raising no babies, going to jail for killing somebody's child, or getting my ass beat and embarrassed. Yes, I can fight, but I'm also smart enough to know not to want smoke with some of these dudes that look like they done crawled out the damn sewer and need a tank to take they ass down.

Thankfully, my son, Taiv, ain't like that and got sense. He does what he's told, doesn't complain, and is working towards a bright future. So nice to have one thing I never have to worry about. The bedroom door bursts open and my heart skips a beat as I spring up with Bae.

"You have to stop Taiv!" Juryni says as she flicks the light on and hurries to our bed, eyes wide. "He's going to kill himself!"

Those words paralyze me. No. Absolutely not. My boy is strong. He wouldn't do that weak shit. Hell, tomorrow's his birthday. But my daughter knows better than to play about that with me. Or interrupt my sleep when she knows I got work in the morning.

"Where is he?" Bae's voice quivers as she throws the covers off and hops up.

"I don't know, but he's trying to stay in this fantasy world and thinks if he's there while he dies in this world he'll stay forever, but he won't."

I stare at her. How can she say all that with a straight face, eyes swimming with tears? One of them acting awards is definitely in her future, but an ass whopping is in her present.

"I'm gone tear you up." I reach for my belt. "You know that shit ain't funny."

Juryni shakes her head of bushy and curly hair. "No! I'm serious! Look!"

She holds out Taiv's phone in one hand and a piece of paper in the other. Covered with Taiv's handwriting:

I'm sorry, but this world isn't enough for me, and never can be.

I have to create. It's my oxygen. I can't lose it. Please, don't be sad.

This isn't because I want to die. It's because I want to live.

I'm happy and free. I hope we meet again one day.

Thank you for everything. Love you.

-Taiv

"Oh my god," Bae whispers as she covers her mouth with one hand and grips my arm with the shaky other. "No. *No.*"

I don't even realize my own hands shake as they hold the paper that arouses memories of the similar one I received years ago. I no longer remember my brother's exact final words, but the pain will always be crystal clear. My knees buckle as my stomach and throat tighten.

No. None of that weak shit. Be strong.

Bae hits my arm. "This is all your fault!"

Her hit does no damage, but her words do along with the hate and disgust on her face. Finally, she admits the way I know she feels.

"The hell you mean this is my fault?" I stare wide-eyed.

She snatches the paper out my hands and pushes it in my face. "Read the fucking words! You're always discouraging him and his talent. And you never show you care."

I raised him for eighteen years. How else am I supposed to show I care? Hug him? Nah. The only flaw with my son is his dream of being a writer like his idol Dre'Mar, but he agreed to put that to the side and focus on achieving a degree to have real, lucrative work so he isn't stuck working as hard or being as miserable as me.

"He agreed it's a waste of time and too risky." I push the paper away. "There's no guarantee. You want him to be one of them struggling homeless people? Because I'm trying to make sure he lives a good life."

"And now he's not going to live at all!"

"Stop!" Juryni comes between us. "You're wasting time! It's not Dad's fault. He's doing this because he doesn't want to leave that world like everyone does when they turn eighteen."

"Stop with this damn fantasy world," I snap.

"But it's real!" Juryni insists. "We have to go there and tell Taiv to stop. It's the only place we can find and talk to him. And we only have until midnight. Please, don't let him die."

"We believe you." Bae glares as if daring me to disagree. "How do we get there?"

Not sure who "we" is, but I bite my tongue. There's no way it's true, but Taiv did often seem lost in his own world. Just like my brother.

"I think I can guide you and pull you in." Juryni sits on the bed and pats for us to join. "Just close your eyes and picture what I tell you and imagine yourself being there."

Bae sits on the bed and I reluctantly join. This feels like a set up, but I'll see where it goes. If they're trying to humiliate me they'll regret it. I close my eyes and focus on Juryni's voice as she tells us to picture a white and pink castle on the coast of the sea in the daytime. I can't, and question specifics of the courtyard, but Juryni doesn't answer.

Her eyes remain closed like Bae's, both their mouths form slight smiles. Yeah, they playing me. My turn. I quietly slip off the bed, grab the covers they sit on, and prepare to yank—

"Stop!" Juryni stares at me confused. "Mom's in and you'll take her out!"

"Really?" I glance at Bae. "Then why is she still here?"

"We don't physically go there," she says obviously. "Just our minds. Now, focus."

"But it doesn't make sense," I say. "It's not clear enough. How big is the courtyard? What shape is it? What's in it? Where is it? How many stories—"

"Dad, stop. You're overthinking it. That doesn't matter. No one imagines the same thing exactly the same. It's distracting when you're so serious. Just let go and imagine how you want."

Yes, because it is so easy to not be serious and let go when either my son is really about to die or my family is trying to humiliate me before they abandon me.

"I can't," I say frustrated. "Just go with her. We're wasting time."

Ten minutes until midnight my alarm clock on my bedside table tells me.

"No, Taiv needs you. If you don't help him I'll never talk to you again."

I doubt she means it, but I can't risk that. I already know how it feels to never speak to someone you love again. I glance at Taiv's note on the bed. I won't lose another person to this.

"Okay." I take a breath and close my eyes. "Go."

I ignore my inner critic to picture Juryni's descriptions — A tug on my arm. My eyes fly open and sunlight temporarily blinds me before it warms my skin. I'm no longer in my bedroom or neighborhood with paved roads and normal houses, but the courtyard of Juryni's magnificent white and pink castle about five stories tall. People race by on clouds, dragons, and broomsticks, or fly on their own in the bright blue sky above as they speed towards other castles sprinkled around different villages and towns in the distance. A slide winds from the courtyard to the sea, on which pirate ships and islands rest, people surf, and mermaid tails and tentacles splash or disappear beneath.

"Finally," Bae says behind us, petting a unicorn and accompanied by two girls Juryni's age in fancy dresses and four boys. Shirtless boys.

"Where the hell they clothes at?" I snarl and fear fills the boys' faces, especially the one with Juryni's name tattooed on his chest. "This what you do here? See if you come back."

"*Dad*," Juryni says embarrassed.

"He really is strict and smothering," says a girl with a tight bun. "Why can't you let her breathe? She is a smart, growing girl. She can take care of herself."

Like hell she can. What else has she said about me?

"You can smother me. I don't need to breathe." A girl with braids winks at me and giggles.

Weird, but I can't help but smile. Bae didn't find it as humorous and neither did Juryni.

"Ew. Shut up." She cringes and the girl instantly stops. "Slap some sense into yourself."

The girl reluctantly smacked herself across the face.

"Juryni," Bae snaps. "I didn't raise no bully."

"It's okay," Juryni says quickly. "They're creations. I can make them forget that. They do whatever we say and want, but it's more fun to let them be their own person," she adds at my suspicious look.

I was about to say that sounds like something that needs to be abolished.

"Well, make these boys find some shirts," I say. "*Now.*"

Juryni sighs and does and they appear on them out of nowhere. Questioning where they came from came to the tip of my tongue, but obviously this is a world of imagination. I instead open my mouth to lecture, but Bae asks if we can return to finding Taiv before I can.

"Yes," Juryni says quickly and turns to her creations. "Who wants to teleport us to the portal room?"

All volunteer, buts she picks the boy with her name tattooed. I want to object, but Bae shoots me a look not to. We grab his outstretched hand, he winces as I squeeze maybe a bit too tight, and in a blink we're in a large spacious, circular room higher up in the castle. The delicious smell of chocolate mixed with the overwhelming scent of perfume and burnt hair assaults our nostrils. At least three floors of archways cover the walls and show different rooms and landscapes with names above them. A snowy path with hanging icicles, a sandy desert, a lava waterfall, and a door made of large playing cards catch my attention the most until we reach Taiv's archway and step through.

A cool chill rolls over us and our nostrils can breathe. I can instantly tell by the dark golden stone walls, navy banners with a detailed crest, suits of armor, and the hanging torches of flickering flames lining the corridor that his world is far more developed. Stars twinkle in the inky night sky from the outside windows as we pass towards a room directly across from the one we left. Noises grow louder as we enter a spacious room filled with trophies in cases and portraits of Taiv over the years in this world—fighting a dragon in the air and sea monsters on a ship, battling in wars, defeating various villains, and many of him smiling with me, both of us wearing crowns and capes. That's my boy.

To the left is a large archway that leads outside to a balcony where a guy, a year or two older than Taiv, with dreads, stands with his back to us, overlooking a courtyard decorated with navy birthday banners and filled with countless people. Some were so fancily dressed that they had to be princes and princesses, knights with their swords, magical ones with wands, others with wings, a number that looked like villains, and a good number who were dressed more modern. Magical creatures I've never seen before like elves, trolls, and more all roam about. At least a dozen dragons loom over the walls and bounce to the beat of a woman singing about how great Taiv is.

"Rheim," Juryni says.

The dreaded guy turns and his eyes flick at us. "You made it."

"Where's my son?" I ask.

Rheim frowns and my stomach tightens as I prepare for the worst. "You just missed him, but he'll be back."

Relief washes over me. *Thank you*.

"Unfortunately, I do not believe he can be persuaded to stop. I told him Juryni went to get you guys, but he didn't care and is committed to this world."

And that relief is sucked back out. Damn. I knew I should've crushed his love of being creative entirely when he first started.

"We'll see about that," I say.

"We won't have much time when he returns," Rheim says. "So, we need to make sure whatever we tell him has a strong enough impact to distract him from this world until midnight passes and he forgets this place."

"Well, what do you suggest?" I ask.

Rheim stares at me and hesitates before saying, "Your death."

"*What*?" I, Bae, and Juryni say, eyes wide.

"I know it sounds crazy—"

Nah, more like completely insane.

"—but when Taiv learns of what you've done he'll know he can't go through with dying and needs to be there for his mother and sister."

"No!" Juryni hugs me tight. "Can't we just lie? I can't lose him."

And I can't lose Taiv.

"You're almost an adult, Juryni, and Taiv will be one in a couple minutes," Rheim says. "Many children lose a parent younger than that.

I wish there was another way, but you know he'll be able to tell. It has to be real."

Damn. Yes, I often considered this route, but never thought I'd ever actually do it. It always seemed a selfish and cowardly act that'll send me straight to Hell, but if it's to save my son then that has to be considered a noble sacrifice and should let me into the good place above. I can't just stand by and let him die, but in a selfish way this is the perfect excuse to make everything stop. No more bills. No more attitudes. No more pain.

"Okay," I say. "I'll do it."

"No!" Juryni and Bae cry.

Juryni squeezes me tighter, as if trying to force the tears burning my eyes to fall but I keep them in. I kiss her forehead and manage an, "It's okay, baby."

"No, we'll find another way," Bae insists, grabbing my arm. "*Please*, don't leave."

She really seems upset. Huh. Have I been wrong about her cheating? Does she really love me? Or is this guilt? Damn. I wish I knew the truth. It'd make everything easier, especially if they didn't care like they've made it seem lately.

"There isn't one," I say. "I'm not letting my son die. Just don't let Taiv blame himself."

I can't watch her cry, especially over me. It makes me want to and I'm not doing that in front of her.

"How do I get out of here?" I ask.

"I can help you." Rheim reaches a hand for me—

A muscular guy bursts in the room and makes us all jump. His face lights up when he sees Bae.

"It really is you!" He sweeps her off her feet and spins her around. "I missed you so much. Mmm you're just as beautiful as when I last saw you."

He kisses her on the mouth and mine drops open. She quickly pushes him off and makes him put her down, but it's too late. Anger burns through me. Lying bitch. I knew it.

"So, this him?" I pull Juryni off me and crack my knuckles.

"What?" Bae asks, flustered. "What're you talking about?"

Here goes the fake ass innocent act.

"Don't play dumb. This is who you've been cheating with and going to leave me for."

Bae rolls her eyes. "Seriously? This again? I am *not* cheating. I have no idea who this is."

"Ah." The muscular guy places a hand on his chest. "My heart. You really don't remember me?"

Bae shakes her head.

"It's me. Prince Handsum. One of your favorite creations. I've waited faithfully for you since you left all those years ago."

Years?

"See?" My wife says obviously. "He's some old childhood thing."

Handsum grabs his chest again. Damn. She might be right. I'm as good as dead so she really has no reason to pretend or lie if she doesn't care about me.

"You're unbelievable." Bae throws her hands up. "I give up. All I do is try to love you, but you don't want it. This is exactly why we're in this mess now and why Taiv is doing what he's doing. Because you suck the life out of everything and are always so damn negative."

"I'm fucking stressed!" I yell obviously. "What is there for me to be happy about? My job is to provide for my family and I bust my ass to do that and everything for your ungrateful asses. You act like you don't want my kisses or gifts. What more do you want from me?"

"I want you!" Bae says obviously. "We all want you!"

The hell is she on?

"I'm right here! I've always been here. I always come home to all of you when I very easily couldn't have. You know how many men can't even be faithful or stick around?"

"What good is being around if you're just an empty shell? You know you never even ask about my day?"

Really? The hell knowing about her day going to do for me?

"Then you shouldn't be sad or miss me," I say. "Sounds like I'm already dead to you."

She sighs as she hugs a sobbing Juryni.

"Get me the hell out of here," I snap at Rheim.

"But you just got here," says a beautiful woman in a pink dress and long dark coily hair as she enters, not taking her eyes off me. "It's really you."

Not again. She fine as hell and the loving look in her eyes is one I haven't seen in my wife's in who knows how long, but there's no time for everyone to come out the woodwork.

"Look, I'm assuming you know me somehow or whatever, but I need to save my son before he kills himself to stay here instead of growing up and leaving like he's supposed to."

"No, he doesn't have to leave," the woman says. "There is a horrible man who tricks Black boys into thinking they have to and that they can kill themselves to stay. He did the same thing to your brother and has wanted to lure you here to kill you. Has anyone here tried to get you to die or kill yourself?"

You have to be fucking kidding.

We all look to Rheim, who smirks. "Almost had you."

"Boy, I'm gone fuck you *up*!" I charge for him and he takes a defensive stance—another guy bursts through the wall and tackles Rheim out over the balcony to the party below. The music ceases and some screams rise as people run out the way of Rheim and the guy throwing blasts of light at each other.

"Now, who is that?" I ask. "Can you all slow down?"

"That's Cuz. He used to be you and your brother's best friend," the woman says. "I used to be your princess. Princess."

A princess named Princess? Yeah, Taiv definitely ain't get his creativity from me. At least ten questions pop in my head, but only one matters. "So, my son can stay?"

She nods. "There is a whole world for the really creative and passionate to continue to. Most don't even make it to eighteen here due to the real world crushing their imagination. So, *he*," she casts a disgusted look at Rheim as he dodges a golden sword Cuz throws at him, "tries to manipulate those that do to gain control of their creations and ideas. He can't have most of us though as long as you live because we were created by your brother *and* you. Well, the others were. I forget I am only your creation sometimes. Your brother used to make me feel like I was one of his after you stopped coming. He was so talented and kind. Anyway, he has most of the others locked up somewhere, and we've been on the run and in hiding from him, but we had to come save you as soon as we felt you were here."

All I heard is my son and I don't have to die.

"A'ight. I'm gonna go beat his ass now. Wait for Taiv," I tell Bae and Juryni before turning to Princess. "Can you get me down there?"

She holds her hand out and I take it. In a blink we are down at the courtyard. Every eye looks to us and some gasp. I don't care and am ready to join the fight, but it's over. Cuz is on the ground, bound by golden rope and pinned by the foot of a man with his back to me wearing a crown and a cape. Rheim stands free, smirking.

"No, stop him." I point. "He's trying to kill Taiv!"

No one looks surprised or moves. Can they not hear? Do they not speak English? They make judging faces full of disgust. Some turn their noses up, others whisper behind their hands, and some outright boo at me. Fine, I'll do it myself. Before I can charge for Rheim, golden ropes pin my arms to my side and my legs together. The same happens to Princess and we fall.

"I've already told them how you're here trying to take Taiv away," Rheim says as we struggle on the cobblestone ground.

"You have a lot of nerve coming here," says the man with his foot on Cuz as he turns to me, disgust all over his face—my face.

It takes a moment for me to overcome the shock of the king who could be my identical twin. "Look, I know we came out of nowhere, but I'm just trying to save my son from him." I nod at Rheim. "If you all care about Taiv, you will help."

"Oh, don't pretend like you care now." The king looks me up and down, snarling. "Why do you think your son doesn't want to leave us? Why do you think he created me to be a better father? You give him nothing and we give him everything. You don't even really know him."

I glance around because I know he not talking to me. "Now wait a minute, buddy, you stepping a little out of line."

"No, you are." The king says. "We've helped him deal with his problems. Cheered him up. Love him. We're his family. And we *will* protect him."

He snaps his fingers and rope covers my mouth, Cuz's, and Princess'. I struggle to free myself, but it's no use. Rheim tells the other creations Bae, Juryni, and Handsum are on the balcony and a couple retrieve them in moments, all struggling against the ropes binding them. They'd pay for touching them.

One of Taiv's creations announces he's coming and we are pulled under the balcony by three soldiers as the rest of his creations cheer and look up at him, beaming.

"Ready?" Rheim smiles up at him and I want to knock every tooth out his mouth.

"Yeah," Taiv's voice comes from above, but I can hear the nervousness.

"You got this," Rheim says. "If I can do it you definitely can."

Taiv's creations agree and egg him on. Fools!

Don't do it, I beg in my mind as I try to free myself. *Don't*!

"Here I go," Taiv says.

No. Blasts of magic rain down as yelling voices fill the air. Many people pour like a waterfall over the balcony, led by Juryni's friend with braids riding the unicorn into Taiv's creations. The dragons roar as Juryni's own fire breathing beasts tackle them and fire fills the night sky. Her four boys come under the balcony. Three of them each take a soldier as the one with Juryni's name tattooed on his chest frees us from our binds, saying he gathered everyone as fast as he could when he received her mental message.

"What is going on?" Taiv asks surprised, now feet from us in the courtyard.

"Taiv!" I run for him, but bump into a golden forcefield Rheim creates over them both.

"Dad?" Taiv spins, wide-eyed as Bae and Juryni run over and pound on the forcefield with me. "Mom? W-What're you doing here?"

"We're saving you. You can stay. He's lying to you." I glare at Rheim. "He wants you dead so he can take your creations. He's done it to so many. He did it to my brother."

Confusion spreads on Taiv's face as he looks to Rheim.

"Don't listen to them, Taiv," he says. "Your dad just wants you to have a boring life and be miserable like him. Don't you want to stay and be free and happy? Or do you want to forget and live in that world where you have to bottle up your feelings? You know you can't. You're not like him. He doesn't care. Doesn't hurt. Doesn't feel like us."

"Yes, I do!" I insist. "I was wrong, son. I'll change. I swear. I hurt too and I do care. More than you can know. And just like you can't lose this place, I can't lose *you*. You are my magic. You and your sister and your mother. You changed my life for the better ever since I met you. And I'm sorry if I have ever made you feel that you are wrong or did anything but that."

Taiv stares at me. His mouth moves as if trying to find the words.

"One minute, Taiv," Rheim says urgently. "If you want to stay, you need to start falling."

Time seems to slow as Taiv looks at me. I plead with my eyes for him to not do it.

"I'm sorry," he says and disappears.

No.

Bae and Juryni scream that same word.

My heart sinks. Tears fill my eyes and I don't even try to contain them as I fall to my knees. Rheim's laugh and superior smirk enrages me as he removes the forcefield, just as much as the cheering of Taiv's creations. How could they be so happy? Fucking fools. This was all their fault. They deserved to die. To suffer. Like I am.

All the pain and feelings I've suppressed behind the dam of my anger breaks through and spill out of me. Literally. I cry out in pain as an endless, formless darkness explodes from me like an atomic bomb and covers the castle and Taiv's world as if I closed my eyes.

Everything silences. So quiet a faint buzzing reaches my ears. Only my cries and the pounding of my heart interrupt it until the voice I long to hear breaks through.

"Now you show you care?" Taiv appears out of the darkness, disgust on his face. "Why didn't you do this when I was alive? Oh, that's right. Men don't do that, right? You should stop. You look weak. Pathetic. Toughen up."

I shake my head. I want to apologize, but can't speak.

"You let me die. You're a failure of a father."

"And a failure of a husband." Bae screams a pleasurable scream as a man much more handsome than me grabs her butt and kisses all over her neck and lips. "Fuck, I can't wait to get away from you. You're so *boring* and an embarrassing excuse of a man. You're right. I don't love you. No one does."

No. She loves me. She said so.

"D-Daddy!" Juryni appears, shaking and holding her tattered clothes to herself, a bloody lip and bruise on her eye. "W-Where were you? Y-You didn't protect me."

"He can't protect anyone."

That voice. I haven't heard in years.

My brother appears, same as when he died at eighteen, but hate was all over his face. "Where were you when I needed you? You should be dead. You deserve to die."

"Die," my son, wife, and daughter join, surrounding me, their voices growing louder as many more join and echo. "Die. *Die. DIE!*"

"Die," I repeat, dejected and hopeless and numb and they all stop. "Okay."

Everyone does eventually, so why continue to suffer in pain when I can end it now? No more bills. No more work taking up all my time. No more people and their attitudes. No more pain. No more fear. No more embarrassment.

No more feelings at all.

"Dad…" Taiv's voice is faint as a small light breaks the darkness far in the distance like a lightning bug. "Dad…"

He is calling me to the afterlife. I'm coming, son.

"Dad…" He sounds closer as the faint light grows—it breaks through, and his face appears, a small oasis in this endless darkness. "Come back. It's okay. I'm still alive."

"What?"

"I didn't do it." He smiles. "I just wanted to see who was telling the truth without Rheim trying any more tricks."

Relief slightly washes over me. He's alive. That's my boy.

I take his hand, but instantly the darkness starts to fill back into me and the weight of pain and feelings weighs me down. I let go and the pain leaves as the numbness returns.

"Leave me." I back away. "I'm no good for you. Any of you."

"Yes, you are." Bae appears and reaches for me as well. "I'm sorry for what I said."

"No, you're right. I'm too broken. I'm fucked up. And I'll do the same to all of you and just hurt you."

"But you're hurting everyone now." Bae gestures around at the darkness.

"I can't take it back," I say. "I don't want to feel that pain again. It's too much. I'm tired of it, tired of being so angry. It's killing me. I can't hold it anymore."

"Then don't. You're human. You feel. And that's good. You're not supposed to hold onto all of that and you don't have to carry that pain alone. Share it with us. That's what people who love and care about you are for. All I've been wanting is for you to be open and communicate. To see your heart like I did when we fell in love. Please. Let us help. We need you."

"We do." Juryni sniffles as she appears, Princess and Cuz behind her.

I stare at them. The peace of this numbness is tempting, *so* tempting, but it's the easy way out. I've never been one for the easy way. They need me. They really need me. I can't abandon them. Can't hurt them. I won't.

I take Bae and Taiv's hands and they pull me into a hug as does Juryni, Princess, and Cuz. The darkness surges back into me and I brace … but it isn't as heavy and the pain isn't as unbearable. It's there, but manageable. The last of the darkness fades and uncovers Taiv's castle.

"Thank you," I tell my family and they smile.

Everyone in the courtyard cheers, except Rheim who roars "NO!" and prepares lightning to attack, but the king with my face punches him and knocks him to the ground.

"Shut it." He glares at him before bowing to me along with all of Taiv's creations in the courtyard. "We humbly apologize. We were misled and didn't want to lose Taiv. We understand if you are angry, but we seek your forgiveness."

"It's okay." I shake his hand and smile. "I think I'm going to give anger a break. Thank you for taking care of my son."

He nods as Rheim attempts to stand, but I punch him in the jaw back down. "That's for my son." I add a kick. "And that's for my brother."

Bae and Juryni get their licks in. Taiv steps to him.

"Why?" he asks. "What do you get out of this?"

Rheim spits blood on the ground and smirks. "You're about to see."

Loud roars, screeches, and battle cries sound as hundreds of different creations surround Taiv's castle, in the air and along the wall of the courtyard. Wizards and witches, soldiers, dragons, trolls, ogres, giant spiders, scorpions and snakes, ice monsters, sea people, rock people, lava people, sentient trees, living fire, and more outnumbering us at least ten times over.

"Like my toys?" Rheim smirks as he stands and dusts himself off. "Now, to add yours," he tells me and Taiv as he strolls around us like a lion. "I think I'll make you forget," he says to Taiv as he holds out his hand and a syringe full of white metallic liquid appears in it, "and you'll end it all in no time. And then this one," he looks to me, "will follow you due to the guilt."

"No!" I beg, thinking quickly as I glance around—Cuz and Princess bring the perfect idea to my mind. "How about a deal?"

Rheim raises an eyebrow. "I'm listening."

"You let my son stay and you can use any creation of his you please whenever you want. Think of all the ones he hasn't even created yet. And I'll make my brother's creations obey you."

An uproar of gasps, objections, and insults towards me immediately raise from Taiv's creations. My family, Princess, and Cuz look at me horrified.

"Silence!" Rheim commands and his stolen creations threaten the others into submission. "I think I can work with that."

"But," I say, "I need to know you will never go back on this and will leave my son alone."

Rheim licks his lips. "Very well. Let's bind it with a spell. You give me control of all your brother's creations or your son forgets. And if I make your son leave, I leave too?"

I nod and ignore all the objections as I shake Rheim's outstretched hand. A sensation shoots up my arm like slime.

"What have you done?" Cuz asks horrified. "You shame your brother!"

I ignore him. "All creations of me and my brother, you obey Rheim now."

Cuz shakes his head. "No, I will never obe—"

"Silence," Rheim says and Cuz did. "Perfect, but unfortunately Taiv's still leaving."

I knew it. "*What*? We had a deal!"

"Yes, that's why Princess will do it," Rheim says. "For an extra sting."

He holds out the syringe and commands Princess to give it to Taiv. She stares at me as she has no choice but to walk, grab it, and raise it above my son. Taiv struggles against Cuz holding him as Bae and Juryni and all of Taiv's creations scream for Rheim to stop. He only smirks as Princess brings it down—and curves it, stabbing Rheim and injecting the liquid.

He gasps and stumbles back, eyes wide as he rips the syringe out, but it's too late. "No. Y-You're supposed to obey me."

I smirk. "But she was never my brother's. Just mine."

"*No-argh*!" Rheim gasps for air as his skin and face shifts and his dreads fall out as he ages to an older man of about sixty.

There are many gasps and my eyes widen at the man I recognize from his photo in his books Taiv loves to read.

"Dre'Mar?" Taiv asks in disbelief. "What? I-I looked up to you. You encourage boys like us. Why would you do this?"

"Please... help me," Dre'Mar begs. "Don't let me go. I didn't want to do it, but I couldn't have a rival. They would have upstaged me. You don't know how hard it is to be a creative. Especially like us. Some waste away never having their stories matter or achieve success, but I took their ideas and told them for them. I give to charity. I'm not bad. *Please*."

"You're right," Taiv says. "You're a coward. We should be uplifting each other, not competing."

He turns his back on him.

"That's my boy," I say proudly. "Bye, fool."

Dre'Mar cries out in pain and holds his head as he fades away. All the stolen creations come to their senses and lay down their weapons. Everyone celebrates and cheers.

"My apologies." Cuz pats me on the back. "You really had me fooled. Your brother would be proud."

I shake his hand and nod as Princess hugs me. Hopefully my brother and all the boys that lost their lives and imagination are at peace. Taiv's creations start singing happy birthday, but he frowns. Realizing your idol ain't shit has to sting.

"It'll be okay, son." I pat him on the shoulder. "Um. How do you feel?"

Taiv shakes his head. "It's not that. It's…"

"You can tell me," I say. "I'm listening."

"What if he's right? What if you are? What if I waste my life on this and nothing comes from it? What if I'm not good enough?"

I want to tell him not to try then, but I made a promise to change and have to stick to it.

"Well, that's not going to happen because you're amazing, but *if* it does, then that's okay. Because it keeps you happy. You deserve to imagine and dream just as much as anyone else. Even if you don't earn one cent from it. And no matter what, I will be just as proud of you as

I have always been. I support you one hundred percent."

Taiv smiles. "Thanks, Dad."

"No, thank you." I pull him into a hug and Bae and Juryni join. "Now, please come home so I can give you a real hug."

He chuckles and tells some creations to introduce themselves while he hurries home. They all had great things to say about him, even his enemies. After a couple minutes he returned and interrupted one of his princesses about to reveal an embarrassing secret.

"My heart shall always burn and yearn for you," Handsum tells Bae on one knee.

"Thank you," she kisses him on the cheek, "but live your own life."

He nods and turns to me as he stands. "Take good care of her."

"I will." I take her hand and smile. "And that goes for all of you," I tell Juryni's boys. "Keep my daughter safe and have fun, but not too much or I'll be back. Got it?"

They salute. "Yes, sir."

Taiv tells Bae and I to close our eyes and we do—

"Happy birthday!" Juryni yells.

I jump and my eyes fly open. Juryni is hugging Taiv at the end of the bed Bae and I sit on. We hop up and wrap our arms around them.

I smile and don't even think to stop my happy tears from falling. "My boy. Happy birthday. Love you, man."

"Thanks, Dad." He melts into me.

"Okay, bed," Bae says after a few moments. "You two aren't going to want to get up and your dad needs his rest for work."

They both laugh as they hurry out the room.

"I love you too, you know," I tell Bae and grab her hand.

She smiles. "I know."

As she makes for the bed, I remember the question I made a mental note to ask daily from now on: "How was your day? You know, other than getting dragged into some fantasy world to save our son."

She turns to me surprised as if I said I was about to kill her. "You really want to know? But don't you need to go back to sleep?"

I shrug. "Eh, it can wait. I really want to know."

She smiles and licks her lips. "How about I tell you after a ride on your Express, Daddy?"

After my initial shock, I laugh and rub my hands together like a fiend. I gently tackle her to the soft sheets as our lips meet and it's like the same blast of lightning from our first kiss, reviving the magic between us as if it never died.

James Gettys II

The_Ninety8 is a Nigerian-American digital illustrator who focuses primarily on Black joy, life, and beauty. Since childhood, she has had a strong love and passion for art and fantasy. Growing up watching shows like Avatar: The Last Airbender and Magical Doremi helped develop her foundation for creating new worlds and characters. This passion was further bolstered by rarely seeing Black people depicted in the art she enjoyed. She seeks to bring more versatile and colorful depictions of Black people to the forefront. Fantasy has always been a genre that she has loved and explored as a creative and will continue to be a strong foundation. More of her work can be found at yewandeart.com and you can contact her for inquiries via email at yewandeart@gmail.com.

James Gettys II's oxygen is writing, especially fantasy led by all types of Black boys and full of fresh, fascinating, and fun surprises. He is determined to help fill that space and encourage imaginations with a range of books he'd wished he could have read growing up. When not being yelled at by the endless characters in his head to tell their stories, he is most likely yelling at soccer matches, some game show, or himself — in a good way, of course.

TO SHAPE THE NIGHT

BY TONJA K. JOHNSON

DARK FANTASY

CONTENT WARNING FOR MISANDRY

When a woman comes to my cottage requesting an impotency jar, I don't ask questions. But when she wants a jar to make a man, who she's never spoken to, fall so deep in love that he won't know his ass from a stray cat, I need answers.

"What do you mean he doesn't know you exist?" I stop grinding herbs, pestle hovering over ancient stoneware. Blended spices burn their way up my nostrils and speckle my sequoia-brown hands in pinks, yellows, and greens.

Yemmi rakes me with a withered gaze. "Stop staring like I grew another pair of tits."

Her words force my eyes to the ample cleavage on display. Skyfire, I'm no better than a man. Face tingling with heat, I smooth my frizzedout edges and cut my focus back to the mixture of pink savory and fresh tarragon. Tears prick as I add a second pinch of turmeric.

"I don't do love jars."

I ignore her groans. The Complete Encyclopedia of Obscure Plant Species lies open on the counter. I lick a finger and turn the page, still not finding anything identifiable. Maybe if I search under species with teeth.

Yemmi reaches over the wooden workspace and clasps my arm.

"Are you even listening? Lovella, please." Her nails dig in.

Tugging free from desperate claws, I ease back.

"Not happening." I carry my supplies to the kitchen counter. A fresh breeze gushes in through the open door and circulates stale air. Bone chimes croon on the breeze. I send a reverent thank-you to the skies for small blessings.

"How about I make you a nice self-love jar instead?" I say, hoping to change the subject.

"What in horned god's hell am I gon' do with that?"

"Don't you ever speak it. Not in my house you don't." I spin to face her. If Momma heard that talk, she'd rise from the dead and mutate us both to star-nosed moles.

"You Arrent women are too superstitious. The horned god ain't real."

If only she knew.

"Which one of those boys got you out of sorts now? You better not be starting any mess."

Her auburn-brown skin lights.

"His name is Harlow Ren." Yemmi practically purrs.

I can't suppress the groan that rumbles from my throat. This isn't the first time I've heard that name. Many girls have beaten down my door for a jar to make Harlow sniff their way.

"If I don't marry him, I'll die." She melts onto worn cedar.

I want the quiet sanctum of my cottage restored. "There's a nice patch of azaleas out back. A spade over there in the corner. You're welcome to start digging."

"Just because your cunny is a dried-up well doesn't mean the rest of us want to end up old and alone." She doesn't hold her punches. "Because you're an Arrent you can't leave the forest, and have to stay shuttered in this creepy old hut?"

Twenty-six is hardly ancient, but by Hollow standards, women without conjure, I am practically a cadaver. I glance around my house. Everything I own fits in this single room. It held such charm moments ago. But now, I inspect my home as Yemmi and the women from town must.

Arrent Cottage is built from the bodies of Arrent Women. Their petrified organs cobble together to create its walls. Their dried sinew wefts its curtains. Their bleached bones make mantle, shingle and frame. Painted skulls form bookcases, candleholders, and bookends. When I die, the next Arrent will add my carcass as adornment.

We waste nothing.

Glass jars wink from afternoon sun pouring in through the

windows. Dried herbs clutter the expanse of one wall.

But this is home. This is safe. Nobody can touch me here.

A hollowness opens in the now tight space.

Yemmi tucks dark curls behind her ear. "How long have I been coming here? Five years? Six? Are you going to die in this room or are you going to go out there and get you some of this life?"

The air hangs thick with static. What does she know about my life? I'm a conjure woman—an Arrent woman—and I belong to the woods just as much as they belong to me. Before I allow evil to use me, I send a silent prayer to the ancestors for endurance.

They don't answer.

Picturing all the ways her greasy organ meat could create potent pestilence jars, I snatch the broom off the wall, and start sweeping her bad juju out the front door.

"Get out," I hiss, patience drier than that damned well.

She stands, huffing like I just insulted her great-grandmother. I have a mind to conjure that gnarled corpse if Yemmi doesn't hurry her boney behind out of here.

She doesn't turn her back to me. Who's the superstitious one now? Her modesty wrap falls to the ground, but she doesn't stop to retrieve it. I trample all over the rich fabric as I stalk her to the door.

As soon as she crosses the threshold, I fist a handful of salt from a pouch nailed to the frame and blow the black crystals with conjured strength. She yelps as salt pelts her backside.

Just as she turns around, eyes slitted with rage, I slam the door in her face.

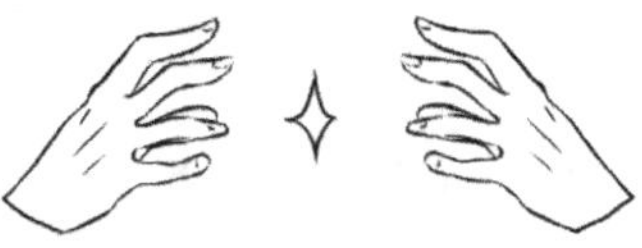

"With service like that, you'll be the first Arrent begging on the streets."

I storm through the house, not bothering to acknowledge Lukyan. Wind snuffs the light jars in my wake. Tension shivers from me in rivulets; the power to destroy right at my fingertips.

He chatters in the background, but my mind is a haze.

"If you want, I can eat her fingers. Or anyone's fingers, really. Just set me on your workstation and I'll do the rest." Lukyan wriggles in his pot, black soil spilling onto the floor.

I duck beneath the crisscross overhang that droops heavy with blackened bones to the counter. Then I'm flipping through the pages of the encyclopedia again.

"All this is useless."

"You're right, a finger is too much. How about a pinky toe?" A slimy inhuman tongue lolls out of his mouth between serrated teeth. "A nail?" His voice is a desperate whine. "A fleck of dried skin that falls off naturally?"

The thought of Yemmi losing a toe to Lukyan drags a lopsided smile from my lips. "If we eat the customers, they'll really send the hunters after us."

"What do you mean, 'we'? I'm not sharing."

I roll my eyes and start shoving supplies back into cabinets. There has to be another book that can describe what kind of creature he is. "Are you gon' tell me?"

Lukyan puckers what could be called lips and blows a kiss with wet smacks. "Now where would be the fun in that?"

Footsteps crunch gravel in the front yard.

"Don't be selfish this time! Let me lick an elbow."

"Shut up," I hiss, tossing him a dried worm. His plant body stretches, stem thick as my wrist, with huge red petals that fan out to capture any debris.

I grab Yemmi's shawl. If she apologizes, then I'll accept. She doesn't haggle like the other women.

I open the door, resolved to be the bigger person. Loose gravel shifts beneath my boots, the crunch swallowing the forest song. Blinding light has me shielding my eyes as the figure approaches.

"Before you take another step, apologize," I say to her silhouette.

She stops, height blocking the sun. "And what am I apologizing for?"

My heart stalls, tight pressure in my chest. That is not Yemmi's voice. Too deep—too resonant, a rattle that shakes my bones.

They step into an angle where shadows fall away and a jagged white scar slices down one eye.

A scream bubbles in my throat but won't release.

He takes another step, reaching toward me, a frown creasing his brows.

A man. A man got through my wards.

Without a word, the scarred man walks right into my space like there isn't supposed to be miles and magic between us. He's all height and dark skin. None of the outer house wards so much as flicker at his invasion.

Our eyes collide. I am adrift, rooted to the spot by one midnight eye and one honey.

The satiny shawl slips from my fingers. "Harlow Ren."

His brows crease, eyes flickering like I shouldn't know him, but how couldn't I when every woman in town has his name on her lips. This exact face is etched in my memory from countless descriptions. A jaw to cut diamonds, eyes that make a woman feel like his only, a mouth that holds the ghost of a smile, and skin so dark it rivals night.

"You got through the wards?" I want to ask how but, "Why?" slips from my mouth first.

He brings his hands to his face, examining shaky fingers.

"I-I don't know. There was a trail, a string of smoke and it gripped me like the noose chokes a dead man. It didn't let go until it brought me to you."

Not possible. What he's talking about is conjure and men can't access that power.

"Leave." My voice is weak even to my ear. Cold sweat breaks out over my spine. I back up several steps until I bump into the bone door.

He takes two forward, hands up as if his presence alone isn't a threat. "Please, I need your help."

"Don't go falling for the tricks of men. Don't no man ever need a woman's help," my mother's warning echoes in my mind, clear as the day she gave it.

"My momma taught me better than that."

Confusion clouds his eyes, but before he can touch me, I invoke the ancestors. Conjure tingles under the layers of my skin and within my blood. With a flash of black light, I thrust that energy into him. Enough to make the lights outside the house flicker.

Dense smoke fills the woods, acrid with the stench of conjure. The air clears in a slow pulling haze. "That should do it." I dust my hands on my hips and admire my handiwork.

My intruder is now a sprout. No way he's unbinding that spell. But to be cautious, I grab a towel hanging out to dry and use it to lift the little plant.

"I think I'll put you next to the azaleas. Not surprising such a pretty boy makes such a pretty plant."

One second, I'm walking with my plant-man, and next he's not a plant anymore, and he's on top of me.

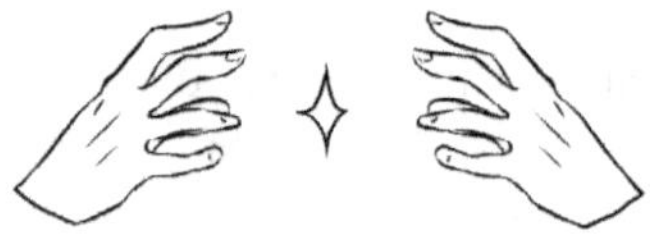

Harlow hovers over me. Body so close we are almost touching. His hands bracket either side of my head, thick thighs straddling mine. I thought I felt something, but the pulse of my conjure still tingles beneath my skin.

I don't dare even breathe.

If I move, we'll touch and if we touch, I'll no longer be a conjure woman.

"So, you think I'm pretty?" His breath is a phantom across my cheek. Lips mere inches from mine.

A fist tightens in my chest. This is the closest I've ever been to a man. Fading sunlight limns the curls framing his face.

That thread, I think I feel it too. I can't breathe.

He's beautiful in a way that makes my body taut, and that is so dangerous. This is why Momma told me to never let men near.

My eyes can't help but chart the scar through his right eye. The urge to trace the jagged line has my hand rising to meet skin even though it shouldn't.

His eyes lock on my mouth.

My lips part. I can't seem to get enough air.

He leans in as if to kiss.

I conjure the strength of the ancestors and blast him to the other side of the clearing.

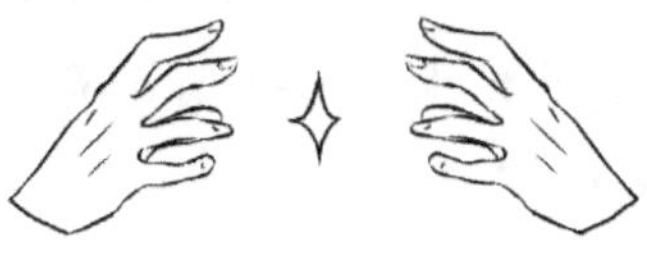

Since Harlow arrived, two things are clear: one, my conjure doesn't completely work on him and two, he's not leaving.

I've mutated him into a snail, a rat, a shrub, even a bobcat—and looking back, that was dumb, but I was stressed—and each time he unbinds himself. Each time the same word passes over his lips, "please".

Whatever he wants, I claim no parts.

Men don't do nothing but take.

"I just want to talk," he yells from outside. He's in the lawn, legs crossed, determination furrowing his brow.

I watch through the window. He's stubborn as a weed. Once he understands I'm not playing his games, he'll leave. And I can pack my house up and take it somewhere he won't find.

Thunder rolls deep in the distance. My eyes tug toward the graying sky.

"Ancestors wash away everything that impedes my path. Let no enemy falter my steps." I smooth a length of braid at the root. This man will not tempt me.

The answering rumble is a sign that Harlow won't be here long.

I kick my feet up and wait.

Rain pours in sheets, so dense it obscures the yard. An icy chill ripples my spine as the deluge pounds petrified organs. Chimes on the front porch rattle, the moan of bone against bone.

I light the hearth and tuck myself into bed. "Everything will be back to normal by morning."

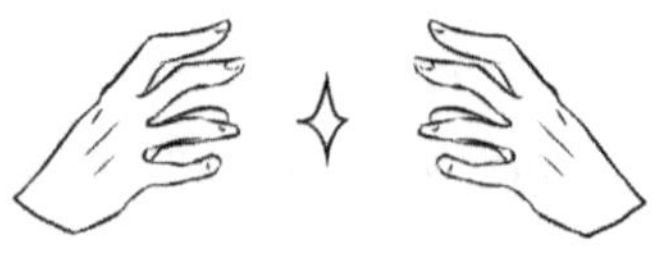

Everything is not back to normal.

Before I rub the sleep from my eyes, I rush to the window. Harlow is curled in a fetal position, smashing my collards. I'm out the door and stomping barefoot down the lawn.

He shivers, likely to catch a chill, but that's not my problem. His eyes crack and that stare pierces me to the core. This feeling, I don't know what it is, and I shift on my feet, suddenly uncomfortable under his steady gaze.

With a groan he sits, arms wrapped tight around his middle. It's so cold out that frost has crystalized on the tips of his curls.

"If you want to kill yourself, do it somewhere else."

He doesn't move. Doesn't even blink. His eyes trail the length of my body. Everywhere his gaze lands feels kissed by lightning. By the time his eyes rest on my face, taking painfully long on my lips, we're both panting.

"Morning." His voice is gravel on silk. A rogue smile tugs the corner of his mouth.

I shudder as his baritone vibrates through me and grit my teeth to stop the jitter.

He leans back on his hands, legs still trembling and takes a moment, tasting his words before he says them. "Are you tempting me, miss?"

My brows pinch. "What're you talking 'bout?"

All he does is nod toward my chest.

I look down. Mortification spreads in waves.

It's a chilly morning, and this shift is thin. Now I'm the one crossing their arms. I should have thrown on my robe, but I'm so used to it being just me.

"Either you talk, or I leave you to freeze."

Harlow straightens, lazy smile gone. He moves to stand, but I put a hand to stop him.

Hells, this man is doing something crazy to my senses.

"I want you to remove this." A thread of gray smoke curls from his palm and slithers over my fingers.

The immediate sensation is warmth as the vapor floods my hand, spreading deep into me. Then that thread clamps down, tightening over my wrist. I flinch and bite back a yelp. And now I'm panicking because what in Skyfire was that? So much is wrong here.

"That's not possible. I can't remove it." My voice is no heavier than the mist undulating over my skin.

A muscle flutters in his jaw like he's trying to hold back that same feeling that's overwhelming me now.

Curiosity pricks the back of my mind. The urge to ask him why he wants to remove the ancestors' greatest gift is strong. But that ain't my business. And what's worse, I don't understand what I just felt or why my body already craves more.

"Then at least show me how to hide it." He sways to his feet.

The urge to help him is fierce enough that I tuck my hands into my armpits. "And if I say no?"

"I can't live like this."

That pleading gaze forces tension from my shoulders. I'm too soft or too dumb. Maybe both. "One day," I say, walking back inside, toes tingling from frost.

"Wait, that's not enough."

"Make it enough."

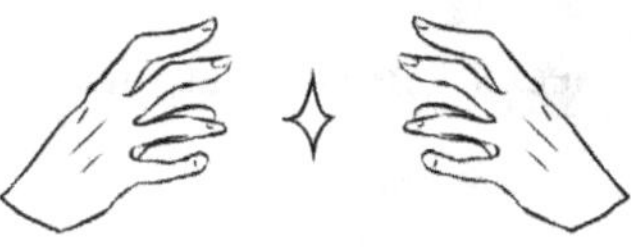

He asked for a week of training, but there was no way a man could stay that long. The risk is already insane. If he so much as touches me, that's it. One day was all he'd get.

I get his blood oath that he won't come back and that seals the deal.

Early morning sun slants through the window. I busy myself, plucking herbs that will help find his affinity.

Harlow leans a hip against the counter, relaxed, as if this space was made for him. I wonder if he walks into every room like he owns it.

"When did you first notice your…abilities?" I say, inhaling spice and wood-smoke that's completely him.

He sets his teacup down and leans both hands on the wood surface. I can't help but notice his nails are trimmed and clean. Separating the manifesting herbs into five stone bowls, I force my attention from the enormous slab of man.

"What's your name?"

I startle as his voice vibrates through me.

"It's only fair, since you already know mine."

My brows pinch. "Let's focus on what's actually important. You aren't going to be here long enough for names to matter." He looms even further over the table, his shadow on my skin like a brand.

"Something tells me you're the most important thing in the world right now."

Heat flooding my cheeks, I look up at him.

And what a colossal mistake.

"Lovella." My name spills like libations over my tongue.

A smile breaks out across his face that crinkles his eyes. "Lovely, Lovella."

I'm a hare in a trap, too stunned to save myself.

He continues as if my heart isn't loud enough for the both of us to hear. "Since I was a boy. But it got worse about a year ago. If my father found out… Well, let's just say he's not a tolerant man." His gaze is a force, stripping me down to bare bones.

"How old are you?"

He scrunches his face as if surprised by the question. "Twenty-five."

"When a conjure woman—person reaches maturity, their powers amplify. Something to do with the brain, that's what Momma said. What you're experiencing is that added sensitivity from your power."

"So, I should learn this relatively quick?"

"I said your power is matured, nothing 'bout your brain capacity."

That lopsided grin returns. "How old are you?"

Now, I'm the one off-guard. "Twenty-six."

"I do like an older woman."

Wildfire spreads down my neck. "Flirting won't change my mind," I say, even as his vapor still twines my skin.

"A man has to try."

"Put your hand over each one of the piles. Slowly."

He's obedient and hovers his palm over each pile. Hissing, Harlow snatches his hand back over the now smoking fireweed.

"Congratulations, Mr. Ren. Your affinity is fire."

"So that means we can suppress it?"

We. It's too easy to think myself a 'we' with him. I clear my throat and ignore his question.

"What's your affinity?"

I hold my hand over the bowl of belladonna, water trickles from my fingertips.

He gapes, staring as if seeing into me. Then that sly smile claims his lips before I can decipher the serious expression beneath.

"I knew you'd be my undoing."

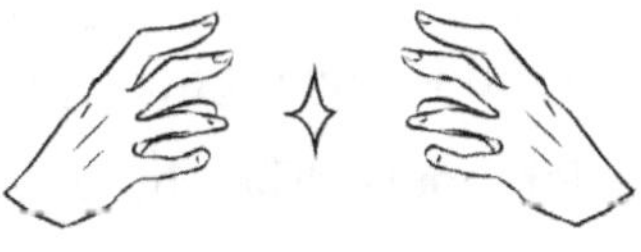

We work, creating potions that subdue fire affinities. Belladonna teas, willow and lotus tonics. And each time Harlow gets his hands on a mixture it belches up in flame.

Poor Lukyan's petals are singed but thankfully he's silent. Which is very much unlike that talkative plant.

"I am trying." Frustration wrinkles Harlow's forehead, biceps flexing as he works the pestle.

"That's too much pressure." The bowl groans and before I realize it, I'm reaching for him.

"If you touch that boy, I swear I'll release all this built-up gas. Every fly and rodent for miles will flock to the stench of rotting flesh."

I falter, lunging for Lukyan instead. Too late, I slap a hand over his pistil, careful to avoid rows of serrated teeth.

Harlow drops the pestle. Stone clatters against bone floors.

Silence stretches taut.

Sweat drips down the curve of my back, heart erratic.

Harlow points a finger at the stupid plant writhing in my hands. "Did that flower just speak?"

Lukyan chomps down on my middle finger. A scream rips from my throat as I stumble away from him. "Vicious little beast."

"Your boyfriend just called me a flower. Tell him to come over so I can bite him."

"Boyfriend?" Harlow and I choke at the same time.

"I've watched y'all for hours. The shy glances." He gags, "The flirting. Makes my stomach sick."

I want to correct him: that one, Harlow is not my boyfriend and two, he doesn't have a damned stomach. But Harlow's skin has gone ashen, his full bottom lip a pale orange instead of its usual pink.

"You're bleeding." He walks towards me, staring at my bloody finger, hands poised to touch.

I dart around the table.

Hurt flickers over his face, before it's quickly replaced by something more playful—something false. "I won't hurt you."

"You couldn't if you tried."

"Then why run every time I get within five feet of you?"

My throat is a fallow, sunbaked field. I can't tell him. "I am an Arrent woman, and we don't touch men."

Powerful arms cross over a broad chest. "Then how do y'all make more Arrent women? Don't tell me a stork delivers your children."

He wants to talk about making babies? Heat rushes to my cheeks. "You think because I live out in the woods, that I don't know the facts of life."

He raises a brow that says that's exactly what he thinks.

Mortification doesn't outweigh my sense of humor. "A man and a woman lay real close, and the male's hormones pollinate her egg."

Harlow stares.

I glare back.

He blinks slow, pinching the flat bridge of his nose as a muted groan slips between gritted teeth. His mouth twitches at a corner then wobbles.

Laughter fills the house, loud and bursting. It plasters over the cracks, so ripe with joy that it tightens my chest. He stalks toward me, this time not stopping when I shrink back.

I scramble onto the mattress until my spine compresses against a cold wall. It was a joke. Something to force him off the subject of why I avoid him. Because I'll never have a man the way other women do.

He pushes into my space, one knee dipping the bed, while a hand braces on the wall behind me. "Oh Lovely, when a man puts a baby inside you," his voice is the rhythm of my heart. The too loud rush of blood through my veins. "It won't be no accident."

Fire flushes my body and coils tight somewhere deep in my belly just waiting to unfurl. "What did you just call me?"

"Lovely."

It takes everything, but I resist the urge to look away. I meet his stare. A slow, wolfish grin overtakes his mouth. My eyes snag on the dart of a pink tongue wetting full lips. I swallow. A doubt can't help but rise to the surface.

When he's had so many beautiful women, why me? But I'll soak my bones in black brine before revealing just how much Harlow Ren affects me.

I force my gaze back up to the most incredible pair of eyes. It's just a whisper. Something in me, something dangerous wants him to push forward, to close the breath's distance.

The conjure in him calls to me. The heat of it curls against my skin, more potent than any touch.

"You feel that? The smoke. That thread never left," he says.

"Are you two going to rub noses? Or whatever the hells it is humans do when they get frisky."

Lukyan's voice is a douse of ice water.

Harlow jumps upright, the tension immediately frayed, and ruffles his ample curls. "I'll keep my distance. Don't want your plant taking a bite out my finger."

Ancestors help me if this man doesn't.

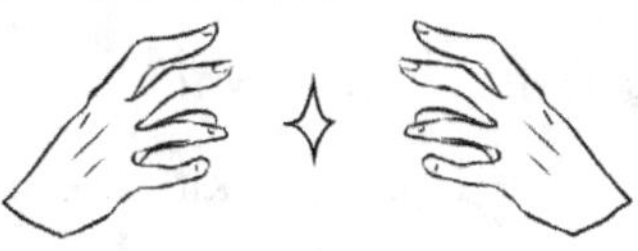

I place Lukyan out in the yard for some sun—his version of a timeout— and that spoiled plant pouts and shrieks the entire time.

Hours pass at a sprint. I teach Harlow the herbs, their functions and how to create more complex conjures that require containing. Jar spells are dangerous, so I teach him how to properly dismantle a user's intentions. I teach him how to find that core of energy inside himself. That it's his ancestors' love stored up, all the way back to his first mother.

But I learn things from him as well, distracting things. Like how his brow furrows when concentrating. I learn he steals glances when he thinks I'm not watching. And his eyes pull to the swell of my hips when I walk. And how he would rather evade questions about himself and turn the subject back to me.

More instances than I care to admit, I lose thoughts mid-sentence as my attention snags on the deadly allure of midnight and honey. Those dual-colored eyes trip me up every time.

"Why do you live out here?" He grimaces on a cold brew of lotus and lemon balm then sets down the cup.

It's a common question, and the answer pours by rote. "Momma died when I was fifteen. And I'm an Arrent woman and Arrent women don't live in town."

He fists dried herbs laid out on the counter, nearly ruining them. "Over ten years you've been on your own?"

"Oh, stop looking at me like I'm a kitten out in the rain." I scoop the mess from the opposite side of the table, careful our fingers don't brush.

He traps me with those eyes. "Trust me, Lovely, there are many things I imagine when I think of you, but a kitten is not one of them."

My skin prickles with warmth. And I don't know if it's his conjure or his words that have me so undone. "You're going to stop flirting with me."

"Yes, ma'am." He inclines his head then goes back to the book spread open before him.

I'm almost disappointed another quip doesn't follow.

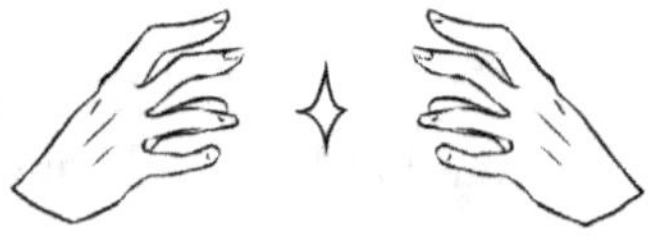

We try more tinctures, make a dozen jars but nothing subdues his conjure for long. Day wanes into night and we grow tense. The air between us thickens the deeper the sun sinks beneath the horizon. He's running out of time. And I can't risk giving him more.

I finally bring Lukyan in and offer him a handful of dead flies and he refuses.

"Next time you plan on leaving me to wither out in the sun to play house with a man, don't." With a groan, Lukyan unfurls rumpled leaves. The hundred tiny suckers on each crimson petal flare and hiss a high-pitched scream. "I need replanting. My soil is ruined. It'll take a month for me to eat again."

Harlow's brows shoot to his hairline.

Somehow, I highly doubt that, but I keep my lips folded over themselves. I wipe his leaves with a dry cloth. He licks salt from my fingers as I polish.

"I'm sorry. I'll get you a new pot. And I'll even let you have my nail clippings for the month."

His stem straightens, petals perking. "You're lying. I can sense it in the air. You get your horny hands on one man and you're already throwing me to the wolves."

The air strips from my lungs. Traitorous little thing.

Harlow's mouth twitches and he straightens his smile before it can slip free.

"You're the real danger," I grit.

Harlow rubs his stubble. "Is it always so...talkative?"

Lukyan laps up the flies from a bowl on the table. "You just want me quiet so you can seduce my mistress in peace."

My mouth falls. Harlow chokes on a cough, but I refuse to look at him.

"That's right, we've heard all about the infamous Harlow Ren." The thousand suckers on his petals flare, revealing teeth. The sharp points glint in the fading light. "Drawls drop wherever you step. You've had a hundred lovers, and your tongue makes women see stars."

I want to die. Combusting into a million bloody fragments would be less painful.

Harlow's eyes flit to mine, that smile finally escaping. "You talk about my tongue?" He claims a step forward, brow arched.

I falter back.

A dark growl rumbles from Lukyan; a sound I've never heard him make. The hairs on my body stand on end. "You won't get that disgusting human mouth anywhere near her. She can't touch a man, or she'll forfeit her power."

Harlow cuts me with a look that slices to bone. "Is that true?" His voice is low.

Another biting laugh. I want to twist Lukyan's stem, but I'm frozen in place by the hurt flickering over Harlow's face.

"You lay one vile finger on her and she'll never conjure again."

The floor opens up, the gaping maw slurping me down, deep down. My secrets splatter out like intestines with no way to sew them back in.

I can't move until Harlow looks away.

Rain falls in sheets outside and I cling to the patter. It's the horned god's hours of the night when we finally find a mix to suppress Harlow's conjure.

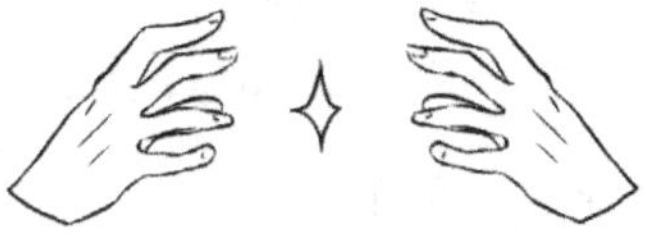

Rain pelts the roof with the hollow tink, tink, tink of water smacking bone. I lay awake. Sleep evasive. I'd mix myself a tonic, but Harlow lays just feet away on the floor. Earlier, we ate in uncomfortable silence. The entire meal he searched my face. And like a coward, I hid in that quiet.

He finally leaves in the morning and I can't wait to see him go. I'll watch until he disappears down my gravel path. I'll watch until his figure is nothing but mist suspended in dawn. I'll watch until the sun burns it all away. And when he's gone, I can finally return to my safe, solitary life.

But the thought doesn't bring the comfort it should.

With the storm bending the wood like fragile reeds, Harlow was forced to sleep inside. And so, I stare at drawings Momma carved into the ceiling.

Some nights we rest, and some nights our minds need extra time to unravel.

Body and mind wound tight, I fear *I'll* unravel, and I don't know where that thread leads.

Thunder rips like the guttural croak of some great beast. An unnatural pulse of lightning illuminates the night.

Harlow shoots up from his pallet like a bloodworm bit him.

"Don't tell me you're scared of a bit of rain?"

"Of course not." He clears his throat, but I can see the whites of his eyes wide in low jar light. The internal flames flicker and wink with the moan of wind blowing over the house.

"Storms are wilder out here. We're safe."

"It's not me I'm afraid for, Lovely."

My breath catches. I sit up on an elbow, conjuring energy to funnel into the light jars. The room fills with a muted glow, enough for me to see every line in his face.

Why be afraid for me? This is my life. The woods are my home. "I'm an Arren–"

"Arrent woman," Harlow finishes on a sarcastic drawl. He sits up, pinning me in place with eyes that will haunt me long after he's gone. "But is that all you are?" He gestures to bones burning like logs in the hearth, the rug made from human skin, and the array of chipped and broken knick-knacks which comprise my home.

"What do you know about me? About who I am?"

"I know that living in the shadow of someone else's fears is like trying to shape the night with your fingers. Darkness slips through the cracks, but you can never hold it. It doesn't belong to you."

The backs of my eyes burn as the light jars wink out all at once. I won't give him my tears. Only shadows remain as the hearth burns low. Harlow slips under his blanket, giving me his back.

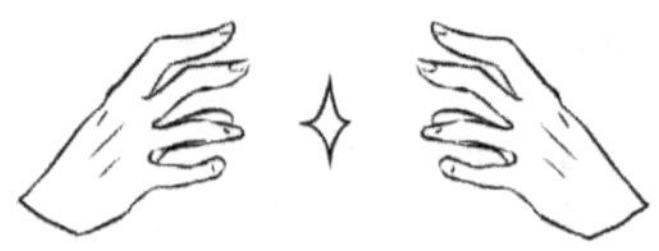

The morning passes in the same uneasy quiet. We have the herbal mixtures to subdue Harlow's conjure, and he knows how to make more. Nothing is keeping us together.

Except that thread, something intangible that makes this goodbye a thousand knives. He stands at the door like he doesn't know what to say, but I'm the one bursting with things unsaid.

"You talked about me hiding, about not knowing myself, but what about you? You see through my glass pane so easily but somehow yours is tinted."

He steps closer. "I may not know why I conjure. But I do know there's something here," he gestures between us. Another step.

My heart aches, cracking from my chest because he's offering me a limb I won't walk out on.

"And I also know you're not ready to admit it."

Harlow smiles like a cat that's been at the milk. And all I can do is exist in this space with him, throat too tight for response.

"I'll uphold my oath. I won't come back."

That promise already seems like a lifetime ago.

His face is expectant, waiting for me to say something. Anything. But everything inside me is so jumbled up and raw I don't know my thoughts from the wind.

My heart is beating fiercely against my ribs, threatening to break me from the inside. This pull, this thread between us, I can't deny it. Both. There has to be a way I can have both. But the words still won't come.

Harlow takes a breath as if resigned. "Goodbye, Lovely." He turns, bundle of jars slung over one shoulder, and opens the front door.

Pale sunlight streams in and a disheveled Yemmi stands outside.

"What're you doing here?" Stepping around Harlow, I walk outside to get a better look at her.

She is silent, wild eyes flitting between Harlow and I. Twigs jut out of her curls. Dirt streaks her dress. She looks like she passed the night in the bramble.

"How long you been out here?" The immediate urge to get her inside and warm has me walking toward her, but her eyes stop me short.

"What's he doing here?" A single tear smears a black trail down her cheek.

At first, I don't know what she's talking about and then realization dawns.

Harlow.

"You've been watching me?"

She staggers forward, and I take cautious steps back. I want to tell her that there's nothing between us, that he means nothing but my throat clenches.

"Witch!" Her mouth twists in a snarl.

Everything in me stops, body jerking as if slapped. My limbs move like they're dragging through honey. That word shouldn't hurt so much, but it does. After all this time, I thought she might be a friend.

Before my anger can even rise, she lunges.

A stinging slap lands on my cheek

Wind bellows through the clearing, whipping braids violently around my face. It's energy sent from the ancestors begging me to protect, urging me to hurt. I try to shove my conjure down, deep down, but it's right at the surface. I won't use my conjure to harm women. It's forbidden. No matter how much Yemmi deserves it.

"I think you'd better gon' home." Harlow's voice is steel at my back. That thread connecting us is what keeps me tethered.

Yemmi ignores his warning, anger still burning in her eyes. "You knew I wanted him, and you just had to take him for yourself." She shouts over the gale. "You think you're so much better than all us normal women because you can conjure."

A piece of me shatters, the control I've held my entire life splintering cell by cell. One moment Harlow plants himself in front of me, and the next Yemmi is barreling through us both.

Their momentum careens into me, and I'm caught in the sprawl. The collision of flesh against flesh is like the crush of a rockslide down a mountain face. Warm, strong arms cradle my neck, but it's too late. My head hits something hard just as jets of black light rip from my fingertips. Golden stars burst in my vision. Before I can mourn what I'm about to lose, the world goes dark.

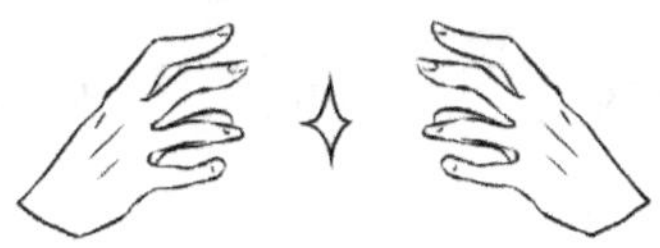

My eyes flicker open to night. A cool breeze wafts through the cottage, my bed is soft, and I'm grateful for small blessings.

"If anything happens to her, I'll feast on your bones." Lukyan's voice is a low growl.

I try to sit up, groggy, but I only manage to prop myself on one elbow. Immediately, Harlow is at my side, resting me against the wall.

"Get out." My throat is hoarse.

"I'm sorry."

"You heard her." The room is dark, but the scrape of Lukyan's pot against the floor tells me he's working his way over.

"Where's Yemmi?" I ask.

"She's gone."

His eyes are sad and pierce through my chest. "Love-"

But I already know what he's about to say and I need to confirm it for myself. On a shaky exhale, I release my conjure to ignite the light jars. But nothing happens. Not a flicker. A man touched me. "I'm no longer a conjure woman."

His hands envelop mine. Warm and solid, but I can't revel in this touch, because the most important part of me is gone.

"Lovely, look at me."

I find his shadow in the dark, but the shape is distorted and then I realize I'm crying.

"Don't worry mistress, I'm coming." Lukyan is still inching over, pot dragging.

Harlow folds a cool glass between my hands, palms covering mine.

"You're still everything. Nothing was taken from you."

I want to scream, throw the jar across the room but he holds me firm.

The prickle of his conjure tickles the back of my hands. "Try."

Hope is a dangerous flame and I dare not ignite it. Like I taught him, I close my eyes and open myself to the ancestors, searching for that coil deep within myself. There is nothing. Only a barren well. Tears burn my eyes. I am about to give up when I feel a pull.

Someone, or many someones, grab my arm and yank me down. Deep within myself. Further than I've ever gone until we collide into a spring of power so overflowing with life that I suck in a breath just to keep myself rooted.

Laughter bubbles from my belly, spilling over and filling the room. The jar between our hands glows, brighter than it's ever been.

All the light jars in Arrent house gleam.

Harlow's smile is luminous. "You always had the power within you. From that moment we first touched you never lost a thing."

My brows dip in confusion. When he fell on top of me, I thought I'd imagined the contact in my fear but now I know, for the barest of seconds his nose brushed mine.

He's right. "But Momma…she didn't want this for me."

His jaw clinches. "Her prejudices don't shape you. What do *you* want?"

My first instinct is to tell him I have everything I want, but that's not true. And I think Harlow knows it too.

He sits on the bed, so close our arms press. He keeps my hands like he's unwilling to let go. His touch is heat and fire, all things right. Heart beating frantically, I lean in, wanting to explore everything, but Harlow stops me, tilting my chin up to meet his eyes.

Breath abandons me in a rush.

"I need the words, Lovely."

There's no more holding back. "I want you." And every word is true.

Lukyan gags in a corner. Harlow's smile cracks first, mine can't help but follow.

A rough hand slides across my cheek to grip the back of my neck, and my senses detonate. "That wasn't so hard was it? Plus, someone needs to defend you from the town crazies."

From the moment I met those midnight and honey eyes, I felt the connection. I was just too afraid to reach out and take what I wanted. But now there is nothing stopping me.

I reach a trembling hand toward his face. At first contact, my body blazes. So acute is the sensation that the air rips from my lungs. I trace hesitant fingers along the angle of his jaw. Stubble tickles my palms as I cup his face in both hands.

The smile that spills over my lips is unstoppable. "Thank you for being my first touch."

He leans in, nose nuzzling mine. "And I'll do everything in my power to be your last."

Soft lips caress, aching for more, I open, and he shows me why

Momma was so afraid of this. The melt of our bodies, of our shared heat, is enough to make anyone lose themselves. I sip the spice of fireweed from between his lips, lap the sting with my tongue.

But I am anything but lost. And I know, the way I know an Arrent woman needs conjure, that I could never be powerless.

Tonja K. Johnson

Tonja K. Johnson is an African American writer of the gothic and the fanatical. Her work honors the rich, diverse culture of her ancestors with their collective voices steeped in every line. When not writing, she can be found reading, drawing and spending precious time with loved ones. She is a recipient of the 2023 MN Write Like Us grant and the winner of the 2024 MN BIPOC Emerging Writer award. Her work can be found in Blue Earth Review.

Other books by Tonja K. Johnson

One to Hang and One to Bind
Voices of Romance
Voices of Christmas

TODAY, WE ARE GENERALS

BY TATIANA OBEY
ART BY PLAIDPUMA

SPACE OPERA

CONTENT WARNINGS FOR DESCRIPTIVE VIOLENCE

There was no enemy like family, and no villain greater than a younger sister.

She glared at me from across the field; standing in her bright steely armor, like some beacon that demanded the attention of everyone around her. But I refused to let my sister outshine me. **Not today.** I surveyed the opportunistic bannermen, the disloyal soldiers, and greedy sellswords that gathered before the gates of *my* city. From atop the ramparts, they looked so small and so insignificant, like unwanted specks of dirt waiting to be cleansed from my home. They thundered towards me with siege ladders to scale my walls, and battering rams to splinter my gates. But no matter what, I would deny them the satisfaction of destroying all that I have built.

I raised my gauntleted hand, and yelled, "FIRE!"

The catapults atop the battlements launched flaming boulders over my head, streaking like meteors before the two moons in the sky, and landed in an explosion of dirt and bodies. The first strike missed its target—one of the encroaching siege towers—and had flattened strips of ground as it rolled down the decline that led away from my city. I knew better than to expect one hundred percent accuracy from the catapults, especially against a nightly assault, but that missed strike rippled through the morale of the soldiers atop the wall. Anxiousness settled into the gut like that of a song begun off-key.

A general's job was to stand steadfast in the face of uncertainty and doubt, and with a practiced calm, I raised my hand and yelled, again, "FIRE!"

Constellations sketched images across the night sky, but the flaming boulders scratched lines through them as they descended. Then the stars disappeared behind the glare of a great bonfire, which swathed across the battlefield as one of the boulders struck a siege tower, expelling a shower of wood in all directions. I released a triumphant cry and the soldiers stationed atop the ramparts joined my cheer. My army contained a mix of all races from across the planet— from big-eyed Dollians to furred Bunnyons—all united in their love of this city that has protected and given them haven.

Despite that success, my sister's army kept rolling forward.

As the aggressor, my sister was at the disadvantage. It was obvious her plan was to throw as many bodies at the problem as possible. That was my sister for you–always so single-minded and starved for attention. I was determined to make sure that her decision to challenge me would cost her everything, and that her audacity would finally be buried alive, choking on grave dirt.

The catapults destroyed half of the siege towers, leaving two who escaped beyond their range.

"ARROWS AT THE READY!" I ordered. On command, the archers who lined the walls drew their longbows. They aimed toward the sky, and they waited on my word to rain down destruction. "FIRE!"

The heavens grew fangs. Arrows took bites out of whole regiments, for my sister had chosen speed over armor and shields, and they were chewed out callously across the hill.

Still, their army kept rolling forward with a single-minded zeal. Why did they follow my sister so religiously when she was so determined to break them against my walls? My spies have reported that she promised her followers plundered riches, and have told them that for many years, I have denied them entry into the city and access to its opportunities. And perhaps that was true. Perhaps my exclusionary practices have led me here today. But I built this city for *my* people, for them to thrive and to flourish. I did not build it for her ugly little toys.

"General." A messenger panted when they reached me. He had long floppy ears tied behind his back and big feet that sprouted from the bottom of his boots, which gave him unnatural speed. "There are updates from the eastern wall. Your presence is requested immediately."

"Keep applying pressure," I told the bowmaster. Then I made my way to the other side, taking stairs down and then back up to reach the eastern wall of the fortifications. I thought over my sister's impulsive strategy and I had begun to think that things were a little too easy. As I approached the wall, I became more and more certain that something else was at play here.

I reached a gathering of scouts, circled around one of my lieutenants. My lieutenant, an armored reptilian, handed me a spyglass once I arrived and I used it to look out over the eastern fields. I could see the blue grass that covered the hills and the purple tops of trees in the distance.

And then, I saw it. A streak of black infesting the land like a poison. Another army.

The banners slowly came into view, hoisted into the air by mounted cavalry. I recognized that offensive swirl of brown on the banners. That emblem belonged to my baby brother. Another unforgivable betrayal.

Up until now, he had taken a neutral stance between mine and my sister's arguments. Perhaps something had changed his mind? Or maybe he was just here to cause chaos as he always did. Regardless, I refused to let these unforeseen circumstances shake me. I was the oldest child, the one who helped change their diapers and shared my snacks when feeling particularly magnanimous. I'll show them the consequences of ganging up on me. Once I took care of my baby brother, then I'd take care of my little sister.

My brother came into view riding a rolling wooden tank, leading the army of cavalry behind him. He didn't command from the back like our sister, but instead, charged recklessly forward. It was his grave.

Time to do some damage.

I crouched to brace my body against what was to come, and then without shame or a self-conscious bone, I screamed at the top of my lungs. The different races of the planet all had their own unique individual traits, and my family had the special ability to summon magic with the sound of our voices.

Lightning flashed in my vision and static crackled around me, raising the small hairs on my arms. The braids of my hair snapped like whips and the cloak of my armor lifted as if gravity could no longer constrain it. I felt weightless with the amount of magic building up in my body. A golden tinge exuded from my skin, and I could only imagine how to others, I had lit up the darkness like a faithful night light.

Then, I jumped.

"General!" My lieutenant shouted after me.

I landed with my fist to the ground, and the planet cratered at the impact. I pulled up my fist, leaving behind an impression of my knuckles in the hard dirt, and faced my brother and his army. He didn't seem intimidated as he continued to charge forward.

I had wanted to preserve my magic, and maybe I wouldn't have enough energy to defeat my sister after this fight, but this was my city, and I would do everything in my power to defend it.

"I don't want to hurt you," I told him, even as I crouched and pressed my hands together. "But if you don't stop, I will give you the spanking that you deserve."

My brother only screamed in response. He waved a metal mace in his right hand, while the entire lower half was consumed by the wooden contraption. It had thunderous wheels and a sharp hungry drill that I could not afford to reach my city walls.

My brother loomed over me and whacked at me with his mace. I evaded the swing, amplifying my speed with the magic I had gathered in my body, but his attacks were equally as fast, and the mace clipped my shoulder. The force of the blow sent me rolling along the ground.

I spit out blue dirt.

My brother raised his metal mace in the air and yelled, summoning magic that caused his black eyes to brighten and his curly black coils to stand on end. The mace glowed with all the magic charged within it, as if he was holding a lightning bolt in his hand. Then, he threw it.

I dived out of the way, using magic to help me leap across the distance. The attack crackled past me, whipping past my hair, and I turned in horror at the sound of a helpless rumble. The magic charged mace had crashed into the city's walls. I watched horrified as the bricks folded and collapsed in a cloud of dust and toil. It had taken what felt like eons to build that wall, and in moments, it had come tumbling down.

I yelled as I picked myself up, and charged forward in my anger and heartbreak. I spun past the sharp drill and set my shoulders against the wooden contraption. I slapped my hands together and pulled them back, pooling all the magic I had summoned to my body to the small point between my palms. I yelled as the condensed ball of magic in my hands grew brighter and brighter. Then, I thrust my hands forward and released all of that pent up anger and grief, all of the energy I had collected, and blasted that dumb contraption and my little brother at point blank range.

I closed my eyes against the blinding light of my own power. My little brother had used magic as a shield, just barely protecting himself, as he went rolling back from the force of the blast. The tank mowed down soldiers that were unlucky enough to be behind it as my brother disappeared into the purple forests beyond the hills.

The exhaustion from the attack weighed down my limbs, but I forced myself to straighten and face the cavalry who continued to bear down on me. Horses clomped through the dirt with a beat I could feel drumming in my chest.

Needing to reserve the rest of my magic, I unsheathed the greatsword I had strapped to my back. With a mighty swing, I cut through the legs of the first steed, an armored unicorn with a horn made from rainbows, and it erupted in a spray of glitter. I kicked the soldier that fell from the saddle squarely in the chest and then turned to deflect the downward stroke of a sword that swept towards my back.

The metal of our swords clashed. I reached to grab the soldier by his breastplate and, with a roar, hauled them off their unicorn and tossed them to the ground. As I stabbed and twisted my greatsword through the soldier's unarmored neck, clouds of fluff sprayed from the wound.

I looked up, with glitter and fluff stuck to my face and yelled a challenge to my next attacker, but my yell was drowned out by a roar from behind me. My army had sent the calvary out through the collapsed section of the wall, and they had come to provide reinforcement. Their bright gleaming armor and pink banners overtook my position.

"General!" The voice of my most trusted lieutenant called out. I turned and grabbed the furry hand he had reached out toward me. I swung up behind him on his stocky gryphon and locked my arms around the waist of the burly lieutenant. Lieutenant Teddy turned to me with the face of a bear, a typical feature of his race.

"We need to get you back. The siege towers have reached the northern wall. The situation is becoming dire."

I nodded in consent, and we left behind the cavalry, trusting them to take care of the situation here. With my little brother no longer in command, it shouldn't take long for my cavalry to rout his forces, and then they could defend the new hole in the wall before my sister could take advantage. My lieutenant and I flew back toward the city.

When we reached the top of the northern wall, we found fighting. My sister's forces had begun to spill over the ramparts. I didn't hesitate to unsheathe my greatsword as we jumped down from the gryphon's back. Once we were noticed, enemies rushed us from both directions. My lieutenant and I pressed back-to-back to brace against their approach. Lieutenant Teddy lifted his fists, wielding spiked metal gauntlets. Then, he cranked back his arm and punched an enemy soldier right over the wall.

"Just like old times, hmm?" I smirked. Lieutenant Teddy and I had been through a lot together, through rigorous classes at the academy and endless campaigns of enduring the Long Nights, a phenomenon when both moons were new and the world was dark.

"Until the sun rises..." Lieutenant Teddy said.

"We slay the night," I finished. I lifted my greatsword over my head and cut through the first foreign soldier standing in my way. They tried to lift their sword to block, and I broke right through the steel. Without armor, they splattered fluff across the walls.

Spearmen stabbed at the enemy pushing out of the siege towers, threatening to overwhelm us with their numbers. A thick of the fighting had congregated before one of these towers, an overwhelming writhing throng of bodies where white had consumed all colors. I slashed my way through, pushing and shoving, and hacking at whatever I could reach. It was chaotic as soldiers screamed in my ear. There was no longer enough room for proper swinging. Just bodies against bodies, trying to make a way.

I pulled whatever soldiers I could find that were wearing my colors to my side and positioned them in preparation for one coordinated attack.

"TOGETHER!" I shouted once I had formed a line. One of the soldiers handed me a burning torch and I lifted it to gather more to my position.

"NOW!" I declared. As one, we pushed forward. Some of our enemies fell off the walls through the crenels. Others were pushed back toward the bridge, but not all could fit on it, and they stumbled off the sides. I stepped onto the wooden planks that connected the wall to the siege tower, and with my soldiers beside me, we kept pushing and pushing, until I could reach the tower.

I thrust out the torch and fed the wooden frame with fire. Smoke burned at my eyes as the flames raced to devour everything it could touch. I retreated back as the heat licked at my face and the tower began collapsing. Some soldiers, in their desperation, jumped to their deaths. Once I reached the safety of the walls, I quickly surveyed the situation. Both of the remaining siege towers were now on fire.

"PREPARE THE OIL!" I called out.

Tubs of oil were distributed to the soldiers on the walls. The soldiers tossed the oil over and it sludged down the bricks, leaving behind a dark stain that scarred the memory of building them.

"NOW!" I shouted. Torches were set to the oil, and in moments, I stood atop a wall of fire. Any ladders leaning on the wall went up in flames. The ditches lit up with heat, and the ensuing fiery river pushed the enemy forces back and back, until a horn wailed through the air, and the enemy finally broke.

My forces cheered at their retreat.

I knew it was just a small moment of respite. My sister wasn't going to give up. No doubt, they will be rerouting toward the eastern wall and the true battle for the city would soon begin.

"General," Lieutenant Teddy said as he pressed a pawed fist to his chest. "Our forces in the east have successfully repelled their cavalry. They are temporarily retreating on all sides."

"Start rerouting our main forces and begin preparing for the next attack. We need to shore up that wall," I said, and dismissed him to execute my orders.

I leaned forward and touched my hands to the aged bricks. They were covered in soot and the color of it stained my palms. The sun began to rise, revealing the true devastation of the battlefield. Scorched fields. Burnt wood. Arrows that stabbed the land. Bodies in the thousands that will fatten the crows. All of this devastation, and for what? Because my sister could never be content with what was hers? Because she couldn't leave me alone and let me have my peace? All our lives, all my sister had ever known was how to destroy.

But I smiled.

For my city stood for one more day.

There was no enemy like family, and no villain greater than an older sister.

I tightened my hands against the wooden table that held the maps of the battlefield, where it showed the position of my forces aimed at a sketch of my older sister's walls. I hated the fact that I had to call a temporary retreat, but the northern wall was on fire, including a good portion of my forces. Not only that, but my brother failed to provide a better distraction. Still, he might have done enough to use to my advantage.

"Are you sure you can't find him?" I asked my lieutenant. Lieutenant Stardust was a tall statuesque woman with large eyes and black frizzy hair plaited down to her waist, but what stood out the most, was the scar drawn down her cheek.

"No one has seen him since his defeat," the lieutenant confirmed.

"What a coward," I said in disgust. "Nothing but a big baby."

I pushed off the table and marched out the open side of the tent to stare at the city that glittered multicolor in the sunrise. My sister loved that city more than she loved me. It was a magnificent model of construction and engineering, and honestly? That was all the more reason to tear it down. Perhaps I was petty, as my advisors whispered. Perhaps I was spiteful, as my mercenaries lauded. Perhaps I was **childish**, as my sister constantly claimed, but at least I would no longer be ignored.

"Tell the soldiers to rest but gather the lieutenants. We attack at sunset."

"Yes, General." Lieutenant Stardust nodded.

The leaders of my army gathered in the command tent, and we spent all day considering tactics and formations that we could aim at the hole in the eastern wall. No doubt my older sister would try to do something to reinforce the break, but her ability was limited by time. She could only do so much in a day.

"General, a message from over the wall."

I greeted the soldier who delivered an arrow into my hands. It had a piece of parchment and a white flag wrapped around the shaft. Was this my sister surrendering? I hoped not. I hadn't gotten the chance to destroy her yet.

I unfolded the sliver of paper, which read, *"Dear little sister, here is a white flag in case you didn't bring one. I will accept no less than the following terms for your surrender..."*

The arrogance! The haughtiness! The audacity! I threw the flag onto the ground and with both feet, jumped on it until dirt and mud discolored the linen. I gave one final stomp, and the twists of my hair fell in front of my eyes as I panted with exhaustion.

Then, I calmly pinned a twist back behind my ear and straightened. My lieutenants were all staring at me, and I glared at them in turn. They swiveled around quickly, quaking in their boots.

"I'll show her," I declared, determined. "I'll show her how all walls come crashing down, and how all cities become ruins."

The next evening, I faced the eastern wall, so wide open for the taking. That city was mine and I couldn't wait to revel in its destruction.

"Charge!" I yelled from atop of my armored steed.

My army marched forward at my command, a pincer toward the rift. Almost immediately, once my army reached the narrow gap, archers appeared from the top to rain down arrows. My big sister had rearranged the debris to create a kill tunnel into the city and my army was dropping like flies.

But throw enough bodies at a problem and anything could be overcome. I turned to my most trusted lieutenant and nodded. Lieutenant Stardust charged forward with the armored cavalry. The infantry parted at the sound of the horns, and the cavalry charged through the opening. Their armor helped to deflect the arrows, and those that survived the initial death trap kept charging until—

The horses tumbled down, hitting ditches that had been dug into the ground. I clenched my fists, hating how my sister seemed to have thought of everything. At this rate, my sister was going to repel me for another day, and I could not have that! I trotted my pegasus forward and the spearmen assigned to protect me followed.

As I came closer, I saw my sister fighting in the kill tunnel, linked pauldron to pauldron with her own regiment of armored spearmen that thrust out their polearms to stop the cavalry's charge. It was a slaughter. I ducked underneath an explosion of rock. One of their catapults from the eastern wall had been repositioned and were now throwing flaming boulders toward my direction.

Something drastic needed to be done if I was to break through.

"SISTER!" My big sister shouted and stared at me defiantly underneath her plumed helmet. Then she lifted Lieutenant Stardust up by her plaited hair and I looked on in horror, feeling helpless to overcome the distance needed to reach her.

"NOO!!!" I yelled and urged my pegasus to fly forward. Not Lieutenant Stardust! We've been through so much together. We shared so many tea dates and accompanied each other on shopping trips. She was more than just a subordinate to me. She was my best friend. And my sister knew this. I dismounted onto the sopping ground where my soldiers had been cut down with arrows and I vaulted over the obstacles that had become of their bodies.

With a steely expression, as if asking, 'Why did you force me to do this?' My sister's grip tightened on Lieutenant Stardust's hair, and then with a flex of muscles, popped Stardust's head right off her shoulders.

NOOOOOO!!!!

I slid to my knees, as tears swelled before my eyes. I was willing to make sacrifices, but this one was too much. I yelled in fury and anger out over the battlefield. All in the same scream, I reached my hand to the sky and summoned the might of my magic.

"MOONSUGAR POWER!"

The magic from my screams threatened to overwhelm me. It transformed me. My armored boots grew wings. A dress flowed down my legs and a skirt of armor clenched around my waist. Gauntleted gloves ratcheted up my arms. Delicate flowers painted my fingernails, and my short twists grew to reach my ankles. A silver helmet materialized over my head, and a staff materialized in my hand. I screamed as bright white wings sprouted from my back.

I flew up into the sky with the light of a star inside of me. I felt powerful. I felt indestructible. I felt invincible. I aimed my staff, and the bauble at the top glowed. The orb released a bright sparkled blast that cleared the tunnel, incinerating everyone on both sides. The two armies seemed to stand frozen in shock, before my side seemed to realize their reversal in fortunes. They cheered and then surged through the cleared tunnel and poured into the city.

I searched for my sister among the tide of people, knowing that the blast wouldn't have killed her, but I couldn't locate her. I had so much magic built up inside of me, and if I couldn't find my sister to release it on, then I would release it on my sister's precious city. I laughed as I flew over the wall that had repelled me just the other day. I laughed as I spun in the air and charged through buildings for them to collapse behind me in my wake. Watching things fall was so much fun and I didn't understand why my sister was so adamant in protecting something that time would soon defeat anyways. Why build something if not to see it destroyed? Why not create fun puzzle pieces from the rubble? And revel in the sound of ruin?

I caught sight of what looked like an armored bear riding through the city, who baited my army toward a trap of crossbow bolts that only I could spy this high in the sky. I recognized that bear. It was my sister's most trusted and faithful lieutenant. I smirked. Ahh. Revenge.

I weaved through the buildings, gaining momentum as my line of sight narrowed on the poor bear in my path. I slammed him right off of his horse, through a building, past a park, and to the ground.

"This is for Lieutenant Stardust!" I cried as I stabbed my staff through the bear's eye. His fluff splattered all over my face.

"Are you done with your temper tantrum?"

I grinned. Leaving the staff behind in the bear's skull, I turned and stared at my big sister. She stood amid the clouds of dust like some proud statue of a war hero waiting for me to knock its head off. I reached behind me, unsheathed my greatsword, and declared, "It is about time you faced me!"

"Are you happy?" My sister asked. "You have destroyed everything that I have built! Everything that I have worked for!"

"All things must end!" I said in turn. "Face me if you dare! For I am the Goddess of Destruction, and you can never stop me!"

My big sister drew back her hands and gathered magic between her palms. Like a mirror, I too gathered my own magic. The wall was broken and the buildings were leveled, but that was not enough.

I was determined to destroy everything.

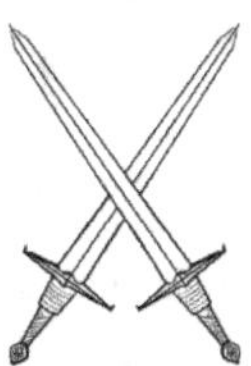

I was determined to save anything.

I thrust my hands forward, and our magic clashed, creating a dome of light that seemed to swallow the city. I screamed and my little sister screamed louder. I screamed louder, and she screamed even more, until the city was drowned under our battle cries.

The magic exploded and we were both propelled backwards. I landed on my back, against a piece of debris ripped up from the city. I coughed as I turned and pushed myself up on both hands. Dust obscured my vision. I saw the vague outline where my sister had stabbed her staff into Lieutenant Teddy's eye, looking like an empty flagpost waiting for a victor to end this madness.

"We slay the night," I whispered.

The dust thinned, and my little sister and I looked at each other. We both found our feet at the same time. We both reached for our magic but found our stores empty. We reached for our greatswords instead. With great roars, we charged at one another.

Our swords clashed, again, and again, and again.

We huffed and panted, staring at each other with wild eyes as our swords dragged our arms to the ground and our strength began to flag. After we caught our breaths, we attacked one another again.

A cry echoed around the ruined square that had become our arena. We paused and turned as something came charging out of the dust, and we barely leapt out the way of the spinning drill. I looked back at our younger brother and felt vindicated at the sight of him. Our brother hadn't betrayed me. He was, as usual, on his own side. If my sister was destruction, and I was creation, then he was undoubtedly chaos.

He charged towards us with his flailing mace, and while dodging out of the way, my sister tripped on a ruptured piece of cobblestone that had been torn by the magical blast. I took that opportunity to lunge toward her. She deflected the attack, but I spun and kneed her in the back and pressed her into the ground.

"No!" She snapped, struggling underneath me. I grabbed the edge of my sister's helmet and ripped it off. I waved it triumphantly overhead just as our brother made a curving turn around and charged towards the both of us.

"Get off of me! He's going to end us!" My sister shouted. Our brother rammed towards our position, drawing closer and closer.

"Then I'll take you down with me!"

"That's dumb! Get off!"

Of course, my little sister yelled in defiance. I yelled in retribution. Our brother yelled just to yell.

"*WHAT IS GOING ON*?!"

The destroyed city became scattered building blocks of assorted colors. Greatswords became pillows. A white flag of surrender became a baby's spitrag. And the helmet that I had torn from my sister's head, became a silver satin bonnet.

"What did I tell you two about using the ship's battle simulator as your playroom?!"

Mom glared at us from the door, with both hands on her hips, in her command uniform. She sent us a glare that would have sent the ship's crew scuttling down the hallways. We jumped away from each other, and our baby brother, in his walker, bounced toward our mother with an excited babble as he waved his rattle in the air.

"Mommy!" I immediately complained. "She keeps destroying my

city! It took me all morning to build!"

"She won't play with me!" my little sister whined.

Our mother immediately rubbed her forehead, and we both knew that gesture meant that we were in trouble. She glared at us both and ordered, "Clean this up, now!"

My sister and I looked at each other, and silently agreed to an alliance. We cleaned up all of the building blocks scattered around the floor. My sister picked up her toys that she would chew and draw all over, and I gathered my pristine and well-cared for stuffed dolls. But not all of the toys had survived.

My sister scooped up Lieutenant Stardust, her favorite doll with a line of purple crayon marked down her face. The doll now had her head popped off, beheaded by my own hands. I clutched poor Lieutenant Teddy to my chest, my teddy bear which had been stabbed in the eye with the end of a suction broom my sister had grabbed from the maintenance closet. Other toys were in pieces about the room, with their stuffing and plastic parts blown about like an asteroid belt. Glitter stained the floor like ship debris. We diligently cleaned up the room under our mother's supervision.

Once it was cleaned to her standards, she gestured for us to follow her out of the room. We carried the remains of our toys in our arms and before we left, we looked back at the empty space that seemed deceptively plain but could make us into anything if only we could imagine it. My sister and I looked at each other with mischievous twin smirks.

Yesterday, we were mermaids.

Tomorrow, we would be pirates.

Donolee Young also known by her online alias 'Plaidpuma' is a Jamaican illustrator and designer whose vivid creations are a hybrid of whimsy, and creativity. Her works usually explore themes of fantasy, storytelling, queerness and the intricacies of human emotions. Plaidpuma draws from her Caribbean culture, and community to craft art that celebrates resilience and the complexity of identity. Their work also serves as a bold affirmation of queer Caribbean existence, portraying love, self-expression, and queer joy through colourful expressive narratives.

For collaborations, commissions, or inquiries, Plaidpuma can be reached via email at pumasstudio@gmail.com

Tatiana Obey writes badass characters slaying dragons. She enjoys combining action with character-driven stories that feature diverse heroes and heroines. She is the author of **Bones to the Wind**, a 2022 BBA Award Winner, and **Sistah Samurai: A Champloo Novella**, a 2023 Indie Ink Award Winner. She has published short stories in various anthologies and Fiyah Literary Magazine, and is a contributing editor to **Magic in the Melanin: A Black Fantasy Anthology**. She taught English in South Korea, studied abroad in Japan, and spent her debut year traveling the world. Learn more about Tatiana at www.tatianaobey.com.

Other books by Tatiana Obey

A Forging of Age Duology

Sistah Samurai: A Champloo Novella

THANK YOU FOR READING

Thank you for reading *Magic in the Melanin: A Black Fantasy Anthology*! We hope you enjoyed reading this collection of short stories. If you did, please tell someone about it and leave us a review on Amazon, Goodreads, Storygraph, or any other platform you'd like! Doing so helps this book find other readers who love Black fantasy of all kinds.

If you would like to read more books by Black authors, check out the Melanin Library website, MelaninLibrary.com. If you would like to support the Melanin Library to help keep it a free resource, consider donating to our cause.

Thank you again for reading our anthology, uplifting Black creatives, and supporting the Melanin Library. We hope all your books are full of melanin!

www.ingramcontent.com/pod-product-compliance
Lightning Source LLC
Chambersburg PA
CBHW072001190726
48293CB00001B/104